East

C000192651

East Lothian
Council

Also by Michael J. Malone
from Five Leaves
Blood Tears

A Taste
for Malice

Michael J. Malone

Five Leaves Publications

www.fiveleaves.co.uk

A Taste for Malice
by Michael J. Malone

Published in 2013 by
Five Leaves Publications,
PO Box 8786, Nottingham NG1 9AW
www.fiveleaves.co.uk

ISBN: 978-1907869754

Five Leaves acknowledges
financial support from
Arts Council England

Cover design: J.T. Lindroos

Design and typesetting
by Four Sheets Design and Print

Printed by Imprint Digital in Exeter

Prologue

The nurse smoothed the sheet over the form on the bed. The quilt cover was bleached of colour and crisply laundered in that way only hospitals manage. The patient's face and hands were also slight of colour having had no sun for some time. As the nurse worked she moved her hands more firmly whenever they touched the patient, testing for a response. But none came. None had for the last six weeks.

She ran the back of her fingers down the patient's cheek. So soft. And not a bruise in sight. What an amazing thing the human body was. This woman had suffered so much damage. Then a long sleep while the body set about healing itself.

The nurse had plenty of other patients; lots of other people demanded her time, but this woman asked nothing of her, only that the various bags, tucked out of sight, were emptied or filled. So she made it her special duty to do what she could to make this young woman comfortable.

'There, there,' said the nurse. 'Aren't you beautiful?' Okay, the blond hair was a tad lifeless and could do with a wash, but the rest of her was so darling, as her favourite actresses used to say. She glided her index finger down the ridge of the woman's nose. It was just the right size for her face; the shell of the nostrils, the line straight and smooth up to the point between finely arched eyebrows. Long, dark lashes rested on her cheek, almost reaching the swell and curve of cheekbones a model would die for.

Lightly, carefully, the nurse caught one eyelid between thumb and forefinger and pulled the eye open. The pupil was a spot of darkness surrounded by an iris that radiated from it in a dazzling blue. *Might have known,* she sighed. *All this and blue eyes too. Lucky bitch.* She relaxed her fingers and allowed the slender layer of skin to fall back into place.

It was all so romantic and tragic, like something from a black and white movie. The beauty asleep on the bed for months. Her only visitor a mysterious, handsome man.

Well not so mysterious really, he was her husband. And not so handsome either. Too skinny. Needed a good feed. There was an element of mystery, however, as on one visit the nurse noticed a certain finger on a certain hand was missing a certain ring. Then when she looked again a couple of minutes later it was back in place, a band of gold snug in its groove of flesh like it had never been missing.

Every day the man turned up to sit on the edge of his chair holding his wife's hand. He stared at her face for the whole hour, silent, as if the energy used in speech would detract from the force he was pouring into the slumbering woman with his eyes.

The nurse sighed and smoothed the corner of the quilt. If only she could attract such devotion. When she first thought of the couple she was reminded of her parents and how they had been lost in each other. Then the incident with the wedding ring had shattered this illusion. In any case no-one could be more devoted to their partner than her parents. Even a small daughter could not impinge on the attention they paid each other.

Her earliest memories were of the floor in the living room being cleared each night after dinner, the scratch and crackle of the stylus before music filled the vacant space and her parents swirled around the room, bodies tight against each other.

She tried to join in, pushing a small hand between their waists. At first her father would gently chide her, throw her in the air and laughing place her on the settee. Then he became more insistent until his laughter changed to shouts. She left the room then in a loud huff to see if they would notice she was gone. They never did.

6

So she put on her pyjamas, brushed her teeth and put herself to bed like a good little girl. In the dark of her bedroom she listened to the music drifting upstairs and imagined the dance and the spinning shapes her parents made as they moved with grace and art around the room below.

The nurse gently pulled a strand of hair away from the patient's face. In another life, they might have been friends. Gone for a coffee and cake, with bags of shopping decorating the space around their feet. They could have talked for hours, about everything and nothing. They could have shared the same love of old Hollywood movies. They could have known what the other meant with a simple look, ending each other's sentences and smiling at the same instant at the same joke.

The husband clearly didn't deserve her. Regret for mistakes made was loud in the shape of his hunched back as he sat by her side day on day. And what was he doing placing the ring on his finger after he arrived at her bedside? Who would benefit from that little display? That pale band of skin where the ring should have nestled was a sign of one thing only.

That was one thing her father would never have done: been uncaring of his wife's feelings. Behaving in this manner to his daughter was another thing entirely. A picture of her father bloomed in her mind. His cropped, grey hair and slim dancer's build. Another picture replaced this, both her parents running down the path of their house towards the car. They turned and waved to her before opening the gate. She kept waving until they were driving down the street. A small act of devotion that her parents missed every time they went off for a weekend's dancing competition.

Mrs Peele, her babysitter, would pull her back from the window, throw her in front of the TV and switch it on.

'Not a sound out of you, you little bitch. I've got Mr Peele's dinner to make and I don't want to be disturbed.'

And there the little girl would sit between meals and

7

bedtimes, terrified to make a sound but eager for the distraction the world of Hollywood could provide. She wasn't good with the names of the movies, but she would always remember a face, a hairstyle or a dress. She studied the way a manicured hand would hold a cigarette, the way a thought could be implied by the simple act of lifting an eyebrow and the way those strong women held power over the people in their lives.

What power those women held, she thought as she again brought her fingers down the ridge of her patient's nose. She placed her thumb on one nostril and, pressing against it, closed off one air-line. With her index finger she touched the other side of the nose. Power was a simple thing. Either you take it or you don't. Either you grab the power or they run over you. She squeezed and brought both fingers tight together.

How long would it take, she wondered.

The patient's eyelids fluttered. Her chest rose.

For then the tragedy would be complete. The errant husband would be hunched over a grave instead of a hospital bed. The world would sympathise with him. His pain would cause others to shed more than a few tears. The music would build to a crescendo and then the camera would pan out, letting the audience see the vastness of the sky behind him.

The skill with power, the nurse thought, was knowing when to use it. She relaxed her fingers, turned with a squeak of her rubber-soled shoes and left the room.

As the sound of her passage faded, it was replaced with loud and panicked breathing. And the rustle of linen as the patient sat up in her bed.

Chapter 1

It's weird being one of the guys again. The Chief Superintendent said that I wasn't to consider it a demotion. I would still have the rank of DI and the privileges it inferred, I would just be "out of sight" until the media had "The Mad Detective" out of their system. Those were his words, incidentally, speaking in headlines was his thing. I was sure the public had very little idea of what had really gone on. He, however, lived in fear of something, anything, causing embarrassment to the police and if one of the hacks in the city got wind of my story it would be the end of his career. The press didn't know I was back.

In the meantime the Super said I should enjoy the rest and the work with DI Peters, who would have the same rank and privileges as me, but who would also have the authority and purpose.

Having your wrists slashed by a homicidal maniac and facing up to some serious childhood demons tends to put a certain perspective on things, so I wasn't too pissed off with the whole charade.

DS Peters, as was, reflected the positive side of the whole "Mad Detective" thing and was subsequently promoted. His calm (for calm, read too slow to pick up on things) demeanour in the face of the shark-feeding frenzy that was the Scottish media, commended him to the powers-that-be as promotion material. My involvement however, gave cause for concern. For the subtext in this read "a fucking embarrassment".

All in all I had to be pleased with the outcome of the investigation into my own actions. I could have been reported to the Procurator Fiscal and charged with perverting the course of justice. This would have led to a jail sentence and a very public dismissal.

My representative argued at my hearing that I had been an excellent public servant with many years of an unblemished career. The circumstances surrounding my actions had been stressful in the extreme; not only had some childhood friends of mine been murdered, but I had been charged with said murders.

He went on to argue that the real killer had been caught, an outcome in which I had a large hand. Furthermore, said killer admitted his guilt to the court meaning that much of the evidence supported my actions. Actions which had been taken with no criminal intent, he added. Actions which had never been made public knowledge. Therefore institutional embarrassment had been kept to a minimum.

Now that DI Ray McBain has recovered from the stress of the situation and from the grievous wounds gained in apprehending the vicious madman, he should be made to suffer no more, allowed to learn from the situation and given the task of using his vast experience to help protect the public.

So there.

The muster room is almost full as we wait for DI Peters to arrive. It's his first day back at work following a holiday, following his promotion. It's also his first day back to be faced with me, still in a job and still a DI.

I am in the back row with Drain and Rossi, trying not to lounge and show disrespect for my new boss, who isn't really my boss. Aye right. I could see through their ploy as clearly as if I had received a typed memo entitled Let's Piss Ray McBain Off — Then He Might Fuck Off and Die. For one thing, it would take more than a promoted and primped DI Peters to hack me off. And for another, there are still a lot of bad guys out there needing locking up. A job that I would need to find a way to do from the purgatory that is admin work.

'Who's going to do it?' Daryl Drain swings round in his chair to face me. He's a walking cliché of male good looks; square jaw, strong nose and full lips. His hair is cropped blond and his eyes are a powerful shade of blue. I must remember to ask him if he wears coloured contacts.

'Should really be you, Ray,' says Alessandra Rossi, hemming me in from the other side. At the same time all three of us turn to face the front of the room and look at the back of a young man's head on the front row.

The object of our attention this morning is a young, very young detective constable by name of Davie Connelly. He's relatively new to the shift and fresh out of uniform. And if I hear him say that Billy Connelly was his dad's cousin one more time, my reactions will be severe and inappropriate.

Did I say that he was also very young? I often think that too much testosterone is wasted on the young. Case in point: DC Connelly. When he's paired with a more experienced male colleague he has one hand on his balls while he attempts to teach them how to do their job. When he's paired with a female colleague, he has one hand on his balls and his eyes fixed on their tits while he attempts to teach them how to do their job.

Today is comeuppance day.

Yesterday, using my questionable authority I handed out a small, yellow-topped sample cup to all of the males in the room with the following scenario:

'A young woman was viciously raped last night between the hours of twelve midnight and one thirty am. She described her attacker as below thirty, white and "quite tall". She also suggested that he must be local by the way he managed to surprise her and subsequently evade capture when she shouted for help. Luckily for us she reported the crime before she cleaned up and the police surgeon was able to take a sample of semen from the young lady's thigh.' I looked around the room and was amazed at how well everyone was keeping their serious faces on. Everyone in the room was aware that this was a prank except the aforementioned DC Connelly.

'We are about to make a request that every male who resides within five square mile of the crime site supplies us with a DNA sample. That request starts here. Given the description of the assailant and the local knowledge he showed, we have to eliminate all of the men in this room from our enquiries. Hence the small cups you have been provided with. We require each of you to return said cup in the morning with a sample of your ejaculate.'

A few of the guys bit down on their lips, but they all nodded their understanding. DC Connelly shifted in his seat, moved through several shades of pink and read the nods of the men around him as a sign that this was a deadly serious matter. Happily, it failed to occur to him that the more usual method of obtaining DNA involved a swab and the inside of the mouth.

Time for a lesson to be learned.

Daryl kicks my foot.

'Do it now before Peters comes in.'

'Aye, okay,' I swallow my grin and walk to the front of the room. I pick up a random piece of paper from the table at the front and turn to face the shift members.

'Morning guys,' I say in my best businesslike manner. 'Yesterday I gave round the sample cups. Most of you have already handed yours in. Just thought I would take in the remainder now before the day starts.' I look down at the piece of paper in my hand and pretend to read. 'And we have everyone's in apart from... DC Connelly.' I look up from the paper.

He looks at the man sitting on his right, who mumbles something along the lines of he gave earlier. Connelly swallows, looks right and left and then stands up. As he walks the three steps between us his face gets pinker and pinker. As he walks his left hand slides into his pocket and draws out a small container, and even from here I can see his semen sliding thinly in the bottom of the cup.

A huge cheer and raucous laughter erupts.

'Connelly, you wanker,' is repeated around the room.

Men and women are in various stages of apoplectic laughter, heads thrown back, holding their sides, wiping tears from their eyes. DC Connelly is rooted to the spot, eyes screwed shut, mouth formed into a grimace.

I pat him on the shoulder on the way back to my seat. 'You'll get over it.'

Just then DI Peters walks in to the room holding a clutch of files. He's wearing his usual expression that suggests he is tired of missing out on the punch line. This time it's for real.

'What's going on?' he asks, with a half-smile.

'Nothing much, sir,' Connelly says as he pockets his tub of semen and sits back down.

Peters' eyes are drawn immediately to mine. He knows I am involved and he is mightily cheesed off that he isn't. I stare back at him with a non-committal expression that I know is going to piss him off even more.

'Right, guys, let's get on with the business of the day.' Peters addresses the room. All laughter dies and we are a room full of cops. Assignments are given, files are handed out and I'm the only one that hasn't been given any work. Those sitting around me offer half-smiles of commiseration. I shrug in return. Could be worse. I could be getting my anus ruptured by a line of power-hungry convicts. All things considered a desk covered in holiday requests and sick notes was not such a poor alternative.

Everyone leaves the room to start work and I am left with Peters. He is sitting on the table in the front of the room. I remain seated at the back.

'Congratulations on the promotion,' I say.

'Right. Thanks.' He wears an expression of surprise, like he had prejudged my response to his promotion and he had fallen way short.

'You've worked hard for it,' I shrug. 'Brown-nose a few journalists, disrespect your fellow officers…'

His expression returns to resignation. 'Ray, I refuse to bandy words with you. Truth of the matter is I am held in

13

high regard. Whereas your career,' he pauses for dramatic effect, 'is fucked.' He leaves the room.

'Fair enough,' I say to the empty space before me. 'Fair enough.'

Cut the guy some slack, I tell myself. He's only following his nature. Much in the same way a snake has to slide on its belly.

Well done, McBain. That episode of the cutting of the slack lasted all of two seconds. I just can't help it; the man is hardwired into my irritation circuit.

A head appears in the doorway.

'Boss,' it's Daryl Drain. 'You awright?'

'Why would I not be?'

'Just fuckin' asking.' He shoots me the finger, grins and then disappears. It would take more than a terse answer from me to get through his thick hide.

Before I head for my office I make myself a coffee. I don't take it from the machine. I make it from scratch. With a kettle and everything. The time taken for this task doubles with this simple choice.

I have kept my old office. No one managed to steal it from me during my absence. As soon as I enter the door I feel the dry, almost oxygen-free heat supplied by our air-conditioning system.

Once I drain my mug of coffee I place it on a once-white coaster stained with ring upon ring of coffee spillage. Is that how they age old police has-beens, I wonder? Count the coffee rings on their coaster?

My email inbox is chocka. Good. That'll take at least an hour to go through.

Internal memo. Internal memo. Internal memo. All fascinating stuff. All completed in that sterile police prose where a Latinate word is seen to be evidence of intelligence. Use words of four syllables or more and you are a fucking genius.

I'm on auto-pilot and barely picking up one word per paragraph when an image grows in my mind. It's Leonard, the real so-called *Stigmata Killer* and he's grinning. My forehead is slick with sweat. My forearms burn as a knife flashes.

I push my seat back and look down at my wrists expecting to see a gush of blood. But of course they are concealed under my shirt sleeves, which are white and detergent clean.

'You alright, Ray?' a head appears in my doorway.

'Of course I'm all-fucking-right,' I answer, then realise it's Alessandra Rossi. If one person doesn't deserve attitude, it's her.

'Sorry, Ale,' I wave her in to the room with one hand while the other wipes sweat from my forehead. 'It's ...' I feel myself about to launch into an hour long moan, 'it's nothing.' Smile. 'Just really warm in here.'

She sits down in front of me, 'Yeah, I understand. Could be better, eh?' We both know she is talking about something else entirely. I notice she has a pad of paper in her hand. Her script fills the page.

'Anything I can help you with?' Then I speak louder for the benefit of anyone lurking outside the room. 'Like holidays? Time off for medical procedures? Counselling after the death of your favourite cat?'

'It's pussy, I'm afraid,' she grins. 'Got something lodged in her throat.'

'Anyone I know?'

'Fuck off, McBain,' she stifles a giggle. Then she sobers. 'Haven't had the chance to say yet, but it's good to have you back, Ray.'

'Thank you,' the new me answers. The old me would have told her to piss off. 'It's good to be back. Kinda.'

She looks at the contents of my desk. 'Know what you mean. You're too good a cop to go to waste, Ray. They'll soon have you back hunting down the psychos.' We both know that the lack of conviction in her voice is there with good reason. Once you are put out to grass, you tend to stay there.

'So is the notepad part of your disguise, or did you bring it in for a reason?' I ask.

'Ah, Inspector Clouseau is mighty perceptive,' she says with a poor French accent.

I lift my eyebrows.

'Ok. Not the best comparison.' Grin. 'But it works for me.'

I smile and drum my fingers on my desk. No one else in the room beyond would dare to talk to me in such an irreverent manner. And I love it.

'It seems Daryl and I are equally out of favour at the moment. There's nothing there but a vague suspicion that we helped you out ...' She and Daryl had kept me in the loop about police movements while I was on the run as the main suspect in the *Stigmata* case.

'And let's keep it vague.'

'Yes. Absolutely. However, it doesn't stop them from giving us the shite.'

'Quite.'

'You are a poet.' She says.

'Don't I know it.'

'And if you get too bored with your ...' she looks around my desk, '...stuff, maybe Daryl and I could provide you with a shovel.'

'For the aforementioned shite.'

'Quite.' This time her grin has cheese on it.

'We'll need to do it on the Q.T. and strictly *entre nous*.' I grow mock serious.

'A technique we have used so well in the past. Daryl will visit you next. He will self-destruct after he has spoken with you.' She sits back in her chair and crosses her legs like a spy handler in a B movie.

'From your mouth to God's ears.'

We share a smile this time.

'How's Maggie,' she asks.

'I owe her a phone call.'

'Mmmm.'

'I know, I know, she deserves more.'

'She's been a good friend to you, Ray.' With that, she stands up and leaves the room.

I can't disagree with her. Maggie has been a great help as I have dealt with the events of the last few months. She turned up out of the blue while I was chasing Leonard and supported me throughout when she barely knew me. She was more of a pal than I deserved. I worried that she was in it for more than my friendship, but in her own inimitable style she told me it was not my dick she was interested in, she simply saw someone in need of help and couldn't ignore them. And then as I recovered from my wounds, both physical and mental she did what she could to remind me I was still a human being. Refusing to take any of my foul moods, she dragged me out of the house any day when the sun shone and quite a few when it didn't.

My scars itch underneath my shirtsleeves. I rub the length of my forearms, giving each arm some attention. A flash of memory. I see the line of skin separate and blood flow like water released from a dam. I shiver and remind myself that it is all over. I am safe. The killer is behind bars.

Except, he's the wrong guy and I'm the only one in this building who knows it.

Chapter 2

The call he'd been simultaneously dreading and praying for came when he was just about to put Ben to bed.

'Mr Hilton, it's the hospital here,' the voice was breathy, filled with the import and drama of the news it was about to pass on, '... your wife has just come round. How soon can you get here?'

His answering pause was so deep the voice queried, 'Mr Hilton, are you there?'

'Right away,' he answered. 'I'll be up right away.'

Jim was not sure which sound jolted him from his thoughts first; the strident note of protest from the telephone which was still in his hand, or the four-year-old asking, 'What's wrong, Daddy?'

'Nothing, wee pal.' He bent forward and placed a kiss on his son's forehead. He would never tire of pressing his lips against that space of fresh, warm skin: a reassuring moment of clarity bubbling up from a chaos of thought.

'But why are you looking so funny?'

Christ. She was actually awake. After three weeks in a coma, Angela was finally awake. Wonderful. Shit. Oh my god. What was he going to do?

'Daaaaad.'

'What, son?'

'You've gone all funny again.' The muscles of his chin were bunched in that pre-warning sign of impending tears.

'Sorry, baby.' He knelt down. 'Daddy doesn't mean to frighten you.' He deliberately brightened his posture and voice. 'That was the hospital. Mummy's awake at last.'

'Yeaaahhhh,' he yelled and jumped up and down. 'Is she coming home? Is she?'

'She's still not well enough, son.' Before Ben's face crumpled he added, 'but we can go and see her now.'

Another yell followed, before his expression altered once again, bottom lip on full tremble. 'But I'm wearing my jammies, Daddy. You have to change me.'

'That's okay, son. They see lots of people in their pyjamas in hospital. It's practically the law.'

All the way to the hospital Ben maintained a torrent of questions from the backseat.

'A coma is a long sleep, isn't it Daddy?'

'Will she have any new teeth?'

'Did she have nice dreams at night and scary ones during the day?'

'Why do you always just say, "Mmmmm" when I ask you something?'

His final question was the one that had been preying on Jim's mind ever since the phone call.

'Will you go back to living with Nana and Papa, Daddy?'

For six months prior to Angela's immobilisation, they were separated and Jim was living with his parents. As soon as the extent of her injuries became clear, he thought it wise to move back into the marital home. It would be best all round, he explained to his parents, less upheaval for Ben. It would be bad enough not seeing his mother without having to move to a new home. An additional benefit was that he would be closer to the hospital, therefore saving time and money on travelling to and fro.

She had sustained multiple injuries during a head-on collision with another car. The nursing staff weren't sure at first if she would pull through, but despite her long list of injuries, her heart kept beating.

Flesh and bones healed faster than her mind and she entered what Jim described to Ben as a very, very long sleep.

'With head injuries like this we have no way of knowing what damage will have been inflicted on the patient.' Dr

Bodrum intoned during one of his early visits. 'Any number of things can have happened, the least of which is memory loss.' Jim thought his smile was meant to be encouraging, a notion that was at odds with the information. 'We must wait and see.' Another smile.

Jim prayed for memory loss. Sounds cruel, but then he could have his family back. He could care for Angela; teach her to fall in love with him again before her memory recovered. Or perhaps, once she was in a better health he could tell her the truth and trust that her reaction would be the best for everyone concerned.

Until he saw an awake and alert Angela he had no idea what to expect. If it turned out that she was suffering from memory loss he had to be the one to tell her the truth of their situation. That meant limiting contact with friends and family until he was in the position to judge the state of her mind.

He leaned down until he was on the same eye level as Ben.

'Mummy might not remember us, buddy. She might not even remember that I was living with Nana and Papa before the accident.' Ben's eyes were large with amazement that this might happen.

'Mummy might be sick for a little longer. We will all need to live together until she's better. But it might make her more sick if she knew that I was not living at home, so can you be like Mummy and forget that ever happened?'

Jim put his arms round Ben and held him close. He felt sick. He closed his eyes tight against the guilt.

And so the lies began.

Chapter 3

There's a line of trees on the road outside my flat. They've got their blossom out. Every time the wind blows, the air downwind is filled with a pink snow. The small flowers then gather in clumps at the side of the pavement like a scattered offering to the gods. When nature does litter it puts on a show.

Didn't sleep much last night. Ate a huge bar of chocolate before I went to bed and it was enough to keep me awake. Eventually I nodded off only to wake up mere minutes later with my eyelids being sunblasted by a bright spring morning.

I stumble into the shower and repeatedly promise myself a set of black-out curtains while the hot water pours over my head and shoulders. I fill my hands with liquid soap and start to work it over my body.

I think of Theresa. I stop working the lather over my chest. You know how it is; you haven't really grown up yet although you are technically an adult, you see the chance of some no-strings-attached shagging. You take it. You take as much as you can. Except something happens that makes you grow up. Then you realise you want more. You catch her scent while sitting watching TV. You think you see her head bobbing in a crowd of people just ahead. Always just ahead.

I did see her just last week in Argyle Street. I was going in to Debenhams, she was on the way out. A man held the door for her. She saw me and a smile stuttered into place. My eyes were drawn down to her full belly and back up to her face. The world slowed and settled. We held each other's gaze. Her eyes read of acceptance and content.

Was there an apology in the lift of her brow? My eyes moved back down to her swollen abdomen. Mine, I wanted to ask?

Real time settled back into place with the bustle of shoppers. My momentum carried me past her and her companion's voice reached me.

'Did you know that guy? Theresa, did you know that guy?'

Her answer was lost among the footfall and charge of rapacious consumers. In a daze I walked on past M&S and towards Trongate and Glasgow Cross. She's pregnant. And by the size of her stomach — and this is a man's judgement — she is due to give birth any second. Which means the baby could be mine. Fuck. I will be a father. Scratch that. I was the sperm donor, nothing more. She has her life all mapped out, I was clearly nothing but a diversion until she found a purpose.

I dry myself and dress. A black coffee and a scan of the news channels later and I am on the way to work.

More emails. I read them while the thought of Theresa being pregnant with my child is like a saccharine hangover that colours my thoughts. For sanity's sake I need to try and get over it. She has clearly decided that I am not parent material.

More emails. More coffee. No-one has a birthday, so I buy some cakes. The clichéd American cop would have a number of doughnuts with a variety of toppings. None of that shite for your Scottish cop. We have a selection of cream cakes, apple turnovers, strawberry tarts, carrot cake, iced gingerbread, iced fruit slice, empire biscuits, snowballs. Just looking at the pile on the table is enough to strip the enamel from your teeth. Daryl raises an eyebrow when he saw me carrying in the cake boxes.

'Shut it,' is my qualified response. 'Besides,' I pull in my belly. 'I am no longer wearing a fat-suit.'

Daryl raises the other eyebrow.

'That's a neat wee trick. How do you do it?' I ask.

'Hours in front of the mirror,' Ale jumps in. 'Don't you know that's his hobby?'

Daryl puckers up for a kiss.

'In your dreams, loser,' says Ale walking back to her desk.

I turn and walk back into my office. Someone follows me and closes the door behind them.

'What can I do for you, Daryl?' I sit down.

'I have a problem with my pussy.' A grin fills his face. He puts a pad of paper on the desk.

'There's a lot of it going around.'

'I need some counselling.' He crosses his arms and leans back in his chair. 'I hear you are the right man with the right set of skills to help me.'

'I hear you will self-destruct when you leave this room.'

'From your mouth to God's ears.' Smile. He sits in silence for a couple of minutes while I read the notes on the paper.

'Anyway,' he stands up, 'I feel so much better now. Bye.'

Several sheets of A4 paper are left on my desk. The hand-writing is too neat to be Daryl's. Alessandra's then. I pull them towards me and read. This is a file from the "Unsolved" pile. A case that has been superseded by a number of other crimes, usually involving murder. Until some parents came looking for answers and someone's conscience was given a prod, considering the fact that young innocents have been damaged. And the worry that it might be happening to others while we focus on more "serious" and immediate crimes.

Due to their past proximity to me, Daryl and Alessandra are clearly ideal candidates to head the investigation of this "cold case" before the parents go running to the press.

We are looking for a young woman. She may have an accomplice. She may have some medical training. What we can say with some degree of certainty is that she has some serious issues.

We know of two families so far that she has destroyed. The pattern of her activity with both was very similar.

She insinuates herself into the bosom of the family. She becomes best friends with the woman and flirts with the man. The children — and both families had young boys — adore her.

To start off with. Then she has some "fun" with them. For fun, read torture and mental cruelty. In each case she disappeared as suddenly as she arrived, and only then do the children tell their parents what happened.

Nice.

Her description varies. In one she is small and round, with long dark hair. In the other she is small and slim with short, blond hair. Another variation was in the way she treated the children. The first family was subjected to what could best be described as mental cruelty. The kids in the next family had similar treatment, but this time it had more of a physical nature. This gave the initial team pause for thought. Was it one assailant or was it two unrelated cases? They asked for photos. There were none.

The time lapse between cases was twelve months. Sufficient time to gain weight and get a hairdo. The name she gave to each family convinced the team that she was one and the same person. Both families said her name was Lucy Hepburn. But she asked that they call her Audrey.

There's an e-fit drawing on file from each family. Computer graphic eyes stare out from the pages. I sit the drawings side by side and study them.

Different people can see the same thing and their brain contrives somehow to create differences. Ask three witnesses to describe the same crime and you can often receive three different accounts. The differences here are largely cosmetic. A change in hair-style and colour is easy enough to explain. One face is rounder than the other. Again, easy to explain.

Both faces have similar shape of eyes and mouth. One has a slightly bigger nose. However, the first team noted that they considered all of this information and were certain that these were the act of one woman.

I would have added that a woman who changes her appearance with both hairstyle and diet is one cunning individual.

And one who is intent on making some form of career for herself.

Below this Alessandra has noted that Sherlock Drain detects some duplicity. All that genius and alliteration as well.

I send Alessandra an email. Drain is copied in.

<<<How far have you guys got with this?>>>

Alessandra replies.

<<<As far as reading the file and distilling the info on to the sheet of paper.>>>

<<<Do we know who initially handled the case?>>>

<<<Dave Holdsworth. He's back in uniform and a sergeant out in the sticks somewhere. Daryl phoned him yesterday for his views. It was his day off.>>>

<<<Daryl, I take it you'll give Dave a call today?>>>

<<<Naw. Too busy filing my nails. ☺ Wee joke. Already called him. He has nothing else to add to the information in the file. Says that suspect's trail went cold after the second family. The addresses are all there in the folder. He seemed an alright guy, but not too helpful.>>>

<<<What next then?>>> I asked.

Before I could receive a reply a bell sounded from my computer. Shit. Have you ever tried to deliberately forget something? Can't be done. I wanted to forget I had an appointment with a counsellor that morning. Tried to banish all thoughts of it from my mind. But what happens with the human mind is that whatever you resist, persists. Every five minutes your mind tells you to remember to forget that appointment. And then you go and make it harder by putting a reminder in your desktop diary. Given the amount of pish that comes out of my head, the wisest thing is probably to go ahead with the meeting after all.

It is part of my agreed recuperation that I download all of my worries to a total stranger paid for by the police.

The name on her card reads Elaine Gibson. It is followed by a bewildering array of letters, like an abstract and truncated alphabet. She must be good then.

Her office is in the other side of town, so at least I get to remove myself from HQ. A taxi ride later and I am looking at a brass plaque pinned to a sandstone wall. "Chalmers, Crowe and Gibson" it reads.

I wait for less than a minute in the reception area before I am guided into an office. If I were to pin a number on the young lady with shoulder length brown hair who walks towards me it would be a ten. As in, out of ten. The new Bo Derek walks towards me with her hand outstretched and a welcoming smile on her face. I estimate her age in the early thirties. Ms Gibson is dressed in a brown, chalk-stripe trouser suit, with a cream blouse underneath. Only one button is open, but this doesn't diminish the view in any way. The material of her suit is being pressed by her flesh in all the right places.

'DI McBain. Nice to meet you.' Her handshake is firm and confident and involves a full grip, not the girly press of thumb and finger on the second knuckle that some women seem to think of as a handshake. Her eye level matches mine. You don't meet too many women as tall as I am.

'Please, DI McBain, have a seat.' She points to a pair of brown, padded chairs that flank a small coffee table.

'Thank you, and you can call me Ray,' I say and my voice seems too loud and masculine in this environment. There's a plant on every available surface and a couple of limited edition prints of flowers hang on the wall. I reconsider my initial impression; the objects in the room are expensive, but as far as gender goes they are nondescript. Any femininity found in this room is coming from its occupant.

We sit; she crosses her legs in a fluid motion and slides a leather folder across the coffee table and on to her lap. I can't take my eyes from her face. She has large eyes framed with dark lashes, an apple-pink blush to her cheeks and her lips are full and curved in a smile. I feel my stomach do a flip when she looks into my eyes. What is it about very beautiful women that make a man feel that he's eleven and obliged to flirt at the same time? Not a winning combination. As your desperation to impress increases, your ability to do so fades in a pre-pubescent fuddle.

'You have a nice office.' Way to go, McBain. That'll have her eating out of your hand in no time. I distract myself from my ineptitude by looking around myself in an exaggerated manner. A six-foot bookcase rests against the far wall. It appears that the top three rows are filled with dull, academic texts if the boring covers and large letters are to be believed. The bottom two rows are filled with brighter covers that suggest more popular and widely available books are stationed here.

'Do you read, Ray?' she asks me.

'If you count Our Willie or the underwear pages of the Next catalogue as reading.' I curse myself. Now she's going to think I'm some kind of pervert.

She smiles and writes something down.

'Sorry,' I offer. 'In my head, that sounded funnier.'

Her answering smile is non-committal. 'Humour is good.' She sets those eyes on me. 'Is that how you deal with things, humour?'

'It beats flagellation.' What's with the sexual undertones, McBain? One syllable answers only from now on. You don't want this beautiful woman to think you are a sicko.

She scratches her pen across the paper on her lap.

'Tell me why you are here.' She lifts her eyes from the paper. 'Please forgive me if I appear distracted. If I didn't write while you spoke I would forget too much.' She smiles and I can refuse her nothing.

'Tell you why I'm here? Because the high-heid-yins want me to talk about my recent trauma.'

'Is that how you would describe it? Trauma?'

'Wouldn't you?'

'Your employers have included in their report what happened. But, no offence, the language your bosses use would cure an insomniac. Why don't you give me the detail?'

'Careful, Ms Gibson. That could be classed as an opinion.'

She smiled. 'It would more accurately be described as a weak attempt to get you onside by being disrespectful to your employers.'

'True. And if I respond you get the bonus of getting me used to doing all of the talking.'

'Does talking represent a challenge to you?'

'Not if it includes a good wine and a well-chosen menu.'

'Has alcohol been a problem in the past?'

'No more than food.'

'You turned to drink when things initially started to go wrong. Why do you think that is?'

'There were too many celebrities doing daft stuff on TV.'

'Tell you what.' She closes her folder, puts it on the table and places her pen on top of that. 'Why don't we stop the verbal tennis and you just give me the highlights.'

'Don't you mean the lowlights?'

She raises her eyebrows in a question. Feeling like an idiot, again, I do as she asks.

I give her the facts in a monotone. When I stop speaking she just sits there and watches me. I'm aware of this technique, in which her aim is to get me to fill in the silence with just a little more detail. In my experience that last piece of added detail can be more telling than everything that has previously been uttered. Most people hate silence and rush to fill it with the first thing they think of and often, with the kind of stress they are feeling, it's the last thing they want to say.

The silence stretches between us. I cross my arms. She crosses hers. I cross my legs at the ankles. She does the same. This is a technique called mirroring and is meant to show the interviewee that on a subliminal level, the other person is on the same wavelength. The trick for the interviewer is to wait until your subject then begins to mirror your body language, because then you have them, they are on-side and you are in charge. She puts her hands on her lap. I keep mine where they are. I ain't that easy.

'What was the worst part of it all?' she asks.

Interesting question, I think.

'What was the worst part?' I search the ceiling for answers and decide I should give her something, then she'll feel she has done a good job. 'The worst part was the loss of control.'

'Loss of control.' She purses her lips and nods. This pursing of the lips thing is very attractive on her. Maybe I should give her more to think about.

'I've been a policeman for a long time. I've been in many dangerous positions. Normally I have the power.' I swallow. My throat feels tight. 'Here I was under the control of a psycho.' Whoa, McBain.

That was maybe a bit too much. The palms of my hands are suddenly slick with sweat. My mind filled with the vision of Leonard's face. A fleck of saliva at the corner of his mouth.

I wipe my hands slowly on my trousers while I speak, trying to disguise my actions. Ms Gibson misses nothing.

'How do you aim to get that power back?'

Another good question. Often people who have been damaged in hugely stressful situations try to regain some of the lost power by turning on people weaker than themselves. By asking this question she is trying to ascertain if I am a further risk to my employers.

'I have no interest in power, Ms Gibson. I just want to do my job and keep the streets safe for ordinary folk like you.'

She doesn't rise to the bait.

'You seem well balanced after everything you've been through ... what did you do to occupy your time while you were convalescing?'

'Went for long walks. Watched old movies, comedies mostly. There's nothing to beat a laugh.' Something Alessandra said earlier tugs at my mind. Something to do with black and white movies.

'Do you sleep well?'

'Like a baby,' I lie.

She lifts her left arm up and turns her wrist so she can look at her watch. It's a chunky silver piece that would look better on me. Its overtly masculine look contrasts perfectly with her slim wrists.

'We have five minutes left. Is there anything you would have preferred we talked about for the time remaining?'

'Your marital status?' I look for a ring. Nothing there.

'Unavailable.'

'If I smile like this?' I give her a three-quarters view of my face, 'People tell me this is my best side.'

'Four minutes left,' a smile tugs at her mouth.

'If someone changes their name, what does that say about them?' I ask.

'That depends. If that someone is you I might have an opinion.'

'Let's say it is.'

She looks at her watch.

'Oh go on. Just this wee crumb of a question?' I smile in a way that is meant to be part flirtatious, but probably ends up with me just looking like a simpleton.

'Depends on the context. I'm guessing this is not you, but a criminal case.' She pauses. 'I thought you were only taking care of administrative tasks for now.'

Warning bell. 'I am. This is actually...' I pretend to act like a daft laddie, '...from a black and white movie.'

'What's it called, I might have seen it.'

'Eeesh, you're asking me the name of a movie, I can barely remember what I had for breakfast.' I raise my eyebrows and this time I'm sure I look like I am in the advanced stages of Alzheimers. 'So what's your professional opinion, 'cos I'm convinced the scriptwriters on this one got it all wrong.'

'Well, without knowing too much about the plot line,' she looks at me with an expression that says she is humouring me, 'It could be any number of things... like a form of fan worship. Or your parents named you Primrose and you turn out to be a six-foot, eighteen-stone rugby player. Or it could mean you have some sort of delusion. Or it could simply mean you have something to hide.'

Chapter 4

'And this is... was the master bedroom,' Jim stuffed his hands into his pockets and stared out of the window, not wishing to observe Angela's reaction. 'I've set up my stuff in the spare room downstairs.' Her answering smile was stiff, but grateful.

'Right,' she said quietly. Her arms were folded tightly across her chest, her top lip pulled tight between her teeth: a mannerism Jim used to love. It occurred to him that her mind may have misplaced the song sheet, but her body still remembered its tune. Its little foibles were obviously noted so deeply that it would take more than a car crash to erase them.

'Come in, come in,' Jim motioned her into the room from the hall.

'This is the biggest bed ever. I can do big frog jumps on it.' Ben's chatter did little to ease the awkwardness between them.

'Shall we ... do you fancy a wee cuppa?' Jim walked past Angela in the small space between the foot of the bed and the wall while doing his utmost not to touch any part of her with any part of him.

'Yes. That would be nice. Thank you.'

'If you're sure.'

'Yes. I'd love one. The tea at the hospital tasted like tar.'

'Or, if you prefer some time ...'

'Some time ... on my own would be nice.'

'Okay ...' What the hell is the etiquette when you're bringing home a wife who has no idea who you are, let alone who she is? There are certainly no books in the

Mind, Body, Spirit section in the shop for that thorny little problem.

'I'll, eh …' He rubbed his palms on the side of his trousers as if …well, he'd no idea why he did it. 'I'll bring you up a cup of tea and you can have a seat. Or a lie down. There's the remote for the telly. Watch the telly. Have a seat.' His face felt hot. Christ, he felt like he was twelve, he didn't know where to put himself.

Ben realising his father was about to leave the room, stood as if his feet were glued to the laminate flooring.

'C'mon, Ben. Let's leave mummy on her own for a wee while.'

'Awww,' his features contorted.

'You can come up later … Ben,' her pause before she said his name made Jim feel that she was about to issue an endearment and then found she couldn't. 'I just need a sleep. I've been very sick in the hospital.'

'I *know* that mummy. I came to see you and you wouldn't wake up. Will you wake up this time?' He ran to her, put his arms round her thighs, which was as high as he could reach, and his head against her stomach. She patted his head.

'Of course I will. Just give me ten minutes. Okay?'

'Let's go and I'll put on *He-Man* cartoons.' Bribery was an essential tool in this parent's toolkit and this was one occasion when it was absolutely necessary. Normally *He-Man* was deemed too violent and kept as a treat for when he was a really good boy.

'Yeah. *He-Man*.' He jumped up and down and then ran from the room.

Angela sat on the edge of the bed while placing as little of herself on it as was possible without falling off. 'Ben, Ben, Ben.' She whispered to herself and then the skin of her face heated as she read Jim's quizzical expression. What had she been doing? Trying to remember his name?

'He …he's a lovely, wee boy. You've done a great job with him.' She ventured a smile.

'*You've* done a great job with him.' He corrected her.

'You gave up work to stay at home with him.'

'Oh,' she responded as if Jim was talking about someone else. 'What did I do before... him?'

'Daddy?' Ben's voice sounded from the living room.

'You were a social worker.'

'Oh.'

'Daddy?' Ben's tone was more strident.

Angela ran her fingers through her hair, 'I'm sorry. It's just that I have so many ...'

'...questions. I know. Let's take it easy for now.' Dr Bodrum's advice as they left the hospital grounds was that Angela should take her time and not overload her brain with information.

'Only answer the question she asks. It would be too much if you gave her all of her life story at the one time.' He said and paused while he deliberated further. 'By all means do look at photographs, videos *et-cet-e-ra*,' he carefully enunciated each syllable. 'It may spark off a memory or even a chain of memories. But do take your time. Too much stimulation too soon will overload her and she will tire very quickly.'

'DADDY.'

'Coming, Ben.' Jim turned to Angela. She had opened a drawer to look at the clothes inside. 'When you want your tea, just give me a shout.'

Wishing he had something stronger, Jim made himself a coffee, with a mug, kettle and spoon all chosen by the woman upstairs. Everything in this house was her; her taste, her personality and none of it was familiar to her. She'd looked through the house as if she were a polite viewer at a house sale. A "that's nice" or "mmm" accompanied each fresh object that she had initially deliberated over and savoured for hours. For Jim this was symbolic of the change in her. Before the accident, well, before the separation, he used to joke that all she needed was two pillows, a throw and ten pounds and she could turn a prison cell at Barlinnie into a display for Homes & Gardens.

34

Her lack of attention paid to Ben was similarly chilling, if a little more understandable. To be suddenly told that you have a four-year-old son would set anyone back on his or her heels, but her calm manner when looking through the house highlighted her estrangement from everything she once held dear.

Angela eventually came downstairs. She looked half-sized and terrified and Jim wanted to hold her until all her questions were answered, until she understood everything, until she stopped shaking. He wanted to lift that strand of hair from her brow and slide it to the side, kiss the space it had covered and reassure her that everything would turn out just perfect.

But he daren't. The brain injury and the damage to her memory meant that he was in effect a stranger: a strange man. *Stranger Danger* is public hazard number one, isn't that what people told their families? And here she was, effectively locked in a house with one. Yes, she could leave, but where would she go? Who would she go with? How would she then start to remember?

Watching her sit on the chair, her eyes now focused on her mug of coffee, Jim's resolve was strengthened: he couldn't tell her that they were separated, on the verge of a divorce. The one adult *in* her life, who was really no longer a part of it? That knowledge would have been just too much for her at that point.

Judging the right time to tell her would be fraught. There never was going to be a right time. Jim just knew it had to wait. He'd give her a few weeks. Until she felt safe they'd sleep in separate rooms. No matter how long it took. Nothing should be allowed to happen to further complicate matters.

Then when she did find out that he'd lied to her from the start, it wouldn't be *too* hard on her. The logic of a desperate man, or what?

He made a mental list of all the people who might say the wrong thing. Angela's parents were both dead and she was an only child. His parents would know the truth and could be trusted, up to a point. Although they had never really taken to Angela, they loved Jim and they absolutely adored Ben; they would do nothing to endanger that regular contact.

Jim's friends and workmates were a different story. He'd have to come up with something believable, something so *ordinary* that they wouldn't feel the need to remark upon it to Angela whenever they saw her.

That left Kirsty: Angela's best friend, pretty much her only real friend. They had grown up together, gone through every major life event together. They were the kind of friends who might not see each other for months and click in together as if only moments had passed since their last meeting.

They always made a point of being together for either one's birthday. Apparently they had made some girlish pact that wherever they were in the world, whoever they were with, they would drop everything and travel to be with the other.

They hadn't managed to maintain this since Ben was born, but in Kirsty's last Christmas card she highlighted her determination that they should get back into the habit.

Kirsty's birthday was in June sometime. That meant Jim had about six weeks to be firmly placed in Angela's life. Six weeks to make a bond that even Kirsty would struggle to break.

And here's the bad news — Kirsty hates Jim's guts. No, that's putting it mildly. She would wear his intestines as a garland and dance the hula over his dying body.

Chapter 5

My taxi-driver goes back to the office the long way. Instead of heading for Pollokshaws Road and then into the city centre, I direct him to go east on the M8, left for Bishopbriggs and then to take the loop through Torrance to Bearsden and head back into the city centre via Clydebank and then on the Great Western Road.

It always feels strange to me that on the fringe of such a conurbation there are actually wee country roads. There are bound to be kids in the inner city areas who will never have seen real live cows and here we are surrounded by them.

In one field the long grass is spotted with lounging sheep, necks tilted up and their long, white faces pointing at the strong, spring sunshine as they take in some rays.

'What happened to the rain we normally get at this time of year,' I ask.

'Aye, I've seen everything noo,' says the taxi-driver. 'Sun-bathing sheep.'

'I hope they're all wearing their sun block.'

'Aye, and they'll all be wearing sun hats next time we go past. Wee baseball caps.'

'And the farmer will bring them wheatgrass cocktails with wee straws and parasols.'

'Don't forget your maraschino cherries.'

'You just took that too far.'

'Sorry.' He looks straight ahead, chewing on a grin.

'Gonnae no.'

'How?'

'Jist. Gonnae no.'

We both laugh. See Glasgow? See the banter? Where else can you chew the fat with a taxi-driver like this?

I feel the sunshine and the laughter lift my spirits. Who needs Prozac?

'You're no bad for polis,' says the driver.

'Thanks. But the next time you give me a lift don't speak to me or I'll bitch-slap you till your gums bleed.'

He laughs so hard I think we're going to crash. Once he recovers his equilibrium I start to think about the events of the morning so far. The therapist was not so bad, easy on the eye and all that, but do I need her? A few laughs with my colleagues, a long run round the streets of my fair city and I will be as right as, well, rain.

I think of Alessandra and Daryl. They could get themselves into trouble again on my behalf. They didn't need my help with this case, but they know I will be crawling up the walls if I am stuck on admin duties for much longer. Bless 'em.

So who is this psycho woman preying on these families? The last time she was heard of was two years ago. I phone Daryl.

'Fancy an early lunch?'

'Why kind sir, are you propositioning me?' He adopts a deep, uber-masculine tone.

'I know it's hard for you to believe that anyone of either gender could find you anything other than appealing, DS Drain, but, naw, it's your brain I'm after. Get your well-toned arse over to the Chinese buffet place in Sauchiehall Street in fifteen minutes. Ask Ale to come along as well.'

They are already seated when I arrive. They have picked a seat by the far wall and Daryl has a plate in front of him that has sufficient food for a family of four. Alessandra is more modest with a matching pair of spring rolls. Guys are such pigs.

'Man, this place is genius,' Daryl speaks through a mouthful of food and sprays some fried rice in my direction. I try to disguise how much he is pissing me off. All that food and he is in great shape.

I fill a plate with some fried rice, some chicken balls in batter, then some more chicken balls in batter. I turn to go over to the seat, pause and turn back. Then I put the extra chicken back in the heated tray. Some bad habits just have to die.

'So,' I place my plate on the table and sit down. 'Any developments?'

'You on a diet, boss?' asks Daryl, as he sizes up the food on my plate.

'Should I be?'

He rests his fork on the side of his plate and looks down at my belly, 'Mmmm. Saying nothing.'

'That's not saying nothing. That's saying "Mmmm" with a tone.'

'Well. We've been talking...' He looks at Alessandra. She throws a-leave-me-out-of-this glare at him. '... and the feeling among the guys is that you're piling on the beef again.'

'It's not that bad,' I say in a huffy tone while patting my belly with my right hand. 'You know, it's people like you who turn people like me into anorexics.'

'A defensive tone is a sign that you hear truth in the other's voice.'

'What, did you get that wee gem out of a fortune cookie?'

Alessandra snorts a laugh and then injects some reality into the conversation. 'Gonnae you two bitches shut up? You're wastin' my lunch.'

'So,' I grin at the guys and move my fork, bearing about three grains of rice, towards my mouth, 'Any developments?'

'I'm thinking we learn from the file, but we really have to start the investigation from scratch,' says Daryl.

I agree, but to give Daryl his head as official chief investigative officer I ask, 'Why?'

'I hate getting too much information second hand from such important witnesses. There's the possibility that some wee nugget of information might be missed,' he replies. Alessandra is looking at him and measuring his answer as if she had just learned something new.

'Do you not trust your colleagues?' I ask.

'It's not that I don't trust them. I just think I might find something they missed.'

'So what you going to do about it?'

'Revisit the families.'

'Under what pretext?' We both know the families are going to be seriously pissed off that we are starting the investigation from scratch.

'No pretext,' he shrugs. 'I've read the file, these are intelligent people. They are going to smell a lie from a mile off. We need to come clean, tell them the previous investigating team all died in a terrible accident, the files were destroyed by an al Qaeda cell and that the A-team has been moved from tracking down a serial killer to find Hell Bitch.'

'That'll do it.' I fork a chicken ball into my mouth.

'Given the personnel we have at our disposal, I think you and Ale should go and see Mr & Mrs Browning. While I go and see Mr & Mrs Greig.'

I nod my head with appreciation at what Daryl is doing. It should be just the two of them and they should be visiting both homes together. Then I turn to Alessandra.

'What do we know about Mr & Mrs Browning?'

'They are in their mid-thirties. They are both dentists, although Mrs Browning is now a stay at home mother. She was diagnosed with M.S. ten years ago. They have two kids, aged three and five.'

Mr & Mrs Browning live in a lower conversion of a sandstone mansion in the south side of the city. Pollokshields is an area of the city that could well have coined the cliché "leafy suburb". The homes are substantial Edwardian or Victorian buildings in what is the United Kingdom's first planned garden suburb. We have Maxwell Park on one side and a number of trees just as substantial as the houses they shelter surround us.

'It must be a bitch to clean up the leaves around here come autumn,' says Alessandra as we slow at the side of the house. She parks her car and our feet scrunch the gravel in unison as we walk towards the grand entrance of the house. A pillar at either end holds up a sweeping sandstone porch. The door is oak and has a small glass window at head height, and a lion's head brass knocker at shoulder height.

The door opens as I lean forward to pull up the lion's chin.

'DI McBain and DC Rossi, I presume?' A sombre-faced man of my own age eyes us both up and down.

'Mr Browning,' I take a step forward with my hand extended. He takes it and shakes. His hand is warm and soft, though the grip is firm. His head is shaven bald and the lower half of his face is covered with a trim goatee. He is of medium height and his slight frame is covered in the uniform of the middle class — chinos and an open necked shirt. Under his shirt I can see a piece of jewellery. Looks like a shark's tooth on a piece of leather. Could he be a bit of a hippy under that middle-class exterior? He turns to Alessandra and gives her the same attention.

We are directed through a large hallway, which is centred with a round table sporting a display of fresh flowers and through a pair of double doors into what I expect is the lounge.

'This is my wife, Liz.' A small, thin woman waves from the end of a large, coffee-coloured leather sofa. The lower half of her body is covered by a red tartan shawl. She beckons us across the expanse of floor with one hand, while she lowers the lid on her laptop with the other.

'Forgive me if I don't get up.'

It's only when I get closer to her that I spot the wheel-chair that has been pulled behind the arm of her seat. We shake hands and her grip is as strong as the light that shines from her eyes. I get the impression that however badly this lady's body may be letting her down, her mind is a force to be reckoned with.

'Which one of you is DI McBain?' asks Mrs Browning,

as Alessandra and I sit on the sofa facing her. I put my hand up.

'Just don't want to make any assumptions that the promoted post would be held by the man,' she smiles.

'Scotland's Police has moved on a great deal in that regard, Mrs Browning,' says Alessandra, mindful of our additional role as public relations officers.

'Aye, right,' Mrs Browning says quietly, still smiling. Then she speaks louder. 'However, my gripe with Strathclyde's finest is not with gender equality issues, but with the lack of attention we have been given over the last year.'

'My wife likes to go straight to the point.' The doleful cast of Mr Browning's eyes suggest the world is about to end. 'I'll just go and fetch the tray from the kitchen.' He excuses himself and leaves the room.

'You have a lovely home, Mrs Browning,' Alessandra says.

'Thank you. Please call me Liz. And himself is Douglas. So...' she drums her fingers on the lid of her computer. '...my letters and phone calls eventually got a response?'

'I could cite lack of manpower, Liz. And too many bad guys lining our streets, but I won't insult your intelligence,' I say. 'We have been tasked with finding the young woman who caused you so much upset.'

'Good. At last.' She leans forward. 'What do you need to know?'

'Shouldn't we wait for Douglas to ...' Alessandra asks.

'Beneath that lugubrious exterior lurks a sharp mind, DC Rossi,' Liz interrupts. 'He'll catch up.'

'Can you explain the circumstances of how you met Lucy Hepburn?'

'Audrey was... sorry, Lucy. I still struggle to use her proper name. She was recommended by a patient of mine. I was a practising dentist before...' she waved her hand over her legs.

'Do you remember the name of your patient?'

'That should be in your report. I have her details

42

written down somewhere.' Her expression is scratched through with irritation at herself. It's like she should have had all the information to hand and is angry with herself for not meeting her own high standards. She doesn't bear any limitation easily, which balances with the wheelchair being tucked out of sight for the moment you gain your initial view of her.

'How many hours did Lucy Hepburn work for you?' asks Alessandra.

'It varied. You see she worked part-time at the Southern General. She was a nurse there. So it depended on her shifts. And I preferred to keep things flexible.'

'What my wife isn't telling you...' at that point Douglas Browning entered the room carrying a tray with an aluminium flask, four mugs and a selection of exotic teas. '...is that she saw the fact she needed a help with the kids as a form of defeat. And it was only when she was absolutely forced to use the help available that she would.'

'I do love it when you talk about me as if I'm not in the room, dear.' Liz's eyes narrow. Then she turns her attention to the tray. 'I hope you don't mind. I've found that caffeine doesn't agree with me so we only have herbal teas in the house.'

'Herbal's fine,' we both chime.

'Just as well, eh?' Liz smiles. 'Anyway. The drugs they force me to take can sometimes make life difficult for me. I can get tired.'

'For tired, read exhausted,' says Douglas as he fills each mug with steaming hot water and offers us the tray to pick from the selection.

She shoots ice at him with her eyes. 'Lucy was a good help at first. The kids took to her very quickly. She had a good manner with them.'

'Yes, there was a childlike quality about her that the children responded to,' adds Douglas, his expression moving from doleful to thoughtful. His voice was very soft and suggested a gentle nature. I'd bet his patients love to be soothed by him. With a drill aimed at their gums, the combination of his sorrowful demeanour and his soothing voice would have people thinking how lucky they were. Hey, how bad could it be, they'd ask. What's a little toothache compared to what's plaguing this little man?'

'When did you realise that everything was not as it should have been?' I ask as I drop a peppermint teabag into my mug.

'The day she left,' Liz says as if it had just occurred to her. She and her husband communicate with a small nod. 'One day, she just didn't bother to turn up. But with the kids there was nothing in particular at first. But looking back it's as if,' she bit her lip, 'It's as if they were lighter somehow. It took a few days for them to realise that she wasn't coming back. Wee snippets would jump from their mouths as we bathed them or put them to bed.' For the first time Liz is wearing a matching expression to her husband. 'Do either of you have kids?'

We both shake our heads.

'As a parent you want only the best for your kids. You'd jump in front of a bullet for them.' Her jaw muscles bunch together. I can almost hear her knuckles crack as she tightens her fists. 'But to sit with the knowledge on a day to day basis that your choices have caused them serious physical and emotional harm. It's almost too much to ...' her voice cracks with emotion. 'That's why ...' she clears her throat '...that's why I have pestered you guys to do something about this. I refuse to accept that a woman like that can betray our trust in such a way and get away with it.'

Douglas pats her on the back of the hand. She pulls her hand away. Their eyes meet for a second, then they both look away as if whatever was broken will never be fixed. For a moment they look lost in their own inability to protect their children. And in their lack of faith in the other to make the right choices. It appears they have each accepted the full blame for what happened while simultaneously finding culpability in the other.

'In what way did she harm them?' I ask.

Liz busies herself with examining the teabag floating in her mug.

'Do we need to go through this again? It's all in the statement we gave your colleague,' says Douglas in the first show of strength of character we've witnessed.

'You know what,' says Liz speaking louder now. '*We* need to go through this again. *We* need to remind ourselves what that woman did.' Her eyes met mine like a challenge. This was her penance and she would gladly pay it.

'From what we can piece together with the benefit of hindsight and what the kids have since told us, it began with little comments, barbs intended to worry and undermine the kids' confidence.' Douglas's eyes are deep in his shame as he speaks. 'The kids would be extra pleased to see me when I came home from work. Relieved to the point of tears. Then, at bedtime, they'd be clinging to my neck saying things like don't die, Daddy, don't die.'

'Dan, the eldest told us later that she used to play a trick on them. She'd pretend to answer the phone and then tell them the police had called to say that their Dad had just been killed in a car crash. Then she'd laugh at their tears and say she was only joking. Then she'd wait a few days and do it all over again.'

'The wee souls wouldn't have known if they were coming or going,' added Liz still stinging with the cruelty. 'The thing is,' her eyes jumped from me to Alessandra, 'and we can only see it now, she was a wonderful actress. Completely believable. She manipulated and deceived Douglas and me with ease. I was completely taken in by her. Two small children were like putty in her hands.'

'So why didn't either of the kids come and tell you what was going on?' asked Alessandra. The same question was on my mind.

'We've asked ourselves that same thing over and over,' answered Douglas. 'Dan, the older of the two, normally can't keep quiet. He talks the way other people breathe.

While Pete is the opposite. He has less to say for himself.'

'Can't get a word in,' says Liz. This prompts a smile of sorts between the couple. 'Dan doesn't give the wee soul time to speak. So maybe,' she pauses '...maybe Pete took his lead from his big brother.'

'Dan did say something not long after Hepburn left,' says Douglas. 'At first when we questioned him he would shake his head and bite his lip. Then as he realised any imagined threats hadn't materialised he began to speak about it.'

'One night I was lying on Dan's bed with one boy on each side telling them a story, when Dan said that he liked my stories better than Audrey's.' She put a hand over her heart. 'I didn't want to seem too keen, but I was dying to drag the words out of him. Then he went on to say that she only had one or two stories and they involved boys who couldn't keep secrets and the terrible things that happened to them when they didn't.'

'From the reports we have it is clear that not all the abuse was mental,' I said. Both of them flinched at the word "abuse".

'Nothing that we can prove though,' answers Douglas. 'Dan tripped and broke his arm. Pete managed to burn himself on the cooker. Neither'll say what really happened. But we know, you know? And of course Audrey was blameless on both occasions.'

'Then there were the bruises.' Liz screws her eyes shut tight against the memory. 'When I think of that innocent face she used to pull,' says Liz. 'I could slap her so hard.' The stress she puts on the last word is so strong I almost expect to see blood drip from each nostril.

'We can't be thinking like that, honey,' Douglas puts his hand on Liz's. Again she moves hers out of reach. He gives a little sigh of frustration and looks at his wife as if to say he would keep on trying to reach her. 'Buddha said that if you pick up a hot coal of revenge to throw at someone, you're the one who ends up getting burned.'

'Oh, fuck you and your little Buddha sayings. If you're

going to get religion, get a man's one. One where you get to take an eye for an eye.' Her face is tight with anger, her lips pale. She takes a deep breath. 'Sorry, officers. Things just get too much for me sometimes.'

For a moment no-one knows where to look.

'Thanks for that, honey.' Douglas voice is barely above a whisper. The muscles in his jaw are wriggling like worms as he fights for control. He addresses us. 'One of the things we didn't admit on the last visit was the games Audrey played with us.'

Liz turns her head towards the fireplace to show her husband the back of her head.

'She wrote a letter to Liz after she left. It was pushed through the letter box, so no postmark, I'm afraid.'

'Do we need to do this, Douglas?' asks Liz.

'She wrote to Liz and told her that we had been having an affair. That while she had her mid-afternoon nap she and I would be on the couch ...what were the words she used, darling.' Douglas is a different man now. 'Fucking like animals. That was it, wasn't it?'

Liz shrinks from the words.

'And my dear wife believed her. Over ten years together. Ten years when I have done nothing to put her trust in me at risk and one madwoman's letter is enough to cast doubt.'

'Mr Browning, did you sleep with Lucy Hepburn?' I ask. This is a question I have to address. If this case ever gets to trial any defence lawyer worth his salt would be raising questions like this, looking for facts that might explain his client's behaviour.

'DC McBain, I will tell you, like the countless times I have told my wife. No, I did not sleep with Lucy Hepburn.'

I may be making the wrong judgement call on this, but I can see how a woman confined to a wheelchair might be riddled with fear that she would lose her able-bodied husband. Hepburn had picked up on that and as a final throw of the dice sent the accusing letter. Perhaps she thought that if the couple fought about this it would detract from the details that would emerge from the kids about how she treated them. What a manipulative bitch. That this continued to be a source of discord in this home was a testament to the power that woman still held over this household.

'What's wrong, Douglas? Weren't you man enough for her? Did you try and she knocked you back?' Liz's expression is cold.

Douglas jumps to his feet and stares down at his wife. There's a look in his eyes that suggests that he has had enough. Police presence or not.

'She wasn't my type, darling. I prefer cripples.' He turns and leaves the room.

People do tend to save the worst of themselves for their loved ones and in my job I get to see plenty of such behaviour, but even I lost breath over the callousness of Douglas's remark.

Liz is wearing an expression that is part profound tiredness and part self-loathing and stares at the glass of the window. Eventually, while Alessandra and I wonder what to do with ourselves, she speaks.

'Sometimes, I think, despite what I really want, all I can do is push him away.'

Chapter 6

Ben was doing his usual budgie impression when Jim collected him from the nursery. He kept up his soprano chatter from the backseat all the way home. He'd been looking at books of dinosaurs and they were the biggest creatures ever to walk on the world he told Jim, his voice tight with awe.

'They're bigger than our house, Daddy.'

'Yeah?'

'Much bigger. The biggest one was a brachiosaurus. He had a long, long neck.' His tone was so emphatic Jim couldn't help but get caught up in it.

'Wow.' If only life could be that simple for everyone: enthuse so completely about one thing and let the rest of the world take care of itself.

'And he ate leaves from the top of giant trees.' The word "giant" never received such great stress. 'Will Mummy want to see me tonight?'

The abrupt change almost caused Jim to miss a red light. Braking in time, he searched for a suitable answer. 'Mummy always wants to see you, son. She's just a bit confused just now. Sometimes that happens when people are in accidents.' He scanned his brain for a parallel in a child's existence and couldn't find one. 'It's like she woke up and found out she was suddenly married to me and had a new son called Ben.'

'But she's always been my mummy, Daddy.' Jim could hear in his tone that Ben was doing his utmost to keep the tears at bay. The car behind blared his horn to let Jim know that the light had changed to green. He used hs horn again. Jim shot him the finger and roared, 'Piss off, prick.'

'What's a prick, Daddy?'

Christ. You need to keep calm, Hilton. He searched for a stupid reply. 'It's a kind of sandwich, son.' Where did that come from? The good thing with that answer was that Ben hated bread, so he was unlikely to ask someone for a prick sandwich. If he did, they'd be on to the social department quicker than you could dial 999.

As soon as Jim could stop the car safely, he did. Then he clambered over into the back seat and sat beside Ben. He unlocked his seat belt and climbed into his father's lap.

'Why does Mummy not love me anymore?' The tears that threatened earlier were now in full flow, the colour of his eyes washed into a pale green. Jim kissed his head and fought back the emotion that was tightening his throat.

'Aww, Ben, Mummy does love you. She'll always love you. It's just that she's not well just now. Remember when you couldn't find your biggest T. Rex toy?'

Ben lifted his head from Jim's chest and looked up into his eyes. A large tear shone, pre-slide, on the long dark lashes that curved on the rim of his lower eyelid.

'Uhuh?'

'Well. You put your T. Rex somewhere and you couldn't remember where. Didn't you?'

'Uhuh.'

'Well, Mummy had an illness that makes her like that. Except she can't remember where she put you and me.'

'That's silly, Daddy. We're here.'

'Yes we are. And Mummy's frightened because she wants to remember who we are, but she can't right now. But we can help her can't we?' Jim was confused by his own logic, but Ben considered it for a moment.

'Yes. I'll say, hello I'm Ben. Every morning.' He brightened at the thought that there was something concrete he could do to help.

Angela had a sleep after Jim made everyone dinner. Once Ben was in bed she stumbled downstairs. Her face lined with fatigue and her hair sticking out at odd angles.

'Are you feeling up to a trip down memory lane?' Jim asked trying to add a jaunty tone to his voice. Angela nodded, her eyes fixed on the floor.

While Jim pulled a photograph album from a cupboard, his actions were haunted by this image of his wife. Where had the vibrant woman he'd fallen in love with gone?

A conversation he'd had with Dr Bodrum popped into his mind.

'I want you to understand what might happen while your wife is in recovery, Mr Hilton,' his sad, brown eyes fixed on Jim's face. 'People in this situation often have dysexecutive problems. This means they struggle with planning and organising their activities, or solving problems and making decisions. In common parlance, the steps that you and I go through in order to make a cup of tea might even be beyond her.'

'Any more good news, Doctor?' asked Jim. He cursed himself for this flippant remark. The doctor was only trying to help, but the implications of all of this were mounting on top of him.

'It's just at this stage, Mr Hilton, you need to be aware that the problems your wife may encounter could have a profound impact on her capacity for independent living.' At this point Dr Bodrum pulled a file out of his drawer. The paper inside was clipped together and headed "Exercises". The first one was a drawing of a maze with instructions for the carer to help the head-injured person complete it.

Jim looked at the Doctor as if to say, are you kidding me.

'This is how far back to the basics we have to go Jim. Make sure your wife is rested. That the room is well lit and you give her plenty of rest. Oh,' he smiled, 'I already said that.'

Side by side at the kitchen table, Jim went through the early years of their relationship. A holiday by the

51

Mediterranean, a friend's engagement party, an author event at the bookshop. As he talked Angela's eyes roved over the pictures. Here and there her hand would slide over the colours and the people as if the act of touching them would make them come alive in her mind.

While he spoke, Angela's gaze eventually made it to Jim's face, something that made him feel more than a little uncomfortable. As he spoke he was aware of the opportunity that this presented: he could give her the Disney version of Jim Hilton. She could discover the nose-picking, farting, real-life version as their relationship deepened, but just then, he had the chance to really sell himself.

But that would be manipulative, a wee bit underhand, and no matter how much he feared it the truth had to be told. And there was no time like the present. He took a deep breath...

'I'm so sorry, Jim.' Angela interrupted his thoughts.

'What?' he exhaled like a trumpet player whose instrument had been whipped away from his mouth.

'This. What a horrible situation to find yourself in. You must really love me. And I've been so ...unappreciative.' She leaned towards him and pressed her hand against his knee. A surge shot from there to his groin.

Whoa. This was not in the script.

'Angela, I'm not a saint or anything ...'

'Jim, you've been wonderful. Patient, understanding ... you haven't even tried to ... make a pass at me. I really appreciate it.' The line of her eyes was soft now. She looked so much like the girl he had met ten years previously. Her hand moved a millimetre forward on to his thigh. Another millimetre and he would be all over her like a clumsy teenager. Oh shit, it was too nice. He sat back in his chair and watched with equal parts of dismay and relief as she placed her hand back on her own thigh.

'Angela. We need to talk. There's something ...'

'DAAAAD!' Ben screamed as if a T. Rex had him in his claws and was about to drop him into his huge mouth.

52

Jim took the stairs three at a time.

Ben was sitting upright in his bed, hair spiky and mouth wide in alarm,

'Dad, I had a horrible dream.'

'But you've only just fallen asleep, son.'

'It was horrible, Daddy,' he answered in his most indignant voice.

Jim spoke in a hushed and soothing tone to the boy and he was soon fast asleep. He rose from the bed and turned to see Angela in the doorway. He made to walk past her.

'What did I do to deserve you?' She placed a hand on his cheek. Jim stepped back.

'Angela. This is too complicated.' She had that *look*.

'Did you feel it when we were downstairs?'

'That was a heavy lorry. We get a lot of traffic in our ...wee... cul de sac.'

Angela laughed, then grew sombre. 'When we were close together downstairs I felt something,' her face flushed and she examined her shoes. She found some certainty and looked back into his eyes. 'A nice something.'

A gallon of blood flooded south from his brain.

'Yeah. Me too. Let's talk about it over a coffee. You want a coffee?' Jim sloped his shoulders in the direction of the stairwell.

She took a step towards him and put a hand on his chest. 'Were we ... good together?' The word *good* had never been imbued with such frisson. The gallon from his head was joined by several pints from his thighs. Feeling that he was about to fall, Jim leaned against the wall. He couldn't remember ever being quite so horny.

'Angela, we can't do this. You're too vulnerable. I'm too bloody desperate. Not a good mix.'

'It's me who's coming on to you, Jim.'

'True,' he nodded, like he was debating a point of housekeeping at the local church's fundraising committee. He shook his head, trying to clear it. A neon sign lit up in his brain.

Bad Idea. Bad Idea. Bad Idea.

It was replaced with an image of Angela reaching behind her to unclasp her bra. He bit the inside of his cheek. Pain. That's what was needed to get his conscience back on the programme.

'It doesn't mean that we are back living ... as a couple. But just for tonight I would like to be with you. But if you ...' She took a step back. Several emotions were vying for attention on her face. She crossed her arms. '...if you'd rather not.' Her voice was quiet. The look of rejection on her face was more than Jim could bear. All she wanted was to make a physical connection. Be skin to skin with another human. He couldn't deny her that. It was what he needed himself.

'What about a hug?' He asked and opened his arms. A hug was safe, right?

Angela rested her cheek against his neck, they held each other and closed their eyes. It could have been hours, it could have been moments, Jim wasn't sure, but he savoured the heat, the presence, the scent of her. Something shifted, something mended and something squeezed at his chest. He sniffed. He'd never felt so ... so much joy, so much relief, or so much pleasure from such a simple act. Her heat, her smell, her closeness had been missing from his life for the best part of a year and here she was, in his arms. He wanted to laugh, he wanted to scream. His emotions were all over the place.

'Jim,' Angela turned her face up to his, 'you're crying.'

His answering laugh was soggy with tears.

'I don't know what I'm doing.'

'Well, it's just as well one part of you does,' she grinned and squeezed his penis, which had all but fossilized. 'Your place or mine?' She asked, nodding her head in the direction of her bedroom.

'Yours,' he answered wondering whose voice that was and why was it so husky. Condoms, he needed some condoms, 'I just need to find ...' He gripped her arms. 'Keep that thought. I'll be with you in a second.'

54

He ran to the bathroom and the cupboard above the sink. Before the split Angela had moved them there for fear of prying little fingers finding them in his bedside cabinet. Jim plucked one from the box, checked the date. Yes, we're on, he thought and ran back to the bedroom.

When he got there Angela was lying fully clothed on top of the bed, curled in the foetal position.

'Angela,' he whispered.

Nothing.

She was fast asleep.

Chapter 7

In the car Alessandra is the first to speak.

'Jeezuz, that was intense.'

I don't respond. I am too busy getting a sense of the woman we are up against. Devious, clever and cruel. She sets out to ruin lives, preying on the weak, getting to know their weak spot before driving home the nail. The effects on that family have been both subtle and far-reaching. Where is she now and where would she draw the line?

'What're you thinking, Ray?' Ale asks.

'We need to meet up with Daryl.'

Ale rummages for her mobile phone in her handbag. 'It's here somewhere.' She lifts a purse out of the way. Then a lipstick and mirror. Then a bunch of hankies. Then some wet-wipes.

'Wet-wipes and hankies?' I ask.

'Got a problem with that?'

'I will only answer that question when my lawyer is present.'

She grimaces, still searching. Then, 'Aaah. There it is.' She plucks out a silver phone and presses a button. A noise sounds.

'I've got a text from Daryl.' She reads. 'He wants to meet us back at the office.'

We meet at the coffee machine. Daryl is fetching one for Alessandra and I just wander up to them with body language that says, here I am, bored out of my skull and wanting to shoot the breeze with some colleagues — and you guys will do.

'Caffeine isn't good for you,' I say.

'Izzat right?' Daryl says it like my opinion isn't worth a dog fart.

'Yeah. Especially women, Alessandra. Leeches the calcium from your bones. Another couple of years of that stuff and you'll know more about osteoporosis than you ever wanted to.'

'Will I get early retirement?' She shrugs, takes a sip and makes an aaaah sound. 'Just what the doctor didn't order.'

'DI Peters,' Daryl says in a quiet voice. 'Called me into his office when I got back in. Wanted to know where you were.'

When you are talking about someone else in your office — your open plan office — and you don't want them to know about it, you have to adopt the correct posture and make the right facial shapes. Backs turned to the room and heads close together is a dead giveaway.

'You're not much good at this secret squirrel stuff, DD,' I say and take a step back opening up my body shape so that it is less exclusive. 'Everyone within a ten-mile radius thinks you're talking about them.'

He sticks his bottom lip out as he considers what I just said. 'I have a cunning plan,' he says, turns and walks back to his desk. Ale follows him, prodding his back with her pen.

An email is waiting for me when I get back to my desk.

<<<Secret Squirrel here. Want to know what happened, ya cheeky b*****rd?>>>

I reply. <<<I meant no offence. A thousand apologies, numb nuts.>>>

<<<Mr & Mrs Craig — what a poor wee couple. He broke his neck in a car accident. Bed bound. Can only move his arms. Mrs Craig works as a teacher. They have one wee boy aged four. Ms Hepburn was recommended by a friend of a friend. One glowing reference. They were so desperate they didn't do much digging into her past. Same pattern as the Brownings. Gains their trust, hurts the kid and moves on. One bad incident. Wee boy nearly

57

died. Half-strangled on the cord of a set of blinds. It was Hepburn that found him apparently. At the time she was a hero. Except the wee boy was terrified of her after that. Wouldn't go near her. She packed up and left and then the wee fella told his parents some other stuff that made them come to us.>>>

<<<Anything substantial that we can prove in a court?>>> It was a horrible situation to be in, but it was almost disappointing that the kid wasn't more seriously hurt.

<<<Just the usual threats and small injuries that are easily explained away in a small boy.>>>

A voice issues from my doorway. 'Everything alright, Ray?' It's Peters.

I slouch and adopt a bored tone. 'Yeah. Just catching up with some correspondence.' I take my time in moving my eyes from the computer screen to his face. He has one hand on the doorknob and the other hangs by his side. Only one foot is in my office. 'Worried about me?'

'Just extending a professional courtesy, Ray. Nothing more.' He walks away. I want to spear him with a pen.

<<<What did DC Peters want?>>> emailed Alessandra.

<<<To see if my numbers came up in the Lottery at the weekend. What occurs to you, Alessandra?>>> I shouldn't dismiss Peters so lightly, but I will be more careful from now on.

<<<Two things. We need to find the friend of a friend that introduced Hepburn. I'll bet the glowing reference was a fake. And oh, thing three ... the Craigs came after the Brownings. She moved from assault to attempted murder. I'm worried that her violence is escalating. What will she do next?>>>

<<<When did she leave the Craigs?>>> I ask.

<<<About five months ago.>>> Alessandra answers.

Then the obvious occurs to me.

<<<The next victim could be getting warmed up right now.>>>

Chapter 8

Didn't sleep too well last night. Took me an age to get over as well. Kept thinking about the Craig boy being held up on the curtain cord and almost strangled. What kind of person thinks that up? It would take a good degree of determination to complete such a task. The wee boy would be struggling, choking, crying for his mum and dad. Did she pretend it was some kind of game at first to get him to comply?

I turned on one side then the other. Kicked the quilt off. Pulled it back over me. Got up for a drink of water and a piss. Then back to bed and back to images of a young boy being held and deliberately tortured.

When sleep eventually pulled me in I had a horrible dream. I was chasing a suspect and all the while I felt someone's eyes were on me. But every time I turned round there was no-one there. I ran down an alley. My legs weren't working properly. They felt as if they belonged to someone else. My breathing was harsh in my ears. My lungs strained to fill with air. The suspect was always just ahead. I knew that without being able to see them.

I kept running. Sweat was blinding me. A foul stench came from somewhere. It smelled of the earth's deepest, blackest cave, of bloodletting and excrement. A place where unnameable creatures hunted. I sniffed looking for a source of the smell. It was me. The stench was made of my fears.

Somehow I was getting closer to the running shape ahead of me. I wanted to turn and run the other way. Every hair on my body was on end. I told my legs, ordered them to stop moving. They didn't. As if through water they moved towards the indistinct form ahead of me.

A feather floated into my hand, small and white and its filament curved with the promise of doomed flight. The man ahead of me stopped. For now I could see it was a man. Most of him was in darkness. Somehow I could see his eyes. They held a peculiar light, one that you knew you could never afford to get lost in. I couldn't see the bottom half of his face, but I knew he was smiling. I also knew his name. Leonard.

I wake up on the couch. Chest heaving and hair soaked with sweat, my body hot in a cold square of moonlight. Sitting on the edge of the sofa, my head in my hands, my mouth closed tight to stop my teeth knocking, I force myself to calm down. How did I manage to get through to the living room? I couldn't remember ever sleep walking.

My quilt is on the floor; I must have carried it through with me. I pick it up and lie back down. The light became grey, and I sleep only for moments before I hear the alarm sounding from my bedroom. I feel like I've slept for five minutes. My eyes are hot with fatigue.

I'm doing that thing again where I walk past the full length mirror in my bedroom while studiously not looking at myself. A sure sign that I know I'm getting fat, and a sure sign that I will do nothing about it. All the skinnies have a big breakfast. This morning I am having a coffee. Followed by a coffee. Caffeine is again the drug of choice this morning.

I need to talk with someone. Would Ms Gibson like to hear the story of my dream, I wonder? Maggie might be a good option; she is always good for a listen on those few occasions I am willing to talk. Na, I'll be a man and keep it to myself.

Theresa no longer fills the position of confidant. Not that we ever had much time for talking. That woman loved sex. Theresa and her bump pop into my mind. The more I think about it the more I'm convinced I am the father. She claimed at the time we were having our affair that she and her husband weren't paying much attention to each other. So it's not like my wee swimmers had to push his out of the way on their way to the egg.

Having an affair is such a genteel way of describing the heartache that is adultery. An affair. A fling. A liaison. Labels that work to disguise the cost of betrayal. Words that soften the guilt. I am a Catholic. Guilt is my middle name. Funny, I didn't feel guilty when I was fucking her. Should I have? Who was the sinner, her or me? She was married, but she couldn't have done it without my help. Does that make her worse? She was the one being dishonest. Perhaps I was as well. I pretended for long enough that it was only sex. Some fun. Nothing beats getting naked with a beautiful woman, does it? I lied to myself and only admitted it when I was on the run. Was my betrayal worse than hers? I fell in love when all she wanted was a little fun.

She told me she was always turning him down when he asked for sex. Stands to reason then, eh? I must be the father.

Can't blame her for preferring her husband to act as the parent. I was on the run for murder at the time. While I stir sugar into my coffee I contemplate life as a father. Sleepless nights. Shitty nappies. Routine and a purpose outside of work. Might not be so bad. My mind conjures up a series of moving pictures. Me and child down by the sea... trousers rolled up and paddling in the slow roll of the waves...kicking a ball to each other with sand and surf spraying as we run for the ball...

Goodness gracious me, Ray McBain ...could you be growing up?

I shut down the images. Who you trying to kid? My life is the Police. How could I force all of that pressure on to children? Daddy's never home, Daddy's always in a bad mood. Daddy's in a good mood now because he caught a bad guy.

I admire the cops who can make it work. Takes a lot of effort, I'm just not sure I have it in me. Maybe I should stay in the shallows of life, find me a woman who is up for some company, romance and unfettered sex … in every sense of the word … and settle for that.

I have some phone calls to make this morning. Well, one. I want to speak to the lovely Ms Gibson. That is not my hormones talking. Well, only partly. I wonder if I should add Theresa to my list. Just to make sure she is okay. What would I say? How are you? Was that a big pregnant bump I noticed last time I saw you? Is it mine?

Or I could be even more direct that that.

Hello. Only me. How about you bin that miserable fucker and let me take care of you and the baby.

I pick the phone from the cradle. A few months from now and another man will be bringing up my child. I take a deep breath; acknowledge the churn in my stomach. My thumb hovers over the buttons.

I pull a note from my wallet, read a number and punch it into my phone. I get through without question. There are still times when using the job title gets you preferential treatment.

'Ms Gibson, I have a question for you.'

'DI McBain, it is a pleasure to hear from you, but can't it wait until our next appointment?'

'No. This is official I'm afraid and doesn't concern my situation. But it will only take a few minutes of your time.'

I hear pages rustle. 'Okay. You have two minutes.'

'It's about power, Ms Gibson.' I outline the situation of Mr & Mrs Craig's son. The abuse he suffered culminating in the fake rescue, if that was indeed what it was.

'What are you looking for DI McBain?'

'Please, call me Ray. All this formal stuff wears me out.'

'Okay, *Ray*. What do you want from me?'

'Be still my beating heart.'

Silence pours into my ear. There is nothing to give me the heads up as to whether she is enjoying my attempts at flirting or if she is scathing of them. The silence continues for another couple of seconds.

'An indication of the character we are dealing with,' I admit a flirting failure. For now.

'Don't you have a profiler linked to your department?'

'Only happens in the movies.' And where we have the money. And in official investigations. 'Speaking of which there's an interesting film on at the Glasgow Film Theatre ...'

'Let's not go any further with that.' Her tone is firm, but not entirely unfriendly. 'You could be right, Ray. Abuse is always about power. In this situation you have to ask yourself a couple of questions. Was this a genuine accident? Was the woman interrupted and diverted from her original plan of murder and then made it look like an accident? Or was this always her plan, to harm the boy and stop just short of murder?'

'That was three questions. What is it with you women and numbers?'

'I thought it was men who had that problem?'

'With numbers we have no problem...first date, second date, etcetera. It's measurements we struggle with. Six inches, twelve inches.'

'DI McBain, you are outrageous,' I can hear a smile in her voice.

'Say we go with the latter explanation. Our sicko always planned to stop just short of killing the boy.'

'That would suggest someone who toys with her power. She revels in it. She has ultimate control in that situation. Let him die or not. She enjoys this, Ray. If that is the real scenario you have a dangerous and manipulative woman to find before she allows herself that final, delicious show of her will. And Ray, if I can offer you one piece of advice?'

'Sure.'

Her voice is full of concern. 'I almost hesitate to say this, Ray. I don't want to tell you how to do your job. But please don't call this woman a sicko. That reduces her to nothing more than a horrible caricature. Nothing more than a label.

'She is more ... much, much more than that.'

Chapter 9

Jim's clothes were neatly folded in three black bin bags on the front path when he came home from work the day Angela decided the marriage was over.

'Don't I at least deserve an explanation?' he remembers asking.

Angela's expression was chipped from granite. 'You can say goodbye to your son and then the next time we speak will be through lawyers.' He looked in the front window to see Ben doing a kangaroo impression from one end of the settee to the other. He hadn't yet picked up any tension.

'Angela, you've got to tell me what I've done,' he grabbed her arm.

She looked at her arm and then into his eyes. He let go.

'What's happened, Angela. What went wrong?'

'I'm done talking, Jim. I don't even have the energy to argue any more. Just, please, say goodbye and then go.' She stepped back into the hallway, looked over her shoulder to Ben and said, 'Come and say goodbye to your dad, Ben. He's going away for a few days.' Her hand moved from her chin to her nose and then rested on her mouth as she struggled to maintain her control. By her actions she was telling Jim that Ben had to be protected at all costs.

Jim went along with the play as scripted by her and stamped a smile on his face in preparation for his goodbye scene.

'Daddy will see you later,' he said while trying not to hold him too tight. "Later" came out of his mouth as if a giant fist had squeezed the last drop of oxygen from his lungs. He pressed his lips against the warm square of

Ben's forehead and turned away from him while he still had some measure of control.

How he made those few steps to the car and remained upright he'd never know. His shoulder shook with huge hiccupping sobs. The view from the car was so blurred as to be indistinct. He made it round the corner before his emotions swamped him. Hugging himself he rocked back and forward in the car seat. Was this feeling ever going to end?

Then it occurred to him that he would no longer be a part of Ben's daily existence. No way would Angela keep him from seeing him, he trusted her on that, but he wouldn't be there every morning when Ben walked through from his bedroom with his pillow-tousled hair. He wouldn't be there every day when Ben complained about having to eat carrots. He wouldn't be there every evening to listen to his son plead for another story. He didn't know how he would cope. A day without Ben in it was simply unthinkable.

What have I done? he had kept asking himself. What have I done? As he left the house Angela almost gave in to his demand for an answer.

Her eyes were heavy with betrayal. 'Look into your conscience, Jim. The answer's there.' As she spoke she slipped something into her back pocket. Jim caught it in his vision for no more than a second. Long enough to see what looked like a letter.

Jim was in his office at the bookshop processing the sales from the previous week. Or he should have been. Instead he was staring at a computer spreadsheet with his mind immersed in his worries. Ever since he returned to work he worried about leaving Angela in the house on her own. Yes, she would spend most of the day sleeping, it seemed she was never done sleeping, but there were a lot of things she'd want to do, things that could mentally trip her, things that might hurt her. She needed constant attention, but he had a job to maintain. A mortgage to pay.

Most of the time it felt like that was the least of his worries however. He was living a perjured life. Every moment of his family's life, every step forward was reaching his brain through the filter of a monumental lie. And it was imprinting its stain on everything. Nothing good would happen without it being tempered, warped or reduced to a cheaper version of itself. No smile or touch would reach him and make its full impact.

And what about last night? They had almost ended up in bed together. He couldn't let that happen again. The chances were that Angela had forgotten all about it and he wasn't about to remind her. The lie of their relationship couldn't be allowed to flounder against the rock of his libido. That would be one betrayal too many to an Angela in full possession of her faculties.

Could he tell the truth? Could he just go home after work and tell her everything? They were too far along the road surely. Surely? If, or when Angela found out, could she go it alone? Maybe she would see that she was too fragile without him. Maybe by then she would be in love with him again and she would forgive the lie knowing it was told with the best of intentions.

To live through the alternative again was just too painful to contemplate.

She was at the psychologists. Her referral had come through at last. Part of her rehabilitation was to work on regaining her long-term memory and improving her short-term memory. Jim had been unable to get time off work to go with her. Any more time off and he was sure his bosses would lose their patience. So he'd ordered a taxi to pick her up and to take her back home. It would do until other arrangements could be made. He'd heard of a local charity that helped people in this situation. He'd give them a call. Perhaps he should phone home to make sure that Angela had gotten home safely. Just as he reached for the phone it rang.

'Jim,' it was Annette down on the shop floor. 'Look on your CCTV monitor.'

'What exactly am I looking for?' He looked at the small black box to the right of his PC, which displayed several views from the shop on its 10-inch screen.

'To the right of the doors. At the three-for-two section.'

'Yeah?' Mr irritable was coming back. There'd better be a point to this.

'Is that...your wife ... Angela?'

'Eh?' He squinted...and there sure enough was his wife picking a book from the shelf. But she looked different, smaller somehow. And as if she'd just stepped fully clothed from a swimming pool.

'I'll be right down.'

When she saw him walking towards her Angela twitched a smile.

'So this is where you work?' Her eyes looked anywhere but into his face. 'Nice. I wrote it down. In case I got lost.' She reached into the pocket of her jeans, while looking into the distance. Her hand came out empty. Her eyes told him that she wasn't sure what she was looking for. 'Must be lovely working with all these books.' She looked around at the well-stacked shelves, her eyes darting from book spine to book spine like a literary bluebottle. Her arms were folded tight across her chest.

'Hey. What are you doing here? What's wrong, honey? How did you get so ...?'

'I felt good. Strong ...you know. I wanted to see where you worked. I wrote it down and everything.' A sob escaped from her lips. 'It's raining ...and I got lost.' She closed her eyes against the flow of tears. Jim drew her into his chest. Her shoulders shook with emotion.

'C'mon. Let's go up to my office and have a wee bit of privacy,' said Jim.

In the office, Jim sat her on a rickety blue computer chair — facing his own rickety blue computer chair. Handing her a cup of water he said in as calm a tone as he could muster, 'Okay. Tell me everything from the start.'

Angela shook her head slowly from side to side, closed her eyes and scrunched up her mouth. Then she bent forward, elbows on her thighs and fingers gripping her head through her soaking hair.

'I can't remember,' she said in a strangled whisper. Then louder. 'I can't fucking remember.' Then a whisper with her head down, as she was examining the carpet. 'Fucking cunt cunt cunt cunt.'

'Your appointment was at ten this morning.' He looked at his watch and ignored the words coming out of Angela's mouth. Pre-accident Angela would have been as likely to say the "C" word as she would have been to give Ben a backhander. 'And it's now two-thirty. How long were you with the doctor for?'

'Can't remember.'

Jim guessed it wouldn't have been longer than an hour. Christ. She'd been walking the streets ever since then.

'You must be ...'

'And on the way back I thought it would be nice to go and look at the shops. You know, act like a normal person instead of a ...freak.' She took a deep breath.

'Then I thought, wouldn't it be nice to come in and see you. Celebrate my return to the big bad world and all that.' She took a sip from her water.

'Is that okay? Would you rather have a coffee?'

'No, this is fine. Thanks.' Another sip. If she could have inhaled it Jim was sure she would have. 'And I couldn't find your shop. Couldn't remember where it was.' Her eyes looked tiny against the mottled pink of her face. Drips from her hair threatened to refill her cup.

'Look, why don't I go and get you a towel,' Jim said and stood up. 'You'll get an attack of the sniffles.'

She pushed a rope of hair thick with moisture away from her face. 'Okay. Thanks.'

Moments later he was back with a towel. Then he noticed staining on the carpet around her feet. 'You really need to get some dry clothes.'

'JIM. Will you sit down and stop fussing? I feel enough of an idiot without you barging around.' Her nostrils flared, her eyes bulged. Then as quickly as the storm blew

68

in, it blew out. She sagged back into her chair.

'Fuck,' she said. This single syllable was drawn out, thick with desperation.

'Sorry, honey. I was just trying to help.'

She closed her eyes. It read to him as if she was fighting a further irritation. Then the flow of tears started up again. 'Jim, it was awful. Do you know what I mean? Terrifying. I didn't know where I was. Barely knew who I was. Couldn't remember the name of the shop. I've been walking up and down this street,' her right arm flew out to the side, she swivelled her head to one side and then to the other, 'or was it that way? It was horrible.'

'Honey, you're here now. Safe.'

'And I kept thinking, what if Ben was with me? I can't be trusted to look after myself, what would have happened to him?'

Apologising to the staff, Jim bundled a still weeping Angela into his car, drove her the fifteen minute journey home, poured a bath and helped her out of her clothes. By this stage, she wasn't giving a thought to the fact she was naked, he didn't think she was capable of thought, she simply obeyed his every request as if she was on automatic.

In the bath, knees gathered to her chest she was like an island of bone jutting out from a sea of foam. Her slight limbs trembling within a translucent layer of skin. He hadn't noticed just how thin she had become. As he soaped her down she gazed into neverland and allowed Jim to move her arms up so he could wash the flesh underneath.

Dropping the sponge through the layer of bubbles to fill up with warm water and then slowly squeezing the contents down the knobbled line of her spine soothed him as much as it did her. It felt like a concrete thing to do, a way to connect with the tired and lost soul somewhere behind those vacant, staring eyes.

Like a child she let him dry her while she sat feet planted on the rug, her backside on the edge of the bath.

Carefully Jim drew the towel across her shoulders, down her back and arms and then across her breasts. Kneeling before her he attended to her feet, her legs and the soft brush of hair at their junction. All the while, Angela stared impassively into the distance.

Then he dressed her in a robe, bound her hair in a towel and led her through to her bedroom. Once she was under the quilt he closed the curtains then walked out of the room. Closing the door behind him, he heard the sigh of the door as its base brushed across the thick pile of the carpet.

In the kitchen, a mug of coffee heating his cupped palms he wondered at the new Jim Hilton and his calm acceptance of what needed to be done. Where did he come from?

Short-term memory loss. That was what the doctors warned him to look out for. Four little words that came nowhere close to describing the chaos they could cause. They did nothing to prepare him for the panic in her eyes, the anger, the exhaustion.

Earlier on that day he had, for the umpteenth time convinced himself that he needed to tell Angela the truth of their relationship. What would the truth do to her right now? She was too fragile. She needed her *husband's* support. She simply couldn't function without it.

What was he going to do? Tell the truth, or continue with the lie? He thought of Angela in the bookshop; fear and uncertainty tattooed into every word that came out of her mouth.

Who was he kidding? There was simply no other option.

The lie was pristine in white and had to remain.

Chapter 10

Those held in Barlinnie Prison are allowed one thirty minute visit between Monday and Friday. The man I'm sitting in front of has had no-one in to visit him since he was locked up several months ago. Bar-L as it is known locally, was built in the late eighteen hundreds to cure the chronic overcrowding problem in Scotland's jails. Ironic that it is now part of the problem.

It is famous for the odd rooftop protest, a certain Libyan diplomat who was found guilty of involvement in the Lockerbie disaster and, until only fairly recently, for forcing the inmates to deposit their overnight excrement into a bucket and then "slopping out" in the morning.

Joseph McCall is looking younger than when I first met him. He looks as if he has lost more than a couple of the twenty-two years he has lived so far. His prison garb is too big for his slight frame and his hair is longer and in need of a wash. His facial hair sums him up, thin and patchy.

'Hi, Joseph,' I say.

He looks at an indeterminate space between us, his eyes dull and unfocused. He does nothing to show that he knows I am sitting in front of him or that I have actually spoken.

'Just thought I'd come and say hi,' I say. And wrestle with a few demons.

He doesn't move.

I look around me. The Visits Hall is pretty busy. Wives and children sit before husbands and fathers, separated by the width of a table. Might as well be a thousand miles. They are a poor bunch. Cheap shoes and overcoats. Plastic bags from supermarket chains at their feet. It strikes me when I look at the people dotted around at the tables that more than a few of the inmates look better fed than their visitors. From exaggerated looks I judge that a few of the convicts "make" me. I must have cop engraved on my forehead.

I consider for a moment that visiting Joseph in the general visiting area might cause him some problems. Then I look at him and change my mind. He looks like he wouldn't care if the whole Scottish legal establishment was sat in front of him.

'They looking after you in here?'

Nothing.

Not for the first time I think about the life this boy has had until now. He is born to a poor, unmarried mother with substance abuse problems. To get her next fix she regularly trades him off to men whose tastes run to the pre-teenage boy. His mother dies and her best friend takes over. He finally manages to make some form of life for himself and gets an education only to find out that his father was a career paedophile. He is then befriended by a serial killer who trains him up as an assistant. To escape this serial killer he takes the blame for several vicious murders and is given life imprisonment. If you watched that story line in a movie it would be titled "Unbelievable".

All this and he's only in his early twenties.

In some ways I feel responsible for him. We are linked in suffering. His mother and I were both victims of the same man. And now he is in jail for the rest of his life because I was unable to convince the powers that be they had locked up the wrong man.

'Can I do anything to help you?' I ask.

'Is there anything you need?' I ask.

It's like I'm speaking to a tailor's dummy for all the reaction I get. I study his face for a clue that there is a shred of something resembling human intelligence within. His eyes are brown, each pupil a small black spot. His eyes look as if they have been dried of life, sand-

72

blasted to nothing but stone.

Concern is clearly not the tactic to reach this man. I try something else.

'Leonard been in to see you yet?'

His nostrils flare slightly as he takes air in to his lungs.

'Didn't think so. How do you think he would thank you for being his bitch?'

A muscle twitches in his jaw line.

'He's probably pissed off, 'cos that means he's got one less target. One less slab of meat to slice open.' I take a deep breath and sit back in my seat. 'What a fucking loser, Joe. Fucked over by everyone who has ever met you.'

His eyes shift focus. From nowhere to me. There's no other movement that I can discern. I feel only sorrow for this sad lump of humanity in front of me and I hate what I am doing. I find the coals of my fear of Leonard and breathe heat into them. I am tired of being chased by my thoughts of this man. I hate what he has made of me and I will no longer take it. And the focus of all that is sitting in front of me.

'Don't you wish they still had the death penalty in this country? Then you could put an end to your pathetic, miserable existence once and for all.' My face is close to his. 'You fucking pisspot. You sorry figure of a man. What could you have been? You got yourself an education despite everything. And here you are. Bet you have a queue of men outside your cell at night beating themselves off at the thought of your lily-white arse.'

He continues to stare at me. The only sign he has heard any of my words is the strange light that has come in to his eyes. There is someone there. He's just been hiding. He opens his mouth to speak and what he says leaves me as the one who has been diminished by my own weapon of choice.

In the car I think about what has just happened. What did I hope to achieve by visiting McCall? Closure?

Redemption? A clue as to where Leonard might be? I got none of that. Instead I allowed a shell of a man to beat me with four words. He said the one thing that would be guaranteed to get through any defences I had managed to construct with my all out attack.

Four syllables: maximum effect.

'At least I'm safe.'

Back at the office, Alessandra is about to get into her car. She tells me Mrs Browning phoned in with the details of the woman that recommended Hepburn as a child-minder.

'Can I come?' I ask with a look that is calculated to make me look like a twelve-year-old whose friends have all pissed off and left him on his own. See me, I've no dignity.

'Can I stop you?' replies Alessandra.

'Not really,' I press the remote to unlock my car and open the passenger door. 'You can drive.'

'Gee. Thanks.'

Mrs Violet Hogg lives in a bungalow in Giffnock. This is a highly desirable part of the city for the upwardly mobile, formerly working class and the recently retired. Nice houses, nice schools, in a nice part of the city. And when we get to Mrs Hogg's house it is, well, nice.

'What was Mrs Browning able to tell you about this woman,' I ask Alessandra as she parks the car in front of a short but well-maintained, monoblocked drive. The border is well populated with the remains of this year's crop of daffodils. The recent loss of small yellow trumpet heads is offset by the flowers of the rhododendron bush that are just bursting into a furious pink bloom.

'Not that much,' replies Alessandra. 'In her mid-forties, widowed in her twenties. Never met anyone else, apparently.'

We walk up the path and ring the doorbell. The door opens immediately, like the owner of the house is desperate to relieve her boredom.

'Come in. Come in.' A smiling woman holds the door open and lets us walk past her into the small square of her hall-way. 'Through to your right.' A well manicured hand points to an open doorway. She's taller than Alessandra I realise as we walk past her. And she looks in her early fifties, wearing tight, black jeans and a pink cardigan that is buttoned all the way up to the top. 'In you go, officers. Have a seat. I expect you'll be wanting a wee cuppa.'

Her face wears the gaunt look of the over-exercised and no amount of make-up will disguise the shadows under her eyes. A recent upset, I imagine.

Alessandra and I walk into a bay-windowed room, bright with sunshine and flowers. Every surface sports a vase with a riot of colour and fragrance spilling from it.

'Have we come at a bad time?' I ask as my eyes adjust to the volume of colour. Did somebody just die, I wonder? Alessandra did say she has been widowed for some years, didn't she?

Mrs Hogg follows my line of vision. 'It's my Tommy's anniversary. It's nineteen years to this day that he passed away.' She's wearing an expression that suggests she's not only a widow, but a martyr to the cause. 'He so loved flowers. Every year at this time,' she makes a sweeping gesture with her right arm, 'I give myself a wee treat. Lovely, isn't it?'

'It's beautiful,' says Alessandra.

I want to say, time to move on, Mrs, makes your house look like a funeral parlour. Instead I nod. The upside is that at least we know how to get on her good side. Something Alessandra also picks up on.

'I bet Mr Hogg is looking down and really appreciates what you're doing,' Alessandra says.

I pass her a look that says, don't overdo it. I realise that I needn't worry when I move my eyes over to Mrs Hogg. She looks like a special effects team have given her the Ready-Brek glow. She beams pure love at Alessandra.

'That's such a sweet thing to say, dear.' She hugs herself. Her waist is so thin she could probably reach round her waist twice. 'I think he would love it. Flowers are such a joy, he used to say.'

'I say it all the time as well.' The words spill out of my mouth before I get the chance to stop them. I cringe and hope Mrs Hogg doesn't think I'm taking the piss. Which of course, I am. I'm just not normally as obvious.

'We often tease DI McBain down at the station, Mrs Hogg,' Alessandra joins in. 'Not many police officers share his enthusiasm for a fine set of blooms.'

Steady, Alessandra.

'Ohh, how lovely to meet a keen horticulturist.'

'Yes, he bought a new greenhouse. Never misses an episode of Beechgrove Garden,' Alessandra's enjoying herself.

Enough, Alessandra.

'He keeps bringing in fresh cuttings off his plants for the rest of the guys. I swear if there was a police equivalent of the "Town in Bloom" competition, we would win it hands down,' she trills.

I resort to an open glare. Then I twist my features into a grimace-cum-smile when I realise that Mrs Hogg is examining me very keenly. She plays with her necklace, sliding a flat, pink stone of some sort back and forth on its fine chain. Then she unfastens the top button of her cardigan. Christ, on a bike. Surely she isn't giving me the glad eye. I sneak a look in Alessandra's direction and she's gone pink. Looks like she is about to burst.

'If we could talk to you about Mrs Browning, please?' Time to direct the conversation on to safer ground.

'Not before I bring through a cuppa for you fine officers,' Mrs Hogg stands up and leaves the room.

Alessandra takes the opportunity to vent some suppressed laughter. Her head is in her hands and her shoulders are shaking.

'You are dead, Rossi.' I say. This only makes her movements more severe. She's saying something. Sounds like Beechgrove Garden. Over and over again. We hear the footfall of Mrs Hogg as she returns to the room. Alessandra corrects her slump and coughs a couple of times. She adopts an expression of pain, like she is reminding herself of every terrible thing that has ever happened in her life in an attempt to sober up. While she does so I look around the room. It strikes me that there is no evidence of children. If Mr Hogg had died some years ago, any issue they had would be in their twenties. There are photographs placed here and there. Mostly black and white. Group photos of grim-faced Glaswegians from the early twentieth century. All dressed in their sombre Sunday best. There are also a couple of photos of who could only be a certain Mr Hogg. One was beside a Ford Cortina, where he wore a smile to suggest the car was his pride and joy. His hair was permed in that style so beloved of footballers during that era, and he sported a moustache that would have gained him entry into every gay club in Glasgow two decades later. What a postscript. Remembered by the fading colours of a fashion disaster and a form of gaydar.

The delectable Mrs Hogg didn't get a chance to produce offspring for the sainted Mr Hogg. And if not, what would be the basis on which Mrs Hogg would recommend a child-minder to her dentist?

I hear the tread of Mrs Hogg approaching the room with the drinks. I hiss at Ale to contain herself. She's still not over the Ray McBain, gardener thing.

'Are you okay, dear,' Mrs Hogg asks as she places a tray down on the marble-topped coffee table. I lean forward to slide a vase out of the way, to give her tray more room. My hands on the vase is enough to make Alessandra snort.

'She has terrible hay fever, I'm afraid, Mrs Hogg,' I say.

Alessandra rubs at her eyes for effect. 'Don't worry,' she says with a weak smile. 'I'll acclimatise.'

Mrs Hogg has a look of mild panic. 'We can go into ... oh, dear. There isn't a room in the house without any flowers.'

'Don't worry yourself, Mrs Hogg,' I say. 'Give her a couple of moments and she'll be right as rain.'

She beams and sits down opposite me and I notice she has released another button. Then I notice that despite being pencil thin, she has quite a rack on her. She is on the edge of her low-slung chair and her legs are demurely crossed in that way only skinny women can cope with. She has one knee leaning on top of the other with the leg stretching down so that the foot belonging to the higher placed knee is wrapped round the other's ankle. There must be a rigorous set of stretches they teach to allow women to do this. My thighs are protesting at the thought of it.

'How can I help you?' Mrs Hogg leans forward, picks up a white china tea pot and pours.

'Mrs Browning, your former dentist, tells us that you recommended Lucy Hepburn to her as a child-minder,' I say.

'Oh, how is Mrs Browning?' she asks. 'You'd never have known that poor woman had such an awful disease. She was always so capable.'

Strange choice of word I think. Having met Mrs Browning I know she would feel horribly patronised by such a comment.

'She's doing well, considering,' I reply.

'Oh …has her condition worsened?' Her face is creased with concern.

'How well do you know Mrs Browning?' asks Alessandra.

'As well as you can do when she has her hand in your mouth whenever you meet,' Mrs Hogg answers with an apologetic smile. With anyone else that might have counted as an attempt at humour.

'But well enough to recommend a child-minder,' I say.

Mrs Hogg smiles in a vague manner. She can't quite place the slight needle in my tone with the smile on my face. 'Anything to help.' She slides a plate full of biscuits over in my direction. 'Not meaning to be cheeky, DI McBain, but you look like a man who enjoys a biscuit.'

I take one when I would rather tip the lot into her mouth.

'How did you come to recommend Ms Hepburn,' asks Alessandra.

'Is there something wrong, dear?' Mrs Hogg is wearing a look of mild alarm.

'Just a routine enquiry, Mrs Hogg,' answers Alessandra. 'I believe that Ms Hepburn took up unofficial child-minding duties with Mrs Browning thanks to your recommendation?'

'Yes. Both of them were able to help the other and I feel happy that I was able to act as a go-between. Lucy is such a lovely girl. Hard-working and keen to please. She worked all the hours in the hospital and then went over to help with the Browning kids.'

'How did you meet Lucy?' I ask.

'It might have been at the church,' she answers staring out the window.

'What church would that be?'

'Or was it the book reading group?' She shrugs. 'I belong to so many social groups it's difficult to keep track.'

'Any other possibilities, Mrs Hogg?' I ask and I am unable to keep the sarcasm from my voice. She doesn't react. That's twice now that someone else might have been needled but she has reacted with all the vim and vigour of a paper plate held under the shower. A word pops into my mind that describes her perfectly. Vapid. She's as insubstantial as a solitary raindrop. She made one splash with her Tommy and has then lived life avoiding any warmth in case she evaporates. Such was her grief that she decided not to allow anything else to affect her. The problem with that approach is that it means you lose out on the good stuff as well. You become like a visitor in your own life.

Instead of feeling sorry for her, I am finding that she irritates me. What does that say about me?

'Time to get honest, Mrs Hogg,' I shift forward on my

79

seat. 'As a result of your actions some children were hurt.'

She gasps. Alessandra stares at me.

'Have you ever heard of Disclosure Scotland?' I don't wait for her to answer; I am getting so worked up. 'It screens out the bad guys so our children are safe.'

'Tommy and I never had kids,' she stares over her shoulder at one of his photos. Then back at me. 'Are you sure it's Lucy you are looking for? She is such a lovely girl. Wouldn't hurt a fly I'm sure.' She takes a sip of her tea. 'And children are so adaptable. They recover so quickly don't they?'

Is this woman for real?

'Mrs Hogg...'

'Mrs Hogg,' Alessandra interrupts with a long meaningful look in my direction. 'This is an early stage in our investigation. Lucy Hepburn is one of the leads we are following. We need to know where to find her so we can eliminate her from our enquiries. Any information you can give us would be appreciated.'

Mrs Hogg sits her cup in its saucer, places her hands in her lap and offers a smile. The world is back on its axis. The moment of confrontation has passed.

'I'm struggling to remember where I met Lucy. But she did help out at a church event. Lovely girl. Really can't imagine her harming anyone. We got friendly as you do when you are in such a situation. Helping others. She mentioned that she was working long hours to earn some extra cash. I remembered being part of a brief conversation with Mrs Browning and her dental nurse about needing help with the children. So I offered to put her in touch with Mrs Browning.'

'How did they get in touch? Do you have a phone number?' I ask knowing that this would just be too easy.

'You know ...' Mrs Hogg strains as she leans over the arm of her chair and pulls at her handbag. 'I got a new phone.' She rummages in her bag and pulls something out. Her phone has its own wee black velvet purse. I'm amazed she didn't knit herself one. 'It's wonderful,' she sings. 'I just love it. Look. How lovely is this?' She slips the phone from its case and displays it to us as if it were a late, great uncle's war medal. 'Anyway. I was worried that I would lose some numbers from the old one. It was so old; it was about the size of a brick.' She laughs. 'But ...' She holds the phone in her left palm and lightly touches the screen with her right hand, '...my numbers were all here. Right. Lucy. Where are you? Here we go...' she reads the number out. Alessandra writes it down.

'Thank you,' I offer.

We stand up to go and Mrs Hogg escorts us to the door. As I stand on her doorstep she asks me. 'Disclosure Scotland?'

'Yes?' I say and notice that her cardigan is buttoned back up to the top.

'Wouldn't that be the parents' job to check up on?' She closes the door.

Chapter 11

Another night. Another nightmare. This time I was in a corridor that never ended. Bare walls and linoleum. The echo of my footsteps. Nothing actually happened, but there was an overriding sense of menace. And the level of my fear increased the closer I got to the end of the corridor. Except suddenly the space in front of me would lengthen again.

I wake up just as tired as I was when I went to bed. At least I have the day off to recover. Over a coffee I make some decisions. Last time I had a series of nightmares I choose booze as my way out. When that didn't work, I went for exercise and meditation. Time to get a grip. I'll skip the booze and go for the healthy body and mind stuff.

And a generation of west of Scotland men spin in their pickled graves.

I chew on a banana while I look for my running shoes and shorts.

I pick up one shoe when my door buzzer rings. I pick up the intercom.

'McBain, let me in,' says Maggie.

When she gets in the door she gives me a hug. 'You're putting weight on.' She looks at the single running shoe in my hand. 'And you are doing... sorry, thinking about doing something about it.'

'Nice to see you too, Maggie.' I walk through to the kitchen and refill the kettle.

'Aah, that would be great,' Maggie leans against a kitchen unit. 'I could kill for a coffee.'

'So you were just passing and you thought you would pop in and call me a fat bastard,' I say.

'Something like that,' Maggie grins. She looks good and

she's lost some weight. Her hair has been lightened and cut fashionably. She's wearing cream linen trousers, a huge brown leather belt slung low on her hips and a lime green blouse is open enough to show a nice bit of cleavage. She challenges me with a look.

I look away from her breasts. 'Sorry.'

We've never had sex and I wonder if we should get it out of the way. I did pick her up once when I was drunk. And we did end up in bed together, but nothing happened because of the state I was in. And the moment passed. Then Maggie did her I'm Intuitive and I Want to Help You thing. Then we became friends. My eyes stray back for another look.

'For god's sake,' Maggie closes a button on her blouse. 'If you can't keep your eyes off the puppies I'm going to have to put them away.'

'Again. Sorry.'

'You need a woman, Ray?'

'You applying for the role?'

'Just a few months ago you were pure worried that I fancied you. Now you're doing your dog in heat thing?'

'Should we just fuck and get it over with?'

'How could a girl refuse such a tempting invitation?' She holds her hands over her heart. Then she gets serious. 'Maybe I have to see what's on offer first.'

'What?'

She takes a step closer to me. 'I read about this latest craze on the internet. Women with clothes on and the men are naked. Displaying the goods. And the women get to touch *everything*.'

I take a step back towards the door.

'So maybe I need to see what Ray McBain has to offer.'

I take another step back.

'Take your trousers off and whip it out big boy. And if I see what I like ...'

'Fuck off.' I grin. 'Nearly got me there.'

'Aye. Now can we dispense with the will we or won't we ever go to bed crap. 'Cos that ship has well and truly sailed.'

She reopens the button on her blouse. 'You can look all you want, Ray. These babies are forever out of your reach.'

We are through in the living room sipping at our coffee in companionable silence. I'm smiling. Glad that we have dealt with this issue so we can concentrate on just being mates.

'Why the cheesey?'

'Nothing.'

'Seen much of Theresa?'

My grin slips. 'Na.'

'You are such a bad liar, McBain.'

Right. I forgot Maggie sees everything. She can read me like a book.

'Well, I did see her and ...'

'And ...'

'And ...it was only for three seconds tops. But it was long enough to see that she was pregnant.'

Maggie takes another sip of her coffee and stares at me intently. I hate when she does that.

'And you think it's yours.'

'Run the numbers, Mags. She wasn't sleeping with him.'

'Ever think that she might have been using you?'

'She's not that kind of girl.'

'Grow up, McBain. She's with this guy for years. No babies. She lets you have your wicked way with her. Biff, baff, boff, she's preggers ...'

'No way.'

'She's pregnant and it's bye, bye Mr sperm donor.'

'I'm telling you she's not like that.'

'I don't doubt that on a conscious level she didn't choose to act in such a way. However, the telling fact is that when faced with a pregnancy, you were not the one she turned to Ray.'

'You have this annoying way of making me face facts, Maggie.'

'You're so welcome,' she smiles sweetly.

I stare out of the window. I can see the tops of the trees

clinging on to the last of their blossom.

'And there's more,' she says.

'What now?'

'What's really troubling you, Ray?' She's doing the staring thing again. It suddenly feels very warm in here. Must be the coffee.

'I've got this case at work.'

'Pants on fire.'

'Christ, do I love it when you visit. My own private therapy hell.'

'You don't have to tell me anything you don't want to,' she sounds hurt.

'Fine.'

'Fine.'

I go back to examining the trees.

'You haven't been sleeping too well have you?' she asks.

'Maggie,' two syllables uttered slowly and invested with maximum whine. 'Gonnae leave me alone.'

'Okay,' she replies quietly.

'Right. Okay. I've been having nightmares again.'

As I recovered from the knife wounds inflicted on me by the real Crucifix Killer, John Leonard, and tried to come to terms with the part he had played in my life, Maggie was the one person I could talk to. She is the only person on the planet who knows the whole story. She knows how I was haunted by dreams while people were being murdered and left with wounds that copied the Crucifixion. She knows that as a child I helped to kill a man I thought had abused me and others. She knows that we killed the wrong man.

The truth was hidden even from me until Leonard went on the rampage. My mind had sealed the memories in the darkest cleft of my mind. It took months of horrifying dreams and Leonard's knife to force them out.

'Why do you think you're having nightmares again, Ray?'

'Dunno.'

She stares at me. This time her eyes have a more gentle light to them. It's empathy in its purest form. She understands as if she had experienced something similar.

'What haven't *you* told *me*, Maggie?'

She sits back in her seat and crosses her legs. 'What would you like to know?'

'Like how come you seem to understand so well?'

'We're all victims, Ray. Anyway, don't try and turn this conversation on to me. This is about you. When do you ever get to talk about you?'

'Mmmmm. One of these days it's going to be all about you.'

'I bloody hope so. And all I ask is that when that happens you listen.'

I can't help but smile. I consider my reluctance to talk to the professional listener paid by my employers and how Maggie can make me feel comfortable enough and yet uncomfortable enough to want to talk.

'I think it's guilt, Maggie. Good old fashioned guilt. I killed a man when I was only a child.' I let the words flow with the tears.

'Oh, Ray.' Maggie moves over to me and pulls my head on to her chest. She puts an arm over my shoulder. I lean into her and feel heavy with fatigue and emotion; heavy with the weight of actions I could never atone for, or take back. Maggie could have told me that I was only a child when it happened. She could have told me that it was the adults around me who let me down. That I was led by stronger minds while I was weak with fear and self-loathing. But she knows that I know all of that. She knows that knowing and acceptance of that knowledge are two different things.

'I killed an innocent man, Maggie,' I cry on to her linen blouse. 'He was old. We murdered him while he slept.'

I recall the group of children round his bed. The feeble movements of his legs when the pillow was held over his face.

The flash of knife.

The blood.

The storm of feathers.

I allow myself to fall into the emotion and while one part of me heaved and sobbed and felt the crush of sorrow, the other noticed the damp of Maggie's blouse cool on the side of my face.

The warmth of her arm on mine.

The scent of her perfume.

We keep up this position for a few more moments. Two humans in close physical contact. Two creatures of flesh and bone taking heat from the other in an ageless method of caring.

'Maggie,' I say.

'What, wee pal?'

'I've got a hard-on.'

'Oh, see you, McBain.' She pushes me away and laughs. 'You are unbelievable.'

Chapter 12

'So tell me about my friends,' Angela broke into Jim's thoughts. He shifted his unfocused stare to her face.

'Your friends,' he corralled his thoughts. '... have not been so good at keeping in touch.'

'Oh.' From the note of her tone he read Angela translating this into a failure on her part.

'It wasn't your fault, or anything. No. It was a combination of things. We moved across here from Edinburgh after Ben was born. You gave up your job to become a full-time mum. Your friends all had babies. Everybody was just too busy in their own lives.' And they all had Facebook to keep them company, so why bother with the effort of talking to real people.

'What about that girl …Kirsty?' Her tone this time was adamant. Adamant that she must have at least one real friend. Kirsty had appeared in more than one of the photographs she had looked through, so Angela had obviously realised her significance. But why hadn't she asked about her until now? Did she sense Jim's unwillingness to talk about her?

Jim hid his reluctance and decided that now was the time to pull Kirsty out from under the carpet and brush her down. He had to give her some part in the story of Angela's life. She was no doubt about to make her own entrance for real soon and it would look better if he prepared the way. A little.

'Kirsty and you were friends at college,' he began. 'You were doing the same nursing course.' But how much to tell?

'Uh huh?' Angela brightened, tucking her feet under her bum and a strand of hair behind an ear. She was getting into a listening position — and Jim thought he'd better have something worthwhile to tell her.

'You and she hit it off almost immediately.'

'Yeah.'

'I think the lack of a father thing was what you shared. You could bitch about men before boyfriends started to let you down.' Jim tried to make a joke of it. Neither of them laughed.

The mirror of memory may have been in 3-D, but Jim had to work at remembering the emotions that surrounded them. They were diluted in the mist that was a time from another age, the energy of youth, the feeling of immortality all bound up in the haze from the pleasure of *now*.

Initially they went around in a threesome. Angela was reluctant to leave Kirsty on her own for some reason. Jim remembered a few arguments over that. How were he and Angela ever going to get intimate with the gooseberry around? Eventually he got used to her presence, as she rarely said much and when she did it tended towards the pithy, so she could be fun. It didn't hurt that under the baggy, student, charity shop clothes and waves of dragged-through-a-hedge hair, Kirsty was actually a very pretty girl doing her best to hide it.

'Again …you kinda lost touch with her after Ben was born. She had a new job in management somewhere in the Health Board and you were busy with the baby.'

Later on that evening, as his two loved ones slept in the rooms above him Jim reflected on the tale of Kirsty. It seemed that Angela had taken some sort of comfort from the telling, as if she was relieved that other than he and Ben she did indeed have someone else in her life. Jim's job now was to effect some sort of introduction that would not endanger his new found family situation. For as difficult and trying as it was he couldn't afford to lose his wife again.

In the meantime, he'd had to help Angela adjust and find some way for her to cope with the hours he spent in the office.

The next day, Jim was confronted with a stranger in his living room when he came home from work.

'Jim, you know...' Angela began.

'Moira.' The small woman sitting in his living room on the settee with his wife helpfully supplied her own name.

'Yeah...' His heart went into freefall behind his ribs. Bugger. Shit. Questions raced through his mind. Who the hell was she? How much did she know? How much had she said? How did this happen? Ignoring the crowd of worries in his head, he donned his best welcome to my humble abode face and said, 'We met ...'

'I'm not sure we did meet, Jim. Angela and I just used to meet at the children's playgroup.' She smiled at Ben, who was hiding behind my leg.

'Hello, Ben. My, you're getting big.'

Who the fuck was she? Did she really meet Angela at the playgroup? Have to get her out, have to get her out. He tried to focus. Right. Was he in any danger? Did she know that he and Angela had split up? If not, why didn't Angela tell her? They couldn't have been such good friends if that was the case.

What was more worrying to Jim was the thought that if Moira did know they had split up, why hasn't she said something? Okay, Jim, calm down. The woman's being sensitive. She probably thinks that they patched things up.

He read Angela's expression. Nothing but naked delight at the fact that someone had come to see her. That and a faint blush of embarrassment that she had forgotten the woman's name.

'M ...she heard that I was out of hospital. The girls at the nursery told her. Isn't that wonderful?' Angela beamed, with only a momentary concern when she chose to go with an initial rather than display her forgetfulness when forgetting Moira's name again.

Oh, bloody marvellous, Jim answered under his breath. Now get her the hell out of here. He sat down while Ben sidled up to his mother. She gathered him in her arms and gave him a kiss.

'Lovely,' Jim said forcing himself to breath nice and slowly. 'I didn't realise you two had been friends.' He aimed a smile at Moira, 'Or I would have got in touch.'

'Oh, that's fine. I understand. You had more to contend with than getting in touch with me,' she hooted and finished off with a snort.

'Moira's been telling me how difficult her life's been recently and not to worry too much. Her husband left her last year.' Angela was keen to be part of the conversation and fought not to make the problems with her memory too obvious.

'...For another woman.' Moira pursed her lips in judgement against all men. Then she turned back to Angela and they smiled at each other as if they'd been comparing miseries and scored around even. What the hell was going on here? This was surreal.

As Moira chattered, explaining how she and Angela used to chat over a coffee after dropping the kids off at nursery, she finished off each sentence with a delighted, solitary note of laughter. Every now and then she added a snort for good measure. Jim searched his memory for any mention of a Moira. None, nothing, zip. The friendship must have begun while Jim and Angela were separated.

If that was the case, why hadn't she alluded to that in her conversation with Angela. Perhaps she had, Jim thought and examined Angela's face for any clues. There was nothing there but delight in having a friend.

Jim examined Moira. She wasn't someone he would have tagged as a friend of Angela's. In his experience people tend to socialise with others who are similar in outlook, habits, beliefs and a myriad of other things. Other than having children in the same nursery he couldn't see any way in which these two women would bond. The pre-accident Angela would have been polite to this woman — but nothing more.

Age-wise he would have put her in her late twenties, early thirties. How would he describe her appearance?

Average. Everything about her was average. Brown hair, medium height, not too thin, small breasts. Even her clothes were non-descript jeans and a brown blouse. She was the kind of woman who would easily blend into a crowd and become indistinguishable from the people around her.

'Oh, the coffees we had,' hoot, 'the chats,' snort. 'We were a fine pair, so we were.'

Aye, right, Jim thought, and my dick's got a bell sown on to the end of it, why don't you pull that? He just couldn't place this woman.

'Where did we go?' Angela was keen to know.

'Oh, here and there,' Moira answered. 'Your favourite was The Honey Pot. You used to love their toffee apple pie, so you did.' Angela did like The Honey Pot, it was a friendly wee cafe with a really good variety of speciality teas. And she had raved about their toffee apple pie. Several times.

'Yes,' continued Moira. 'And you loved their cappuccino, so you did.'

'Can I make you both another coffee just now?' Jim asked, so that he could leave the room without appearing too rude. Who was this woman? And in any case, a worrying smell was coming from the kitchen. Angela must have been trying to make the dinner and Jim thought he should take care of it rather than leave Angela to place another tick in her *fail* column.

'No thanks, Jim. I've had enough for now.' Angela smiled. Then she was on her feet, expression tight with alarm. 'Shit. The dinner.' She ran into the kitchen. We heard the oven door opening. 'Shit.' A strong smell of burning meat. And then the oven door was slammed shut.

'Something else was burning when I came in an hour ago,' Moira said under her breath. She smiled weakly and then shrugged as if apologising for distracting my wife. 'I think that's version number two.' She smiled again.

How dare you smile at my wife's accidents, Jim wanted to say. Instead he stood up and said. 'Well, thank you for visiting Angela,' and waited for her to do likewise. Walking towards the door, he added, 'perhaps you could come again.'

'Oh, right,' Moira looked at her feet for her handbag. And stood up. 'Perhaps I should leave you two alone. A hard day at work and all that.'

With a 'See you later, Angela,' winging into the kitchen, Moira followed Jim to the door.

Angela appeared at my shoulder, 'You don't have to go so soon.'

Moira glanced at Jim, read the expression on his face and faced Angela. 'I really should go and get Erskine from his granny's. She'll be tearing her hair out trying to deal with the little darling.'

Yeah. Go on. Piss off, Jim thought.

'That's a shame,' he said. 'I mean, that you have to go.'

'It was lovely to see you, Angela,' Moira leaned past me and kissed Angela on the cheek. 'I'll call in again, soon.'

'That would be lovely.' Angela looked lost. Her new friend was going away. Would she really come back, was that the question in her eyes?

'Yeay. Do come back. Next time bring Erskine and he and Ben can play together.' Jim found himself saying. Why the hell did he say that? Guilty conscience was intruding on his plans.

Standing there watching Angela's expressions range from pleasure to little girl lost made him feel like the worst husband on the planet. But he couldn't allow this woman too close. What did she know? And if she did know something, why didn't she say?

Moira was now on the path leading to the gate. Facing them, instead of the way to her car, clutching her handbag to her belly. 'You're looking so well, Angela. I can't believe it ...after everything.' She lifted her shoulders and gave a wee squeal. 'What a brave woman you are.'

Oh good Christ, she's going to cry now, thought Jim. But then she reined in her emotions and looked around her at the too long grass and bare brown earth of the borders that were needing a spot of colour.

'Lovely garden, Jim.'

'Thanks,' he said. 'I like the minimalist look.' Right, go on, beat it. She must be one of those women who take an hour to say cheerio.

'Toffee apple pie,' said Angela. 'We could meet up at that place and have coffee.'

'I'd love that,' said Moira.

In the doorway, Jim placed an arm over Angela's shoulder. It stopped him from grabbing a handful of brown blouse and dragging Moira to her car.

'Right. Bye,' said Moira. And then they had another round of kisses.

In the kitchen as Angela and Jim viewed the brown and black lump that had been their dinner, she said. 'What a nice friendly wee woman she was.'

'Aye.' It was all he could do not to wipe sweat from his brow with relief. Result. Disaster averted. 'She obviously cared about you.'

Angela smiled in response. 'It would be nice if she could come over sometime with her son. Let the boys get to know each other. Or, did they know each other before?'

'If they were at the same nursery then I guess they should do. Anyway ...' Jim clapped his hands while thinking about his ruined dinner. 'Who fancies some sweet and sour chicken?'

During the meal Angela opened her mouth only to pop in some puffs of battered chicken, her eyes focused somewhere on the surface of the table, between the aluminium tubs of food. She'd moved on from delight at finding a friend to ...he wasn't sure where. Must be exhausted after all the excitement.

'She seemed nice,' he tried to engage Angela in conversation. 'Moira. Nice steady name that.' There were several times during their short conversation when

Angela clearly struggled to remember the woman's name. A wee reminder might help.

'Oh very subtle, Jim. Why don't you remind your wife how crap her memory is.' Angela's expression was melting into a puddle of shame.

'Sorry,' he offered, feeling awful. 'Just trying to help.'

'Can't even remember an old friend's name. How embarrassing is that?' Angela flung her fork down on to the table.

'It's only a name.' He couldn't quite understand what was so important.

'A name? Just a name?' Angela screamed. A tiny piece of chicken hit his right cheek. 'It's polite ...it's manners. How on earth can I function socially when I can't remember anybody's names?' Her voice rose in pitch throughout the sentence. She punctuated the last word with a slap at a tub of food. 'Fuck.' She screamed again.

Red sauce splattered over the floor and half way up a cupboard door. Ben, face white, slid off his chair and with a whimper ran out of the room.

'Ben ...' Angela reached for his back. 'I'm sorry.' Her temper crashed in on itself and was replaced by tears.

Fighting to keep the irritation from his voice Jim said, 'It's just a name. Not worth scaring Ben for. I'll go and check on the wee man.'

'No. Let me,' Angela walked past him, almost shouldering him back onto his chair. 'I need to clear up my own mess.' Fine, Jim thought. Pardon me for trying to help.

As he listened to her feet pad upstairs he looked at the mess on the floor and wondered if he should leave that for her as well. Deciding that he was tired of being Mr Nice Guy, he walked past it, careful not to slip and on in to the living room. What a night, he thought as he bent forward to switch on the TV.

Kicking his feet up on to a footstool he considered what he should do. This wasn't the first time that Angela had thrown a fit. But it was the first time she'd done so while Ben was in the room and the first time she'd actually thrown something. Jim wanted to help, but Angela's temper was getting worse and in the face of that it was difficult to keep calm and offer assistance.

She was right about Ben, however. The fright had come from her, so she should be the one to placate him. Similarly with the floor. Would she clean it up if Jim threw his dinner over it? No way. And there was no need to snap. He just wanted to help.

All over a bloody name — for a bloody nobody. Moira who? And what was she all about? Weaselling in here to speak to his wife. Pretending to care. Probably didn't have a life of her own and wanted to steal someone else's. What were the chances Jim would find her rifling through his garbage, trying to find out more about them so she could infiltrate their lives.

Whoa, big guy. Time to get off the bus before it arrives at Paranoia City.

Chapter 13

Where are you, Ms Hepburn? The curtain is falling. Your time on stage is almost up. Okay, I'm getting fanciful, but it is four o'clock in the morning and I can't sleep.

I can understand a name change when you are trying to hide your nefarious deeds, but why choose a famous name? The first thing is that we are dealing with damaged goods. There are few people who can act in such a vicious way without being a victim themselves. It's way too early for the nature/nurture debate, McBain, but it feels right. Something terrible happened to her so she's regaining power by passing that tag of victim on to someone else. Several someone elses. Which suggests she gets something from it.

What do psychiatrists say when it comes to motivation? We move away from pain or towards pleasure. Does she really find pleasure in what she does, or is she so full of pain that the only relief she can achieve is to pass that pain on to someone else?

These thoughts are going over and over in my mind in a loop. Enough with the cottage industry psychology, McBain, get some sleep.

Tomorrow I go for a run. Perhaps then I will sleep when I go to bed. Exercise, that's what's called for. And a diet. Even Maggie remarked on my weight gain.

Monday is a great day to start a diet. That gives me the whole of tomorrow, well today, to enjoy my food. A huge fry-up for breakfast. The works. Black pudding and everything. Then choccy biscuits with my coffee at elevenses. I love Kit-Kats. A couple of sausage rolls for lunch. A slice of cake with afternoon tea. Has to be carrot cake. And then a curry for dinner. With a sweet naan.

Then a bag of Maltesers while I watch a late movie.

I chuckle at my intensity. My belly is groaning at the thought of all those calories. Perhaps I will just settle for a cooked breakfast and see what the rest of the day brings.

It's eleven o'clock Sunday morning and the door goes. I press the intercom. Recognise the voice and let him in.

It's Kenny, my favourite career criminal. When I was on the run from the police, my employers, Kenny was one of the few people I could turn to. The irony of that was not lost on either of us. Our paths have crossed several times over the years, first as boys and then as young men. Each time began with me saving his expensively clad arse. So he owes me, he thinks. I think the debt is all-square after he saved me recently. Without his intervention while I was under the knife of Leonard I would no doubt be dead.

'Let me guess. It was a toss-up between church and me. And I lost?'

'Haven't seen you for a wee while, big man. Just thought I'd give you another chance to thank me for saving you from a homicidal maniac.'

'You should have found me before the heid-case slashed my wrists. How thick are you? I left enough clues to fill an edition of Junior Cluedo.'

'Once again,' he punches my arm. 'You are welcome.'

He's looking good. The bastard. Every inch the success-ful and wealthy businessman. Except his business is on the shady side. And whatever it is I don't want to know; bonds forged in war of boyhood are often the hardest to break. He's wearing a pair of jeans that probably cost more than my favourite suit and a shirt which I am guessing is from his preferred shop, Thomas Pink. He walks ahead of me into the living room in that loose-limbed, athletic way of his. He is broad-shouldered and lean. Moves like he is totally at ease in his body. I think I hate him.

'You'll be making me a coffee?'

98

'One pinch of arsenic or two?'

'Bitch.'

I make us coffee and bring it through to the sitting room. He's sitting on a sofa like he designed it. Arms open wide and resting along the top, his right foot placed on his left knee.

'So what's the haps? What is the famous detective investigating these days?'

'None of your business.' I hand him a hot mug.

'Oh c'mon. Tell me.'

'Nothing, really.' I shrug. 'I've been benched. I'm on the subs bench. They don't want me working on anything until the public has well and truly forgotten all about the Stigmata thing.'

'Ah,' he nods sagely, 'McBain The Embarrassment.'

'Remind me why we are friends?'

'You need someone to look down on. I need a break from the monotony of making loads of cash.'

We grin at each other. Don't know why I am so sanguine with this situation. If the bosses knew he was my friend, I wouldn't even be on the subs bench. Given that I don't have a garden, I can't go on gardening leave, I'd have to call it Window Box Leave.

'Getting any?' he asks in that caring male way.

'None of your business.'

'That'll be a no.'

'I've decided to be celibate. Women are just too much trouble.'

'Theresa. That was her name wasn't it?' What is that in his eyes? Concern?

'Mmmm.'

He thinks for a moment. It's as if he has something to tell me and he's not sure that he should. Eventually he opens his mouth. 'She's pregnant.'

'I know.'

'He knows. Fuck me, mate. I've had this news for weeks. Been too worried to tell you, and you know.' He pauses. 'Is it yours? How do you know?'

'The more pertinent question is how do you know?'

'Want me to do something about him?'

Him would be the husband, I assume. 'Na. I'm the polis remember. We don't do stuff like that.'

'Aye. Right.'

'So how come you know about this?' I ask again.

'Information and the trade thereof is how I make my money, old son.' He replies in a theatrical manner. 'And I have an interest in making sure that my friends are looked after.'

'Don't tell me anything else,' I shudder to think what Kenny knows and what he does with that knowledge. For a moment I think about Theresa's husband. With him out of the way, minor damage only of course, severe memory loss for example, I could waltz back in there and be a father to our child.

A boyish devilment dances in Kenny's eyes. 'You're thinking about it, aren't you?'

'Machiavelli was never my role-model.'

'Right enough, Baden-Powell was more your scene. If you ever get tired of protecting the great unwashed, come and see me. I'll make you rich, my boy.'

'So information is your thing these days?' I ask.

'People and their many and varied vices are my thing, Ray.' He lifts up his half-full mug and toasts them all. 'Information brings me to them. It's amazing what the right piece of information in the wrong hands can achieve.'

'Tell me no more.'

'Bet you I could find out something about the good folks of Glasgow quicker that you could with all your high-falutin' policeman stuff.'

I take sip from my mug. There just might be some mileage here.

'So you'd become a police informer.'

He shuddered violently. 'Wash your mouth out with vim. No. I'm talking about the type of people you deal with. You know, the happily deranged and the psychos.

100

I'll be an unofficial adjunct to your investigation.'

'Right enough. We've got to have our standards.' I aim somewhere between sarcasm and irony. I am always amazed at how those involved in financial crime regards themselves as above the violent in the criminal pecking order. The human mind in all its glory. If the Afrikaners could use the Bible to excuse apartheid then we can manage to reason almost anything into the justifiable.

'How's Maggie?' he changes the subject.

'Happy that she hasn't crossed paths with you.'

'She doesn't like me?' He actually manages to look wounded.

'Let me try and remember how she described you. Ah yes. If he was chocolate he would have nibbled his own knob down to a nub.'

'Good work with the alliteration. A good brain and nice tits.' He nods his head slowly. 'Why haven't you shagged her yet?'

'Friends don't get all groiny with each other.'

'Platonic friendships, my arse,' Kenny the Philosopher dismisses a world of friendship. 'Unless one of you is pig-ugly.' Smile. 'You could qualify for that title in your little two-some.' His eyes are momentarily lost in a picture he has summoned into his mind. 'Maggie is one fine looking woman. Pity she doesn't charge for it.' Kenny has a thing for prostitutes. The kind that have their own appointment system and a waiting list. His thinking is that sex is nothing but a form of transaction and when he pays for it at least it's honest.

'Away an' howl at the moon, ya numpty. You're doing my head in.'

Monday morning, it's only ten o'clock and I am lunch-time hungry. May have something to do with eating breakfast at six o'clock. Couldn't sleep and when I did my dreams were enough to make sleep the last thing I ever want to do again.

I am in my office on my own. Daryl and Alessandra are out on a job and I'm doing the good little banished detective thing. Posting holiday requests and sick-notes is not my idea of policing. Still, someone has to keep Human Resources up to date.

The only thing I've done this morning that might resemble my actual job is to read an email from Alessandra. She checked out the mobile number we got from Mrs Hogg. It was dead. Surprise, surprise. *Pay as you go* phone numbers are ideal for the transient and wannabe untraceable elements of our society.

Coffee. I'll have another coffee. Go into a café and look at the skinny people. They'll all be drinking coffee. The fatties will have tea and cake in front of them. Ergo, to lose weight, drink shit-loads of coffee.

See me. See flawed thinking. I'm a genius at it.

It's now eleven o'clock and Daryl and Alessandra aren't back yet. I'm having another coffee and I'm beyond hungry. Next thing I see with a pulse is going to get speared, skinned and roasted.

The thing about boredom is it makes you think about your next meal and the next snack. Find a boring job and you'll find a fat bastard doing it.

Enough is enough. Think I'll take me and my mobile phone a wee walk for some fresh air. I walk up Pitt Street, take a right into West George Street and walk down to Blythswood Square.

Here, a square shaped garden is surrounded by Edwardian terraced houses, most of which are now offices. At the far end with a whole block to itself is the former RAC club. Now a hotel that should have swanky in its name. I make my way into the square and find a bench. I pluck my phone from a pocket and dial a number.

'Had a re-think about my offer?' Kenny answers immediately.

'You been waiting for my call?'

'My breath has been bated since last we spoke. Wassup, partner?'

I tell him what I need. He promises to get back to me as soon as. We hang up.

I lean back in my seat, kick my feet out in front of me. The sun is strong on my forehead. Traffic is busy going around the square, but the lines of trees and bushes are enough to give the illusion of an oasis. Right. That's enough non-movement, McBain. Who can you phone next?

'Ray?' Daryl answers the phone immediately.

'Hey good buddy. What's the haps? Howzit hanging?'

I can hear him talking to someone else. 'DI McBain is bored out of his tiny mind.'

'Yes and any crumb of police work would be gratefully nibbled on,' I reply. Alessandra chuckles in the background. 'What you got?' I ask.

'Dead end, Ray. We've just been up at the Southern General. They've had no staff working there going by the name of Lucy Hepburn. Or Audrey Hepburn for that matter.'

'Mrs Hogg was sure it was the Southern General she was working in. What about the other city hospitals?'

'We already tried them. And nothing going there either.'

'Maybe we need to spread our enquiries to other regions?' I suggest.

'But, Ray,' I can hear Alessandra over Daryl's shoulder. 'It can't be too far away. Hepburn had to do her shift at the hospital and then go and do her second job.'

'Well spotted, Ale.' I pause. A woman sits beside me. She sits as far away from me as she can without sitting on the bench's arm. She is wearing a navy blue business suit and a white shirt. She is carrying a dun-coloured woven bag which she places on her lap. She pulls out a silver flask and sits it to her left. Then she pulls out a plastic tub full of salad and a plastic fork. Is everyone on the planet on a diet? I'm sure she can hear my belly grumble.

'Ray? Ray? You still there?' Daryl speaks in my ear.

'Sorry. Got distracted. Have we tried the private hospitals in the area?'

'Not yet, Ray,' says Daryl. 'We'll add that to the list.'

'One thing that bothers me. Nurses have qualifications. You have to prove who you are to sit qualifications these days. You can't just dance into a hospital and pretend to be a nurse.'

'So?'

'So maybe she's using her real name at work and the name she gave to Mrs Hogg and the families are bogus.'

'The fact that she retains the first name might be a clue. We need to get a hold of all the nurses in the west of Scotland with the first name of Lucy,' Alessandra jumps in.

'Let's get on it,' I say and hang up.

'Lovely day,' the woman beside me speaks.

I look at the food on her lap and the fruit spilling out of her bag and think it all looks very healthy. I need healthy.

I smile and say, 'I'll give you twenty quid for the lot.'

Chapter 14

'Why don't I have a brother and sister?' Ben asked, turning away from a cartoon. One of the characters in the show was about to get a new little sister and was all excited about it.

Angela looked up from her purple notebook — it was a present Moira had given her that afternoon over coffee at The Honey Pot and in it she could record all the new information she received each day — the question of having other children was something she hadn't yet considered, judging from the expression on her face.

'Because ...' Jim sat down on the floor beside Ben, gathered him in his arms and kissed his forehead. 'When we got you, you were so perfect we thought it would be too greedy to ask God to give us more children.'

'Oh.' Ben smiled, pleased with the answer. Then his attention went back to the TV. 'But I only want a brother. 'Cos then I have somebody to play with.'

Once Ben was in bed Angela repeated the question.

'Why did we only have one?'

'This is a bottle of wine story,' Jim answered.

'That bad?' Angela asked, folding her arms in anticipation of some discomfort.

Jim sat beside her, put his arm over her shoulder. She shrank from his touch and then faced him.

'Sorry,' she offered.

Jim pulled his arm away, dampening his irritation that even this form of contact was not allowed. Only the other night she was doing her best to tempt him into bed, but that was a road he could not, would not allow himself to go down. If physical contact of all kinds was banned, then he would just have to learn to live with it.

105

'It's not easy listening, honey. Why don't you let me go and get a bottle and ...'

'Just tell me, Jim,' her voice was quiet but firm.

He took a deep breath. 'Okay ...' This was not an easy story to tell. They'd had a difficult time successfully trying for a child and then there were some added complications that would have to be edited out.

For the full and true story they had to go back to the weeks before and after Angela's mother's funeral. However, the heavily edited story Jim told Angela was this: they had been lovers for just over a year when it happened. He dropped Angela off home after an evening at the cinema when she invited him in to the house for a quick cuppa.

As they walked up the path, Angela wondered why the house was in darkness. It didn't make sense to her; her mum was a poor sleeper and would sit up in bed with a barely glanced-at book until she knew Angela was back safe in the house.

Under the tired light of the street lamp, Angela checked her watch.

'It's just gone eleven. Surely Mum's not gone to bed already?'

Slipping her key in the lock, she pushed the door open. 'Mum. I'm home,' she announced. Nothing. She turned to Jim, all colour washed from her face by concern.

'Mum?' She ran upstairs. The stair light went on. He stood by the front door and listened to Angela's feet tread across the ceiling into her mother's bedroom. Silence, then her feet thundered across the carpet and down the stairs.

'Mum's not in her bed, Jim. What's going on? The house is empty. This isn't like her.' Her hands were at her throat.

'Maybe there'll be a note somewhere. Where would your mum leave you a note if she had to go out,' he asked.

'The kitchen table.' She spun and half-walked, half-ran into the kitchen. Jim followed and all but ran her down

106

when she came to an abrupt halt.

'Oh my God,' Angela's whisper was like a shout in the still of the room.

'Oh my God,' she repeated. Her mother was slumped across the kitchen table, as if she was sleeping. For months Jim would see the colours every time he closed his eyes: the red of her cardigan, the white of the table and the sepia tint from the spilled tea that puddled in her grey-blond hair.

Sue was only fifty-five when she suffered a massive stroke.

The next piece of information, Jim decided to keep to himself: the real set of circumstances surrounding the discovery of her mother's body. It was time for another white lie. What would be the point in telling Angela that they had ended their relationship?

They had actually fallen out a couple of weeks before Angela, on her own, found her mother dead in the kitchen. Prior to this they were getting to what he referred to as the point of no return. Either they made some form of commitment to each other, or they ended it and went their separate ways. Jim was just twenty-two, the same age as Angela and felt strongly that he was too young to settle down. Yes, Angela was a great girl. Yes, they had a great time together. But a lifetime commitment? Not at that point.

On discovering her mum and not knowing what to do, Angela phoned Kirsty. She wasn't in. Next she tried Jim. He couldn't refuse the panic in her voice and drove over to hers straight away. Well, after he dropped his new girlfriend off at her own house.

When Jim arrived, Angela was a tight bundle of limbs on the floor, head resting on her mother's feet. After he helped her on to a chair he phoned 999.

Angela and he were still seated by the kitchen table after Sue's body had been taken away.

'Stay with me tonight,' she pleaded. The need for

company was naked in her expression, her voice so small, that Jim simply couldn't say no.

They sat up for hours drinking from Sue's favourite stainless steel teapot. Sometimes Angela would talk about her mum, but mostly they sat in silence. At some point, Jim couldn't remember when or how, they ended up on the couch together. Perhaps Angela wanted to feel someone's arms around her. It was important to her to feel the solidity, the *thereness* of another person.

What could he say about the inevitability of what happened next? Even now as he reels them off they sound like really weak excuses. They were twenty-two, lying face to face on a couch that had seen much *face to face* action previously.

There was no agenda, no calculation, no aforethought. He can remember being stirred by her nearness, breathing in the apple scent of her hair. One soft press of lips on her cheek, led to one on her neck, to one at the corner of her mouth. She turned to ease his reach. Then it became urgent, pressing, squeezing, touching, grabbing.

'What are ...we can't ...?' He straightened his arms and pushed himself off her.

'Please. Don't stop,' whispered Angela.

'But...' a particularly delicious movement of her tongue on his froze the thought.

Clothes were forced aside.

They thrust at each other, until everything tightened ...and then loosened in a sharp, molten exhalation. Like a last, valued breath.

He remembers rolling off the couch on to the floor, panting like a pup. Guilt was an indistinct mass rolling in on the next emotional front, but he didn't want to pay too much attention just yet. Nerve ends were still snapping.

Breathing now regulated, sitting up, he leaned over and held Angela's hand.

'You okay with this,' he asked, not really knowing what the right thing to say was. Or the right thing to do.

Should he go? Should they go back to cuddling? She looked at him as if to say *what the fuck just happened there*? Then she sat up, gathered her knees to her chin, and stared into the near space.

'That was ...' from her expression she didn't know what it was. Silence reclaimed the room. A silence thick enough to be grated. A silence that words retreated from.

They dressed facing away from each other, modesty a symptom of their new sense of unease. Not moments before they were two healthy animals caught up in a ...what? A bodily reaction? Now they were all thought, reason and dissemblement.

Angela just looked at Jim as he walked backwards out of the room. A big shovel would have been handy at that point. Then he could have just kept on digging.

'Let me know when the funeral is?' he said at the door. Just as he pulled at the handle it flew open and in charged Kirsty.

'Oww,' he rubbed at his knuckles, but it seemed churlish in the extreme to complain.

'What's wrong,' she asked, not even seeing Jim. 'Mum said you were looking for me.' Her face was pink with alarm and uncertainty. She walked towards Angela, her arms held out. 'Angela?'

Jim closed the door behind him on the way out, feeling it was best that the two girls be left on their own.

Of course, all these years later this goes unsaid. It comes in under the heading of *Too Much Information*. Then there's the sub-heading *How Could I*? From the distance of time Jim was less than proud of his actions. Immaturity can only excuse so much; what manner of man was he to take advantage of Angela in that state? With an internal cringe that was souring every moment, he realised that history was repeating itself. And what's more he was as unable now as he was then to stop himself.

Jim and Angela had hugged like near-strangers after the service, exchanged words over a sandwich at the Funeral Tea, and said what seemed like a final farewell at the door to the hotel where the Tea was held.

Some weeks later, Angela appeared, pale, thin and tired at Jim's parents' house. Her timing was impeccable he had just arrived home after a game of squash with his new girlfriend.

'We need to talk,' she said. Not a good sign, but he was not quite fully present. His girlfriend was upstairs. The same girl he'd left on her own to go and help Angela on the night of her mother's death. He didn't tell her about his session on Angela's couch, nor had he told Angela that he was seeing someone else.

'I'm kind of ...in the middle of ...' he said.

'Jim. I wouldn't just come round if it wasn't important.' Something in her tone and in her eyes sent a bead of sweat on a slow slide down the length of his spine.

'Right.' He wondered what he should do. There was something really, really wrong here. 'Let me ...' He looked behind him into the house. 'Give me ...' God, what should he do?

Angela mentioned a pub in the town. 'I'll meet you there in fifteen minutes.'

'Right.' Oh shit. He could do without this complication. 'Okay, see you in fifteen.'

His girlfriend was lying on his bed with Lucky, the family cat. She was less than enamoured. 'You're going for a drink with Angela?' She jumped to her feet, furious. Lucky fled from the room. 'I had something important to tell you.'

'Can't it wait for a couple of hours? Something's up. I can tell.' He shrugged an apology.

'You haven't told her about us yet, have you?'

'Look. Not now. Okay? Her mother just died, for chrissake. She needs ...'

'What?' She demanded. 'You're *my* boyfriend now, Jim. I feel just as bad as you about her losing her mother. And

110

I know when she finds out about us she'll be less than pleased ...but you can't just run off when she clicks her fingers.'

'Just this once. Okay?' He kissed the tip of her nose. 'There's nothing to worry about, sweetheart. You're the one,' Jim paused. 'The one I'm with. Okay?'

Angela had a seat by the window, her fingertips on the stem of her wine glass that was more of a prop than a drinking utensil. Her expression was neutral, her eyes studying the knots and swirls of the pine surface of the table.

While he waited for a pint at the bar Jim wondered what he was about to get hit with. Did Angela want them to get back together?

He sat his pint on the table, careful not to spill anything. Before he could meet Angela's gaze, she spoke.

'I'm pregnant, Jim.'

His new girlfriend was still in his bedroom when he returned home. Thankfully, his parents were down at the bowling club and didn't witness all this to-ing and fro-ing.

'Angela's what?' she asked.

Jim sat down on the bed, elbows on his knees, head in his hands. 'What a fucking mess.'

Silence.

'Oh my god.' She paced back and forward. 'How is she?' She looked at him, 'Don't answer that. You probably didn't even notice.'

Silence.

'But we've been together for a couple of months. How far gone is she?'

'Five weeks.' Jim answered.

'You bastard.' She slapped him. 'You utter bastard. You were sleeping with both of us at the same time.'

He nursed his face. 'No it was just the once. It was an accident.'

'Oh. Well that's all right then.' She shouted in his face,

'So what happened? You accidentally fell on top of her …and through four layers of clothing your dick managed to …what…accidentally slide into her vagina where it accidentally left behind some semen?'

'Something like that,' he mumbled.

'You prick. You bastard,' she shouted and kicked at a pile of his records. Then she turned to face him. 'So what really happened? You went round to give your condolences and gave her one for old times sake while you were at it?'

'Something like that.' His chin was resting on his chest.

'That is the worst …' she screamed a short burst of anger. 'You are unbelievable.'

'I know.'

'That girl was in mourning and you …' again she screamed. 'That is the lowest, the worst thing I have ever heard.'

'It wasn't like that,' he tried to defend the indefensible. 'We just …I was comforting her. She needed a shoulder. I …we cuddled on the couch …and it just happened.'

'She needed a shoulder, Jim. Not your dick.' She looked him in the eye. 'And to think I'm …' Her eyes brightened with tears.

'You're what?'

She shook her head to dispel the tears and ignored his question. 'So how did you and Angela leave things?'

For all Jim knew Angela was still at the bar, still holding the stem of the wineglass with her fingertips, still waiting to hear his response.

Jim had just looked at her when she stopped speaking. Pregnant, the word echoed through the blank landscape of his brain. Angela was pregnant. He probed for an emotion. How did he feel? Did he want her? Did he want her and the baby?

Pregnant?

Oh shit.

'You don't have to say anything, Jim.' Angela appeared so calm, so together. 'You needed to know.' But god only knew what was going through her mind.

112

In his bedroom, his girlfriend stared at him in disbelief. 'So you just left her there on her own?' she asked.

'What was I supposed to do? Go down on one knee? Offer to pay for an abortion? What?'

'You're supposed to talk about it. Re-assure her. Help her cope with this.'

'How can I do that when I don't even know what to think myself?'

'What's there to think about? You're going to be a father. Either you take responsibility or you don't. She didn't have the luxury of time to think. She'd just be presented with the fact.'

Kirsty walked to the door. 'And to think I was falling in love with you. I'd never have come into this relationship if I'd known what a bastard you are.' She shivered. 'You've made me feel so cheap.'

'Where are you going?' Jim asked when she pulled the door open.

'I'm going as far away from you as possible.' She took a step out of the door, stopped and turned. 'If I ever see you again, I hope it's in a coffin.' Jim would never forget the look on her face.

'But ...' Let me think about this, Jim wanted to say. Give me time to wrestle down all of these thoughts and emotions into some sort of coherent shape.

'But nothing, Jim. Grow up. Be a man. And be grateful you're still breathing.' With that last comment Kirsty walked out of the room, throwing him a look of the purest hate.

Over the years since, Jim had given little thought to Kirsty and the state of their brief relationship, but now it filtered through. After his initial split with Angela, she'd pursued him with a vigour that both surprised and flattered him. There were phone calls and chance meetings in places where she must have known he would be. Why not, he thought at the time. They were both single.

Kirsty sealed it with a wondrous handjob in an alley down the side of Jim's favourite pub. Kirsty had said she was too hot, would he mind going outside to keep her company?

She walked ahead and as soon as they were in the dark of the lane his trousers were round his ankles. Later Jim had no idea how it happened so quickly. It seemed one second he was at the bar and the next he was feeling the most intense pleasurable experience of his life. She worked at his belt and zipper and then turned Jim round till he was facing away from her. Her hand reached round and pumped at his cock, while she was pressed against his back. For a brief moment Jim felt as if this whole exercise was for her benefit alone. As if she was imagining the dick in her hands belonged to her.

Then he disengaged his brain and allowed the pleasure to take over. Keeping the speed of her hand movement consistent, Kirsty moved. Still behind him, she was on her knees. Jim felt something warm and wet probe the cleft of his arse.

'Ohmygod,' he shuddered, grunted and it was all over.

Jim reviewed in his head just what had happened. 'Fuck.' Was all he could manage. He wanted it again. No-one in his limited sexual history so far had appeared quite this keen. He was completely, fully, head over heels in lust.

This incident became the pattern of their brief relationship. Within seconds of meeting, Jim's trousers would be at his ankles and Kirsty would have her full focus on his cock. She couldn't get enough of it. Strangely, she rarely let him touch her. He could play with her breasts as much as he liked and on a number of occasions she allowed him to slide his cock between them until he came over her chin and cheeks, but she wouldn't allow him to go below her waist. Full fucking was a no no.

Aren't you having enough fun, she would demand? On one occasion Jim tried not to take no for an answer. His cock was so hard only the heat and moisture between her legs could satisfy him.

No matter how much he cajoled, pressed or pestered Kirsty remained resolute. The answer was no.

'Why?' Jim asked, pulling at the buckle of her belt.

'Just leave it, Jim. The answer is no.'

'Oh, c'mon,' he pleaded. 'We've done everything else.'

'Jim, you're starting to really piss me off.' Her lips were pursed tight. Her face was white, her body stiff with anger. She turned and walked towards the door. Jim moved quicker, not bothered that he was naked from the waist down. He reached the door before her and barred her exit.

'What is it, do you want to be a virgin when you get married? Is that it?'

She clenched a fist in front of Jim's face. He raised an eyebrow in defiance. His look said, go on try it. I don't hit girls, but I won't let you hurt me. She looked uncertain. For the first time she was not the one in control. Her shoulders slumped and she moved back to the bed. She sat down, eyes brimming with tears. This was a first. Jim had rarely seen emotion on Kirsty's face. She mumbled something and a tear shone on her cheek. Jim's ardour was flattened by the weight of Kirsty's discomfort. He felt like the world's biggest arsehole.

'Oh, babe,' said Jim. 'I'm so sorry.' What on earth had happened to this girl to make her so keen for cock but unable to deal with him getting into her pants? And what was she mumbling? Sounded like she was saying, *dirty, dirty, dirty*. Over and over again.

Minutes later her mood had swung back to having fun. Jim was naked. It would be a shame to waste it. Then she encouraged him to masturbate in front of her, giggling as his semen shot on to her face and hair. She even turned it into a game and gave him points for how far the first spurt reached, or giving him the target of her upper lip, her right eyebrow or her nose to aim at.

Part of his mind noted this was the only time he saw Kirsty smile; really smile. Apart from when she was involved in her other fixation, Simon Le Bon. The remainder of his mind was caught up in the erotic charge of it all and he set the issue aside as something to think on in the cold half-light of the morning after.

Tenderness was another issue. In public, Kirsty was happy for Jim to hold her hand or place an arm over her shoulder. It was as if that was a badge of normality. But whenever they were on their own it was a different matter and if Jim tried to hold her hand or hug her, she would move out of reach or distract him by tugging at his belt and stroking his balls through his jeans.

Nor did she enjoy the sort of languorous kissing sessions that he and Angela used to pass hours in. Kissing Kirsty was a thrusting and brief affair, all tongues and almost bruised lips.

Sure, he rarely passed a minute in Kirsty's company without a hard-on, and what guy wouldn't like that amount of attention on his groin, but her intensity wore him out and he began to worry where it was all going to end. He worried that he had no free will. He was Kirsty's plaything, a penis on a stick, she once called him, laughing at his slight frame. He was simply snared within the glare of Kirsty's need and no matter how his concerns rumbled in his mind, he could no more walk away from her than he could willingly donate both kidneys.

Chapter 15

Kenny phones me back. Gives me a number to call. Says he's thinking about opening up an office as a private investigator. I tell him to turn off the TV and go rob some more rich people.

I dial the number.

'Hello?' The voice sounds young and female. And scared.

'I'm told you can get me some information I need,' I say.

'God. If anyone finds out about this I am pure fucked, mister.'

'No one will find out, sweetheart,' I say in my best soothing tones. 'Just think about it as a public service. One that could save a child's life.'

'Right. Okay. That's got to be a good thing, eh? Me, pure saving a wean?'

'Where can we meet?'

'You know the McDonald's at Govan? Be there at twelve-thirty. Mine's a Big Mac.' She hung up.

I retrieve my car from the car park and jump on to the M8 and head towards Govan. I take the exit at Ibrox and with the football stadium behind me, I drive towards the Southern General and from there head for McDonald's and its car park. The traffic is minimal at this time of day so I arrive a good fifteen minutes early.

Standing at the service point I think long and hard about what I'm going to have. I've never really been a fan of these fast food chains. I prefer good old-fashioned grease shops with Italian names above the door, where if you don't eat deep-fried you leave hungry.

There is a so-called healthy option. A salad that looks wonderful on the poster, but pathetic in its little perspex box. A member of staff in his sub-Americana uniform sidles up to the till-point. He raises his eyebrows by way of offering me his undivided attention. It's a wonder the movement doesn't set off an explosion of pus on his forehead. It's less like he suffers from acne, more like he has the plague.

I open my mouth to speak. Then close it. I've been really careful so far today. Not eaten anything fattening. Why did that woman have to want to meet here? I could just have a coffee. I open my mouth again. And close it. My stomach does a fair impression of a rottweiler warning off a burglar. I need more than a coffee. And more than that sorry-looking salad.

'Can I help you, mister? Before the prices go up?'

I smile. 'If you want to keep your job, mate, let the customers do the funnies. A Big Mac meal, please.'

'Want to go Large?'

'Not really, but is that not what happens anyway when you eat in places like this?'

'It's murder on the complexion as well.' He presses a few buttons on his screen, his mouth half-forming a smile.

With my food on a tray, I choose a seat in the far corner of the shop, where I can see everyone who comes in. The fries drop straight into my stomach, I barely chew on them I am so hungry. The burger takes a little longer. I wash it down with some fizz.

With a thought aimed in the direction of my abdomen I judge the status of my stomach. Still hungry. Should I have one of those cardboard apple turnover things and a coffee?

The door opens. A couple walk in. They'll both be going "Large" I expect. They are a matching pair. Same height, same shape and wearing pretty much the same clothes; navy sweatshirts and sweatpants. I can't imagine them doing much sweating, unless it's while running to catch the ice cream van. It just occurs to me that when both sexes beef up to that extent their body shape ends up matching. Fat softens the musculature and the curves into a kind of middle sex. The only way I can recognise the male is with the hairstyles. His head is shaven, she has a ponytail.

The door opens again and a young woman walks in. She's holding her head high like it is costing her a month's wages in effort. She looks round the room and sees me.

'You started without me,' she looks at the remains of my meal. A smile is shoe-horned into her expression.

'Sorry. That was rude,' I say. 'I was unsure what the etiquette might be.'

'Eat first. Ask questions later.' Her hair is out-of-a-bottle-blond and the skin on her face sports an out-of-the-can-tan. Under her black raincoat I can make out a hospital type uniform. She looks as if she is in her early twenties. She has the pinched features of poverty, her eyes sunken and dark. She sits and puts a small leather bag on the table.

'If you want a photo, mate, I can arrange it.' Whatever is worrying her is putting an aggressive tone in her voice.

'Big Mac?' Without waiting for her to answer I walk up to the till. My young friend is still serving. The eyebrows go up and I want to duck for cover, but no explosion ensues. I ask for the same again and pause.

'Anything else for you, sir?'

'Aye, okay. A chocolate muffin and a coffee.'

The girl and I eat in silence. I finish first, even if the muffin gets more chewing action than the first part of my meal.

'So who's the kid that I'm helping?'

'What's your name?'

'Jasmine.'

'Ok, Jasmine. You work in the hospital in an admin capacity I am told.'

She nods and chews. While she eats her feet are drumming on the floor. She's wired.

'I need to find someone. A nurse someone.'

'There are official ways to do that, mister,' she says and then sucks on her straw.

'Tried that. Got nowhere.'

She measures me with a look. 'Mebbe that's 'cos there's nothing for you to get.'

Over Jasmine's head I can see a man is walking away from the counter towards the door. Something about him is familiar. Where had I seen that face before?

'Hello?' says Jasmine. 'You alright?'

'Yeah,' I answer as I watch the man leave the store and walk to the car park. Something about him.

'Sure? 'Cos you look spooked mate.'

I shiver. Then notice she hasn't touched her fries. I steal one. 'Anyway back to you. I have a hunch.' I tell her what I want. She slumps back in her chair.

'But that's going to take me ages.'

'We don't have ages. A child's life is at stake.'

'Let me get this straight. You want me to search all the hospitals in the Glasgow area for a member of staff with a famous name that just might include the first name Lucy?'

'You got it.'

'C'mon tae fuck, man. Do you know how many people work for the NHS?' She leans forward into my space.

'Just what does Kenny have on you?' I stay where I am and ask.

She sits back again, a hole punched in her street tough demeanour. She looks out of the window. Fear tightens her features. Inwardly I cringe. I don't want to play a part in someone else's misery. This is not what I had in mind when I asked for Kenny's help. I should have thought it through some more before giving him the call. God only knows how deep the shit is this girl is in. And you've then got to wonder, how much is Kenny stirring the pot?

'When do you want it?' she sounds defeated and her street mask has slipped making her look young enough to have just recently left school.

'As soon as.' I answer while my conscience screams vile names at me.

Back at the office Daryl and Alessandra are at their desks. Time for a mingle at the coffee machine I think. I aim a wink in their direction and press the button for a cappuccino served in a tan, plastic cup. It is released into my hands and the froth is as thin as saliva. I swear, every time the machine issues one a groan sounds from the world's Italian population.

Alessandra joins me. 'I'm your help for the day. Gimme a mocca with a chocolate swizzle stick, please.'

'A white coffee then?'

'As long as it's warm and wet.'

I pause.

'See how I'm holding my tongue?'

'Impressive.' She takes a sip and judging by her expression she's mentally giving the drink a score. Settles for, 'better than nothing'.

We're just two colleagues shooting the breeze, with a body stance that says, look how relaxed and friendly we are and not talking about anything suspicious. I scan the room. Peters is in his office, face locked on his computer screen. His hand darts to the side of his keyboard and plucks a brown sandwich from a pocket of tinfoil. He looks at it as if it is covered in shit and throws it back into the foil.

'What's eating his gusset?' I ask and debate whether or not to liberate the sandwich.

'The Super was in Peters' office not long before you came in. Looking for results. Not getting any. It's the skull they found in that city centre building site. Turns out it was Tony Kay.'

'Right. And the high heid yins are worried we'll have a gang war on our hands,' I fill in the blanks. The former bearer of said skull was the favoured son of a prominent gangster in the city. Prostitution, drugs and money laundering were said to be his thing. He was yet to lose a day's freedom for it. But it may have cost him his son.

'Not a happy chappy.' Alessandra takes another sip of coffee while her eyes skim over the top of her cup in to Peters' office.

'Moral of the story; be careful what you wish for. You might not like it when you get it.' All the while I was Peters' superior officer, he made it very clear that he resented my promotion over him. All the years he spent on the force and he only had a sergeant's ticket to show for it. Look at him now; all smoke and mirrors. Take away the bluster and you are left with an adequate professional who is so far out of his depth he should have been handed a snorkel and flippers with the promotion.

For a moment I consider walking into his room and acting like a sounding board for him. Maybe all he needs is someone to help him make a decision. He's not the kind to ask for help. He would see that as some form of failure. Na, fuck him. If he wants help, he'll ask for it.

'We should gossip, Ale,' I say.

She just looks at me.

'Seriously. Small talk is good. An affirmative method of bonding in the workplace.'

'And what about the poor sap who's the object of the goss?'

'He, or indeed she, will see it as character forming in his or her quieter moments.'

'You're on a diet again aren't you?' she asks.

I screw my eyes up. 'Any chocolate in your desk?'

'If I give you some, will you stop talking crap?'

'Indubitably.'

'Jesus. That word itself deserves a Mars bar.' The noise of our laughter is enough to force Peters from his thoughts. He looks in our direction and aims an expression of non-interest at us.

Alessandra walks over to her desk, rummages in her drawer and comes back bearing the familiar shape in the outstretched palm of her right hand.

'The diet starts for real tomorrow,' I pluck it from her

hand and tear it open. I have an instant mouth orgasm. 'Mmmmm.' I can feel a thread of soft caramel on my chin. Don't care. 'Anyway,' I mumble. 'Get anywhere this morning?'

'Zip, zilch, zero. Daryl's been on to the private hospitals as well. Nada, nil, nothing.'

'What's with the alliteration?'

'You're not the only one that can talk crap.'

I look over at Daryl. He waves with one hand while the other holds the phone at his ear.

'He's gone back to talking to the people at the Victoria,' says Alessandra. 'He's hoping he gets somebody different this time and that they know more than the last person.'

'Worth a go.' I'm still chewing.

'What were you up to this morning when we talked on the phone?' asks Alessandra.

'Trying to buy a woman's lunch from her in Blythswood Square.'

'Did somebody start off a new slang word for procuring prostitutes and not tell me?' She crosses her arms in fake displeasure.

'I was actually...' I stop talking. However I describe it, it doesn't sound too good. I shrug. 'Just needed to get out of the office.' I debate whether I should tell her about Jasmine. And decide not to. I've not quite squared that off in my conscience yet. If I talk about it to another cop I'll just feel even worse.

My mobile rings. I aim an 'Excuse me' at Alessandra and turn into my office.

'Okay, big man. I've something for you.' It's Jasmine.

'That didn't take you too long.' I say.

'It took me way too long, Mr. If anyone hears about this I am out of a job.' She reads me the names and addresses of five Lucys. Then she reads me their job titles. Except for Lucy number five. Then I hear some clicks from a computer keyboard. 'Scratch that last one, mate,' she says with as much emotion as she might inject into a comment about the colour of the walls. 'She's deid.'

I send Daryl and Alessandra an email.

<<<I've got a list of four Lucys that work for the Greater Glasgow Health Board.>>>

<<<How the buggery did you manage that?>>>replies Daryl.

I'm trying not to feel too superior. After all he has only been on the phone for the last couple of days.

<<<You just need to speak to the right people>>>

<<<How do you give somebody the finger over an email? I'm *thinking* the middle digit of both hands>>>

<<<I'm thinking I've got the message.>>> I type the names and addresses of two of the women.

<<<Do you two want to have a look at these ones and I'll take the other two? A division of labour will keep Peters off our case.>>>

<<<You got a camera, Ray? We'll need to get a positive ID won't we?>>> types Daryl.

<<<On the button, Daryl. I will get a fine piece of technology from Boots. Eight quid for a disposable should do the job.>>>

<<<I've a digital one, Ray.>>> sends Alessandra. <<<Means we don't have to wait for the film to get processed. We can come straight into the office and upload on to the computer.>>>

<<<Ooooh, get you. Do you happen to have two?>>>

<<<You'll have to wait until we get back.>>> writes Daryl. <<<Feeling superior now?>>>

I don't bother with email; I walk to my office door, hands at chest level with the required fingers aimed at the ceiling.

So I'm waiting again. I search the news agencies online for details of the Kay case. Nothing there that I don't know already. I'd come across Tony once at a charity dinner in the days when I gave a fuck about playing the game. He was at my table with his wife/girlfriend and another couple. All of the women around us were suddenly more alert and more attentive whenever he spoke.

And more prone than usual throughout the meal to rushing off to the ladies room to touch up their lipstick. He was your stereotypical Italian, tall dark and yes, handsome and when he did open up his mouth to speak what came out was reasoned and articulate. It was said that he wasn't in the same life as his father. He was an accountant for a large public company through in Edinburgh. It seemed that some apples do fall far from the tree. Unfortunately for him the life found a way to reel him back in. Permanently.

This made me think of the young girl I met earlier. Any contact with the underworld can be enough to make you lose your head, literally or metaphorically. It still bothers me that I attempted to use her. I phone Kenny.

'Silver Investigations,' he answers. Silver is not his surname, but a name he said he might choose if he ever became a porn star. Obviously he had decided it was an appellation with franchise possibilities.

'Tell me about Jasmine.' Small talk is way over-rated.

'Somebody's ticked off. Somebody should be more grateful.'

'I didn't enjoy being part of her problem, Kenny.'

'Get the plank of wood out your arse, big man. Keep your eyes on the prize.' Then he hung up.

I rub at my eyes, suddenly more tired than I deserve to be.

Eventually my colleagues return, looking all flushed with purpose. I realise I am grinding my teeth while Daryl is talking to me about the two women he has just photographed. He is full of wild conjecture about one of them. She is in her early thirties and a midwife. An excellent opportunity to gain the trust of desperate families.

'It's too early for all that, Daryl. Let's wait until we show all the photos to the families and get an ID.'

At my tone Alessandra looks at me sharply. 'Everything alright, Ray?'

'Fucking peachy.'

Just then DI Peters comes out of his office and walks towards us. 'Can I see you in your office, Ray?'

'Talk to me here.' I turn and face him.

He swallows and after some internal dialogue he moves closer. His voice is low and aimed at my ears only, although everyone in the room can read the tension between us.

'You've been warned, Ray. Your duties are to be administrative only. Until further notice.' The last three words are pronounced with care.

I want to sink my teeth into the fleshy lump at the end of his nose. Instead I fish in my pocket, find a coin and throw it to him. 'Here's twenty pence. Phone somebody that gives a fuck.'

I brush past him. Lift the camera off Daryl's desk and walk out of the room.

I'm not sure where I'm going I only know that I need to get away from Peters before I split his skull. I go and sit in my car and will the blood in my veins to recede from boiling point. I take several deep breaths and go through the meditation exercise that Theresa taught me.

I need to repeat it several times before my muscles relax.

I try to focus on a prism of crystal in my mind's eye. I try to watch the colours split. Instead, an image of the Craig boy being hung on the blind cord fills my head. This is followed by an image of me around ten. I'm in the convent orphanage, at the back of the gardens hiding under a bush. I'm shaking. It's a warm summer's evening and I'm shaking. It will soon be bedtime and I don't want to go to bed. Because then the bad man might come for me. Again. I see a cloud of feathers. Then an arch of blood. I shake my head the way a dog might do to try and shed water from its coat.

Then I see the man walking out of McDonalds.

Nah. It couldn't be.

Leonard?

Chapter 16

'So you stuck by me?' Angela asked.

Jim could only nod and stare at the floor, feeling completely unworthy of the look of appreciation she was wearing.

'Must have been difficult for you ...what were you, twenty-two?

He shrugged.

'What about your parents ...' she continued. 'How did they feel about it all?'

'Dad was giving it all this crap about the piper having to be paid for his tune. Mum was happy as long as I was happy.'

'And were you happy, Jim?' Angela bent forward, her gaze searching his.

'Yes.' He forced a smile.

'You could be a little bit more convincing.' She said, her eyebrows all but meeting in the middle.

'Well,' he exhaled a heavy sigh. 'We were happy for a time...'

'Of course.' Angela sat back in her chair, stunned by what had just occurred to her. Jim's chest felt too tight. She'd worked it out. She realised that he was not really in love with her at the time. His face felt hot. Think, Hilton. Think.

'I've just worked this out ...this was what, over ten, twelve years ago? We don't have a twelve year old.' Her face whitened, she clutched at her throat. Jim tried to disguise his sigh of relief at her being wrong, and summon the effort to tell the next part of their story.

'What happened to my baby, Jim?'

The memories stormed back. The rushed wedding minus the bride's parents, but with Kirsty as chief bridesmaid. Her thinly disguised hostility and her departure as soon as the band played their last note.

The long night in the hospital. The fear that Angela might not survive the miscarriage. The doctor said the grief and the pregnancy were too much and she lost the child at twelve weeks.

Angela had been writing furiously in her purple notebook since Jim started speaking, only pausing here and there to ask for clarification. Again, the facts of his relationship with Kirsty were excluded, along with the troubling events afterwards, but otherwise the story was a piece of non-fiction. In his new career as a liar Jim had come to realise that the best form of lying is to stick as closely as is comfortable to the truth.

'It would have been another four or five years until Ben was born ...did we not try again?' Angela tapped her pen on her chin.

'Yes,' Jim grinned. 'We tried plenty.' Then he considered the current state of his sex life and looked at the floor. 'But nothing happened till Ben.' He paused. 'I was offered the post of shop manager over here. It gave us a new start, away from all the bad memories. And the extra money from the promotion allowed you to give up your work.'

At this statement Angela nodded. After all the agony she had gone through to get him she could understand why she would have wanted to provide full time care for Ben herself.

'And then we lived happily ever after?' Angela asked.

'Yes,' Jim smiled. 'Just like in a fairytale.' By now he didn't even have to think of the lie. It had become as solid as truth.

Later, while Angela slept, other memories, sinister memories joined those of the baby. Kirsty all but disappeared from their lives only keeping in touch with Angela with the odd phone call.

Strange things began to happen. A nail was driven through all four of his tyres. Once they were replaced a key was dragged along the bodywork of his car.

Jim suspected it might have been Kirsty, but kept the thoughts to himself. The next event he was sure wouldn't have been her, after all she loved Lucky, but one morning he left the house to find his mother's cat on the doorstep unconscious through loss of blood and pain. His tail had been sliced off with a very sharp knife.

Then there was the time he'd come home from a night at the local club and taken off his new leather jacket to find a knife had been slashed across his back. If the jacket hadn't been so thick, he was sure it would have drawn blood.

When he discovered the damage to his car he instantly thought of Kirsty as the culprit. The cat and his jacket couldn't have been her. They were both put down to vicious youths. It was surely a coincidence that both of those events happened so soon after he broke up with Kirsty. Wasn't it?

Chapter 17

Alessandra catches up with me in the car park. Her eyes are full of concern.

'What's up, Ray? What's really bothering you?'

I pace before her. Words zip in and out of reach. I try to pluck out a few and use them, but I can no more speak than I can find a reason for my behaviour. It's like I've been taken over by evil me. I went from just-filled kettle to boiling over in jig time.

It's all fucked.

I rub at my arms. My scars suddenly itch.

Leonard is out there.

'Ray,' she says and puts a hand on my arm. I stop. 'Ray, what's going on? Are you...'

'Thanks for your concern, Alessandra. But everything is fine.'

'Aye. Right.' She doesn't look convinced. 'You've really not been the same since you came back to work.'

I look at her, quietly stunned.

'You haven't. Not really. Oh, you do the jokes and the banter as well as the rest of us...' She looks deep into my eyes, 'but it's like you're ...oh, I don't know...there's an edge to you, Ray. Even more so than before.' She stops and looks away at a space somewhere over my left shoulder. 'Sorry,' she is now looking at her feet. 'I've said too much.' She turns away. Then turns back.

'You're not over all of that ...' she waves her hand in the air at some nebulous object, 'stuff yet.'

I'm doing the thousand yard stare. I can feel her eyes on me but I don't want any sympathy.

'How do you use this thing?' I hold the camera out.

'Give it here.' She takes it from me. Presses a few

buttons. 'It's good to go, Ray.' She holds it before me. 'All you need to do is aim and press here.'

'Thanks.'

'Ray, should you...'

'I need to be doing something, Alessandra.' My face is burning as I unlock my car door and take a seat. I brush off feelings of guilt that bunch in my shoulders. Daryl and Alessandra will be in the firing line for my behaviour. Again. I drive away.

The first address is just off Paisley Road West. This Lucy should be coming home off her shift soon. I wait just down the street from her house trying to look as inconspicuous as a man can who is hiding in a car with a digital camera.

It's a good job that I have a purpose or I would be out of the car and pacing. Peters is bound to go up the line. What will the big boys do with me? The worst they can do now is pension me off.

Get a friendly doctor and have him report that due to stress I am unfit for duty. Maybe they'll just ignore me? Yeah, what are you worrying about, McBain? Maybe they'll just let me continue with the administrative duties. Mind you, with Peters on my case that is highly unlikely. He'll be in Chief Superintendent Hamilton's office right now bending his ear, telling him what a flake I am.

A woman is walking up the street. She looks like she is in her mid-forties. She is short, two-stones overweight and carrying a bag of shopping. I've worked out that I won't know who the right woman is until she has entered the path to her home and by that stage it will be too late. So I'll have to take the picture of every woman who walks up this street, watch which door number she approaches and then delete the wrong ones. I'm hoping that this doesn't take too long. There's a Neighbourhood Watch sign on a couple of the houses and they'll soon realise that this is a stranger's car. The act of using a camera will also set off a few alarm bells. Luckily with a digital, the photographic action isn't so obvious.

Woman number one goes to door number 81. I want door number 85.

A tone sounds from my mobile phone. I've got a text. It's from Daryl. I've to come in and see Hamilton. I reply that as soon as I'm finished I will do so.

He replies that Hamilton wants me to drop everything and come back to the office immediately. I switch my phone off and on again. It's a shame that the service to my phone in this area is so patchy.

I've now been here twenty minutes, taken another four photos and deleted them all. I've had another text from Daryl. He told Hamilton I'm driving on the way back to the office and that's why I am not replying.

The next woman is of average height and build. She has a child with her, a girl of around ten. The woman's face is etched with strain. The girl is skipping, she knocks into the woman and earns a rebuke. I'm no lip-reader but that was a fuck that was aimed at that wee girl. I take her photograph and hope she goes into 85 and then proves to be the one. In fact I want to get out of the car and throw a few swear words at her.

I hear a knock at my window. I turn in my seat and as I do so I roll my window down.

'Whit do you think you're doing, mate?' An old man says. He has a full head of white hair and is wearing one of those cardigans that they must dish out to Scots men who reach seventy-five.

'I'm selling double glazing,' I open the car door and get out.

He measures me with a frank stare. Here is a man who sees it as a virtue to protect his neighbours.

'Double-glazing my arse,' he says and sticks a finger in my chest. 'You're one of they paedophiles. I saw you taking a photo of that wee girl. I've just phoned the police and given them your registration number. So you better piss off, pronto.'

'Away and check your colostomy bag, auld-yin and give me peace,' I snarl in his face. He backs off spluttering

132

with righteous fury, then turns and wags a finger at me before going into a house. My attention has already returned to the woman I last aimed my camera at. Yes. She has gone to the right door. I climb in the car, switch on the car engine, put on my seat belt and prepare to face the music.

Chief Superintendent Hamilton is on my office. Sitting in my seat.

I move towards the same side of the desk as him. I'm thinking that this will be a less adversarial stance to take. He's not having it and points to the seat on the other side of the desk.

'Sit.'

Like a good hound I do as I'm told. I open my mouth to speak, but decide against it and close it again. He leans forward so that his elbows are on the desk. He picks up one of my pens. Clicks up the nib. Clicks it shut again. Puts the pen down.

'I'm actually speechless, DI McBain.' He cocks his head to the side in the way a dog might do as it looks for understanding. 'Speechless.'

I lean forward in my seat. 'Sir?'

'Just let me get this straight,' he fiddles with the cufflink on his right sleeve. 'You're just back from ... three months was it?' He doesn't wait for me to confirm. 'And you are ordered to keep a low profile. What do you do? You trick a young, gullible officer into handing over a semen sample. You make an official visit to a woman who has written more letters to the Chief Constable than the other eight hundred thousand Glaswegians put together. You forget to go to your meeting with a counsellor, which I might add was a condition of your continued service.' I cringe. Shit. I had forgotten about that. 'You insult and demean a colleague who tries to help you. Then when I order you to come back to the office you ignore me. And don't try to tell me the service was poor on your mobile. Don't kid a kidder, DI McBain. And then we have the icing on the proverbial cake when an active member of a local neighbourhood watch scheme phones in your car registration and claims the driver is taking photographs of young girls.' All the while he is speaking I watch his face. His nostrils are dilated and the lines round his eyes are tight with the effort of keeping his voice low. 'Is there any part of this list of actions that might come under the heading of keeping a low fucking profile, Ray?'

'Sir, there is a crazy woman out there hurting kids. We're just beginning to get somewhere.'

'Ah, yes. I forgot about that. You also enlist the help of a couple of your colleagues. Putting their coats on the same shuggly peg as yours.'

There are times when you just have to take the hit, when you have to brace yourself and let the boss ram his indignation up your arse. I chew on my frustration knowing that a huge well of anger is close to boiling over. I study the backs of my hands; trace the line of my veins with my eyes. Keep it down, Ray. Keep calm and let the moment slide.

'In any case, both of them have been re-assigned. They are on the Kay ...'

'You have got to be fucking kidding me. A dead accountant is more important than a...'

'McBain, how dare you speak to me in that manner.'

I can hear my breath as I exhale through my nostrils in an attempt to keep control.

'Think about it, Ray.' He thinks I'm under his thumb now; he's going for a more conciliatory tone. 'Would the Browning case ever make it to court? What do you have? A mother's paranoia and a nasty bedtime story from a child. You have nothing, Ray. Nothing.'

'Sir, there is a child out there in danger.' I stand up. 'Forgive me for thinking that a policeman's job is to protect the more vulnerable members of our society.' I'm at the tipping point. There are times when you take the bullet and there are times when you say fuck it.

'Do not presume to tell me what our job is. A big part of

our job is to follow orders. A part that you seem to struggle with.'

'This is shit. Total fucking shit.' I am shouting now and I don't care. 'This is all about politics and it stinks. The press are all over this gangster's dead son and the suits are shitting themselves. Let's fend off some media headlines rather than actually save some lives, why don't we?'

'McBain. Sit down and shut the fuck up.'

'How dare *you* speak to me like that? What crimes have you actually solved in your career, Hamilton? You get a degree, take a march up the ladder and think that makes you a policeman. You're an administrator. Away and do some filing and leave the police work to those who know what the fuck they're doing.'

'McBain, that's enough. You're too much trouble. I don't want to see you in this office again.'

We are both standing now. Toe to toe. Snarling in each other's faces. I want to hit him. I swear I want to bury my fist in his stomach. It's this realisation that calms me down. Without another word I walk out of the room.

In the corridor, I hear someone's feet hitting the floor as they chase me.

It's Daryl. He pulls on my arm so that I am facing him. 'Ray, what the fuck are you doing?'

'I'm going to the off-licence and I am going to get shitfaced, rat-arsed, deep in the gutter drunk.'

Chapter 18

I feel almost untouched by memories of my father, as if they originally belonged to someone else and they became mine in the telling. He was a tall man, with a dark bush of hair and my adult mind translates his physical slightness as the thinness of an addict.

There were times of absence and times when he filled my world with his presence. His voice was deep and warm and I was fascinated by the way his adam's apple would bob up and down in his throat as he read to me at bedtime. He read from the classics, running his vocal chords across the words of Stevenson and Dickens. Jekyll and Hyde was a favourite of his. Perhaps he saw the parallels between the desperate pain Stevenson's character doled out to himself and his own attraction to the bottle.

He'd start off a happy drunk, dancing and singing, throwing me in the air and I was a boy flush with the warmth of his father's attention. Perhaps Mum felt left out as Dad's focus was on me. Her smile would grow brittle and crack, falling off her face in shards sharp enough to lacerate as they fell around her feet. Then she'd throw accusations at him like lances. Sentences calculated to maim.

The fights could go on for days, or so it seemed to me. When my father picked up a can of beer for his breakfast, my mother would pick up the threads of last night's fight and weave them into a fog of reason my father could not see through. He was no match for her. His replies, even to me, sounded like faint efforts at vindication. I remember hiding behind a piece of furniture while they roared at each other. From my viewpoint all I could see was my father's foot, part of his leg and a hand flexing in and out of a fist. Eventually when he ran out of words he walked out.

His disappearances lasted longer than the fights and while he was gone my life was filled with the soft, supportive tones of women. I wanted the growl and rasp of a man's vocals to circle the air above my head. While he was away I remember being in an agony of waiting until my mother slapped me into the moment.

'Go out and play,' she'd say. 'Uncle Joe's coming over for his tea and he doesn't want a wee boy running around and tripping him up.' I remember a series of silent men coming to visit. In my mind they all share the same face and they all look at me for the shortest of moments and then turn away as if I hurt their eyes. What was the purpose of these men's visits? As a child I didn't think it strange that mum had a lot of men friends, at least it made her happy. She always had a smile for a day after each visit and there was always fresh, not tinned food on the table for a couple more. Until once again she stiffened with loneliness and her face creased into furrows of worry.

Once I remember being in bed for three days following a visit from father. It was like I was sickening for his return. Mother's slaps didn't work and, desperate for a reaction, she told me he had died. She immediately recanted when she saw the look of grief on my face.

I allowed her to cajole me back to life and pulled my body from the blankets. While I dressed I asked myself which parent I should hate the most.

I name emotions as I recount this time, but it's the adult who has spliced them into memory. The child wears a distance from them like a shield. One thing I am certain of is the cause of all this pain was alcohol. This was reinforced by the nuns at the convent orphanage who wasted no time in telling me what a sodden drunk my father was and how he had run my poor, sainted mother into an early grave. They then went on to prescribe my future with a harsh tone and with the certainty of an oracle.

'Mark my words, Ray McBain, one day you'll turn out to be a worthless drunk just like your father.'

All this goes through my mind as I stand at the super-market till waiting to be served, a month's worth of booze in my trolley. I have locked myself on to a course of action and I can no more turn back from it than I can halt the moon's slow slide up into the night sky. I know I am ful-filling the potential as passed on to me by my father, but reason and emotion have fled into that corner of my mind, behind the shields I built as a boy.

'Having a wee party?' the till attendant chirrups. I ignore her and place the bags of bottles back in my trolley.

At home, it takes two runs from the car and up the stairs to my flat to empty the boot. I'm on the second run when I sense a presence at my elbow. It's Maggie. From her face she knew what to expect and doesn't react to the clink of the bottles as I continue to walk.

'What do you want?' I am gruff with the need to be on my own. I all but march upstairs.

'Alessandra phoned me. She's worried about you.' I can hear Maggie huffing as she keeps up.

'So you thought you'd come and check up on me like a good fucking Samaritan.'

We're at the door to my flat. I leave it open for the return trip and Maggie skips in ahead of me. She walks to the kitchen door, turns and pulls the bag from me and sets it on the floor.

'Ray,' her face is turned up to mine. I expect to see sym-pathy and I prepare to growl. Instead her eyebrows are raised, her mouth shaped into the suggestion of a smile. A smile that hints at understanding. Her face is infused with genuine warmth and concern.

'Ray,' she says again, her hand on my arm. I move to her left, an action that brings us closer together. I sag as the weight of fury leaves me.

'C'mere,' she holds her arms out and I lean into her. Her heat calms me further. My nose is filled with the

138

scent of her hair, as if a breeze had brought with it the gift of flowers. I notice the press of her breasts against my stomach and the weight of her against my thighs. I am hard now and shift away from her. She moves and fills the space.

'Ray ...' her face turns up to mine, her lips parted with need.

Chapter 19

'Is the food okay?' asked Moira before they'd even brought the first spoonful to their mouths. It was Sunday dinner at Moira's house. In her own environment she was a different woman. She did less snorting, was a little more open in how she talked to Jim and she didn't seem to be trying so hard to be liked. Whatever synergy the two women shared, it was of mutual benefit. So who was he to sneer? As long as his secret was secure they could do whatever they wanted.

It was safe, wasn't it?

If Moira had any knowledge of their prior situation she was keeping quiet. So, perhaps Jim could assume she knew nothing. In any case she was a great help to him and Angela, particularly now he was back at work. In fact, he was beginning to wonder what he would do without her.

The menu was a watery soup à la Weight Watchers, followed by melon, followed by grilled chicken breasts with vegetables, followed by a fruit salad. All very healthy.

The house itself was a bog-standard three bedroomed, newly built, detached villa. The rooms were all small, but furnished with care. Every available surface had a vase, or an ornament, or a photograph on it. Moira must really dote on Erskine, Jim thought. Every single photograph contained him, and only him. No mum, dad or other relatives, just Erskine.

The talk ranged from their respective sons, to soft furnishings to the price of local houses and back again to their sons. Now and again Jim joined the boys in the garden just to get the merest whiff of testosterone — they had finished their dinner of tomato soup and chicken

140

nuggets in record time — then he would go back into the house.

'We're going to have a girly day tomorrow.' Angela clutched her ever-present purple notebook to her chest when Jim sat down with them for coffee.

'Oh,' he politely requested more information; delighted he would be nowhere near.

'Yes. We're going to have our nails done. And our hair.' Moira squealed with excitement.

Just then Ben and Erskine came running in. 'Moira, Moira. Moira,' chanted Erskine, 'Ben called me a bad name. He said I was stupid,' Erskine's face had almost folded in on itself with anger at Ben. Then it occured to Jim that he had just called his mum by her first name.

'He's going through a wee phase,' Moira smiled and shrugged. 'Refuses to call me anything but Moira.' We all share a smile at the idiosyncrasies of children.

'Ben,' Jim spoke in a warning tone. 'What do you say to Erskine?'

Ben pouted at his father. Looked at Erskine. Then he looked back at Jim.

'Sorry, Erskine,' offered Ben. He walked over to the other boy and pulled him into a quick hug. 'You're only a little bit stupid.'

Erskine paused, weighing this up and then placing his hand on Ben's back he returned the hug. Then he tugged at Ben's hand.

'C'mon and see my new dinosaur. It's an Allosaurus.'

Ben's eyes widened and both boys issued a long, 'Oooooo' then charged from the room and towards the stairs.

'That'll be a lovely day out for you, sweetheart.' Jim brought the conversation back to Angela and her imminent trip while admiring how children can at times move past insults so quickly.

'I know. We're going to a trendy new place,' Angela opened her book and flicked over a couple of pages. 'Palmer-Douglas it's called. Everyone's talking about it.

Apparently they're really good.'

'Yes,' smiled Moira. 'It's about time I had a new me.'

Angela was in the kitchen; rested after an hour's nap, but despite the late spring heat she was warming her hands on a full mug of coffee. Something about her shape as she hunched over the table made Jim pause.

'You okay, babe?' he asked.

She looked at him and sucked on her top lip before speaking. 'Am I difficult to live with?' She looked like tears were close.

'No, honey. Not really.' Jim groaned inwardly as the last two words came out of his mouth, too late for an edit.

'Not really? What does that mean?' Tears were now giving way to irritation.

'It means that yes, you are difficult at times,' he maintained an easy tone. 'But no, you are not too difficult to live with.'

Then Angela burst into tears. She covered her face with her hands. Something resembling words fought their way through the wall of her hands.

Jim walked over to her and put his arms around her.

'You have been such a help, Jim. I don't know what I would have done without you. Don't know what I would *do* without you. Please don't take any notice of what I say. I just get so frustrated at not remembering stuff that I lash out. I know it's not fair on you. I just can't help myself.' Then she added a list of her faults; it sounded like a litany of self-hate.

'I'm a crap mother. A shit wife. I have no friends but Moira, and another woman called Kirsty who never gets in touch. What is it about me? Why am I such a failure at everything?'

'Hey, hey, hey.' Jim hunkered down so that he was at eye level with her. 'You are not a shit wife and you are certainly not a crap mother. Ben loves you to bits. He adores you. And it's only natural that when you move away from your hometown and devote your life to your child that you lose touch with people. Right?'

Angela nodded, completely malleable now as if pleased to have someone else do her thinking for her.

'In any case,' Jim said, 'Moira is enough of a friend to be the equivalent of ten. Not sure what we'd do without her.' The words were sincere when they formed in his mind and intended as reassurance. But once given sound they soured like yoghurt left to sit too long in the sun.

Chapter 20

As a man, what more can you ask for than to go to sleep with a smile, make like a catatonic for eight hours and wake up in the morning with a hard-on? Maggie is on her side facing away from me. I press against her, feeling the sweet ache as my penis touches the swell of her buttock. A groan escapes from my mouth. Maggie turns her head to face me.

'Can you not hear my belly growling? People in the next flat are about to call the RSPCA for fear there's an animal in here getting mistreated.'

I grind against her. 'There is. Me.'

She turns on her side, her mouth forming a pout, reaches down and sticks a finger in my stomach.

'I need food.'

'OK,' I jump out of bed, pull on a pair of jeans that were lying in a heap on the floor, just for such an occasion, rummage in a drawer for a T-shirt, slip on a pair of shoes and find my wallet in yesterday's trousers in another pile of clothes.

'Right. I'm going commando for breakfast,' I swivel my hips.

'Sticky commando,' says Maggie as she sits up in bed. I notice she pulls the quilt with her and holds it in front of her breasts.

'I'll shower when I get back.' I lean forward and aim to give her a kiss. Her forehead is the only place I can reach.

The corner shop is empty save for me and the shop-keeper, Amir. He is in his mid-fifties and sports a thatch of thick white hair. Whenever his wife is working in the shop with him, he loves to tell his customers how his hair was as black as a crow's wing until he met her.

'Having a wee lie-in, Mr McBain,' he asks, his accent as broad Scots as mine.

'There's no pulling the wool over your eyes.'

He raises his eyebrows in that bored expression he is so fond of. I'm sure he stands in front of a mirror and practises. The only hint that he is in fact quite happy with his lot is the glint in his eyes that he is unable to disguise. 'What morsels can I tempt you with this morning?' He moves his left hand, palm up, in a grand sweeping gesture, as if his shop were filled with the finest goods the world would ever see.

'I have a need for square sausage, Amir. Is there any other country in the world that flattens its sausage meat into a square shape, do you think?' I'm feeling expansive this morning. Wonder why?

'Dunno,' he shrugs. 'We Scots have some strange culinary habits, mate. How many slices of such sausage will satisfy your appetites this morning?'

'Four. And four rolls as well, please Amir.'

'So, Mr McBain is not breakfasting alone this fine morning?' His doleful expression lightens at the prospect of some gossip.

I struggle to keep the grin from my face. 'Should I fill out a wee postcard and stick it in your window?'

'Ah,' he clutches his hands before his heart. 'Affairs of the heart should stay between a man and his lover. Don't sully my windows with tales of fornication.' He pauses. 'Anybody I might know?'

'Fornication? Who is talking about fornication in my shop?' A small round woman enters from behind a beaded curtain at the rear of the shop. Nisha is Amir's wife and her voice is still filled with the mountains of Pakistan, despite over forty years in this country.

'My shop, dear,' says Amir. 'And it's Mr McBain from number 79. He's here to buy rolls for his breakfast.' His tone and the way he tilts his head suggests there is more than just food involved.

Nisha's face transforms with a smile.

145

'I remember the first flush of romance, Mr McBain.' She looks over my shoulder, her eyes fixed on a spot that must be so wonderful I feel forced to turn and see what is in her line of vision. 'Didn't last long.' She narrows her eyes at Amir. Then her face softens as she turns back to me. 'Have you known this lady long? Is she very beautiful?'

This middle-aged couple are now standing side by side, like matching bookends, wearing identical smiles and waiting to hear of my romance. The only difference is while Nisha has her hands clasped in front of her heart, Amir is holding a plastic bag containing my breakfast.

'She's gorgeous. I've known her for about a year and can I have my food please?'

'Sure, sure.' Amir is all business now. He names the price, I pull out my wallet and hand over a note. While Amir counts out the coins of my change he fixes me with a look.

'Savour this moment, Mr McBain. The world turns, people grow old ...' His eyes shift to the side. 'And eat too much chocolate.' He winks at me.

'Enjoy your breakfast, Mr McBain,' says Nisha. 'And my advice is not to listen to bitter men who grow old before their time.' Her smile is as sweet as sugared almonds.

Walking back to the flat I slow my pace as I think about last night. What do Maggie and I mean to each other? I've always suspected her feelings for me were stronger than mine. Could I love her back? My head was too full of Theresa, and running away from my colleagues to find a serial killer before I was locked up. But that was then. And now?

An image of her smiling at me pops into my head. I feel my face shape itself into a smile of response. One thing is for sure, she makes me feel good. Is that enough? After spending a night with the woman I love, I should be dancing along this street, throwing my joy into the world. Instead I'm wondering whether I could love her or not.

146

She is a wonderful woman. I enjoy her company. She makes me laugh. The sex last night was better than good. Most couples would view all of these things as mandatory.

Yes.

Me and Maggie. Maggie and me. It could work.

I ignore the wee voice that intones; *you're kidding yourself, McBain.*

Back in the flat, Maggie is all business. She has dressed and showered and is standing waiting with her hand out for whatever food I am carrying.

We each avoid the other's eyes.

'Have a shower, Ray and I'll prepare the breakfast.'

Clean and dressed, the smell of cooked meat invites me through to the kitchen. The table is set with mugs of steaming tea and a plate piled with breakfast. A voice drones out from the small TV set that sits on top of the fridge. It's the Scottish news. There's been a shooting in the east of the city. Two men approached a parked car and shot the occupant. He died at the scene. The speculation is that it is linked to the dead accountant.

For once it's none of my concern, I pick up a roll and sausage and take a bite. Thinking one of us should speak, I say, 'Just realised how hungry I am.'

Maggie's eyes are on the screen.

The next news story has me paying attention however. A test case had gone before the courts to decide whether the former residents of orphanages run by nuns of the same religious order as had looked after me were due for some compensation. Over four hundred and fifty people had complained about abuse at the hands of these nuns between the years 1961 and 1977 and wanted compensation for the treatment they received. The reporter went on to say that the judges had rejected the three test cases with the view that their actions became time-barred past 1990.

It's like getting good news and bad news all at the same time. Firstly, I could have actually sued for damages. I could have gone to the courts and seen that the women who treated me in such a way, under the cloak of religion, were punished. Then I learn it's too late. Some judges have decided that there is a time limit on the effects of abuse. Put the clock on it for twenty-one years and it appears the impact of your treatment will have lessened sufficiently for you to believe that it never really happened. Aye right.

'Bugger me,' I say and then look at Maggie. 'These rolls are just what the doctor ordered.'

Maggie is chewing and nodding her agreement. We eat in silence. I finish one roll and pick up another. Maggie satisfies herself with one.

'I thought you were hungry? Did you sleep OK? I slept like a log. The best sleep I've had in ages.'

'Ray, we need to talk.'

My heart lurches. I know I'm doing the male thing of ignoring the elephant in the room and hoping that it goes away. Equally I know we should talk about what happened last night and what it means to our relationship.

'What's wrong?'

'You're an easy man to fall in love with, Ray McBain,' she lifts her head up and meets my gaze. I see a tear shine, trapped in the web of her lower lashes.

'And that's a bad thing because?'

'What would you have done last night if I hadn't been here?'

'I would have got drunk.' I lean back in my chair and try to work out what to say. Which is difficult when I don't know what I want.

'And the next time you feel like going on a bender will I be expected to turn up again?'

'So last night was a sympathy shag? Poor McBain is going off the rails. Some pussy is what's needed to keep him on the straight and narrow.'

'Don't be crude, Ray. And last night had nothing to do with sympathy. I came over here to talk sense into you. Not to fuck sense into you. The ... stuff just happened.'

148

'Who's being crude now?' I stare at the dregs of my coffee, a dribble of brown liquid is drying to form a dark circle at the bottom of the mug.

'Do you even love me?' she asks.

I pause searching for the right words. Do I love her? Before last night I would have said that I was very fond of her. What's more she is very attractive and highly desirable. But, do I love her?

'Enough said.' I barely hear her words.

'I didn't even say anything,' I defend myself knowing that it is a waste of time. Maggie is wearing the expression of someone who has a firm idea of what she wants.

'Your pause was too long. Your answer should have been instant,' her smile is weak. A smile of commiseration. We could have had something, it said, but the time has past. 'Last night was a mistake. A lovely mistake...' she says. 'But I deserve better, Ray. You deserve better. I don't want to fill the gap in your life until somebody who is not me comes along.'

'But...' I interrupt. It's not like that, I want to say. We are good pals. We could have something. Arranged marriages are built on less. We could work at it. Instead I say nothing, my vocal cords as redundant as a black and white TV.

Chapter 21

'Next, please?'

Jim was on the front till of the bookshop serving the few customers that were about on a Monday afternoon. He should have been in the office checking through last week's orders but he had a staff shortage due to illness. Half of the staff were no doubt sick of working.

The middle-aged woman approaching the counter was wearing an uncertain smile and her hands were empty. Not a good sign. This meant she was looking for something. Often with customers it was like a game of charades. "It has a bright cover." "The title has the word Red in it." "It's by that guy that wrote the other one." Usually Jim enjoyed the challenge, but today he was tired. Tired of work, tired of home, tired of everything.

The woman opened her mouth to begin. Then closed it, looked away, then back. 'If I want to buy a book,' she said. 'Do I just bring it to you?'

A thousand witticisms crowded into Jim's head. After a long pause of disbelief, he settled for, 'Yes.'

He was watching the woman walk away when Moira approached the counter.

'Can we talk, Jim?' she said while pulling a strand of her hair behind an ear. Jim took a step to the side, trying to ignore the flare of worry in his stomach.

'I'm worried about your Angela,' she said, all but wringing her hands.

'What happened?' he asked.

'Today. This morning. I met Angela, just like we arranged…and we went for a walk. I thought it would be a great idea. I mean what could go wrong with a simple walk?'

'And …' Jim read the very real worry in Moira's face and began to feel his resistance to her crumble a little more.

'What is wrong with her, Jim? What has this head injury thing done to her?'

'Well … lots of different things,' he answered while thinking what the hell happened?

'She stepped out in front of a car. Just like that. The driver just managed to stop in time. I nearly messed my pants.'

'She stepped out in front of a car?' said Jim needlessly. 'Why would she step in front of a car?' He was doing all he could to help, wasn't he? Jim leaned both elbows on the counter top. He wasn't hearing this. Surely she wasn't feeling suicidal?

'She said that she keeps forgetting to look. She steps down from the pavement and forgets to look for the cars.'

'Eh?'

'What would have happened if Ben was with us? What would happen if a car …' Her face was stretched tight with the horror of it. The rest of the sentence was too terrible for her to finish.

'That won't happen, Moira. Angela doesn't feel strong enough to take Ben out on her own yet.'

She sagged into herself and pressed a hand to her chest as if giving permission to her heart to slow down its beat. 'Oh.' She thought some more. 'Poor woman. Imagine being too frightened to take your child out for a walk.'

Holy shit, thought Jim. She forgot to look for any cars before she crossed the road. But that was elementary. What part of her brain has switched off to make her forget that?

Jim was a mental inch from giving in. He wasn't an expert. He didn't know how to handle people with all these kinds of problems. He could barely look after himself, for chrissake.

'Sorry, Jim.' Moira placed a small, warm hand over his. 'Work must be the place where you get a break from all that stuff.' She realised that she had overstepped some

151

sort of social boundary and removed her hand. 'I …It was just such a shock.' Moira bent forward and lowered her voice as if aware for the first time that there were other people about. 'I knew she was forgetful and that, but you don't really stop and think of the consequences …' her speech tailed off as she did so. 'What else does she struggle with?'

'Lots of stuff.' Jim really didn't want to do this. Talk. He didn't have the energy; a nice soft bed would have come in handy. He could lie on his side, draw his knees up to his chin and sleep for a decade or however long it took to sort this all out.

'Oh, Jim,' said Moira. 'Poor you.'

Simultaneously Jim mentally thanked Moira for voicing this — and hated her for it.

He needed to get away from his own thoughts. This was new to him, having to worry. Worry was something he viewed in the same way as masturbation. It was a solitary pursuit to be done late at night when there was nothing on the TV.

Chapter 22

Daryl is worried about me, although that is not what he says. What he does say is, get your arse out of bed and answer your phone when we ring you. Alessandra is worried about me and wonders if I can get her camera back to her. Kenny drove by the other morning and spotted Maggie leaving my flat. Did you shag her, was his polite enquiry.

Me and Maggie.

Maggie and me.

What should happen next? I've never had sex with a mate before. Have I in some way let her down?

She appears to have dealt with it more easily than me. And anyway, who says that men have a more practical view of sex?

It's been two days since I walked out on Hamilton. Ha! Told him. However, wondering about whether I had a job or not wasn't even on my radar. Eating and sleeping was performed on automatic pilot. As was interaction with anyone who came into my orbit. There's an old Scottish word for this kind of dream state ... a dwam, and for most people it will last seconds while they perhaps wonder what they might do if they won the lottery. Yet it enveloped my mind like a semi-permanent fog.

Why did my mind produce such a state? Perhaps it was to remove the temptation of slipping back to the booze. Up until my last and only slip, I had an aversion to drink that made some of my fellow officers question my sexuality to my face. Can't be a real man and not take a drink. Unless you were a recovering alcoholic, of course. Then you'd earned your scars and your reticence

was completely understandable, if not totally regrett-
able.

I also found myself continually rubbing at my real
scars. The ones cut into my wrists by Scullion. There's no
way that was him in McDonald's. Who would be so
brazen?

Kenny left a message. Can't be arsed answering the
phone to anyone. Instead I drive across the city and visit
the Kelvingrove Art Gallery. The newspapers said it was
the most visited attraction in the whole of Scotland that
summer. With my fog as companion I thought I should go
along.

The museum is a massive building of red sandstone and
the guide says that it has been constructed in various
styles. Like a new parent it struggles to come up with a
name; the best they can come up with is Spanish Baroque
style. It houses an amazing variety of objects from stuffed
animals to the remains of a dinosaur, from Rembrandt to
Picasso and it's just what I need in this mood.

A place of wonder and the everyday; bustle and quiet;
old and new. Somewhere I can be part of the machine and
not be affected.

I'm standing reading an information board in the
Natural History section. Here we have a number of
animals that have achieved record-breaker status. I'm
reading up about this swordfish. It's the fastest creature
in the ocean. Moves in a stream-lined, liquid blur. I
become aware of two little boys standing at my side. One
is open-mouthed. The other is less impressed and tries to
climb on to the exhibit. A mother's voice warns the boy
down. She sounds familiar. I speak to the boy on behalf of
this familiarity in a tone I hope is friendly. As I do so part
of my mind is asking, how do you speak to a stranger's
kids nowadays, without them rushing off to phone
Childline? I hear the woman's voice again, but it's not the
boy she's talking to, it's me. I turn to face her. There's no-

154

one in my immediate line of sight. Then I look down to the woman seated on an electric wheelchair.

'DI McBain?' She's saying. Her face pale and livid at the same time. It's the attitude I recognise first.

'Mrs Browning. Nice day isn't it?'

'It might be if I knew my children were safe.'

I turn back to the fish. Doesn't she ever let it go? I take a deep breath and speak to one of the boys.

'Cool, innit?'

He nods, his button-nose wrinkled in delight.

'Pete,' her tone is one of warning, her voice too loud in this space. 'Come here.' I sense a shift in atmosphere around me as a number of adults turn to stare, while reaching out to grab their own children.

Pete ignores his mother, something tells him he is safe in such a place and with me. He tugs at my trouser leg and points to another creature of stuffed flesh and glassy eye.

'Whassat?'

His brother is more heedful of his mum and goes to stand beside her chair.

'Pete, c'mere,' the older boy warns, but Pete is too interested. I look down at his wide eyes, the small smudge of dirt on his cheek. A cheek that looks as fresh as if the boy slept in a fairy world at night only to come out and dazzle the humans during the day. My fog lifts as quickly as if someone had pulled a blanket from over my head. I look at his mother and then back at the boy. Her worry. His surety that the world holds nothing in it for him but wonder. The older boy has a strained expression on his face and it suddenly shames me that after all he had been through with Ms Hepburn that I should be the cause of further concern.

'Pete,' I nod over at his mother. 'Maybe you should go and see your mummy.' He shrugs an okay and does as I ask.

'Sorry to trouble you,' I say to Mrs Browning and turn away.

I need space. I need to be on my own. I need to process all of this. Seconds later I am in the toilet. The door bangs with the resonance of a gunshot. I lock it and sit on the seat.

Where has my head been the last few days? Chief Superintendent Hamilton has a go at me and I lose it? Time to grow a pair, McBain. The woman who harmed those kids is still out there and you're acting like a child yourself.

A picture enters my mind. Pete's little face turned up to me, curiosity a bright light in his eyes. A strange feeling had come over me as he tugged at my leg. One that I had never felt before. I had won his attention easily, but as he held my trouser at the knee I wanted to keep it. I wanted to make him laugh, show him the meaning of fun. I wanted to engage him in the give and take of a conversation. I wanted to do something that made him laugh. I wanted him to like me.

And now I want to make sure what happened to him and his brother doesn't happen to anyone else.

I open the cubicle door and at the sink throw some water over my face. Time to figuratively and literally grow up, McBain, I tell my reflection. He grimaces back at me, his face older than I remember.

Where will the kids want to go? Natural History? They've already been there. I make for the Egyptian section. Children love mummies don't they? A quick scan in that room reveals nothing. Next.

I try the polar pears. A small room has been set aside to show the environment such an animal might live in, complete with fake snow. Nope. The Brownings aren't here either.

I take a lightning quick tour of the massive building and can't find them. Perhaps they were at the end of their tour and decided to go home. I make a quick decision. If I leave now and make my way over to their home, it might freak them out. I wouldn't put it past Mrs Browning to phone the police and complain about me while I was standing at her door. No, I need to let her calm down a little and then she might be prepared to listen.

Downstairs now in the café, I order an Americano, with a little jug of milk on the side. A row of home-baking winks at me. Mentally I stick my tongue out at it and decide the coffee will do.

My watch tells me it's two-thirty. If I wait for an hour, they should be home and relaxed by then. A voice distracts me.

'DI McBain, I'm sorry I was so rude to you upstairs,' says Mrs Browning. When I turn to face her she's at my eye level this time.

I choke a little at the surprise and wipe a dribble of coffee from my chin with a napkin. 'No apology necessary.' I can see the older boy, Dan, behind his mother's wheelchair. Pete's smiley face appears in a peek-a-boo action behind his brother.

'Can I get you a coffee and something for the boys ...'

'That won't be necessary. I'm sorry to trouble you on your ...' she looks me up and down as if she finds something missing. 'Day off.'

'Please, Mrs Browning. I would like to talk to you,' I hear myself say before I have the chance to really consider what to say. 'I do want to help you. It's just things have become a little complicated recently.'

'It's Liz, please. And I'm no fool, DI McBain. I'm well aware how stretched resources are and how the recent murder of that gangster's son might take precedence. After all,' her shoulders slump and her face takes on a tired, defeated look. 'It's not like we have an identifiable, proveable case here.'

'I'm afraid life has become even more complicated than that.'

Her eyebrows lift and she makes a small 'O' of enquiry.

'Before I tell you, I have to buy you a drink. And the boys too if you'll let me.'

She shakes her head and prepares to verbally refuse me, but the boys are too fast.

157

'Can I have a coke, please Mum?' says Dan.

'Me too, please Mum,' says Pete.

She makes a rueful face. 'Mind you, it would be nice to actually get something out of Strathclyde's finest for once.'

'Two cokes and a ...?'

'Tea, please. Earl Grey.'

Shortly, I return to the table with the drinks as requested. The boys are both very polite and thank me.

'Don't tell Dad,' Liz leans forward towards the boys.

I nod in understanding while I wonder how much to tell her of the recent situation.

'I practically grew up in here,' she says as she lifts her head up and gazes across the room. 'We lived five minutes walk away and my parents used to bring me regularly. I love the grandeur of the place. I love how it can be busy and have wee pockets of quiet at the same time.' She pauses. 'I love what they've done with it.' She refers to the recent renovation.

'I have little memory to compare it with. I think I only visited the place once.'

'Not from Glasgow then?' Her tone said that if you were from the city then you were more than likely to have been a regular to this place over the years.

'I spent some time in Ayrshire as a boy. But most of my adult life has been in the city. I just had other pre-occupations.'

'Celtic or Rangers?'

'Neither. Can't be arsed with all that.' Not used to being in the company of children, I realise what I've said and make a grimace as an apology. 'My time has been used up in the employ of Strathclyde Police. Not had time for much else.'

Her face softens as the implications within the answer become clear to her. Married to the job. Nothing else in his life. Sad and lonely.

'So,' she takes a sip of her tea. 'You mentioned complications?' Sympathy for DI Ray McBain now dispensed with, she's looking for information. I decide to tell her the story, the whole story and nothing but the story of the last few weeks. Apart from me and Maggie sleeping together. Although, I have felt the urge to talk to somebody, anybody about that.

Once I've finished talking I turn to the boys to see how they have dealt with all of this inactivity. They are having a mini sword fight, with their straws as swords. Even the 'Oooo' and 'Urrrgh' sounds they make as they receive an imaginary wound are in miniature.

'So let me get this straight?' says Liz with an unreadable expression. 'You are on sick leave. No-one else is interested and you are all we've got, 'cos you really, really want to help.'

I nod.

'And if your bosses find out you have investigated this case while you are on sick leave, you may end up losing your job?'

I nod again.

'What's in it for you, DI McBain?'

I look at her expression. It reads of a judgement on pause and for some reason I can't fathom, I want her approval. 'I was once in a kind of similar situation to your boys, Liz. In an orphanage run by a religious order. Because of the treatment we received, one of the boys there quite literally turned into the Bogeyman.' My tone leaves no doubt that said Bogeyman was a very dangerous man indeed.

'Oh.'

Dan and Pete stop their mini-fight and look at me and then at each other. They both give a delighted shiver. 'Ooooh. The Bogeyman.' They each try to outdo the other with the force of their scary sound effects.

'That's enough, boys,' says Liz. With the flash of a stripey straw, they go back to playing mini Zorro.

'I live with the effects of that everyday, Liz. I don't want another cycle of violence to begin.'

Chapter 23

'Have you had a good day, honey?' Jim asked when he got home, pretending that he knew nothing about Angela's escape from the grille of a car. She was sitting cross-armed, cross-legged, as if lost in the corner of the sofa. She was like a collection of angled bones among the warmly cushioned soft corners. She looked as if she'd been sitting there since Moira left her.

'Yes, thanks,' Angela answered his question distractedly and bent forward to collect Ben as he raced into her arms. The force of his run made her fall back into the depth of the seat

'Mummy,' he cheered like she'd won some sort of award. Angela's answering laugh was just a little too forced.

'Hungry?' Jim asked, feeling the nip of annoyance. 'I'll just put something on.' Without waiting for an answer he walked towards the kitchen. Rummaging through the freezer, he located some meals that would be ready with minimum effort. Ben's was nuked in the microwave and Angela's meal was thrown on to a tray with his and stuck in the oven. How would madam care for some Chicken Plastique à la Rubber Sauce? Well, too bad. It was all he could cope with.

Watching the goo of Ben's pizza melt in the maw of his hunger, Jim felt guilty again. He shouldn't be feeding his son this crap. Ditto for Angela.

But, she'd been sitting on her arse all afternoon and he still had to come home and make the dinner. So sang Mr Angry perched on his right shoulder. Mr Calm and Reasonable, on the other hand, had noticed the worn expression with the hint of panic on Angela's face and read that she had lost a good deal of confidence after her escapade this morning with Moira. She had surely forgotten the detail, but the mood would hang over her like the fog of a bad dream.

If Jim could just have five minutes on his own to relax.

The doorbell rang just as Angela and he sat down to eat.

'I'll get it,' Jim offered and walked from the room thinking, if this is any religious tossers expecting a convert they'll get a boot up the backside.

'Jim, how nice to see you. I was just passing and I thought I'd come in and say hello.' It was Moira. He stood to the side and let her in. The way she brushed past him, the tightness of her shoulders and the speed of her step towards Angela all caused Jim concern. What the hell was going on? Before Jim closed the door, he saw a taxi drive off. Where was her car, he wondered?

By the time he caught up with her and stepped in through the doorway of the living room Moira was in a heap on the sofa and Angela had an arm over her shoulder. Moira's head bobbed up and down with the force of her emotion, her sobbing coming in great whoops as if being issued from diseased lungs.

'Moira, what on earth's wrong?' Angela was trying to meet Moira at face level in an attempt to offer some form of reassurance. Her head bobbed up and down in time with Moira's.

'A glass of water,' Jim said out loud, not sure how to help. Then he realised Ben was watching, his head peeping out from the kitchen door. His mouth was open in naked amazement and not a little fear.

'You want to go up to your room, buddy?' Jim asked quietly. This was not suitable viewing for a four year-old. He nodded and fled across the carpet as if he couldn't bear the thought of Moira's eyes lighting on his back for even a second.

After the stress of Angela's day Jim didn't think she would be able to cope with Moira in this state on her own for too long, so he quickly filled a glass with water and returned to the living room, where Moira's sobs were winding down.

'There you go,' he stretched out his hand with the glass. Moira ignored it, or she didn't see it. Instead Angela reached for it and sent him a look of gratitude.

'He's got her son, Jim.' Angela said. She sounded drunk and she looked like she was suffering from sleep deprivation. On top of the day she'd already had this was too much. In the struggle to help her rebuild her memory, fatigue was enemy number one. The more tired she became, the less she was able to cope. Things that happened only moments ago would not be recorded. Events would not separate into cause and effect and from there action would fail to realise a reaction. Angela held the glass in both hands. She knew that it was important, but she wasn't sure what she should do with it.

Jim nodded in Moira's direction.

Angela's eyes sparked with realisation and she offered the drink to her friend. Moira accepted the glass and gulped a mouthful. The swallow she attempted didn't coincide with her ragged breathing pattern and she choked out some frenzied coughs.

'What's wrong, Moira?' Angela asked.

Jim faced Moira. 'Okay, Moira...' he purposely deepened his voice, softened his tone and removed any trace of emotion from it. 'Tell us in your own time what happened.'

'Ersk...Ersk...they came and took Erskine.'

'Moira. Who came and took Erskine?'

She grabbed the glass from Angela took a slower sip this time and answered. 'His dad and his grandpa. They just ... came and took him.' The sobs began to grow in stature again. 'And his dad even took his car back.'

'Is he in any danger?' Jim asked. Angela's face whitened at the thought.

'No.' Moira answered, a little calmer. 'They both love him to bits. It's me they want to have a go at. They would

162

happily see me in a coffin. Him, they love. Precious fucking Erskine.' Sob.

'My precious Erskine. I'll fucking kill them if they harm one hair on his head.' A mad light flickered in her eyes and then faded as she stared into the glass of water.

Chapter 24

Away from their mother the boys are quieter. Pete is happy to hold my hand, while Dan walks by my side. I reasoned with Liz that I should speak to the boys on their own. Children tend to perform for their parents in these situations. Almost always seeking approval and looking for some form of guidance in what to say and how to act. Even as a non-parent I have observed that children are masters at reading non-verbal language. A minute change in expression, a tiny lift of the eyebrow, a pause in speech, all of these can send signals to a child that can be interpreted in any number of ways. Ways that are designed to appease or please the parent, but ways that will inevitably obfuscate the truth.

'Enjoy your tea,' I told Liz. 'And I'll take the boys for a wee walk.' I'd spotted a room full of armour on my patrol earlier and immediately thought of it when I suggested that the boys should speak to me alone.

'In most crimes, the criminal leaves something of themselves behind,' I attempted to explain my reasoning to Liz. 'And normally that's where the forensics team come in. Whether there is a fingerprint, a microscopic element of bodily fluid etcetera, it can be found. But here all we have to go on is memories. Locked inside those boys' heads is a piece of information that is going to help us find this woman.' We both look over at the boys who play on, oblivious to our attention. 'There is no such thing as the perfect crime. That woman left something behind. We just have to find it.'

As I walk with the boys I find I enjoy the sensation of looking after them. To people around us we could be just any other family. What could be more natural than a

164

father taking his two boys for an educational visit to a museum? For the briefest of moments my mind drifts to Theresa and her unborn child. Is it mine? Could I be taking our child along these halls one day? As I look down at the boys I find that thought warms me.

Then I notice that Dan has a limp.

'Did you enjoy your cokes, boys?' I ask.

'Yeah,' says Pete looking up at me. 'Daddy doesn't let us have it.'

"Cos they're bad for our teeth,' Dan defends his father and sends a look of warning to his brother. Pete isn't caring. He's having way too much fun. He's pulling me forward while Dan is slowing me down. My feeling is that his pace is not just to do with his limp. He keeps looking over his shoulder as if expecting his mother to appear.

'Mum's just having a cup of tea, Dan. So I thought it would be nice to show you some more stuff upstairs.'

'Stuff. What kind of stuff?' He's too polite to be sullen, but he's skirting on the edge.

'I saw you and Pete playing with the straws. Do you like swords?'

'S'pose,' says Dan.

'Yeah,' sings Pete. 'I love swords.' Then he points his arm out and slashes an imaginary sword in the air.

'There's a room upstairs full of them. Wanna go and see it?'

'Yeah,' says Pete and walks faster.

'Okay,' says Dan allowing his brother's enthusiasm to touch him.

As soon as we enter the weapons room, both boys emit a "Wow" softened with wonder. With eyes as big as moons, they turn their heads together on a slow axis to take in all of the objects in the room. Then they are off, darting here and there, tugging at each other's sleeves as they pull the other to another object that has them bright with delight. I can't help but be caught up in their excitement and trip after them like a deranged minder, always just off the pace and a touch reticent. I feel I'm like the nice but dim cousin, twice removed on the father's side, who only gets involved in the family once a year and only then to do a spot of babysitting. The reticence comes from the fact that I am showing two boys who have been the victim of violence an exhibit that is a paean to the violence man has carried out on his neighbours over the centuries. Swords, spears, shields, armour, arrows all arranged like works of art. The strange beauty of the various objects belying their terrible intent. Some of the weapons weren't just made to kill. They were made to inflict terrifying wounds, to maim and cause mayhem. I tell myself to relax. The boys don't see the severed limbs, spilled intestines or piles of bodies. They see playtime on a grand scale.

'This is cool,' says Dan. He has now accepted me and several times over the last twenty minutes was quite happy to tug on my sleeve to attract me to another exhibit.

'Awesome,' says Pete with a huge smile.

The common sense part of my brain then insists we go and see something quieter. The boys grow quiet when I suggest we move on, but don't argue. We take the long way round and I give them both the chance to see over the sandstone banister down into the grand hall, where they can see a Spitfire suspended from the ceiling.

Walking back down towards the café I decide the time is right to speak to the boys.

'Do you guys know what I do?' I have one small hand in each of mine. They both turn their head up to look at me. Both expressions are blank.

'Mum said you were a policeman,' says Dan as the memory presents itself to him. Pete nods, thinks for a moment then asks, 'Have you shot anyone?'

'Good grief, no,' I answer. 'Most policemen don't have guns in this country. And I for one hope it stays that way.'

'Have you put anyone in jail, Ray?' asks Dan. This is the first time he has used my name and I can't help but feel touched by it.

'Lots of people. Lots of very bad people.'

166

Both boys are big-eyed and long-faced.

'Do you ever get scared?' Dan asks again. He looks at me and then his eyes slip to the side as his thoughts take him on a private journey.

'Of course I do. All the time. I meet some scary people in this job. But I also get to meet nice people like you guys.' I tighten my grip on each hand for emphasis. 'I also get to protect nice people like you from bad men.' And in this case, women.

'Dan's my big brother,' says Pete. 'He 'tects me from bad people.' Pete's small chest is puffed with pleasure that his big brother can be measured against an adult like me. His eyes move as he speaks. I follow the line of his sight. Children learn to lie at a very young age. But it can take years to control your body language so that it matches the words that come out of your mouth. As Pete spoke his eyes darted over to Dan's legs. The question occurs to me, does Dan's protection have something to with the injury to his leg?

'How did he protect you, Pete?' I ask and look from him to Dan. Dan is studying something in the distance. He looks content that we are talking about him, but is too modest to take part.

'When the lady...'

'Pete,' Dan turns on him, his voice a harsh whisper. 'It's a secret. She told us not to tell.'

Pete's head sinks into his shoulders, like a tortoise retreating from a threat.

'What did she say?' I ask Dan.

'She said she'd come back and really hurt us if we told on her,' says Pete.

'Shut up, Pete,' says Dan.

'Sorry.'

'Listen you guys,' I kneel down so that I am on the same eye level as them both. 'No one is going to hurt you. She told you those things so you wouldn't tell and then she wouldn't get punished for hurting you. But she's gone somewhere else now and she won't come back. Ever.'

167

'Can you punish her?' asks Dan. His eyes narrow and his lips tighten against remembered pain. His left arm hangs by his side, his hand reaching down his leg. Subconsciously, he pulls at his left arm with his right. As if at some level he's aware that he is about to betray himself.

'Yes. I'll make sure she never hurts a little boy again.'

'Will you make her cry?' asks Pete.

I ruffle his hair and consider a response that meets with the truth and a child's sensibilities. 'Oh, she'll cry alright. And she won't stop for about ten years.'

Pete nods as if that is good enough for him and looks at Dan to judge his state of mind. 'Dan. Tell him.'

'But how do we know she won't come back?'

'Do you think your parents would let her in the door of your house? Your dad would be straight on the phone to the police.'

'She said Dad was her special friend and that he would be on her side,' says Pete.

'What else did she say, Pete?' I ask.

'She said she would break my arm if I didn't punch Dan in the willie.'

'Pete,' Dan warns and moves towards his brother. 'We promised. It's a secret.'

'What happened?'

'Nothing,' Pete says in a small voice, steps back and looks at the floor.

I turn to his brother. 'Dan, you've got to believe me, mate. This woman is out of your lives for good. She has hurt you guys for the last time. I promise you that.'

I don't know if it was my tone, or the use of the word "promise" but something shifted in Dan's eyes.

'Listen, you were silent to protect your brother and yourself and it worked.' I can feel I have some sort of inroads. Now it's time to press home the advantage. 'A secret is a special thing. Something magic. Something powerful. Take the power away from this secret and tell me.' I look at him as an equal.

'Some secrets just don't deserve to be secrets, Dan.'

Chapter 25

'Angela, why don't you go to bed and have some sleep. You look done in,' said Jim. Angela shook her head and walked through to the spare bedroom. Several times through the evening Angela popped in to see how Moira was coping. The repetition of this event had as much to do with concern as it did with forgetfulness. Each time Jim would hear a soft mumble as the two women conversed. He ignored the impulse to shout at Angela to leave the poor woman alone. She would be feeling bad enough without someone else reminding her how awful the situation was every five minutes.

By the time the nine o'clock news was on Angela's movements were slow and deliberate, her speech slurred and her expression as slack as a drunk's.

'Honey,' Jim held her hand as she made another move in the direction of Moira. 'You look about dead on your feet. Get ready for bed and I'll see to Moira one last time before we turn in.'

Too tired to speak, she simply nodded and clutching her notebook to her chest as if it was a battery for her heart, she slouched towards the bottom of the stairs.

Moira's room, or rather, the room that until now Jim had slept in, was in darkness. From the light provided by the hallway he could see a mound under the quilt. It was facing the wall to his far left.

'Only me,' Jim whispered. 'Can I get you anything?'

No answer.

From the absolute stillness of the body under the quilt he guessed that Moira was still awake. If she didn't want to speak to him he wasn't going to persuade her otherwise.

By the time he arrived in Angela's bedroom she too was asleep. The depth of her breathing and the slow rise and fall of her chest were proof of that. Jim looked down at her in sleep and wondered at how young she looked when the worry about being alive was tethered to the land of daylight. Even her skin looked softer.

For a moment he wondered what to do. Should he just go and sleep on the couch? They hadn't really talked about the sleeping arrangements. He didn't want her to feel uncomfortable, nor did he want to allow Moira any insight as to what life was really like in their house.

Looking at Angela from the side of the bed he realised that he was wasting his time worrying: King Kong could have picked Angela up from her bed, carried her around the town for an hour and she wouldn't have noticed. Besides, he was getting too old for sleeping on couches.

He checked on Ben before he turned in. His son was lying on his back, the quilt pulled up to his nose. The only visible features were a pair of large, hazel eyes and a tuft of hair.

'Are you not asleep yet?' Jim asked, somewhat unnecessarily. 'You should be asleep at this time.'

'Is Mummy's friend upset?' he asked.

'She misses Erskine, son. He's staying with his daddy for a few days.'

'His daddy took him. I heard her say that.' Ben had obviously not missed much. He started to sob. 'You're not going to take me away, are you?'

'Of course not, baby. This is our home.' Jim leaned forward and pulled him in to his arms. Ben's hair was damp on his forehead. The wee soul must have been working himself up with worry for the last two hours since he put him in bed.

'Aw, son. Don't cry. Daddy's not taking you anywhere.' Jim pulled the quilt back and slid in beside him. 'Do you want me to sleep with you until you feel better?'

He could feel Ben's answering nod against his chest.

170

Very quickly Ben's breathing settled into a pattern that in turn soothed his father. He thought he would give it five minutes to make sure Ben was asleep and then he'd go through to the master bedroom.

Just five minutes... poor Moira, enjoying the connection and the warmth from Ben's back, Jim couldn't imagine the pain he would feel if someone were to take Ben from him. It must be the worst thing that could happen to a parent.

For the first time that day Jim felt good about himself. Despite the fact that he didn't like the woman, he had been human enough to offer her some support when she was at her lowest. You're not so bad after all, Jim Hilton. Another five minutes and then I'll go and join Angela. This was just so comfortable. Just five ...

Jim woke up with a start. From deep sleep to skin prickling alert in a second. He could sense the presence of someone else. He slowly lifted his head up to scan the room. He could make out the shape of a figure hunched in the far corner of the room.

'Moira?' Jim whispered as his eyes adjusted to the gloom.

Nothing.

Jim couldn't see her face as it was in the shadows, but something told him that her eyes were open.

'Moira,' he said louder and sat up. 'What's going on?'

'Just looking,' Moira said and leaned forward into the grey slice of moonlight coming in from the window. 'I should have that. I should be able to slip into bed with my child. I should ...'

'You should go back to your own room. You'll wake everyone up.'

'I just checked in to see if Ben was okay.' She sniffed back a tear. 'I was sure I heard Erskine crying ...' she paused and corrected her emotion. '...And then I remembered where I was. And that he wasn't here.' Another pause, another gathering of strength. 'So I thought I'd

171

check on Ben.' The faint light from the street lamps outside highlighted her brief smile. 'You both looked so happy and safe ... It was hypnotic. I couldn't tear myself away.'

She stood up and it appeared to Jim that something shifted in the process: a mask had slipped back into place.

Chapter 26

One of the frustrations I remember having as a boy was not being in control. All the adults around me held the power and I moved about on their orders. I watched both boys as my words took seed in their minds and flowered into realization. Dan and Pete could both see that this was their opportunity to take back a little bit of that power from the adults.

Dan looks up at me. Through the window of his eyes I can almost see words taking shape in his mind. He opens his mouth to speak and then closes it again. His chin scrunches up. His mouth taking on the shape of an upturned U. His bottom lip trembling.

'I'm scared,' he says. Before I know it he is in my arms, his small shoulders shaking with the force of his emotion. Pete is soon overcome and joins in. Both boys are in my arms and part of my brain asks if I don't need clearance from Disclosure Scotland before giving other people's children a hug?

At first I feel reluctant. I am male and alone with a stranger's children and I have my arms around them. Cue an angry mob and accusations of paedophilia.

Bollocks to that. These little boys need consoling and I am the only one here able to do it. Dan's head is buried in my shoulder. Pete's eyes are awash with tears, but he doesn't stop watching his brother. With one hand he is rubbing his big brother's shoulder and saying his name over and over again.

'Hey guys,' I say. 'You're perfectly safe. I'm the Police. No one is going to hurt you ever again.' There I am thinking Dan is about to open up and then his fear of the Bogeywoman takes over. Anger tightens my jaw. That

173

bitch has done a good job on these boys and it's going to take more than a wee pep talk from me to break down their reserves.

Time for a shift in focus.

'Dan, Pete, I'm sorry I made you guys cry. It's all my fault. But if your mother sees you both like this she is going to break into that weapons room back there, steal a huge sword from the display and whack me with it. Then she's going to stamp all over my dead body.' I jump up and down on an imaginary corpse for good measure.

Both boys laugh. Dan's giggle has a little hangover of a tear in it, but Pete is completely sold into laughter, his little body shaking as his brother's had done only moments ago, except this time it's with mirth.

There is one last trick up my sleeve to complete the boys' transformation from tears to happiness. Desperate times call for the promise of more sugar.

'Who fancies an ice cream?'

The boys sing "Yay," in agreement. They both jump up and down. Call me irresponsible, but, hey, it works.

Before long, both boys have their bellies full of confectionery and their faces washed and I present them to their mother as if we have just had the most wonderful time. Which we did, apart from the five minutes of abject terror and tears.

I observe her in an unguarded moment as I walk across the café, before both boys shout "Mum" and run into her arms. The features of her face sag with fatigue and her shoulders are slumped against the need to ignore the requirement for rest and a darkened room. When she sees the boys running towards her, she sits up and her face transforms with borrowed energy. I don't know much about her condition, but her fortitude impresses me and more than ever I want to help.

'Wow, you guys look like you had a great time,' she kisses them both on the cheek and looks over their heads at me. Her eyes are asking the question. Did I get anywhere? I shake my head. She wilts with disappointment and then rallies again. 'Tell me what you saw,' she says to the boys.

The boys try to outdo each other with descriptions of the weapons they just looked at. They both run out of arm's length as they try to describe the scale of the swords. While words jostle and leap from their mouths, mum looks on with a rapt expression, as if there was no other place on the planet she would rather be.

'I wish I had my camera with me. You guys look so excited,' Liz says and touches both boys lightly on the chest. For the briefest of moments she holds a hand over each boy's heart. They glow with the warmth of their mother's obvious affection.

I'm feeling like a spare part and decide it is time I left. Then I remember the digital camera Alessandra and I used to take photographs of the various Lucys who worked at the Southern General. It must still be in the glove box of my car.

'Liz,' I say. 'There's something in my car I'd like you to have a look at.'

'OK,' she replies with a question in her expression.

'Anybody want to come for a walk to my car with me?' I ask the boys. Dan looks at me while moving even closer to his mother. He has had more than enough excitement for the day, thank you very much.

'Me,' Pete sticks his left hand up as if in school.

'It's a camera,' I say to Liz. 'It has photos you might be interested in.'

Pete and I walk out of the café and out towards the car park. He takes my hand automatically and all the way keeps up a stream of chatter. He talks about the animals he's seen and the weapons on display. He refers to Dan constantly. Every boy should have a hero and it seems especially worthy that it should be his brother.

'He's a good brother to you, isn't he?' I say.

Pete nods. He's my big brother, why shouldn't he be a good one, the nod tells me.

'I'm sorry I made you guys cry. I just want to know more about this woman before she hurts other kids.'

'She's mean,' says Pete. 'Horrible.' His delicate features are scrunched up with the memory. 'She should be ...' he stamps his feet as he walks, not quite sure what punishment she deserves. 'She should be hurt.'

'Believe me, one day she will be, wee man. But first we have to find her.' I aim a smile at him. 'Did she ever take you guys out anywhere? Did she ever do anything nice with you?' I am wondering how she managed to make both boys keep their mouths shut for so long. The threat of violence could only do so much. Unless that threat didn't materialize until she had first won their trust.

We've reached the car and we stop walking. I reach into my pocket for the car keys.

'Dunno,' Pete says. 'The park round the corner.' He shrugs. 'Watched cartoons. She told scary stories.'

'Do you remember any of the stories?' I ask. I wonder if the stories were one of the ways she kept the boys in line.

'Some bad boys did some bad things and got punished. There was one about pirates and goblins.' He shivers dramatically, playing to his audience of one.

'Yeah?'

He launches into a story, his eyes big with excitement. The stories become safe in the re-telling, here in this most public of places, and to me a policeman. In the telling of them, Pete becomes something more and be less affected by them. And as he does so I could see the fear fade away.

He is talking about a castle, some caves below it and a secret cottage with one hundred and forty one steps down to the shore. He struggles with the name of the path. Calls it the snuggels path. I take in the all of the images he has used and translate.

'The Smuggler's Path?' I ask. He looks at me as if to ask, is that not what I just said? While he continues talking I reach into the glove box and remove the camera.

'Pete,' I crouch down to his height. 'Did the woman hurt Dan's leg?'

He bites his bottom lip and gives an almost imperceptible nod of his head. 'She said to say he fell down the stairs.'

'But she did it?'

Another nod.

'You don't have to tell me if you don't want to.'

'She wanted Dan to push me down the stairs. Said it would be funny.'

I pull a memory of their house into my mind. The stairs were wide and carpeted, but steep. The soft bones of a child would easily fracture in that fall.

'But he wouldn't do it?'

Oh, Dan. I realize my teeth are clenched in anger.

'So what did she do to his leg?'

'She said a bad word. Lots of bad words.'

'You don't use those bad words, do you?'

His face is a portrait of saintliness as he moves his head from side to side.

'What about his leg?'

'Kicked it,' says Pete. His face screws tight with defiance. He is going to tell the truth and he doesn't care if Dan is annoyed with him.

'Can you show me where?'

Pete points at my knee and then sucks in his top lip as if this was an inadequate description. Then he stands by my side and makes a motion with his arm towards my leg. Next he places his hand on the side of my knee. I can feel the heat of his anger transfer from the skin of his hand through the fabric of my trousers.

'She kicked him there. Really hard.' He puts a hand to his mouth and talks behind it. 'And she pushed him down the stairs.'

I tried to imagine the event. Dan trying to protect his brother. Hepburn screaming at him, cursing him, telling him all kinds of horrible things trying to provoke a reaction. Only Dan refused. Pete was his brother. Most kids,

177

some adults for that matter would have bowed under such pressure. What made Dan different? Did his mother's condition force a level of maturity on to those slim shoulders?

Then Hepburn would have to come good with the threat or the screaming and shouting was all for nothing. I considered the blow she gave the boy. Was it the product of deliberation or an impromptu strike? Whatever it was it was one that would cause maximum damage. A blow to the side of the knee like that could possibly cause ligament, muscle and bone damage. What's certain is that it would cause a lot of hurt and would take a long time to heal in a child, if ever. For her it would mean minimum effort, maximum pain.

Except on that occasion her plan didn't work. No long-term damage. So she throws him down the stairs.

I ruffle Pete's head. 'You have one brave brother there, wee man.'

His smile wipes away the look of worry on his face.

'You did the right thing, Pete. We need to know what this woman is capable of. She's very clever and we are only going to catch her with the help of brave little soldiers like you and Dan.'

I realize that this last sentence might sound a little patronizing, so I squeeze his shoulder with my right hand. An act that may be viewed as equally patronizing. Jeez, talking to kids is difficult.

'Let's go back to your mum.'

Back in the café I hand the camera to Liz.

'Do you recognize any of these women?' I ask her, once she has received a hug from Pete. She eyes me over his head and takes the camera from my hand.

'Scroll through the images and tell me if anyone jumps out at you.'

She shakes her head slowly as she does so. 'Should I know them? Who are these women?'

'We don't have any pictures of Hepburn. On a hunch I

got some women photographed.'

'Judging from their clothing these women work in one of the local hospitals?'

I nod.

She continues to shake her head as she scrolls through the photographs. 'Sorry, Ray. None of these women are her.' She hands the camera back to me. 'Sorry.'

'It was the Southern General she worked, wasn't it?' I ask.

'That's what she said.'

'It's what someone else told us as well.'

'Ooh?' She sits forward. 'Do you have a witness? Is there another family you know of?'

'It was Mrs Hogg. The woman who introduced her to you.'

'Oh, her,' she sat back and pulled her lips into thin threads. 'Remind me to thank her next time I see her.' She sighs. 'Hepburn could be anywhere. She could have worked in any one of the city hospitals. Why on earth would she tell the truth about that?'

'Can we go home now, Mum,' says Dan. 'I'm bored.'

'Me too,' Pete borrows a pout from his brother.

'In a minute, boys,' Liz answers. 'What did you make of Mrs Hogg? Do you think she knows more than she is letting on?'

I shrug. 'How well do you know her?'

'Don't worry about offending me if that's why you ask,' she smiles. 'As well as being a patient of mine I used to come across her at charity events. I always found her to be ...how do I put this without sounding like a bitch?' She scratches the side of her face. 'Nice but touched.'

I nod. 'Sounds about right.'

'Do you know any of her friends? Are there any other people who might know more about her?'

'Possibly,' she screws her mouth to the side as she thinks. 'Patricia Conroy. She's with the local MS fund-raising committee. She's had more dealings with our Mrs Hogg than I have.'

Chapter 27

'Couldn't you sleep?' Moira's voice coming up from behind him set Jim's skin prickling with fright. After waking up to see Moira looking over him and Ben, he was standing out in the back garden looking up at the dark swathe of sky.

'Sorry, did I give you a fright?' She asked. She was wearing one of his jackets over her nightclothes and her arms were crossed over her breasts against the autumn chill. Her fingers were barely visible at the end of the length of sleeve as she swept a strand of hair from her eyes.

Jim shivered as if Moira wearing a jacket had just reminded him of the chill. He was still wearing the shirt he had on to work that day. The only concession he had made to coming home was to open the top three buttons.

She was standing too close to him, so Jim took a step away and returned his view to the sky.

'You should be sleeping,' he said.

'I lost my son today,' she replied. 'Sleep isn't on the agenda.' Her gaze followed his and in silence they both looked up at the blue-black of the sky.

A cat wailed in the distance. Or could it have been a child? Moira shivered and stepped closer to Jim. Thinking it would be rude to move too soon, Jim took a count of twenty and then increased the space between them.

She coughed. 'Thank you.' Her voice was weak, sounded like it travelled between the earth and the clouds before reaching his ears.

'It's nothing,' Jim shrugged, suddenly feeling bone weary.

'It's a good deal more than nothing,' Moira looked up into his eyes. From the way she then set her gaze to her feet Jim was able to see how much this was costing her. She cleared emotion from her throat with a cough. 'A woman you barely know is having a horrible time and without a quibble you offer her your home.'

'Yeah,' he managed a smile. 'Didn't know I had it in me.'

'You really are a lovely man, Jim Hilton.'

'I have my moments,' he said and looked at her as if for the first time. The curve of her eyes, the line of her nose, the swell of her lips. Then he considered who she was. The sudden shift in her mood when he found her staring at him and Ben. What did they really know about this woman they had let into their lives?

'Tell me about Angela,' she said. 'I only knew her for a brief time before the accident. Barely got to know her, other than as a mother.'

There was something about the way she asked the question, something about the night air and the quality of the silvery light that made Jim cast aside that part of his masculinity that demanded he suffer in silence and want to talk. He was just as important as Angela, wasn't he? Didn't he need an understanding ear?

'She was a clever woman. Full of ideas and energy. She loved her job. Loved helping people,' Jim spoke up to the stars.

'You really love her, don't you?'

Jim nodded. 'It is so difficult to see the woman that she has become. He made a grimace at Moira. 'Sorry. It must be the moonlight, making me go all ... '

She stepped forward and put a hand on his bare skin, where neck stretched into chest. Just below the curve and junction of his clavicle, just above his heart.

'If I can do anything... *Anything*. Let me know.'

Chapter 28

When I am back at the flat I change into my running gear. In the car on the way home I promised myself that I would make better choices. To start with immediate effect.

I run up the Saltmarket and then up the hill to the Cathedral and the Necropolis. When I get there I am panting like a labrador who's been left inside a car on a hot day. My legs feel like they belong to someone else. A ninety-year-old someone else. Just six months ago I could have kept running all the way up to the John Knox memorial without a problem. Today it might as well be Everest. So I turn and make my way back home.

There's something on the floor behind the door when I arrive back at the flat. I bend down to pick it up. It's a book. It has a blue cover with some red writing on the cover. It's called *Happiness*. I turn it over and read the blurb on the back. The author is a Buddhist monk and his schtick is that happiness is a skill that we can learn.

Only one person would have thought to leave this: Maggie. She must have arrived when I was out for my run. With my heart beating a little harder I move through to the front room and look out the window to the left and the right. No sign of her.

Did she wait for me to leave before posting it through the letter box? I throw the book on the sofa. I'll get round to reading it sometime.

A quick shower, shave and a change of clothes and I'm ready for action. The book and Maggie posted to the back of my mind. I have a sick woman to find. Something tells me that our Mrs Hogg knows more than she's telling me, but before I pay her another visit I'll speak to her friend Patricia Conroy.

Mrs Conroy lives in a modest mid-terraced ex-local authority house in the west of the city. Her small front garden consists of a square patch of grass bordered by rows of blue and white flowers.

A trellis is placed to the right of her front door and wears an explosion of large purple flowers.

The door opens before I can reach it and a tall, severely thin woman smiles as she invites me into her home. She appears to be in her mid-fifties, has a short blond bob and is wearing a bright red dress, covered in yellow flowers. She is all cheekbones and chin. The line of her hipbones can be seen under the sheer material of her dress.

'Okay, officer,' her face is large with a tight smile. 'What can I do for you?' She is sitting facing me, back as straight as an army sergeant's, legs crossed and curiosity bright in her expression.

I explain that I am in the middle of an ongoing enquiry about which I can't give her too many details, but any information she could give me would be very helpful.

'I believe you are friendly with Mrs Hogg?' I say.

'I know Mrs Hogg. Friendly is not the word to describe our relationship.' She flashes her teeth at me.

'What would be a more adequate word?' I ask, matching her smile.

'Not sure.' She twists her face to the side. One eyebrow moves up. 'Colleagues? I've known Violet for a few years. We have ...' she pauses '...causes in common. Violet is not one to make friends.'

'Oh?'

'Right. Okay. Coffee,' she says and stands up so abruptly it takes me by surprise. 'Let me put the kettle on.' She wags a finger at me. 'I need coffee. And something tells me this is going to be more than a one cup conversation.'

Mrs Conroy returns carrying a tray. 'Would you mind sitting at the table? I prefer to stand and it feels odd if you are sitting low on the sofa. The dining room chair is not as bad.'

I move over to the dining table.

'Also do you mind if I dispense with the DI thing and just call you McBain?' she smiles and holds out a mug of coffee to me. 'Help yourself to milk and sugar.'

'Not at all,' I say as I take the mug and consider the abbreviation of my name and title. This might have felt rude with someone else, but it seems to match her staccato delivery and speed of movement.

'I'll sit for a minute,' she sits. 'But don't be alarmed if I stand up. Car crash. Back injury. The pain is bloody awful if I stay in the one place too long.'

I realize that murmurs of empathy won't interest this woman so I go straight back to the reason I am here.

'I believe you and Mrs Hogg both help raise money for MS?'

'My husband suffered from it. Not sure why she got involved, but yes, that's how we know each other.'

'Did you ever get to meet her friend, a Miss Hepburn?'

'Something always struck me as odd about that relationship. And if her name is Audrey Hepburn then I'm Grace Kelly.' She takes another long drink.

'What makes you say that?'

'Everything about that girl is false. Never trust anyone with a famous namesake, McBain. Apart from me. Or yourself even,' she laughs. A sharp note in the air. I realize, not only does she bullet point her speech, she does the same with her laughter. Maybe it hurts her to laugh on a more prolonged basis. 'Let me tell you about Violet Hogg. Okay, she does this woe is me widow thing to perfection, but she's as sharp as a blade. Whatever that girl is up to, Violet Hogg is aware of it.'

'My husband had a particularly aggressive form of MS. His decline was rapid. The day after his funeral Violet Hogg came to see me. She sat in that chair where you are sitting now and with the expression of a kindly aunt she told me that she had also been through the death of a husband while she was still young. She then told me that I was in for a long and lonely life. Best get

184

used to it.'

'Lovely lady,' I say.

'Describes the woman to a T,' she says and stands up.

'Why did you say there was something odd about her relationship with Hepburn?'

'Just that Violet Hogg doesn't tend to make friends. Everyone is kept at arm's length while she acts at caring. And here there was this young woman regularly in her company. Odd.'

'What we know of this young woman is that she is extremely manipulative. Could she be pulling the wool over Mrs Hogg's eyes?'

'Anything is possible, McBain. Violet may have been taken in partly. But not all the way. She would have been aware something didn't quite add up.'

'What did you get to learn about Hepburn?' I ask and my eyes are momentarily drawn out of the back window. The house has a long and narrow back garden, bordered by a dark brown ranch-style fence. The grass is trim and appears to be weed-free as do the borders that are planted with a variety of small trees, shrubs and flowers. The sky is cloudless and the sun shines hard on the garden, glinting off the metal table and chairs on the patio down the far end.

'Only that she worked at the Southern General. Not sure in what capacity. She made me feel uncomfortable so I didn't spend much time in her company.'

'Uncomfortable? In what way?'

'The way she looked at me.' She sits back down again, reaches out for the cafetiere and tops up her mug. She then takes a long drink. Her eyes cloud over and then brighten again. 'As if she was ...I dunno ...measuring me for a coffin.' She grimaces at the dramatic impact of her words. 'I'm sure the poor woman has some redeeming characteristics.'

'Did you ever get drawn into a conversation with her?'

'Once or twice.'

'Anything of interest?'

'My recollection is that we talked about the disease. Or rather, I talked and she asked questions.' She looked at the ceiling above my head briefly. 'I remember thinking it wasn't unusual for people to want to know more about the disease, but her whole demeanour was …it was like she was less looking for information and more trying to …I dunno …it was all about what an MS patient might not be able to do. People usually come to us to work out what they can do. Goodness me.' She laughs. 'The police come to visit and you come over all drama queen, Patricia.' She made a face of apology. Then her eyes probe mine, looking to see if I understand.

I understand perfectly. Hepburn would have been working with the Brownings at the time. A predator can save itself much energy if it understands the weakness of its prey.

Chapter 29

'Coffee?' asked Jim. He turned and half-faced the back door, his mind full of questions. What was that?

Anything.

Was it a genuine offer of help? A come-on? He could still feel the heat from Moira's hand on his chest.

'Hot milk,' said Moira. 'We both need some sleep.' She walked ahead of him into the house. His steps were slow and measured. Deliberately so. He needed time to think. He preferred the distant Moira, the one who appeared to have a thing about his wife. The hot milk and sympathy Moira was much more difficult to deal with. That meant being alert. Jim wasn't doing *alert* much these days.

When he stepped into the kitchen, Moira had a pot of milk warming above a gas ring. He sat down. No one spoke until the milk was served. Jim sipped. Moira must have added some sugar. Nice. His mother used to do this for him when he was a boy on the rare occasion he was out late. He picked up a teaspoon and skimmed a layer of skin from the top of his milk like a welcome memory; he examined it and draped it over the side of his mug.

'I owe you ... you both, an explanation,' said Moira. Her expression was grim and full of self-loathing.

'You don't need ...'

Moira ignored him and began to speak. The words were delivered in a monotone as if the act of speaking itself was taking up the last reserves of her energy. She took a deep breath, held on to it as if coming to a decision and then let it out in a long, slow exhalation. 'The thing is, Jim ...I haven't been completely honest with you and Angela ...' she paused and stared into a fixed point in the distance. 'And you guys have been so good to me. I feel so bad about it.

'Erskine's father and I had a bit of a falling out. When Erskine was just a baby.' Her hands were balled into fists on her lap. 'I had a great pregnancy. A wonderful birth. He was all I could have wished for, you know? The right numbers of limbs and digits.' She sniffed. 'But I was tired, know what I mean? I was in labour for about twelve hours. I actually cried when the doctors handed him to me. This little screwed up face, pissed off at the world for pulling him out of his cocoon. How much energy he could use just to scream! He never stopped.'

Where was this going, Jim wondered? What kind of falling out had she had? If it was true why was she not marching straight to the police station?

'The thing is, you guys have been so nice, so helpful.' She looked over at him, 'And you ... you must have had your suspicions about me. You'd never met me before and suddenly I was all over your wife and son, sticking my big oar in,' her smile of apology shamed Jim.

'Not at all,' he argued. 'I ...' She had voiced his concerns and hearing them aired so frankly made him feel unsure of himself.

'It's okay, Jim, really. I would have been the same. I just feel so bad about misleading you both. You'll think I'm some sort of nutter.'

'Not at all,' he repeated, and the words sounded forced even to his ears.

'Anyway ... when they put the little bundle of energy in my arms, I cried. And I didn't stop for about six months.

'Post natal depression is a terrible thing. It was like looking into the world from the end of a black hole. And poor Erskine. No matter how much I tried I felt nothing for him. How can I even say that?' She sobbed. 'I was a mother who felt nothing for her son.' She steeled herself to continue her story. 'When Erskine was six months old I was hospitalized. Six months of therapy later I was released back into the big, bad world,' she took a deep breath, 'only to find that my husband and son had disappeared.'

'Oh my god. How terrible.' Jim commiserated. Was this the truth? What did he really know about this woman? There was something in the cast of her eyes; the way one finger rubbed at a non-existent stain on the tabletop.

Surely she couldn't be lying about this. Jim had really worked at lying over the last few weeks and months. He well knew the effort it took.

Would she tell such a lie?

His mind was a jumble of thoughts. His body ached with fatigue.

Surely she was telling the truth. It was bad enough to be so ill, but to work at getting better for months, only to get such a kicking. Poor woman.

The question thrust itself out through his mouth before he could consider it.

'But how...Erskine... How did you...did you win him back?'

She turned away from him to look out of the window. Silence was ticked off in the room by the clicking and quiet groaning from the fridge.

'Please don't think badly of me when I tell you this...' Moira edged into the silence, her voice becoming louder with each word. '...I didn't win him back. I *took* him back.'

'Oh.'

'I found where he and his father were staying. I didn't intend stealing him at first. I just wanted to see my son, you know?'

Who wouldn't? Jim thought. A thought that of course led on to the question, what would he do in the same situation? Anger and an equal measure of fear surged through him at the thought of someone taking Ben.

She can't possibly be lying, he thought. There was just too much happening here.

'Listen, Moira, I'm not going to sit here in judgement of you. You were being denied a fundamental right you have as a parent. And you did something about it.' Jim moved his focus from his mug to her and saw that she was pleased with his words.

189

'So, you went along to have a look at your son?'

'Yes. It was all a bit cloak and dagger at first,' she grimaced at the memory, 'hiding behind bushes and all that stuff. Anyway, I quickly found out that Bob was taking Erskine to a nursery. A nice place. It had a wee garden in the front with swings and stuff. I used to park my car just around the corner, where I could get a reasonable view and where I wouldn't rouse any suspicions. I'd sit there for hours waiting for just a glimpse of him.' She sniffed and wiped away a tear prompted by the memory with the back of her hand.

'Could you do me a wee favour,' she asked. 'I don't want Angela to know any of this.'

'Why not?'

'She has enough on her plate.'

'We're husband and wife, Moira. You're staying with us. She's going to want to know what's going on.'

'I hear what you're saying, Jim, but please, don't tell her anything. I couldn't bear it if it made her think badly of me.'

'Why do you think she would take it like that? Even the most level-headed person would have done the same thing.'

'Please, Jim. I'm begging you. I don't want Angela to know.' The force of her expression surprised him.

'Well ...if that's the way you want it ...'

'I drove over to the nursery to watch Erskine for days and days. Can you imagine how desperate I was to hold him? I would spend hours in that car imagining what it would be like to just walk up to him, see him smile in welcome and hold out his arms for me to pick him up. But I couldn't. I wasn't worried about what Bob and his lawyers might do. It was Erskine that worried me. He wouldn't know me. He'd never known me. What if he saw this strange woman walking towards him and started screaming?' Tears rose fresh along her lower eyelid. 'My son didn't know me, Jim. We'd never met.'

Jim felt himself respond to her pain. No one was this

good at lying. He reached out and placed a hand on hers. He was simply another parent sharing her pain.

'So, one day ...it was a beautiful summer's day, all of the kids were in the garden with about one member of staff to three children. Ben... sorry Erskine ...' she smiled an apology for her lapse, '...was crying. I don't know why. Probably something silly. Before I knew it I was out of the car and striding across the road towards the garden. Then came a terrible commotion from inside of the house. All the staff ran indoors and started carrying out more children. Each one carrying one or more screaming kids. I heard someone say a fire had started somewhere inside. Anyway, and I'm not proud of this, Jim, I leaned over the fence and picked Erskine up. And he did start to cry. But what was one more screaming child in that melée. I stood there holding him, trying to keep him calm in the face of all the noise. I was just one more woman holding a crying child, no-one noticed, so I turned and made for the car.' She paused. 'It was easy. Frighteningly easy.'

They sat quietly as Moira waited for some sort of reaction from Jim.

'So how long did you have Erskine before his dad snatched him back?'

'Two years.'

Two years is a long time in a child's life. A long time without his father.

'Wasn't there a way for you guys to work this out?' Jim asked. 'Couldn't you find a way to share him?'

'I asked myself that very thing a thousand times. The loser in all of this is ultimately Erskine. She looked into the distance, rubbed at her face and turned to him. 'I've been there, Jim. I've asked all of those questions, but Bob just wasn't listening. He wanted Erskine all to himself and me as far away as possible. Preferably behind bars.' Her eyes searched Jim's, looking for understanding. 'So now you know why I haven't gone to the police.'

'Surely there's something you can do? Some kind of help you can get from the legal system?'

191

Moira didn't respond. She simply stared at her mug of milk.

Jim thought of Angela. She should know this, but could she take it in? This was all quite a story and Moira was probably right, there was no way of knowing how Angela would react. This would certainly be a case of too much information.

'Look, I won't say anything to Angela, but if it ever looks like this information is going to compromise my relationship with her then I'll have to.'

'Thank you, Jim.'

'And don't worry about where you're going to stay. You can stay with us for as long you it takes to get yourself back on your feet.'

'Thank you, Jim. I appreciate it. Really.' Her bottom lip quivered and it looked like fresh tears were about to fall.

'Hey, that's enough,' he squeezed her hand. 'No more crying. We'll get you sorted.'

After Moira had gone to bed, Jim found that he was still unable to sleep. So he made himself a coffee and moved through to the sitting room, where he turned on the TV.

An Arab man was stumbling across the screen, carrying a body while a newsreader explained the scene of destruction behind him. Another suicide bomber had struck. The death toll was not yet clear. What was clear was the man's anguish.

His eyes were staring ahead, his mouth shaped in a silent, endless scream, his face streaked with blood, sweat, soot and tears. Jim crossed his arms, trying to heat himself against the depth and chill of the man's despair. The body in his arms was covered with a blanket; age and gender both indeterminate, but Jim could see that the body was long and slight. The body he is carrying must be his child, thought Jim. Only the death of a child could draw that amount of anguish on to the screen of your face.

Chapter 30

Back in the car, I roll down the windows to let out the heat and let in some cooler air. I switch on my mobile phone. Force of habit. I don't expect anyone to be looking for me. Oh, lucky me. I have voicemail. I connect and the voice of Elaine Gibson fills my ear.

'DI McBain, this is Elaine Gibson. Wondered if we could meet up soon? You missed our last session and I wondered if this Friday at ten suited. Give my office a call will you? Thanks.'

I look at the clock on the dashboard. Six forty-five. She will have gone home for the day. Just as well really. Attractive females turn my brain to mush these days. Five minutes in her company and I'll be down on one knee and promising her my pension.

At home I fix myself a salad of lettuce leaves, avocado and smoked salmon. I grate some fresh ginger over it and squeeze out half of a lime. It tastes lovely. And it's healthy. Yay me.

There's nothing on the TV. Over one hundred channels of nothing worth watching. How does that happen? I switch it off and move over to my stereo. I bought myself one classical music CD over ten years ago in an attempt at education. It's been on the player twice, maximum. Let's give it another go.

The sound of violins swirl in the air around me. Very nice. It occurs to me that I have been very urbane today. First a visit at the museum, then I admire flowers and now I have Mozart for company. Maybe I should put my hands down my trousers, give my balls a good scratch and reassert the caveman in me.

The big purple flowers, Mrs Conroy had told me after

193

we had finished speaking about Hepburn, were clematis.

'The hybrid is called Comtesse du Bouchard, I believe.' She raised her eyebrows. 'I must have been feeling grandiose the day I bought them.' Then she bunched her features into the middle of her face. 'I'm now going to worry about what I said about Violet Hogg for the rest of the evening.'

'You were a great help, Mrs Conroy. There's no need to feel guilty about telling the truth.'

'The truth can sometimes be over-rated, McBain.' She took a long, deep breath. Her eyes dimmed with pain. 'She does a lot of good, McBain. It's her motivation I question. I do what I can because I want to help. But with her it's like she's keeping some sort of moral scorecard. She's going to hand it to Saint Peter at the gates and say — see, I raised thousands for MS that day, let a lost young girl sleep over at my house that day, made postcards for ....'

'Can we rewind a little bit? A girl slept over at her house? Was that Hepburn?'

'Yes. I can remember thinking, how odd. She always struck me as wishing to be one step removed from her good deeds.'

'Do you think anything untoward might have happened?'

'Not that I'm aware of. Apparently Audrey had rent problems. Violet has a spare room,' she shrugged as if to say it made perfect sense to somebody.

'How long?'

'Not entirely sure. A couple of months or so, I think.' She studied my expression. 'You don't think there would have been more? Some romance between them?'

'She said it herself, she's had a long and lonely life. Who's to blame her if she takes a little comfort here and there?'

'You men,' she laughed. 'See sex everywhere.' Another laugh. 'If Violet Hogg is ...more than familiar with this young woman good luck to her, but I'd happily eat everything on this trellis, petal by petal if that were true.'

So, we men see sex everywhere? I look down at my lap. There ain't nothing goin' on down there. Thinking about the nuns at Bethlehem House and their mantra "The Devil makes work for idle hands" I decide to go for a walk.

The feeling that Leonard is around refuses to leave me, no matter how much logic I try to apply. However, I'm fucked if I'm letting him keep me indoors.

The early summer sunshine beats down on me. It's still warm even at this time of night. Love it. Mediterranean weather in Glasgow. A marriage made in my own personal heaven. I look at the walls of the buildings around me. At one time Glasgow was the British Empire's second city and when you're not dodging the raindrops it's easy to see why.

Soon, I find myself in Argyll Street among Glasgow's newest claim to fame, her shops. I now live, as is argued by some, in Britain's second best shopping destination. At its peak Napoleon derided the British as nothing but merchants. Now we're content to hand over the work of the merchant to a giant corporation and become a bunch of shoppers.

'Hello rerr, officer.' A voice interrupts my mental diarrhoea. A bald man in his mid to late fifties scowls at me from a doorway. He's standing behind a newspaper stand. There are very few people around me or there is no way he would have given me that title.

'Daniel James Donovan. How the hell are you?' I reply and then walk over to his stand. When I arrest someone and write their names on countless reports, I often find it difficult to use anything other than their full title when I speak to them.

'Any better, officer and I would be twins.' He grins. If teeth were houses his would have been torn down a long time ago. The acne-scarred skin, bulbous red nose and a belly pregnant with the passing of decades of beer make up the rest of the assault on the eyes that is Dan Donovan.

'What are you selling today then?' I ask. To the passer-by this might seem a ridiculous question when the only thing in front of him is a large pile of newspapers with the title

195

Evening Times. However, our Dan has another string to his bow.

'Just the paper these days, son,' he says and then nods as if this adds weight to his statement.

I pick one up. The lead story is about a shooting in the east of the city. Two men walk up to a car and shoot the single occupant in the head. The police are appealing for witnesses. The reporter speculates that the killing has something to do with the gangster's dead son.

'How much?' I ask. He names a price and I hand him a twenty pound note. He hands me a paper and pockets the note.

'What do you think?' I fold the newspaper so that I can easily hold it in the grip of one hand and point it at his chest. We haven't done this for a number of years so I wonder if Dan is getting rusty. I feel the loss in my pocket where the change from my twenty should be resting around now. The man in front of me had a career in crime that stalled at the edges of the underworld for a number of years. Petty theft, petty violence, and reset gave him a number of stays at Her Majesty's leisure. Then he discovered the power of information. Perhaps I should introduce him to Kenny. Strike that. They undoubtedly know each other.

'Pile of pish,' he says and stabs the headline in front of him with a thick digit. 'Gang war my arse.'

He turns the top newspaper over on to its face and aims a look at the sports pages. Which as usual is talking about Celtic and Rangers. 'That new player. The Italian fella. He's at it. Thinks he's got them all tricked.' He is speaking louder now. He taps the side of his nose with a finger three times. I expect if he did it once more it would burst like an over-ripe strawberry. 'Young man's got them Tally good looks the women go for. Mair fool them, he should be playing for the other side.'

He closes his mouth. I know that look. It means he will need me to buy another newspaper and the price has rocketed.

'Not my game,' I answer. 'All that Old Firm stuff leaves me cold.' I raise an eyebrow and turn to walk away.

'Come back and get your news anytime, young man. I'm sure we'll have other stories to tempt ye.'

I retrace my steps back to the flat and try to unpick the information I've just been given. Dan is in a highly visible situation and to pass on his knowledge without raising the suspicion of fellow criminals is key — if he wants to carry on breathing unaided that is. He has therefore developed shorthand. Once you get on his wavelength it's fairly easy. The title of Brain of Britain won't be going his way any day soon. But what Dan has got is street smarts and loads of it.

The football was clearly a distraction. Celtic and Rangers are such a part of everyday life in this city that to talk about them is almost like verbal wallpaper to any passer-by. We started talking about gang warfare. He dismissed it. Then the Italian having tricked people. The young man would have attracted female attention. Past tense. Would have. He's talking about the dead son. Why would the women be fools?

Oh. Right. It all suddenly makes sense. Playing for the other side. The son was gay. So the "Italian" would be code for the gangster. The father of the dead man, a certain Mr Kay. Who has he tricked? Is that to do with the gang stuff? What would be in it for him? Crimes are committed for three reasons; money, sex and power. Make that one thing. With the power comes money and sex.

The sex here is of a different flavour. One that the old man wouldn't be comfortable with. He's the old school. To him a gay man would be lower than a pickpocket.

The money involved will be colossal. He could be fighting for control of the city under the guise of revenge.

I wonder whether I should give Daryl and Alessandra a call and pass this info on.

So what, I can hear them say. The dead son is gay. The father is using his death as an excuse to start a war to gain more power in the city. Doesn't help them bring the case to a close, does it?

Back at the flat, I open up a tin of tomatoes; add some breast of chicken and some herbs and garlic. Boil up some pasta and we have a cheap and delicious meal.

There's nothing on TV. I flick through the channels. Nothing. If I liked watching so-called celebrities I could gorge on that. They're doing everything from pretending to fall in love, to driving cars, to eating kangaroo testicles. Some people must be really keen to stay in the public eye. I can't remember TV ever being this bad. Did someone turn up while I was busy catching criminals and decide that the populace didn't have a brain cell between them?

At ten-thirty, feeling bloated on desperation, but having been entertained by it in some way for the last few hours, I decide enough is enough and I go to bed.

On the way through to the bedroom I see the book that Maggie posted through the door. *Happiness* is lying abandoned in the hallway. I pick it up to take it to bed with me. The movement forces the pages to flutter open and something falls from the pages.

I bend down to pick it up.

A solitary, white, feather.

Chapter 31

'My name is Derek Boyd and my job is to help you guys ...' the man seated at the desk said to Jim and Angela. He paused and searched the ceiling for the right words, 'I am here to help you guys deal with the situation you find yourself in. Give you the information you need.' He pursed his lips and exhaled as if the task was monumental. 'And how are we, Angela?'

She nodded as if keen to please. 'I'm fine.' Her legs were crossed, and her ever-present notebook on her lap, its edges frayed with the effort of containing all the information within.

'And how are we all coping with things?' It was obviously just a way into a conversation, but it seemed such a fatuous question Jim wanted to slap him. Instead he answered in the same vein as Angela. 'Fine. We're fine.'

He looked at Jim, held his gaze for a moment and sucked on his top lip as if finding him somehow wanting.

'The meeting today will be short. So that we don't get too tired. Consider this as a starting point on the journey of reclaiming your memory, Angela. But we don't want to go too far too soon or we will cause more damage than good. Okay?' He nodded fiercely in anticipation of a positive response. Jim and Angela complied, nodding back.

'So, questions?'

Questions. Two syllables deep with possibility. Angela and Jim swapped a look of uncertainty; where do we start? Her eyes pleaded with Jim for some sort of direction.

'We need some help, basically,' he said. 'Angela is tired, confused and feeling more than a little helpless ...'

'I know,' said Derek, 'It's not easy. But we will learn to deal with this and although the light at the end of the

199

tunnel seems to be very far away, it is there.'

His use of the collective "we" was starting to get on Jim's tits. Ignore it, he told himself. He really was trying to help.

Although he had planned for this meeting and complained that it had taken so long to organise, he wished that it hadn't happened today. He had enough to think about with Moira. And the message on his answer phone saying that Kirsty was on her way.

At breakfast Angela looked up from her notebook. 'Tell me about Kirsty.'

'Again?'

Angela just looked at him.

'What did she say when you answered the phone?'

'Jim.' From the way Angela elongated the syllable it showed she was fighting back her frustrations. 'I wrote in my book ...' She flicked it open and read, '...Kirsty called. Coming up next weekend. Jim to call her back. She sounded really friendly.'

She closed the book, pushed it to the side and pulled her coffee mug closer to her as if she wanted to seek comfort from its heat. She mumbled something down on to the table top.

'Sorry?' he said.

'I also wrote here, was she Jim's friend?' She tore her gaze from the mug, 'There's some memory of her. I can see her face. It's like a movie camera that's broken. I see her and you. Then the camera freezes.'

Damn.

'But that's good, honey. You're starting to remember stuff,' he hid behind his pleasure for her, 'that's wonderful.' He grabbed her hand and rubbed it. 'We did go over this not long after you got out of hospital. But, you've had to deal with so much, no wonder you can't remember. You're right in that Kirsty started off as my friend. But then the three of us became good pals after her boyfriend dumped her. And then it was a case of girl power, matching menstrual cycles and all that stuff. Poor me with the testosterone didn't get a look in.' He laughed too loudly at his weak joke and mentally scanned the words that had just come out of his mouth. Did they match what he told her the last time they talked about Kirsty?

'So was she my best friend?'

He nodded.

'Why has she waited till now to get in touch?' She sounded hurt, like she was being blown about like a seed in a hurricane, praying that the wind would drop soon and allow her somewhere to land.

'She's busy. She's something in NHS management. She finds it difficult, nigh on impossible to get time off.'

'Right,' Angela regained her fascination with her mug, her disappointment palpable. If that was all she could hope for from her best friend, what did it say about her pre-accident? A voice interrupted his thoughts.

'What do you think of that?' asked Derek. The two of them were looking at Jim.

'Eh, sorry …eh'm that sounds good,' he said and nodded, praying that it was an appropriate answer.

'Post traumatic amnesia is very common in these situations, in relation to short-term memory. Long-term memory tends to return more quickly. When it does, it helps us enormously. But we still have the challenges with short term stuff, which affects our lives on a day-to-day basis.'

Nod.

They nodded back. And Jim wondered what was it about health professionals that has us all reverting to children.

'How are your long term memories coming along, Angela?'

She studied the floor and didn't answer.

'Angela?'

She lifted her head up and avoided Jim's eyes. 'You know …it's difficult.' Her eyes shone with suppressed tears. Something about the delay in her answer set Jim on edge.

Was she lying?

'Don't worry about it,' Derek forced gaiety into his voice. 'It will find you again.'

As Derek spoke Jim continued to question Angela's reaction. Why couldn't she meet his gaze? Was she hiding something from him? Could she remember more than she was letting on? He forced himself to listen to Derek.

'...way of looking at it is to think of the memory like a filing cabinet. Most people have lots of wee drawers in the short-term section ...it's kinda like a temporary section? Then from there the information gets tipped into the long-term drawer. What can happen in people who suffer head injuries is that they lose access to the short-term drawers ...' He looks at the ceiling again. Jim's eyes follow Derek's as if he would find a series of scripts tacked to the white artex. '...I might have about thirty or so of these drawers, but you only have the one. So for you ...when a new piece of information comes along it forces out the earlier chunk. Then the next piece of information does the same and so on.'

Jim looked at Angela. Her eyes were screwed shut as if forcing this new detail into a fresh new drawer.

'You must get really tired?' Derek asked her.

She opened her eyes and nodded. Her eyes then moved back and forwards as if searching internally for what he said just a moment ago about the drawers.

'Don't worry about it,' he said. 'Most patients expend so much energy fighting to remember stuff that they get exceedingly tired.' His attention turned to Jim. 'Loved ones need to appreciate how tiring this can all be. I had one patient who described it as being wrapped in a blanket of fatigue. The simplest thing can tire you out, reading a book, a journey to the shop, a room full of strangers. And you have to learn to plan for it. So, if you are going over to your parents' say for Sunday dinner, make sure that you have time afterwards for Angela to recuperate.' Another nod. 'Yes?'

'Right, I think that's enough for today.' He rubbed his

shaven head vigorously with the palm of his right hand and stood up. 'Let me walk you guys to your car.'

The car was parked down the side of the building and the three of them walked in silence. Jim opened the car door for Angela and moved round to the driver's side. Derek walked with him.

'You looking after yourself, Jim?' he asked.

'As best I can.' He made a face in a *you know how it is* kind of way.

'Take time out for yourself, Jim. Angela needs you, I know, but she also needs you to be effective. And you won't be if you are stressed and knackered all the time.'

Jim looked at him; mouth open and worthless, because what he wanted to say was 'go and bugger yourself, baldy' — but the manners his mother had taught him cut off the link from his brain to his mouth.

'I know, I know,' Derek said. 'That might have sounded callous. I'm not saying that you are somehow lacking, I just know from watching others how difficult this all can be and if the carer doesn't care for themselves everyone suffers. Half an hour at the gym, an hour down the pub with your mates, and you'll feel better.'

At work, after he dropped Angela home, Jim viewed the morning's mail with something well short of enthusiasm and stared out of the window at some newly planted trees. He exhaled long and hard and tried not to feel sorry for himself. This was all getting too much for him. He didn't have two women and a child in his home, he had two kids and a stranger. It seemed more and more that Angela had regressed to some childlike state. She was completely docile, unsure of what she should do or say. He was at a loss as to how he should deal with her. The fact that Moira was about was a blessing.

A doctor had warned about the personality changes that head injuries could cause. Some people exhibit their fear and uncertainty in some inappropriate ways, they become wild and rambling and even violent at times.

Others withdraw, become passive, wanting their carer to do everything for them.

An image of Angela sitting on the edge of the chair in the office that morning thrust itself into Jim's mind. She kept rubbing her fingers along the back of her hand as if trying to remove a layer of skin. Her uncertainty was large in her expression and when she wasn't busy with her notebook, her arms were tight around her as if terrified that her guts would spill out on to the floor at her feet.

What was he doing? How could he feel sorry for himself when she was in this state? Jim still had access to a world of trees blowing in the breeze and ranks of books on a shelf. All she had was acres of empty space in her mind that she feared she would never be able to fill.

Chapter 32

Isn't the act of waking a curious thing? One second you are oblivious to your surroundings. Then awareness thrusts itself upon you with the suddenness of a heartbeat. You're in bed. You enjoy the warmth of the quilt. Or maybe a foot has got loose and is the one spot of chill in your body.

Which of the senses fire up first? Touch or hearing? Or are the senses always there, suspended, waiting for the first loud bang, or the kiss of a lover to stir you into sentience?

I get out of bed and make for the toilet.

Bladder empty, I make for the kitchen and the kettle. A coffee in my hand I move into the living room and put on the morning news. I almost feel absurd being naked and watching the TV. While I was a boy in the convent, nudity was on a par with theft. If any of the girls were to see a penis then their next step would surely take them to the fires of hell. You can take the boy out of the Catholic orphanage ...you know the rest.

As the news presenters chat to each other my mind drifts. I'll go and visit Mrs Hogg today and work at getting more information from her. There's something she's not telling me. She holds the key to us finding Hepburn, I'm sure of it. I just need to find the right words to get her to open up. The last time we spoke I made sure I mentioned the kids that have been hurt. I might as well have been talking about the dangers of drinking diet drinks for all the interest she showed. She'd never had children and perhaps she didn't care for them.

She adopted causes, is what Patricia Conroy said. I need to find her a cause.

Mrs Violet Hogg opens the door to me and directs me into her lounge.

'On your own today,' she asks as we sit down facing each other. 'No nice young police woman to keep you company?' Her features are composed into a smile, her eyes almost serene.

'I'm really sorry to trouble you again, Mrs Hogg. I just thought we could go through some more details concerning Ms Hepburn?'

'I'll obviously help in any way I can, DI McBain.' She crosses her legs. At this point on my first visit she would have been on her way to the kitchen to make me a cup of tea. Now, she rests her elbows on the arms of her seat and steeples her fingers.

I notice a book by her elbow. It is covered in red leather and has a cross on the front. It's too slim to be a Bible. A hymn book, perhaps?

'You do a lot of good work, Mrs Hogg.' As I say this I think of people like Liz Browning who might benefit from her fundraising. By doing so I aim for authenticity in my voice. All part of the buttering up process.

'Why, thank you, DI McBain,' she replies. Her tone is heartfelt with a touch of surprise and a little quizzical. She didn't expect this from me and she wonders where I am going with it. 'I do what I can.'

'Our community would be lost without people like you doing their bit.' I smile. 'We all owe you a huge debt of gratitude.'

'Again. Thank you.' Her eyes are filled with a strange light. Like she expects canonisation any minute.

'I assume you are religious?' I ask.

She nods.

'Church of Scotland?'

Another nod. 'My local church kept me going when my husband died. Don't know what I would have done without the good people there.' She allows her hands to fall on to her lap. 'Forgive me for asking, but I can't imagine you're here simply to thank me for doing my duty? And I've told you everything I know about Audrey.'

I look out of the window to my right, then down to the hands on my lap, and lastly move my eyes back to her face. I take a deep breath and exhale slowly. Her eyes bore into me as if she is trying to read my soul.

'We often double back over old ground, Mrs Hogg.' I cross my legs and hold my hands in my lap as she has done. In posture we are the mirror image of each other. As I speak next I decide to slow the delivery of my speech to match hers. 'To be honest with you, Mrs Hogg, I'm struggling with this one.' Perhaps a little display of vulnerability might help. I rub my eyes and aim for a weary expression. 'With the best will in the world we often forget small details. I thought another wee chat might reveal ...' I allow my voice to tail off.

'Are you feeling alright, DI McBain. Would you like a drink of water?'

Make her work for it.

'Thank you for the offer, Mrs Hogg. Very kind. But I'm okay.' I shake my head slowly and smile. I allow my eyes to drift off to the floor at my side.

'When Ms Hepburn stayed with you did you guys spend much time together?'

'Oh, dear no. She was a young, busy woman with two jobs. Mostly she used the house like a bed and breakfast.'

'Doesn't seem much of a reward for your kindness.'

'Being in the position to help was reward enough.'

'Few of us have the capacity to act in such a selfless manner, Mrs Hogg.'

She sat up straight. 'Are you sure I can't get you something to drink?'

'Actually, now that you mention it, a cup of tea would go down a treat.'

She beams at me and stands up. 'Give me a moment.'

When she is out of the room I take a moment to congratulate myself. There is little that is selfless about this woman. Yes, she does good things and yes, a lot of people benefit from them. But she takes a good deal of personal validation from them. I would bet that the bulk of her self-worth is bound up in the recognition she receives from others in the face of her charity. The pay off for her is not an easier path to salvation, but the appreciation of her peers. In and of itself I guess this is not a bad thing. The net effect is the same, people get help. However, it does give me a window into her soul and from there I might be able to win her over to my side.

Her loyalty to Hepburn thus far, I find a little perplexing. What kind of hold does that young woman have over her? And how can I break down that resolve? At least now she is more receptive to me, I think, as I watch her place a tray on the coffee table between us.

She sips at her tea as if she were in the Queen's drawing room. 'Forgive me if I am being a little too nosey, DI McBain,' her face creases with concern. 'But you don't seem yourself today. Not quite as brash.'

I make an expression of surprise, one that also says that I am comfortable with her honesty.

'Sometimes we get so focussed on a case that we forget the people who are offering their help. I'm sure you'll have experienced something similar,' I say. She raises her eyebrows in a you-don't-know-the-half-of-it motion.

'Apologies about the brash comment. I forget myself sometimes. But you do strike me as a little pre-occupied today.'

'You'll know scripture, Mrs Hogg.' I take a gamble. She won't expect a man like me just to blurt out what's on his mind. I'll go for an oblique approach. 'When I was a boy I went to mass every day. You know how it can be to a child. Pretty boring. I used to imagine I had some toys with me. Anyway one day the priest said something that grabbed my attention. Matthew verse something or other, he reports Jesus as saying "Suffer little children" — I can't remember the rest. But those words used to rattle in my brain as I tried to sleep. Used to think that it was ...I dunno ...a command?'

'Goodness me, no,' Mrs Hogg holds her hands over her heart. 'Whatever happened to you as a boy to make you think Jesus would want children to suffer?'

'It seemed to me that we were all here to suffer, Mrs Hogg. The nuns never tired of saying that we were born with the mark of original sin on our souls. If Jesus said we were to suffer it kind of made sense.' I stare at the floor. 'But it didn't tie in with the man who helped all those dying and hungry people.'

'Matthew, chapter 19, verse 14. Jesus said to his disciples to suffer the little children and forbid them not, to come unto me. He was telling off his disciples for scaring away the children. The actual use of the word *suffer* comes from the old English translation, I believe.'

'Did you regret never having children, Mrs Hogg?'

'No.' She crosses her arms, a hand cupping each elbow. She smiles, but the light in her eyes didn't change. Didn't reveal the thought behind the smile. 'Children were not in my gift, DI McBain.' Her stare is strong and forceful. A stare that tried to inform that she never wanted children.

She takes a sip from her cup and places it on the saucer with a gentle clink. 'That's one of the nicest sounds in the world,' she says. Her expression goes through a number of changes. It finishes with one that says she wants to know more about me.

'I'm guessing you didn't have an easy time as a child?' she asks. I consider the motivation for the question. Her demeanour shows interest, but lacks real compassion. Even as she asks a very personal question I can sense a distance. Perhaps the role she has given herself necessitates she behaved in this manner. It's as if she has tried to learn how to empathise from a book.

'I refuse to see myself as a victim, Mrs Hogg. I'm a survivor.' Jeez, that was a bit dramatic. I sound like someone on Oprah. Need to rein it in a little. 'How many of us can say we had an idyllic childhood? We like to portray childhood in a certain way, don't we? But it's largely the figment of our collective imagination. Especially if you're in the care system. Our society doesn't do well with the vulnerable.' Now for some fiction of my own. Serve up lies with a dollop of truth and it works everytime. 'I never knew my parents, Mrs Hogg and I was placed in an orphanage run by nuns. Mostly they were good women. One or two of them should have been stripped of their habit and locked up.' I pause and allow her imagination to fill in the blanks.

'You surprise me, DI McBain,' she says. My heart gives a jolt when I think this means she doesn't believe me. 'You don't present yourself as someone with a troubled past.'

'I was lucky, Mrs Hogg.' I hide my relief and prepare for some more fiction. 'I was adopted by an elderly couple. Good church-goers like yourself.' I allow a far away smile to grow on my face. 'Don't know where I would be today without them.' I pick up my cup and sip. My tea has gone cold. 'I'm guessing that's what drew you to Audrey? You recognised a troubled soul and tried to help.'

'I did help, DI McBain,' she replies quickly and I gain a flash of insight. She refuses to accept failure. She sought to, and succeeded in, offering a solution for Hepburn's basic human needs. Her emotional ones were not her responsibility. A roof, heating and food were freely on offer. Love and affection had dried up in this woman on the day her husband died.

'I'm sure you did, Mrs Hogg. And it's a shame Hepburn's subsequent actions didn't repay that kindness,' I say and move on before she can protest. 'Tell me about the first time you met Audrey.'

'It was a church do. We needed money for the roof.' She laughs. 'That's such a cliché in fund-raising terms, don't you think? I was working on the book stall. Up to my eyes in books by writers like Margaret Thomson Davis and Jessica Stirling. It was as if people wanted to prove how Scottish they were by donating books by local authors.' She issues a small huff of disapproval. This suggests she is one of those people who, in that uniquely Scottish way, think that if something comes from Scotland then it can't be up to much. 'One of the ladies, can't remember who, brought Audrey over to my stall. Said she was my help for the day.' She pauses and exhales on the first word of her next sentence. 'She didn't say much for a few hours. One syllable answers. Then I managed to get through.' As she says this one hand strokes the bare flesh of the other arm. She looks at me, completely unaware of the movement of her hand. Long fingers slowly move the length of her upper forearm to the wrist as if she is remembering the touch of a lover. 'And we became firm friends.'

Oh good Christ, I see it now. The old woman fell in love with the girl. Not that she would ever have described it as such. In her youth "gay" had a completely different connotation. She would never have recognised the feelings the younger woman stirred in her, nor would she have acted on them. However, she would have acted on her need to be near Hepburn and what better and more innocent way than to offer food and shelter. Hogg was lonely and unfulfilled. She was ripe for the picking and would immediately fall on to the radar of a predator like Hepburn.

It all makes sense now. This explains her reluctance to pass on more information. Out of some sense of loyalty she refuses to believe that someone she felt a strong connection to would behave in such a dangerous and hurtful manner.

'You asked me what was wrong with me, Mrs Hogg. The truth is I really am struggling with this case. I was harmed as a child. As I'm sure Audrey was.' I pause. 'But she has gone on to harm others in turn. Three little boys that we know of.' I look out of the window trying to pick my words with care, but reason and wit are failing me. Old hurts surface with a speed that frightens me. 'The crimes we inflict on each other more often than not go unpunished.' I stop. 'Our legal system places crimes into pigeon holes that fail miserably when it comes to taking into account the effects on the victims. Rape and abuse, are after all just words. Sure, they strike fear in us. But unless we have experienced them for ourselves we can't really understand.

'We might gasp in horror, consider briefly "what if" and then go back to our tea and toast. They're categories that do nothing to describe the humiliation, pain or emotional injury. The effects of these crimes go way beyond the court case and the jail sentence.

'Did you know the law applies a time-bar to bringing a prosecution? Twenty-one years. The clock goes ping and things that happened to me as child are supposed to fade into somewhere beyond memory. Twenty-one years …' Whoa, McBain, getting way more personal than you expected.

I rub my forehead and eyes with both hands. 'Sorry.' I say. 'You didn't need to hear that. It's just so …I feel betrayed. I was betrayed by those I trusted as a child. And that betrayal carries on even now when I am an adult.' I take a deep breath. Calm down, McBain. I look at Mrs Hogg. She seems rapt in my behaviour and my story. So there is a person in there somewhere.

Her face is pale and her eyes shine just a little too much. Could that be a tear?

My words are having an effect and even though my emotion takes me by surprise, I decide to go with it and allow a little more to leak through.

'Sorry,' I say, and hear the feeling in my voice. 'Seeing those kids. Listening to what happened to them brings it all back.'

'Audrey wouldn't hurt a fly.' Mrs Hogg's voice is small and full of uncertainty.

'Betrayal can hurt more than a knife wound, can't it, Mrs Hogg?'

She looks at me, her face thick with denial. She mouths a silent "No".

'The blood stops dripping, the skin grows back. But when someone betrays our trust we lose a little of our soul. We're lessened by someone else's actions and that's part of the tragedy.'

'I don't know what you are talking about,' she says and stands up. Her face is white, her mouth pinched with suppressed emotion. 'Please leave.'

'We surprised you with what we said the last time. But now you can see the truth.'

'Please leave now, DI McBain.'

I stand up and move closer to her. 'She betrayed your Christian trust and kindness, Mrs Hogg. While she was living under your roof she went to work and hurt three innocent little boys ...that we know of.'

'Shut up,' she has her hands over her ears.

'She hung one wee boy on a curtain wire until he almost died and then pretended to save him.'

'Shut up.'

'Can you imagine the effort that must have taken? To hold the wee boy down, with the cord round his neck while he kicked and screamed ...'

'Please ...' her eyes are shut tight as if she is fighting against the mental images my words bring.

'Another she threw down some stairs because he refused to hurt his brother. He broke his arm in the fall. He was only ten.'

Her voice is nothing but a whimper. 'Go please. Go.' She falls on to her chair.

'Please help me, Mrs Hogg. Help me find Hepburn before she harms another innocent.'

Chapter 33

After I leave Mrs Hogg's house I go straight home, change into my running gear, do three sets of thirty press-ups and the same of ab-crunches and then I go for a run. Without conscious thought I make towards the Necropolis on Cathedral Hill.

It's one of those overcast days that Scotland seems to specialise in. The clouds are low and uniform grey, the rain falls in a constant deceptive drizzle. Smirr we call it. A mist of rain that falls like a light shower, barely registering, barely touching skin. It's only as the minutes pass that you realise the world is more than damp and your clothes are stuck to you like a second skin.

In the summer months it's great weather to run in. Today my muscles feel strong. My breathing is even and my heart is beating in a rhythm I know will last me to the end of my run. My thighs only protest after I cross the Bridge of Sighs into the old cemetery and work at the sharp ascent to the top of the hill.

The view from the top across the city has been dimmed by the weather. Looking around me it appears that the world of grey has brought the city in closer. The Glasgow conurbation has shrunk in the rain. I stand under the John Knox memorial and with a nod of apology to the spirit of the man above me, I lean against the plinth and give each hamstring a wee stretch.

On the way down, the angle is harder on my knees so I take my time. My thoughts turn to my meeting with Mrs Hogg and those large, dark eyes of hers as she considered the truth in my words.

'There are families out there who have been destroyed

by this woman,' I said. 'I need your help to make sure no one else ...'

'She laughed at me once,' Mrs Hogg interrupted me. Slumped in her chair, shoulders low, hands between her knees. 'I can't remember why, what caused it. And it only lasted moments.' She brought the fingers of her left hand up to her mouth. 'It happened so quickly I dismissed it.' She shook her head. 'I imagined it, I kept telling myself.

'Don't get me wrong, I do have a sense of humour, DI McBain. And I can handle it if the joke's at my expense. But this was different. This wasn't a friend laughing with a friend. There was no humour in that laugh whatsoever. It was a moment. A glimpse into the real person. And I ignored it like a silly old woman.' She sat back in her chair and brought her arms to her waist, like she was hugging herself. The changes in her eyes highlighted the emotions that scored through her mind.

'She was using me, wasn't she?'

I said nothing, but offered a small smile of commiseration.

'I thought we had, you know, a connection? It's just ...I remember that laugh. The coldness in her eyes ... for only a moment and I know...' Her voice is just above a whisper as she fights back the tears, I know she could be capable of those terrible, terrible things.' She looked away sharply to her left. I felt deeply uncomfortable as if it was me who was responsible for her feelings.

'Her room,' she paused. 'The *spare* room is just as she left it. I've only been in to hoover and dust it.'

'Did she leave anything behind?' I asked more in hope than expectation.

She shook her head. 'She never had much in the first place. Just a hold-all with casual clothes and a toilet bag. You can go and have a look if you want, but it'll tell you more about me than it will about her.'

'If you don't mind ...' I stood up.

'Up the stairs. It's a loft conversion.'

I walked out of the room and the muscles in my back

flexed as if expecting a blow. The role of messenger has never been an easy one and I'll have to move quickly and get what I need before she turns her resentment outwards and aims it at the only other person present.

The stairs were tucked away at the back of the hall. I climbed them and found myself in a room with a large floor space, but little headroom. I had to walk down the middle of the room as at either side the roof sloped sharply. The room contained little but a double bed, a matching pair of bedside cabinets and a bookcase. I looked through the cabinets and under the bed. There was nothing. Fuck. Surely she had left something of herself behind. No one was that careful.

I looked at the bed and tried to imagine Hepburn lying there in the dark of night, thinking about her latest actions and taking delight in them. Did she lie there and hug herself at the thought of the pain she inflicted? Did she plan her next deception? Conjure up ways to hurt the parents as well?

What would make a young woman behave in such a way? Her victims are all boys so far, so who is she enacting revenge on? Her father? Uncle? Brother? Or just the world and men in general? Had she been abused herself? There has been no sexual element to the crimes so far, so does that mean the abuse she suffered was physical? The twisted way in which she treated the Browning boys would suggest there had also been some mental abuse.

The bookcase had three shelves. I turned my head to the side to read the spines. These would give nothing away as they would have been Mrs Hogg's choice. They were mostly classics; Austen, Brontë and Stevenson, with a couple of books that looked like they had been bought at one of the charity book stalls Mrs Hogg mentioned earlier. One has been pushed further in. The obsessive compulsive in me slid it back into line. It's called *Resolution* and it's by Denise Mina. I pulled it out and opened the cover. According to the writing in pencil it sold for "50p".

I examined the script and wondered if it was Hepburn who wrote it. If it did, the lettering wouldn't give us too much to work on. Two numbers and a consonant.

'Find anything, DI McBain?' Mrs Hogg's voice gave me a start.

'Jings,' I held my hand to my chest. 'You gave me a fright.'

Her arms were crossed and her eyes looked anywhere but directly at me, 'She just started that book while she was here. Like most young people nowadays, books didn't interest her.' She walked towards me and plucked the book from my hand. She thumbed quickly through the pages. 'I gave it to her thinking that because it was modern and it was based in Glasgow that she might read it. Are you a reader, DI McBain?'

Her question momentarily threw me as I was questioning why she had been so hasty in taking the book from me. 'For two weeks of the year, on holiday I'm rarely without a book in my hand. At home I never look at them. Haven't read that one though. Could I borrow it? I've heard she's really good.'

'OK,' she said but it looked like it was the last thing she wanted to do.

'Thank you,' I said and took it back. I wasn't that bothered about reading it, as I knew it would just gather dust in my hall, but there was something about her reluctance to let me have the book that needed to be explored.

'You don't turn over the corners, do you?' She looked worried. 'That's what man invented bookmarks for. And please tell me,' her face coloured. '...that you don't read while you are sitting in the loo?'

'I won't from now on. I'll look after this book as if it were my flesh and blood.' I said. That explained her behaviour, she was afraid I would make a mess of her book. 'A bookmark for me it is.' I ran my thumb across the edge of the pages so that they fanned out, don't know why. Perhaps I wanted to stress her out a little. 'And no toilet.'

'Sorry, I don't mean to be ...Oh. What's that?'

Something was dislodged by my actions and fell to the floor. I bent down to pick it up.

'What's this?' said Mrs Hogg. She held out her hand as if to take it. 'Audrey must have used that as a bookmark.'

I held on to it and examined the item. It was an envelope, folded tightly into a rectangle and as Mrs Hogg surmised the shape of it suggested that it had been used as a bookmark. Carefully, I unfolded the creases. The envelope once opened was about half A4 size and had a window, through which an address might appear. Through it I could only see a piece of blank paper. But it was thin and through it I could see the script was on the other side. The envelope had been torn open and I separated the tear and pulled out the paper inside. The familiar layout struck me immediately. The two columns; payments and deductions. The National Insurance number. The employer's name, the Greater Glasgow Health Board. Finally, the employee's name, Lucy Hepburn.

'Oh. That's odd,' said Mrs Hogg as she moved round to stand by my side. 'Why would Audrey put that in there?'

'Perhaps she was terrified to turn the corner of the page down?' I tried to make it sound like a joke but her features remained pinched as if in irritation. 'Still,' I said and put it back in the book and moved my hand to my side. My movements stating my intention to hold on to it. 'She won't be needing it now. Unless her tax return is overdue.'

I walked out of the room, down the stairs and over to the front door, while Mrs Hogg followed me.

At the door, I turned to thank her for her time. She misjudged my movements and bumped into me. Pink blotches in her throat warned me of her state of mind. I had forced her to face an uncomfortable truth, a role usually reserved for best friends, not a member of the local police force.

'Glad to be of help, DI McBain,' she said before I could say anything. She reached beyond me and pulled the door open. 'Goodbye.'

Before I walked over the threshold I turned to ask one more question. Again, more in hope than expectation.

'You didn't manage to take any photos of Audrey while she was staying with you?'

'She is an unattractive woman, DI McBain.' She bit off each word with care. 'Women like that tend to avoid cameras at all costs.'

Chapter 34

'A drink, Jim?' asked Moira.

Jim shook his head not moving his eyes from the screen. An American crime drama was on. They were after a serial killer. Again.

'Thanks. Had enough.'

He turned to watch Moira leaving the room. She'd lost some weight over the last week, and who could blame her after everything that had gone on.

Ben and Angela had been sleeping for the last couple of hours and he and Moira had slipped into the habit of watching late night TV. Both of them had trouble sleeping.

He no longer tried to hide the fact that the sofa was his bed while Moira stayed with them. What was the point? She wasn't stupid. As soon as she realised she became all flustered and refused to go upstairs. Jim responded by saying that she could have the floor, 'cos he'd resigned himself to giving up his bed, but he wasn't giving up the sofa. They both laughed and Moira caved in.

This then became their guilty secret. Warm drinks, TV and chat until the small hours. Although the conversations were mostly one-sided; Moira had an easy way of drawing information from someone and Jim had never had such a willing audience.

Whenever he did try to engage Moira more fully in the give and take of their chats she would answer his question with a question. So skilfully did she do this that it was only later that Jim would notice that once again he had been the biggest contributor to their conversations.

'Tell me about the first time you guys met?'

'Tell me about the day Ben was born?'

'Tell me about any other girlfriends you had.'

That particular evening he found himself talking about Kirsty, minus her name of course. Telling Moira things that he had never told anyone else. Despite his warning bells of conscience he enjoyed how specific details made him sound. This had been an attractive woman after all and she couldn't keep her hands off him.

'Must be difficult for you,' mused Moira. 'Living with the woman you love and unable to ...you know.'

Jim said nothing. The switch from past to present was too painful.

'Sorry,' said Moira. 'None of my business. Forget I said anything.'

Jim eyed the screen. The bad guy got shot and the credits rolled.

Moira offered a shy good night and left the room.

Despite the hour it took Jim an age to get to sleep. Talk of Kirsty sent his mind wandering. Eventually he slept and dreamed of her. Her hands on him. Teasing him, building his excitement up to levels approaching pain.

This carried on for some time until he realised he wasn't dreaming. He opened his eyes. His midriff was bare and his quilt was down at his feet.

'Moira,' he sat up. 'What the ...'

'Sssh,' she said and with one hand pushed him back down on to the sofa. Her other hand continued stroking his balls. A finger slid down to the crack of his arse and pushed its way into his anus. This along with the rhythm of her hand was almost unbearable. Just before he came, he felt her mouth on him, ready to take his semen. He came hot and hard.

She pulled the quilt over him and ghosted from the room like smoke from a delusion.

In the morning Moira was so calm and unresponsive that Jim wondered, did he imagine it? He was a bit old for wet dreams, wasn't he?

Chapter 35

Showered and changed after my run, I'm back in the car and driving to the other side of the city. I go on to Kilmarnock Road and make towards Rouken Glen. From there I take the road that takes me across the M77, from there I coast past Bellahouston Park and House for An Art Lover.

Almost every time I drive this section of road there are a handful of joggers stretching their lycra'd legs and drumming their expensively clad feet on the pavements. Must be something in the water in these parts.

We have learned that the Greater Glasgow Health Board had five employees with the name of Lucy. It's not a deeply unusual name, so perhaps five women sharing this name is statistically possible.

Mrs Browning confirmed that none of the four women I showed her on the camera was the woman who hurt her kids. Jasmine, my health board mole, informed me that the fifth woman had died. What do we deduct from that?

She is missing someone out.

The question I want an answer to is, did she deliberately miss one out or was she just plain sloppy? When we met she appeared to be a little nervous. However if I were in her position with Kenny breathing down my neck, I might be the same.

Sloppy or deliberate? Did nerves play a part? But surely she would know if she was deliberately holding out we would find out and one of us would pay her another visit. In that case, we have to ask, what's in it for her?

Does she have a connection with this woman as well?

For fuckssake, McBain. Rein your neck in. Speak to the woman before you start jumping to mad conclusions.

Chances are she was just being lazy. She probably did the least she could in the smallest possible time to get me off her back.

Approaching Ibrox stadium and in the time it takes to blink, we move past the sandstone mansions of yester-year and towards housing that was built for a less exacting clientele. Take the flyover running across the M8 and you leave houses behind you that might sell for upwards of half a million pounds. The flats that face you, you couldn't give away. And if you see anyone running in these parts, they'll be wearing jeans not lycra, they'll be around forty pounds overweight and late for the kick-off.

From there I take a left and on to the Southern General Hospital. I look at the clock on my dashboard. 15:35. It's a Wednesday. Chances are Jasmine will be working. And this time she'd better tell me the truth.

The scale of this place never fails to jolt me. If you were to drop an alien in the middle of this location, they'd be sure to get the impression that sickness and disease was one of our greatest industries. They might even be right. The place is huge. A wide avenue scores down the middle of a medley of building styles from Victorian to modern. Apparently the place started off as a poorhouse and then had a stint as part hospital, part lunatic asylum.

As I drive past the first of the large Victorian buildings I crane my neck to get a good look. Some poor bastards in the nineteenth century would have been locked up in here in the asylum.

Signs. I get my attention back to the job in hand. And just in good time before I run into the back of that ambulance. Look for a sign. There are plenty of signs and they all tell a depressing tale of the human body's inadequacies. Makes me grateful I am in good health. Give or take a few cakes and bars of chocolate. Maybe they should put a lane in this avenue for sightseers and make it a prescription for anybody that's overweight and drinks too much to drive down here. It would give them a great deal of perspective.

There must be a sign for medical records. I move my head from side to side as I drive down the road, like a spectator at a mobile tennis game. More buildings. A sign for the helipad. A big patch of grass. More buildings. And then, yay, more fucking buildings. The road sweeps to the left and I see a library, a restaurant, a nursery. They even have a nursery? Makes sense, I guess.

I park the car in front of the nursery. It feels like I could drive up and down these roads until the planet runs out of fossil fuels and still never find the sign I'm looking for. I drum my fingers on the steering wheel and look in my rear-view mirror at the nursery. An adult face appears at a window. Probably wondering if I am a parent who's just finished their shift and has come to pick up their precious darling. Time to play the daft laddie.

The nursery is in an old, grey building, much smaller than those around it. To make up for the lack of ability and/or imagination on the architect's part, the nursery staff had placed brightly coloured posters on the windows.

The door has an intercom system. I press the buzzer and wait.

'Yes?' A female voice enquires from the speaker. Sounds young.

'Sorry to bother you...'

'You're not a parent are you?'

'No. I'm sorry to...'

'You're lost, I suppose?' Her voice is polite, but under-lined with a hint of irritation. This isn't the first time this has happened.

'This is going to sound a little bit crazy, but, I'm looking for love.'

'Excuse me?'

'I met a girl the other night. She says she works here ...'

'Are you right in the head? Go away or I'll call the polis.'

'Oh for godsake don't do that. Then she'll never agree to go out with me.'

She moves her face away from the mouthpiece at her end and I can hear her talking quietly to someone else. Then some smothered laughter.

'Look. I'm really sorry and I wouldn't trouble you otherwise, but I'm desperate.' Shit. Wrong choice of word, McBain. She'll think you're some kind of mad stalker. 'Could you just come to the door for a second? You wouldn't want love to spoil before it gets a chance would you?'

I can hear someone egg her on. The speaker goes dead and the door opens slightly, just enough for me to see the head and outline of a woman in her late thirties or early forties. She's around five-foot tall, with shoulder-length blond hair and a pair of large green eyes.

'Well?' she asks. I give her my million-pound smile. The one that says you're going to just love me. She raises her eyebrows in a question. Not impressed.

'We met the other night in *King Tut's*.' As I speak I change to a more humble tone. This is a pretty woman in front of me and she'll have met a few charmers in her time. 'She gave me her number and I lost it. I've been kicking myself ever since.'

She allows the door to open a little more and leans against the upright, crossing her arms as she does so. This has the effect of squeezing her breasts together and means she is now displaying about two inches of cleavage. Her red T-shirt is low at the front, modestly so in this day and age, but a pleasing amount is on show none the less. Men and tits. You'd think we'd get over that, wouldn't you?

'You know how it is. It's been a while.' Oops, that didn't come out right. I look for a ring on her finger. Nothing. At her age, she must have been in one or two relationships. Not in one at the moment. Perhaps I can play on that. '...it's been a while since I met someone who was so much like me ...you know?' I look away. 'She was nice.'

'So what makes you think she works here?'

'She said she was in medical records. She didn't say which hospital.'

'Aah.'

'This is the third one I've tried.'

'Ooh.' She tried to disguise a smile. 'That's determination.'

I shrug in a self-deprecating way.

'She must be nice,' she says. Her voice is wistful. A strand of hair is breeze-blown over her eyes and she tugs it behind an ear. Her expression changes as something occurs to her. 'How do I know that you're not some kind of sick psycho?'

A car draws up behind me. I hear the handbrake being ratcheted tight. A door opens and shuts. Footsteps.

'My eyebrows.' I point. 'They don't meet in the middle.'

She laughs. 'Right.'

'A well-known fact. Neither do I have a hunch,' I say and turn to the side to display my straight back.

She's grinning broadly now. 'And you're not wearing a mask like Hannibal Lector.'

'You must be well up on your killer types.'

'I've met a few assholes in my time.'

I sense someone at my side. 'Excuse me,' I hear a woman say. I apologise and move out of the way. 'Afternoon, Leigh. How's Joe been today?'

'He's been a wee darling,' Leigh answers and smiles, slightly abashed at using a word like *assholes* in front of a mother. She moves aside to let her in and mouths "Better go" to me.

Before she shuts the door she says, 'Try Zone 1, Block D.'

I smile, raise my hand in thanks and turn to go away. The door shuts. I go back and knock on it. She opens it straight away.

'Yes?' She looks kind of pleased to see me.

'If she's not there, what are you doing tonight?'

'Not playing second choice.' Smile.

She closes the door.

Chapter 36

'Jim, I'm leaving,' Angela was standing at the door when he came home from work, a holdall by her side and a white-faced Ben clinging on to her arm.

'What?' Jim shut the front door behind him as if that would close off the thought in Angela's head.

'My long-term memory is fine, Jim. I can remember everything, Jim. *Everything.*' Her face was in his, eyes all but popping from her head, her skin a deep pink. She handed him something. He opened his hand; it now held a condom. He could feel the waxy skin of it and its squishy little deposit at the end. He let it fall, disgusted.

'I'm sure a DNA test would reveal who filled it,' said Angela.

'Ben, go to your room,' said Jim, partly as a delaying tactic and mostly because he didn't want his son to hear what was coming next.

'Moira told me everything. You bastard.' Her saliva sprayed on to his cheek. 'In her moment of weakness you ...' her hand shot out and smashed into his cheek.

'Mind you, there is a pattern there, isn't there? You and vulnerable women. You just can't help yourself, can you?'

'What are you on about? A pattern?' Jim was mystified. Unless she had remembered the day her mother died. She doesn't remember that, does she?

He held a hand to his face trying to think. This wasn't happening. This can't be happening. Not again.

Angela lifted her bag and pushed him.

'Where will you go? You can't go. You can't look after yourself. Can't we talk this through?' He held her arms. She shrugged him off. He looked around for Moira, but she was nowhere to be seen.

'Angela, what's got into you?' He held out the condom wrapper. 'I can explain this.'

'Don't you dare tell me any more lies, Jim Hilton. I've had enough.' She stood in front of him every inch of her vibrating with rage. She lashed out with her foot and caught him on the knee.

'Oww. That hurt,' he rubbed at it. 'Angela. Listen to me. It's not what you think.'

'I remember everything, Jim. My long-term memory has been fine for days,' she was smiling like a mad-woman. 'I remember that we were split up before the accident. I remember why we split up before the accident. But you were being so nice. So considerate that I believed you were a changed man.' She slapped him again. She grunted with the effort, like a tennis player might during a long rally. He took it without complaint.

'What is it with my friends? Kirsty not enough for you, you have to go and fuck Moira as well?'

'But she ...'

'She what, Jim? Was lonely and vulnerable? Just the kind of woman you like?'

She seduced me, he wanted to say but he knew as soon as the words were out of his mouth they would damn him. His mind wasn't working properly. Not only was she the one who seduced him, but they didn't use a condom. They didn't even have full sex. So where did that come from? And what was that about Kirsty?

'But Angela ...'

She pushed past him and stretched for her bag. She was determined and nothing Jim could say would rein her in.

'I'll go,' he heard himself say. 'You can't. You've nowhere to go.'

She stopped at the door, facing the wood. 'Why, Jim? Why?'

'But I'm taking Ben,' Jim said. 'You can barely look after yourself.'

Angela rounded on him. 'My son is staying with me.'

'No way,' said Jim. He was not going through that again.

Angela opened the door and took a step out. Jim pulled her back in. She screamed at him. He shut the door.

'Get your fucking hands off me.'

Jim took a step back. He was lost against the violence of her anger. 'You can't leave,' he said. 'It should be me.'

'Too right,' said Angela. 'And if you think you are taking Ben, you are seriously mistaken.'

'I am not leaving here without my son,' Jim shouted.

'Dad. Mum. Please don't.' Jim could hear Ben screaming from the top of the stairs.

'I am not leaving here without my son,' Jim shouted again, losing all restraint.

'Fine, then I'll go.' Angela made for the door again. Jim pulled her back again.

'Don't ...' punch, 'touch ...', punch, 'me.'

A heavy knock sounded on the door. Angela opened it. It was a uniformed policeman and woman.

Angela and Jim were both stunned into silence. Who called them and how did they get here so quickly? They had barely begun to argue.

'We were called in because there was a fight,' the male said. While he did so the female stood by Angela like a private guard.

'What's going on?' she asked.

Angela and Jim both spoke at the same time. Their anger at the other made the words flow out of their mouths, hot and dangerous.

'Mr Hilton, you should pack a few things and leave,' said the female. 'Your wife is clearly ill and should have the minimum disturbance. I think it's best all round if you both take some time out.'

'What about Ben? You said it, she's ill ...' a distant thought remained unexpressed. How did the policewoman know Angela was ill? '...She can't look after herself let alone a four year old.'

'I can help there,' a voice said and Moira appeared from the kitchen.

'You fucking witch,' Jim roared and stepped towards her.

'Sir, if you don't calm down I'll have to arrest you,' said the policewoman.

Chapter 37

As I face the girl on reception in Zone 1 Block D I can't help but wonder what the Latin might be for "Harassed but Helpful". Whatever it is it should be formed into a coat of arms and stuck above every sign for the National Health Service.

Her desk is a curved slab of pale wood. It contains the ubiquitous computer screen and piles of folders that could have once amounted to a small forest. Despite her obvious workload the girl's smile is genuine. She knows she has a shitload of work and she knows that she'll get round to it eventually.

'Can I help?'

'Yes please,' I read her badge, 'Caroline. I'm looking for Jasmine?'

'Does Jasmine have a second name?' She has long brown hair caught in a neat ponytail, a square shaped face and I can't see much else of her because she's wearing a uniform and sitting down. Looks to be around the same age as Jasmine. Chances are they might be friends.

'I'm positively sure that she does.' I nod. 'I just forgot to ask her.' I give the million-pound smile another outing.

'If this is a personal call, sir, I'm not sure I can help you,' she picks up a pen and fiddles with it. A good sign. Displacement activity that shows me she is a girl who doesn't like to say no.

'It's not personal.' I reach into my back pocket and pull out my wallet. From a section in the middle I select my warrant card and show it to her. 'It's business.'

'I'll see if she's in,' she says and then fiddles about with her computer screen via her mouse. While she searches

231

for what I assume is an extension number I look around me. What I see is mostly bare and functional. An essay in the necessity of industrial drabness. The walls are a blue-grey and the floor is a similar colour. At least the ceiling is white. Broken only by a small closed-circuit camera aimed at the desk.

Caroline then punches a number into her phone. She's too far away from me to hear any of the other side of her conversation. She asks for Jasmine. Then pauses. Looks at me. Makes an uh-huh sound. Then another pause. A nod. Then says, 'Right. OK.'

She looks up at me. 'The girls in her office are going to look for her. They think she's gone out for an errand to one of the other wards.'

Errand. Do people actually use that word nowadays? It seems curiously out-dated coming out of this young girl's lips.

'How well do you know Jasmine?' I ask.

'OK,' she tucks a strand of hair that's come loose from her ponytail behind her ear. 'Wouldn't say we were best buddies or anything. She's a bit ...' Caroline looks quickly to the side as she thinks of a word. 'Rough.' Then colours slightly as if afraid I might think she's a bitch.

'Would you say you know her well enough to lie for her?'

'Sorry?' Her blush works at her cheeks and flows up to her eye line.

'She told you to keep me waiting while she did a runner, didn't she?' I swivel round to point at the camera. 'She can see me on that, can't she?'

Caroline studies a file on her desk and mumbles something. Sounds like sorry.

'Does she have a car?'

Nod.

'Where do staff members park their cars in this place?'

'Anywhere.' She shrugs.

'What kind of car does she have?'

'A Clio. Red.' Her expression sours against the thought she's grassing on a mate.

'Fuck!' I turn to move away and then turn back. 'Don't go away, young lady. I want to speak to you again.'

I race out of the reception area and back to my car. As I run to the car park I keep my eyes open for a red Renault Clio. Nothing. Then I spot her just as I reach my car. From where I am parked I can see a line of cars queuing to get out of the hospital grounds. Just then a car that answers the description Caroline gave me turns right into traffic and out of sight. Fuck! This calls for a quick decision. If I get in the car and try to catch up with her I have no way of knowing which way she has gone. This is a well-connected hospital. From here and driving in that direction, she could have made her way to Govan and from there anywhere to the south of the river or she could have made for the Clyde Tunnel and from there anywhere north.

Time to have another wee chat with Caroline.

On the way back to her office I give Kenny a call. He answers immediately.

'McBain. I was just thinking about you.'

'Having a wank?'

'That would be a no ... unless you've had a back, sack and crack done since we last spoke.'

'Jasmine,' I say, thinking I've had enough banter. 'You got her address?'

'Does the Pope wear a funny hat, does a bear shit in the woods, does a one-legged duck ...'

'Do you ever just give a straight answer? Can you meet me at mine in half an hour?'

'No can do, big guy. Crime doesn't only pay, it's calling me.'

'Don't need to hear any more. Send me a text with the address, will you?'

I close the connection without saying goodbye. He's got broad shoulders. He can take it.

Back at Zone 1 Block D, Caroline has been replaced by a man. He looks like he is in his early thirties, his hair is "styled" in what could best be described as a reverse

Mohican and he is wearing a brown tie like it houses MRSA. His badge reads "Bob".

'Can I speak to Caroline, please?'

'You'll be the policeman who was bothering our staff?' A faint scent reaches me from across the desk. Aftershave. Smells familiar, but I can't place it.

'You'll be the jobs-worth who tries to get in my way.'

We size each other up. If we were dogs he'd be pissing in every corner of the room.

'How can we be of assistance, officer?'

'It's Detective Inspector McBain.'

He deflates just slightly under the weight of my full title. Then he rallies. 'Do you have a warrant?'

'This isn't Hollywood, Bob. And we're just at the stage of making some enquiries. Have you ever had to help the police with their enquiries, Bob?' As I speak I move closer to the desk. He's sitting at the other side and I tower over him.

He stands up. I still tower over him.

It's good to be the king.

'As I said, we'll do whatever we can to help the police. We are kind of busy.' He's being apologetic. Building his case for letting me down. 'We're in the middle of an audit.' He makes a face. 'As long as whatever you are looking for doesn't compromise our own legal responsibilities, I am more than happy to help.' His smile is merely a curve to his mouth. His eyes are full of uncertainty, topped off with a desire to impress any staff member who is watching on the CCTV. However, he's alluding to Data Protection and that's a line I don't want him to stick with. Time to crank up the pressure.

'You don't seem to be bothered that one of your staff legged it as soon as the police arrived.'

'She was going off duty and whatever our staff do in their own time is not under our control.'

'It should be if it involves stolen prescription pads.' Don't know where that came from, but I'll run with it.

His adam's apple bobbed in his neck. 'That's eh...'

'That's a story the press would love. I'm not above going to the newspapers if it flushes out the bad guy. Are you a bad guy, Bob?'

'Certainly not,' he says and bristles. His scalp gleams and the tufts on the side of his head are on full alert. He pushes the knot in his tie closer to his neck. Several thoughts play across his features. It would not look good if a story like this was real. He's not to know that occasionally I take the truth for a wee walk, come back and leave it behind.

'As I said, how can I help?' He asks and attempts a look of calm. Looks more like he's constipated.

'Now I don't want Miss...'

'Toner.'

'To lose her job. She simply got frightened. Between me and you we think it was her ...'

'Boyfriend?'

'You catch on quick, Bob. Yes, boyfriend, who got her mixed up in this. Anyway, she was helping us with our enquiries, just as you have so kindly offered to, except she managed to miss out some important information. Now the fact that she does a runner when I show up suggests she deliberately misled an official investigation. Doesn't look good, Bob. Does it?'

He coughs. 'No. However ...' He stands up to his full five feet six inches and puffs out his chest.

'Forget the however, Bob. I need your help and I can't be arsed with the posturing. Take me to your office.'

'Right.' He harrumphs as if egging himself on to defy me. I simply stand and stare.

'Gimme a second,' he says and with every syllable he takes his indignation down a notch. What's the point, he's saying to himself, I'll only lose. He picks up the phone, dials a number. 'Can you come back to the front desk, please?' he asks whoever answers. I'm guessing it's Caroline. His tone piques my interest. The name of the scent pops into my head.

'I thought they stopped making Brut years ago.'

His head snaps up. 'What?'

'Nothing,' I smile and Caroline appears. Bob gives her all of his attention. Makes like he's in control. Then it occurs to me; the aftershave, the attitude, the tone ...the poor guy thinks he's got a chance with the cute receptionist. Isn't the male ego something to behold?

He leads, I follow. We go along a corridor, round a bend, along another corridor and through a brown door. It is all so nondescript and minus any recognisable features that it would be incredibly easy to get lost in these halls.

Bob has a fairly large office with a central desk. The wall behind the door has a row of filing cabinets against it. A couple of them have drawers that barely shut they are so full. Another has all its drawers closed, but slightly askew as if the weight of paper has pushed the drawer from its runner.

Before he can take a seat I speak.

'Staff records ... where are they?'

'I ...eh...' he cocks his head to the side and pushes out his chest.

'Bob. I really don't have time for this. You have a woman by the name of Lucy Hepburn working with you. She is hurting little boys. We need to stop her.

'Now we can do this the hard way, which means this woman damages another wee boy and this hospital's name gets dragged through the media mud. Or you save us all a lot of heartache and punch a few keys on your keyboard right now.'

'I could get the sack for doing this without the proper ...'

'Bob. I know. And I really am sorry to put you in this position,' I interrupt him. His features soften as he tries to read my new approach. 'Five minutes and I'll be out of your hair. Forever.'

I pull the wage slip from my pocket and slide it across the desk towards him. 'You might find this useful,' I say.

He sits down and pulls his chair closer to the desk. He

unfolds the wage slip. His fingers flash across the key-board and several menus come and go on his screen.

'If anyone gets wind of this my career is on the line.'

'Who's to know?' I hold my arms out in a saint-like gesture. 'I'm not telling anyone.'

As he looks at the screen he sucks on his teeth. I bite down on my irritation. We're best friends now and besides, I don't want to antagonise the guy any further.

'Right,' he says and writes something down. Then he sucks on his teeth some more and writes down something else. He takes a deep breath and pushes the paper towards me and stands up.

'If you look at that while I go out the room ...'

'Bob, you watch way too much TV. We're beyond that.' I motion him down. 'Sit on your arse. And while I'm on this honesty malarkey will you please stop sucking on your teeth. It's getting on my tits.'

'You've been reading that book again, haven't you?' Bob purses his lips, clasps his hands and places them on the desk in front of him.

'Eh? What book?'

'How to Win Friends and Influence People.'

See Glasgow? Full of comedians.

'By the way, she's dead. Died, what, four months ago.' He peers into his screen more. 'That's odd.'

'What is?'

'There's a flag against her name. Like we are missing some information.' He moves his mouth as if he is going to suck his teeth and stops when they get close to just a pout. Not a good look on him. He stands up. 'Give me a second, will you?' He quickly walks out of the room.

As soon as I am on my own I am out of the chair and facing his computer screen. It details her name and date of birth as 10th March 1988. Makes her in her early twenties. A young age to die.

There are a number of letters I am guessing are her nursing qualifications. Her most recent address is noted. It's just off Kilmarnock Road in Shawlands. I sit down again just before Bob re-enters the room.

'I ...that's very odd. I can't find her file.'

'You said there was information missing. What might that be?'

'Without the file I can't say for sure. But there are certain things we should have on here ... like a note that a copy of the death certificate is on file. Without it we can't do things like apportion any of her pension rights and death benefits.'

'Is that at all unusual? To be missing the information for such a long time?'

'Unusual, but not unheard of.' He looks at the screen, clicks the mouse. 'Normally the nearest and dearest are flocking to see what's going to come their way, so they are happy to supply the necessary.' A couple more clicks of the mouse. 'But this girl ... it seems, has no next of kin.'

I considered the implications of that. Alone in the world at her age. Poor girl. Didn't even have someone to send in her death certificate.

Unless ...

There's something about this whole thing that bothers me. What do we have? A dead Hepburn minus a death certificate, a missing file and a member of staff who works in the medical records department goes AWOL just as I come for a visit.

Jasmine clearly has something to hide.

Could this woman actually be alive and be the Lucy Hepburn we're looking for?

'DI McBain?' Bob says.

'Aye?' I realise I look odd as I sit staring into space.

'Can you sling your hook now? I've got work to do.'

'Sure, Bob. Sorry.' I stand up. 'When you get this file ...if there's anything you think we should know will you give us a call?'

'Absolutely.'

I give him my card. 'I want to know how this girl died and who notified you of her death. Can you do that for me?'

He nods, more than happy to help now that he knows he is about to get rid of me.

Bob escorts me back out to reception. Caroline is at her desk busy at the monitor. I give her a smile. I pat him on the shoulder and speak loudly for Caroline's benefit.

'I'm sorry I troubled your staff, Bob. And you're right I was a bit harsh. Thanks for your time. You've been a great help.' For good measure I shake his hand.

He looks at me as if I've just spoken to him in Flemish.

Then I say quietly in his ear. 'She's cute, Bob. I think you've got a wee chance there. But a word from the wise. Bald guys shave their head these days and nobody's worn Brut since Abba broke up.'

Chapter 38

Leaving the hospital grounds, I quickly look at my mobile. True to his word, Kenny has left me a text. Quick decision time. Do I head for Jasmine's or go to the dead Hepburns'. The latter isn't going anywhere, that's for sure. Jasmine however, might well be long gone. If I was her I'd be expecting a visit. I don't remember telling her that I was with the police. So she'll either be out or she'll have called in some pals to back her up.

Hepburns' it is. I aim the car back the way I came, to Shawlands. From there I head back into town. I find the address easily. Typical Glasgow tenement flats. Four floors of brown sandstone and hardly a space to park your car. The people on the streets are also fairly typical of Glasgow these days; lots of brown faces with an equal measure of pale Celt. Mothers are pushing prams, kids are kicking a ball, older people are carrying plastic bags full of shopping. Just a normal street, in a bog-standard part of the city. And it may hold the key to finding a very dangerous young woman.

Number 176 has a glass panel about head height and is clearly a secured entrance. The giveaway is the neat aluminium box with a row of buttons to the right of the door. Some of the buttons have names on them. None say *Hepburn*.

Chances are, if I press any or all of the buttons and say who I am no-one will let me in. More Glasgow bluster is called for. If I'm lucky, somebody might be expecting someone back in and allow me in without vetting me, so I press all the buzzers. No-one answers. I buzz again and wait. Nothing. This time I press each one for thirty seconds. Before I get to the top a voice issues from the box.

'Who is it? What d'ye want?'

'For chrissake, it's me. Let me in,' I say. The lock buzzes and I'm in. The hallway is dark, but there is enough light to see a stone staircase and two doors on either side of it, giving entrance to the ground floor flats. To the left of the stair a passage runs to the back of the building, where no doubt there will be a door that opens out to a drying green and a collection of bins.

A door opens somewhere above me. A man's voice calls, 'Who is it?' Their tone suggests a wee bit of humour and a little concern. The worry might come from their having second thoughts about who the owner of the voice on the intercom was. The humour would be in place to suggest that they knew who it was all along and they were just having them on.

I need to get rid of them.

'Sorry.' I call up. 'All the doors in this street look the same. I've pressed the wrong door. What a numpty. Sorry mate.' I turn, walk back to the door, open and close it while staying inside. This satisfies the person upstairs and I hear their door close.

Now I'm in, I need to decide how to go about finding Hepburn's former abode. Two doors on each floor. Four floors. Best to start from the top. The stairs are steep so I take my time. As I pass each door I try to assess what the owner might be like. The bottom two doors each have a nameplate. "King" on one side and "Banks" on the other. King has a doormat and a wooden cat. Banks has a flowerpot on a wicker stand outside his/her door. The flower is a red thing. I'm guessing these flats are single occupancy. Old people, perhaps.

My footsteps echo in the stairwell as I head upwards. The first-floor owners have given more effort to their doors. Less chance of their stuff getting stolen? Bigger plants are on display here and where the door on my left has a kid's bike leaning against the wall, the one on my right has a small, white wicker chair. Comes under the heading, Seemed Like a Good Idea At the Time. Begs the

241

question, why would you want to sit out here? The door with the chair has two small brass nameplates. Again, neither is Hepburn. The other door has nothing.

Moving up, I notice my breathing is getting shallower. Slow down, McBain. Don't want to knock on the door and be panting like I've just run away from a mugger.

This floor is more promising. The first door is covered in a pristine gloss. It has three white, plastic nametags, but none are Hepburn. The next door has one plastic name tag, Connor, but below it are three strips of paper sellotaped to the wood. Welcome to Bed-sit Land. This one would make sense. If Hepburn was on her own, good accommodation might be hard to find. Especially on a nurse's pay packet. The paper tags suggest transience. Apart from Mr or Mrs Connor, no-one else tends to stick around.

None of the pieces of paper say Hepburn, but I wouldn't expect that. Space is money here. As soon as it was vacated the room would be up for grabs.

Without thinking. I rap my knuckles on the door. Footsteps approach the other side; I reach for my wallet and pull out my warrant card. The feet stop, links of a chain sound and the door opens slightly. A man's face peers out.

'Mr Connor?' I ask and hold my card out.

'Go away. I'm not buying anything,' he says. His face is covered in a lattice of deep lines. A flop of fringe hangs before his eyes. It is white, with a tan, nicotine streak down the middle. The top of his head is about level with my chin.

'I'm DI McBain from Strathclyde Police. I need to speak to you about a former tenant, Mr Connor.'

Alarm flows through his features. 'Them students are gone now, officer. If I had known aboot the drugs I would never huv let them in.' His voice is low and quiet and strung through with a tremor. Old age? Nerves?

'It's about the nurse. Hepburn.' I make a calculated guess. If she didn't stay with him, he might know where

242

she did stay.

'Whit? The wan that died?'

'Yes, Mr Connor.'

'But she's deid.' He looks at me as if I am the most stupid person on the planet. 'Died months ago.'

I hear the noise of the other door on the landing open behind me. Mr Connor cranes his head to the side in an effort to see past me. Then he looks back at me. He seems uncertain what to do next.

'It might be best if you let me in,' I say quietly. 'You don't want the neighbours to hear your business.'

'Aye. Aye,' he says. He looks at the ground as if searching for instruction. 'Right.' He fumbles with the chain. 'In ye come.'

He leaves the door and shuffles away from me. I enter and close the door behind me. The hall is carpeted and deceptively spacious. The carpet is brown, with yellow flowers and looks like it has been there since the seventies. The walls are covered in woodchip wallpaper that has been painted in vanilla. Where the walls join the ceiling I can see some spots of blue that the painter failed to cover. There are two doors on my left and one on my right, then the passageway takes a short dog-leg to the right where there is another door. The old man stops in front of this one. I hear the clink of keys, he picks one, inserts it and enters. I follow.

Chapter 39

Since we entered the flat Mr Connor hasn't spoken a word. He's standing by a double bed, hands in his trouser pockets and eyes on the floor while he waits for me to speak.

The bed is bare. It's simply a mattress on top of a wooden frame. The far side of it is lined by a blue, velour three-seater sofa. A dark brown table has been pushed against the window and four chairs sit round it. None of them match the other.

Another, smaller table is pushed against a different wall. There are three chairs around it. The next wall has two wardrobes pushed against it. Both have double doors. Both are different colours of wood. This is more like a storeroom than a bedroom.

I assess what I've seen of the flat so far. There are another four doors leading off the hall. One must be the kitchen and one the toilet. The other two might be for tenants. Which means this is where Mr Connor lives.

It takes me a second to realise what's missing. Apart from a TV, of course. It's the clutter. There are no ornaments, no plants, no pictures or paintings.

He's still standing in front of me. His expression suggests he is having an internal debate. While he does so I give him the once over, trying to make sense of him and his space. He's wearing a blue, padded overcoat, brown trousers and a pair of black, leather moccasin slippers. If I was to analyse the stains on the coat it might tell me everything he's had to eat over the last six months, as I doubt that he ever takes it off. Perhaps that's why there are no covers on the bed? He wears it.

'Could you tell me what you know about Lucy Hepburn, Mr Connor?'

'She's deid,' he says as his mouth takes on a line of distaste.

'Before that?'

'I had to chuck her oot. Didnae pay her rent.'

'Then how do you know she died?'

'S'pose you'd better have a wee seat, son,' he says and points to the table at the window. He walks over and sits. I chose a seat across from him and sit as he does. Knees tight together, hands clasped in his lap. From here I can see his trousers are as stained as his coat.

'Have ye been in the polis long, son?'

'Too long,' I answer.

'You're lucky, but. There's no many people has a job that can make a difference.'

'True.' I sense he wants to chat. It might help to get more information if I comply. 'You retired?' I fully expect the answer to be yes, but it won't do any harm to flatter. He looks as if he might be in his early seventies.

'A long time ago, but.' He fumbles in the front pocket of his coat and brings out a red pocket book. He opens it in the middle and puts it on the table. The pages are well thumbed and from here I can see there are lines of dates and amounts that might appear on a ledger. Or an order book.

'I was a salesman, son.'

'Right.' I can't imagine him selling anything. Unless it's uppers. One look at his face and you'd be in the need of false cheer. I look over and see that the numbers stop half way down the second page. The last date is 12th March 1967.

'Aye, I sold flies and bait and stuff to huntin' and fishin' shops.' He stretches into another pocket and brings out a wad of paper. He unfolds it and pushes it flat on the table. It's a map of Scotland. 'Used to go all over the country. You name it and I've been there.'

'Excellent,' I say and do some quick sums. His tone suggests this was his last job, which means he "retired" forty years ago.

'The world's gone to the dogs, son. The dogs.' He picks up the map and carefully folds it. 'What with the drugs and the homersexuals.'

Here we go. It's time to call a halt to our wee chat.

'I had a wee part-time job last year when I lost some tenants. A public toilet in one o' the parks.' He purses his lips, which has the effect of making his face look like it has collapsed in on itself. 'Druggies and homos.' He gives a big shrug. 'I'm telling you, son, it was a breath of fresh air when somebody came in for a shite.'

I'm getting the feeling that if I don't steer the conversation away from him I could be here all day.

'About Miss Hepburn, did she take drugs?'

'No that I know of, son. Mind you,' he raises his left eyebrow, 'she could have been up to anything behind that door. Especially given what I seen later.'

'When was the last time you saw her?'

'I cannae mind when, son. But it was the same day I changed the lock on her door. She hadn't paid her rent for four weeks and nobody takes a loan of Ian Connor.' He nods once and clasps his hands on his lap. His expression changes and grows thoughtful. 'That was the strange thing, but. Her stuff. I told her she could have it all back if she paid me my money. She just stood there and grinned like I was doing her a favour. I never saw her again.'

'Did she leave much stuff?'

'A few clothes, toiletries...' he crossed his arms and his legs. His eyes move to the side and examine the pile of the carpet.

'Anything else?' I ask.

'That's why you're here, isn't it?'

'Sorry?'

'You hear aboot it all the time, but. Famous people, n'at, getting done for strange pictures. That woman tried to get it all off me, but I said to her to prove she was legally entitled. Once she did that and once she paid the outstanding rent, she would get it.'

'Mr Connor,' I lean towards him. 'Excuse my slow wee brain, but you've lost me. Could you start at the beginning and tell me about the woman and the pictures.'

He examines me as if seeing me for the first time. 'I thought you polis guys were smart,' he mumbles. 'The woman who told me that the lassie was deid. She came for the wee lassy's things.' He stands up.

'Did you see her death certificate?'

'No yet. Although that wummin promised to send me it.'

'The woman that came for her things?' I ask. As far as I'm aware she has no next of kin. Could it have been another nurse at the hospital?

'That's how I know she's deid. Nobody's that good an actress. The poor woman was distraught. Grief's an awfa thing, son.'

'Could you describe this woman?'

'Needed a good feed. Medium height. Dark hair. Well dressed. Like a toff. She was wearing sunglasses, which was strange given that we were in the middle of winter. I expect it was to hide her eyes. You know how women get when they've been greetin'. She came back twice more. Each time she was more and more upset. Said she was the lassie's adopted mother. Explains why she was greetin'.'

He turns and walks to one of the wardrobes. He picks the keys from his trouser pocket, takes one and inserts it in the lock. Once opened, he allows the door to fall wide. Despite myself I have a look at what it contains. Mr Connor still has his back to me as he bends forward to pick something up. Beyond him I can see that the floor of the wardrobe is covered in three waist high piles of paper. It looks like envelopes, paper folders and formal pieces of paper. I can see the logo of a well-known bank on one and the name of an investment house on another. Well, well. Mr Connor has himself a wee treasure trove.

If he ever spends any of it, the first thing he should buy himself is a new coat. Or maybe a jumper, then he can save his coat for when he actually goes outside.

He turns holding a black bag to his chest. Like the kind of bag people keep laptop computers in.

'How do you guys track these things, satellite?' he asks.

'Yes. We have some very sophisticated technology these days,' I say. I have no idea what he is getting at but I get the feeling it will help my cause if I agree.

He slowly puts the bag on the table. 'I was going to bring it in, you understand. But I was holding it until I got my money.' He sighs. 'Looks like that's no going to happen any day soon.'

While he's pulling a black laptop computer from the bag I ask about the mystery woman.

'What exactly did this woman say?'

'Just that the lassie had passed away and 'cos she was her next of kin she should get all of her stuff.'

'And when you said no?'

'Then she started shouting at me. Said it was all of a great emotional value. Then the tears started. A big fat wan rolled down her cheek from behind her specs,' he says with a great deal of feeling. 'The poor wummin was in a state. Felt right sorry for her, so I did.' He opens the lid. 'There you go.'

Not sorry enough to give her all of Hepburn's belongings, I think.

'I let her have the clothes and stuff. Then she came back the next day saying that she didnae get everything and that I was a thieving old bastard.' He's wearing a face to suggest he was mortally offended. 'But I did my research. This machine would score a couple of hundred second hand and the wee deid nurse owed me about that. So I told her that I wiznae playing. Nae cash. Nae computer.' He patted the keyboard for emphasis.

It's your run of the mill laptop. IBM issue. There's a small blue "nipple" in the middle of the keyboard that I'm guessing is in place of a mouse. Blue-brown would be a closer description as it's dirty. This machine has been about a bit. A couple of stickers advertising technological parts are only half complete suggesting heavy use. Perhaps the dead Hepburn got it second hand.

He presses a button and the machine whirrs into action.

'How did this woman sound? Was she local?'

'Aye. From a posher part of the city, but. She spoke properly. Nae slang.' The familiar music of Microsoft Windows sounds from the machine and a blue page fills the screen.

'When I first tried it I was terrified. I'd never seen anything like this in my puff. Had a few classes down at the library...' as he speaks he's wearing a proud smile displaying a set of teeth any self-respecting dentist would run a mile from. '...and now I'm getting quite good. When I first worked out what I was doing I had a wee nosey.' He studies me. 'I hope you don't blush easy?'

'I'm in the police, remember? We get to see all kinds of things.'

'No like this you won't. I've never seen the like in my life.'

If he doesn't get to the point double quick I'm going to yell at the old fucker.

'Ah. Right.' His hand moves with careful deliberation. 'Nearly there. Right.' He clicks and a picture fills the screen. It takes me a couple of seconds to make sense of the image. The central space is filled with a three-quarter view of a woman's head. Her eyes are half shut and her mouth is half-open. Her expression is filled with what I can only describe as lust. There's some white, almost pearly stuff strung over her nose and one eye is almost completely obscured. Some of it is coming out of her mouth.

'Ah'd never have thought it. But she looks like she's having a great time,' says Mr Connor. The way he says it suggests he didn't believe that a woman could enjoy a sexual practice like the one we see before us. Because sexual it quite clearly is. The big clue is coming in from the corner of the screen. The angry, thick head of a penis that is just shooting a fresh load of semen on to the woman's face.

'There's no way all of that semen has come from the one man,' I realise that I've just spoken out loud.

'Aye,' Mr Connor nods in agreement. 'Doesn't she look like she's havin' a great time, but?'

'Aye, she does,' I agree with him. Then we are both silent as we study the picture some more. Takes all kinds, I guess, but the more I look at the picture the more it turns my stomach.

Questions assert themselves in my mind. Why would someone keep this picture? Who is the woman who was so keen to retrieve it?

I look closer at the picture. Beneath the semen you can see that the woman is at least middle aged. Her clear eye is thick with mascara, some of which is running onto her cheek. Her hair is pulled back out of the way and is long and blond. It doesn't match the face ...too young, which suggests it is a wig. Her bare neck has that stringy look. I look at the face again. There is something about it.

'You married?' Mr Connor asks.

'Nope. Never had that good fortune.' Whatever was on my mind has vanished, slipped from my grasp like the smoke of a dream.

'Me neither,' his eyes haven't left the picture. He looks like he's just learned the most valuable lesson of his life and it's too late to use it. 'It's changed days right enough, son. In my time it was lights out, knickers off, before her parents caught you. Now you young yins have got all ...' he ran out of words. '...this.'

Chapter 40

'Can I get you anything, son?' Jim's mother leaned into his room, the lines of her face deepened with concern. He had brought a few things over from his house and taken up residence in his old bedroom. This had become his refuge when he and Angela first split up. It felt like he had never left, that all the work and effort of the last few weeks and months had been completely in vain.

'Do you think she'll let you see Ben today?'

Jim shrugged. Then shook his head. He didn't know. Every day for the last week he had turned up at the house hoping to see Ben and every day the door remained shut to him.

Yesterday, a little white face appeared at the upstairs window. Jim shouted, 'Ben,' and the face disappeared. It was all he could do not to kick in the door. Every instinct he owned urged him to run at the door, shoulder his way in and pull Ben out.

If he did so he knew that the police would be quick on his heels. Then he would be put under a restraining order or an ASBO or something and he would never see Ben again.

'Jim, you can't just lie there all the time, son.' His mum remained by the door as if her son's despondency restricted her movement. 'Eat something. You have to eat.'

Jim lay back on the bed and pulled a pillow over his face. Into its softness he roared his frustration and anger. He heard his mother's footsteps as she moved away. He wanted to go after her. Apologise. He was rooted to the spot. He'd never felt so hopeless.

Or so angry.

He'd gone over every second he had spent with Moira since she elbowed her way into their lives and each time he did so he became increasingly alarmed at her actions and his inability to do anything about it.

At first there were suspicions. Why the hell didn't he pay them more attention? Then there was the concern she showed for Angela, the attention she lavished on her. Then she had turned her charm on Jim, and wasn't he a prize dickhead for not seeing through it.

She engaged his sympathy with the story of Erskine, a tale she wove with the skill of a novelist. She left in just enough of her own *regrets* for him to see that she was a real, three-dimensional woman in a difficult situation. Sure, she acted to snatch her own child back, who wouldn't?

What about the condom? That was a masterstroke in her plan. If truth be told, the one flaw that allowed Jim to see what was really going on. He hadn't worn a condom that night. She must have kept his semen warm in her mouth, climbed the stairs to the bathroom and then spat it into a condom from the bathroom cabinet.

If her actions hadn't such a hurtful outcome, he might be impressed at her cunning.

Then there was the police. How did they get to his door so quickly? They had barely began to argue when they turned up.

Moira must have phoned in when she knew he was on his way home from work, hoping that by the time they arrived he would have had enough time to meet Angela's revelation. And blow a fuse.

Jim's mother was right. He sat up. He couldn't just lie here and twist in his own despondency. He had to do something. But what?

The police weren't interested. He'd been to see them three times. Each time he'd been shown the door. The report the two constables filed on him wasn't complimentary. He was recorded clearly as the aggressor and if he made any more allegations of kidnap he'd be charged with wasting police time.

He started at the beginning of Moira's story and began picking at it. Was there anything that came out of her mouth that was truthful? They had been in her house. Was it really her house? Was Erskine even her son?

Chapter 41

Back at my place I power up the laptop and link it to my printer. I open the file and press print. As the machine chugs away at the paper I think about Mr Connor's expression as he watched me pack the computer up.

'Once we're finished with it, I'll get it back to you.'

'Right,' he said and looked out of the window.

'Don't know how long that might be though. It has to be logged as evidence and then we have to wait for trial.'

'There's gonnae be a trial?'

'We don't know for sure, but the rest of the evidence points to it,' I said. Just one more lie to add to the day's tally.

The doorbell rings.

It's Kenny.

'Dear me, Ray McBain as I live and breathe. Caught in the act of masturbation,' he says with an air of schoolboy delight when he sees the image on the computer.

'It's not what ...' I realise as the words trip from my mouth that it doesn't matter what I say. This will go down in Kenny history as the Time He Caught McBain Wanking.

'Interesting little fetish you have here as well,' he says in the manner of someone appraising an antique.

'It's a fetish?'

'Of sorts. Bukkake.'

'Is that not a mushroom?'

He sat on the chair next to me. 'Imbecile. It's Japanese. The literal translation is to splash.' I look at him amazed that he knows this stuff. He studies my expression. 'So if you weren't having a wank what were you doing?'

'First off, it does nothing for me. Secondly, I'm on a case.'

'Explain.'

'This is where the Kenny Criminal Investigation thing falls down. This is a police thing and I can't be telling you all this stuff.'

'Who's to know? And besides,' he leans back in his chair, 'you want to know where to find Jasmine?'

I tell him everything.

'Call me at confused dot com,' he says. 'You have a dead nurse who is your only lead. A girl who ran away from you at the hospital. A woman with a face full of come and another woman trying to get this laptop back.' He blows air out of his mouth. 'Put the kettle on will you?'

I make him his coffee and sit back down.

'What do we do now?' he asks.

'I, not we, follow each trail back to where they meet. Then we find Hepburn and lock her the fuck up.'

'That's a bit woolly, my man. Give me some specifics.'

'Fuck you and your specifics. I need to go and visit this Jasmine.'

'Can I drive?'

The reason that Kenny wants to drive is that Kenny has a new car. It's a Mercedes. Black. Leather seats.

Once inside he pats the steering wheel. 'The Germans certainly know how to build cars.'

I just look at him. 'By fuck, am I in the wrong job.'

We coast along the road in silence as I try to make sense of the various strands of evidence. Just what is happening here eludes me for the moment. All of these women are connected in some way, and one of them will lead me to Audrey/Lucy Hepburn. I'm sure of it.

We're just off Paisley Road West in a council estate. I scan the street on the way in. No sign of a red Clio. The house is red brick, mid-terraced and has a small, neat front garden. The door opens at the first knock.

'Yes?' a woman says from the partially opened door-way.

'Can I speak to Jasmine, please?' I ask.

255

The woman has the same shape of face and eyes as Jasmine and the same bleached hair, tanned face look, except her hair's styled shorter and she's about four stones heavier. She's wearing a pink halter-neck top. There's a gap between her top and her trousers, from which juts an apron of belly, complete with piercing. I want to tell her that it is less than flattering, but I'm barely the real police, who made me the fashion police?

'Sorry, guys. She is not in,' she says in that exaggerated way some people do when they are making an effort not to speak in slang, where every syllable is carefully uttered. Her eyes move from me to Kenny. Her smile wavers when she looks at him. 'Sorry, gentlemen. If you will excuse me,' she's shutting the door as she speaks. 'I'm in the middle of my favourite TV programme.'

Kenny brushes past me and puts a hand out to stop the door from closing.

'What programme's that, doll? I've got you down as a woman who likes her Casualty, or Holby City. One of those programmes where people end up in the hospital.'

She is quicker to pick up on the threat in the words than I am. Her face pales under her tan and her hand moves to her throat. 'No, The Bill is more my sort of thing.' If she's intimated by Kenny she's doing an okay job of hiding it.

I turn side on to Kenny and glare at him. My eyes are telling him that this is not the way I do things. He shrugs and steps back as if to say, okay we'll do it your way.

'When are you expecting her back?'

'You know these young girls. Do as they please nowadays,' she laughs. Her laugh is high and nervous.

'Do you know where she's gone or when she's coming back?' I ask.

'Not a clue.' Another laugh which is just as brittle as the first. 'Whenever she feels like it I s'pose.'

'Who's she with?'

'Dunno.'

'So you're telling me your daughter is out God knows

where, with God knows who you don't know when she'll be back?'

'She's a bloody grown up, mate. She can look eftur hursel'.'

'Sure she can,' I say. 'That's why we're at your door.' Her turn to get the glare. Short of barging past her into the house and holding her down until she tells us something, we're not going to get anywhere here. 'I'll be back.'

We're walking up the path to the car and Kenny speaks out of the side of his mouth. 'Bastard. I wanted to say that.'

'Say what?' I turn to look at him.

He stands tall, stretches out his chest and speaks in a Germanic accent, 'I'll be back.'

We sit in the car for a debrief.

'That was shite, man,' says Kenny. 'Thank fuck I'm not in the police.'

'What would you have done?'

'Pretended I was going to slap her around until she told me.'

'We can't go around intimidating the public.'

'How are the conviction rates?' Kenny asks as he starts the car.

'Could probably be better.'

'I rest my case, your honour.'

Just then a small blue car pulls up in front of us. It's a Vauxhall. From here I can see that the inside has been given the girlie treatment, pink fluffy dice, pink steering wheel cover and pink seat covers. A girl gets out of the car, locks it, hoists her handbag straps through her arm and over her shoulder and walks down the path of the house two doors down from the one we were just in.

'Where to now, big stuff?' asks Kenny.

'Turn off the engine,' I say. This girl looks like she could be the same age as Jasmine. Before I've articulated the need for action I am out of the car and walking towards

257

her. I reach her just as she pushes open her door.

'Excuse me,' I say.

'Aye,' she turns. She has long brown hair that looks like it's been polished. Her outfit is similar to Jasmine's mother, but on this girl it all fits.

'Are you friends with Jasmine from number 62?'

'Who's asking?' She pulls her door shut and faces me.

'Strathclyde Police. Is she a friend of yours?'

'That skanky bitch? You must be joking, mate. If she was on fire I'd be throwing lighter fuel over her.'

'Boy trouble?' I ask.

She gives a smart-alec smile in response and asks, 'What other kind of trouble is there?'

'Her mother says she's not in,' I look over at the door as if Jasmine might materialise in front of it. 'Do you know where she might be?'

'Do I know where she is? I can give you the bloody post-code, mate. She's with my ex-boyfriend and she's bloody welcome to him. Bloody waster.'

I pull out my notepad. 'Name and address?'

She tells me while a smile shines on her face. Ah sweet revenge. 'That's Darren with a double R. And you need to watch out for him. Mean bastard. Muscles out to here,' she holds her hands out wide, 'and he's a black belt. We were finished anyway. She's welcome to him,' as she says this she pulls her hair behind her ear.

'So why are you sounding so pissed off?' I smile at her energy.

She looks at me as if I am from another species. 'There's etiquette, man. You do not go out with a friend's ex-boyfriend until a decent pre-determined period has passed. Anyway ...' she pushes open her door and gives me an impish smile, '...tell them I said hi.'

When I get back to the car Kenny is on his mobile. He's listening and occasionally grunting an acknowledgement that he understands what the other person is saying. He cuts off the call.

'I'll drop you off at yours. Something's come up,' he says. His eyes are aimed straight ahead as he drives but his mind is elsewhere. I study his profile and not for the first time wonder what depths my friend reaches in his other life. The reaction from Jasmine's mother gives only a hint, I'm guessing.

The next door I rap my knuckles on is back across in the Govan area of the city. Another tenement. Another security entrance, but the last person to use it has allowed the door to close itself and therefore it's not properly shut. Darren with a double R lives on the top floor so I'm taking my time walking up the stairs. As I've said before, panting is not a good look when you're asking questions.

The heavy bass of dance music thumps down the stairwell and gets louder as I move upstairs. When I get to the door I have to give a heavy thump so that I'm heard above the noise. The music goes off. I hear a gruff male voice.

'Was that the door?'

I knock again for good measure. Heavy footsteps move across a hall and the door opens. A huge shape fills the space. He's wearing a tight, white T-shirt and pair of denims low on his hips. His arms and shoulders are all exaggerated muscle, with the pipe of a vein showing on his arm here and there. His chest, moulded by his T-shirt is like twin plates of meat. From there he tapers down to a small waist. His hair is short, blond and gelled into spikes, his face clean-shaven and even-featured; handsome even. If he has a black-belt in karate it happened before the muscle, but he looks like a man who can still handle himself.

I've never needed to get involved in many fights. My motto is get in hard and fast and get back out again. At the first sign of trouble I'll aim for his nose. A good-looking guy like him will be keen to save his profile. Rather than hit me back he'll be off to the nearest casualty ward to get his nose set.

'Can I speak to Jasmine, please?' I'll start off being polite.

'You the police?' He appraises me.

'You a bouncer?' I ask. Now I recognise the stance. Confidence, calmness and an air of don't fuck with me goes a long way in fending off a threat. This is good news. Bouncers rely on a good relationship with the police in case things get a bit hairy in the pubs and clubs. Therefore he's not going to want to antagonise me.

He smiles. 'You got me. Come in,' he says and moves out of the way. He guides me into a living room that is purely male and functional.

Jasmine is there and she is standing up and shouting at Darren. 'What the fuck are you doing?' she flings an arm in my direction. 'I came here so you could protect me and you invite him in!'

'Jas, honey. You didn't tell me he was the polis.'

She pulls her neck in. 'You're the polis? How did you find me?' Her expression grows thoughtful. 'You didn't say you were a policeman? What were you doing with that Kenny character?'

'Yes. One of your neighbours. You didn't ask. And none of your business,' I answer each question in turn.

'Colleen told you where I was? What a bitch!'

A smile tugs at the sides of Darren's mouth.

'Jasmine, have a seat,' I say. With a look of surprise that she is actually doing what I say, Jasmine sits. Darren sits beside her, puts an arm over her shoulder and I sit on the chair opposite.

'Am I in trouble? And how do you know Kenny O'Neill? I could pure kill that Colleen. Bet she couldn't wait to get her own back. Cannae bear the thought of you and me together, Darren.' Jasmine says. 'Did she look miserable?' she asks me. 'Bet she was pure miserable.' She turns to Darren and punches his arm. 'And did you just smile when Colleen's name was mentioned?'

'No offence, Jasmine, but do you ever shut up?' I say.

'Kenny?' asks Darren with a thoughtful look. 'Kenny

O'Neill?' He pulls his arm away. 'What are you doing with Kenny O'Neill? That man's trouble.' Darren looks angry. And a little worried.

'Jasmine, you might well be in trouble if you don't tell me what you know about Lucy Hepburn.' I need to get this meeting on track before these two combust.

'She's dead. What else is there to know?' she answers and flicks an invisible something from her leg.

'Last time we spoke you gave me the details of five different women with that name. How did you know I was talking about the one that died?'

'Just made sense,' she mumbles.

'Why?'

'Dunno,' she answers eventually. The sleeves of her jumper are long enough to cover her hands. The only part that is showing are the tips of her fingers. She's picking at a nail, looking half her age.

'Jasmine, what I told you the first time we met wasn't a lie. A child's life could be in danger if you don't tell me what you know.'

She says nothing. Just stares at her hands. This makes me realise how young this girl really is. Barely out of her teens and she still displays a teenage response.

'Jas,' says Darren. 'Help the man.'

'Jasmine. Look at me,' I say. She lifts her head up and does so. 'Do you understand what I'm saying?'

'Yes.'

'Can't hear you.'

'YES.'

'So tell me.'

'We got a letter through to say that this woman had died. Natural causes.'

'Didn't it strike you as odd that someone that age, who was healthy enough to hold down a job, had died of natural causes?' I ask.

'Nope. You see all sorts of things in that place. Besides you don't have time to ask questions. You just fill in forms and keep the piles of papers down as low as you can.'

'What next?'

She exhales sharply. 'Then we sent off a request for the death certificate, and diarised a chaser.'

'Do you remember the address you sent it to? Or the person who sent in the letter?'

'You kidding? Do you have any idea how much paper I touch in a day in that place?'

'Then what?' I keep my focus on Jasmine, but I can see that Darren is edging further and further away from her.

'Then,' she exhales, long and slow, 'then a woman came up to me in the car park at the hospital. Gave me one hundred pounds and asked me to get rid of the Hepburn file.' She looks at me and then Darren. 'Easy money, right? What's the harm?'

I allow this information to sink into my subconscious; I don't want to focus on it just yet. The implications are important, but I need more from Jasmine first.

'Could you describe this woman?'

'Average height, short dark hair,' she makes a face, 'dressed expensively but pure frumpy. Sunglasses. Big sunglasses that covered half her face and it wasn't even sunny.'

'A local accent?' I ask.

She studies me, 'Aye, but she was posher 'n me.'

'How did she know to pick you?' I ask. 'There are any number of people who work in that place who might like an extra hundred pounds. Why you?'

'Dunno what you mean. What are you tryin' to say, mister?' She's sitting tall in her chair and her mouth is pinched tight as she speaks.

'Had you met Hepburn before she died?'

She doesn't answer me.

'Were you mates with Hepburn?'

'Nut,' she screws up her eyes and tries to stare me down.

'You were. That's why this woman chose you. She knew you would do it.'

'That's no true, mister. You're doin' that thing where...'

'Hepburn was your mate and she knew she could call on you to help. Man are you in trouble.'

'Nah, mate you've got it all wrang,' she's leaning forwards towards me.

'We're talking child abuse. You've aided and abetted. Prison sentence ...' I suck at my teeth, '...ten years. And those that harm kiddies get a nasty time in prison.'

'For fucksake, Jas,' says Darren. 'What the fuck's going on?'

'Darren. Darren,' she reaches for his hand. He pulls away from her. 'It was only a wee bit of smack. That's all. Just a wee ...'

'Fuck me,' he jumps to his feet. 'You're dealing. In a fucking hospital.' He rubs his head and looks at me. 'Man, I had no idea about this. I am totally clean. Totally.'

I believe him on the recreational drug front, but I wonder what a test on steroids would show.

'Darren,' Jasmine is pleading.

'Izzat how you know Kenny O'Neill? Fuck. Jasmine. You brought drugs to my door!'

'Guys,' I interrupt. 'We need to get this straight before you go into meltdown. Jasmine, am I right in saying that you sold drugs to Hepburn.'

'Aye,' she nods, defeated.

'How many times?'

'A couple.'

'So the hundred quid was a sweetener. The real issue was that this woman would grass you up to the authorities if you didn't do as she asked.'

She nods.

Darren has walked out of the room. Jasmine follows him with her eyes. She rubs at her left eye. Then her right. She has gone several shades lighter.

'What did you do with the file?

'Put it in along with patient files. In among the Macs.'

Chapter 42

'Who the hell are you?' asked the man who came out of the door to accost Jim. He appeared to be in his mid-thirties, wearing a pair of dark blue trousers and an open necked shirt over his slim build. He had a long, thin face that was pale apart from the dark shadows under his eyes. 'Are you from a newspaper? You vultures do my head in. Away and piss off. It's no as if we've had enough to deal with.'

Jim prepared to speak back to him in the same manner when the part of his brain that was still working spotted the man's stance, his certainty, and allowed what he said to sink in. From a newspaper?

Jim's confidence in his mission evaporated and he wondered what in hell he had just walked into. 'Do you live …I was here just a …' he shook his head as if trying to make sense of everything that had happened over the last few days. The way things were going he wouldn't be surprised if gravity reversed and he went floating up into the sky.

The man walked out of his doorway and stepped into the grass patch that had moments ago given Jim visual access to his living room. 'Are you looking for someone, mate?' His earlier aggression had softened a little, but there was a degree of concern in his tone.

There was no car in the drive and there had been no sign of movement with the house's walls or Jim would never have dreamed of peering in the window.

'I'm sorry,' said Jim. 'I must be confused. I thought I had dinner here the other week with a friend called Moira and her son Erskine,' said Jim.

'Erskine? You say *her* son's name was Erskine?' the

man asked, his voice rising in alarm.

Jim took a step back and held up his hand. 'I'm really sorry, mate. There's been some sort of misunderstanding.' He turned and walked towards his car.

'How do you know my son's name?'

'I was here just the other week. Moira invited my wife and I for ...'

'Moira? Moira Shearer?'

'Is that her surname?' Jim inwardly grimaced. He hadn't even bothered to find out the woman's surname. 'So you'll be Mr Shearer then.' He relaxed.

'What? My name's McKee. Rob McKee. And Erskine is not Moira's son.'

'I ...eh...but ...' began Jim. Will somebody please tell me what the fuck is going on, he thought.

'I think you'd better come in,' said Rob.

The interior was just as Jim remembered from his last visit. Rob guided him in to the living room and watched him as he viewed the room.

Rob studied him for a moment and then asked. 'You've been in here before, haven't you?'

Jim nodded. The room was pretty much the same. Everything about it was recognisable. It was the same room. The same house, after all. There was something not quite right though, but he couldn't pinpoint what it was.

'As I said, Moira invited my wife and me over for dinner.'

'And you came over here to see if you could see Moira?' asked Bob.

'Oh I know where Moira is, Rob,' said Jim. 'What I need to know is what she's up to.'

'Want a beer, Jim?' asked Rob. 'I've got a feeling that this is going to take some time.'

Rob vanished, then returned with a bottle of Stella Artois for each of them. Between gulps from his bottle, Jim told Rob his story.

'So she told you Erskine was her son and that I, or some mythical person had stolen him from her?' Rob was

265

sitting forward in his chair, pointing his empty bottle at Jim. He leaned back in his chair, his mouth pursed in thought. 'Bloody hell. She seemed all right, like. A bit flirty, but good with Erskine.'

Jim rubbed his forehead, feeling the shame of his submission to this flirting.

'You know, what you're saying throws everything she told me up in the air. As well as making me think of the similarities between us. We are both working fathers, struggling with a solitary child, a boy, both our wives are having a tough time.'

'Your wife ...?' Jim assessed Rob afresh. Now that he mentioned the situation with his wife, Jim noted again the strain in his face, the pouches of grey under his eyes.

'She's in hospital. Head injury. Would you believe she fell down some stairs? In a shopping centre of all places. She hates lifts. I told her I would see her on the top floor. Try explaining all of that to the police.'

'How's Erskine taking it?'

'The wee soul's doing okay. Well he was until ...he had his accident.' Rob swallowed and shifted his view from Jim to the floor, to the window and back again, clearly uncomfortable. 'That's why I got it into my head you were a journalist. Those pricks just prey on bad news to good people.'

Bad news, thought Jim. What's going on here?

'Come to think of it that was the last day I saw Moira,' said Rob as if he was having half a conversation out loud and half internally. 'I was convinced she blamed herself. Just a couple of weeks ago.'

'What happened?' asked Jim. 'Where is Erskine?'

'He's sleeping. He...' Rob paused as if he had trouble forming the words, '... lost his eye. His right one. And it's all my stupid fault.' Rob rubbed his forehead, then his chin, agitation running through his muscles like a current. 'I should know better than to go off to work leaving planks of wood and tools lying in the garden. I was building him a den, you know. Something to cheer

266

him up while his mother was …' Rob broke off, his voice thick with emotion. 'I can't tell you how awful …' his voice broke.

Jim could feel Rob's anguish. 'Man, that is terrible,' he offered, not knowing what to say. What could he say that might help?

'It seems he was running and he tripped and fell into the …I left a pile of old planks …I was going to build a den among the bushes at the back of the garden. Boys love that kind of thing right?'

Jim nodded.

'He tripped and fell. A nail was embedded in his eye …I wasn't even here and I can still hear his screams.' Rob stared off into some indefinable distance, heating his thoughts on a guilt that would never wear down.

'Man that is tough,' said Jim and decided he'd already said something similar, so he'd best just shut up for a while. The two men sat for minutes in silence, each lost in their own thoughts. Something occurred to Jim.

'When did it happen?' Jim asked.

'Not sure. A couple of weeks ago. Three weeks maybe. It was a Monday, I'm sure of that.'

Monday, thought Jim. It was a Monday when Moira came over to his claiming that her son had been stolen from her by his father.

'I know what's different, in here. The photos. There's loads more photos.' Jim looked around himself. Different sizes and different frames. Different family members.

'It's always like this,' said Rob. 'My missus loves a house full of photos. Says it makes up for only having one child.'

'Yes, but they were evidence that Moira was not who she claimed to be. So she hid half of them that day we came for dinner.'

'Crafty bitch,' said Rob as if impressed despite himself.

Jim thought some more. A thought that chilled him to the marrow and made him want to rush out and visit his family. 'Rob, are you sure Erskine's trip was an accident?'

'Oh, c'mon man. Now you're getting a bit weird on me.

Okay, I think we can both agree that Moira has lied and schemed. But to deliberately hurt Erskine like that? No. I'm sure that's not her game. She just wants free room and board.'

'Ben liked...sorry, likes her. Did Erskine get on okay with her?'

'Yes,' Rob said almost automatically. Then he thought about it some more. 'Yes, he did. I think he enjoyed the female company given that his mum wasn't available.' Rob gave a weak smile, as if he had only a few left and he didn't want to be wasteful. 'He loved bedtimes. He enjoyed her stories about pirates and smugglers in caves. He kept badgering her about when she was going to take him to see the caves.'

They both fell silent again. Another thought occurred to Jim.

'How did you meet Moira? How did she get to be your part-time nanny?'

'Somebody at the hospital I got talking to recommended her. I can't remember her name,' he paused. 'It might have been Lilly? Lucy? It began with an L.'

Chapter 43

Driving away from Darren and Jasmine's flat I look at the clock on the dashboard. Just gone five pm. If I phone Bob at the Southern General Hospital and tell him what Jasmine has to say, he might just have time to have a quick look for the Hepburn file before he finishes for the day.

I park the car on the side of the road and pull my phone from my pocket. I have a missed call. No number has been stored in the memory, which suggests it was a phone call from a place of work. I try my answering service. Whoever it was chose not to leave a message. Couldn't have been that important then. Daryl or Alessandra maybe?

Na. The bastards will be so delighted to have a real case they've probably forgotten I exist.

From the directory I get a number for the hospital. I ask to get put through to medical records. The phone rings out. They've probably all gone home.

Back at the flat I change out of my suit and put on shorts and a T-shirt. Then I throw some chicken, pak choi, beansprouts and garlic into the wok. I wash it down with some tap water. All very tasty and healthy. There is however a very large bar of chocolate in the kitchen cupboard calling my name.

I put on the TV and watch the news. War and famine. Violence on women and children. People dying from heat exhaustion during a heatwave in Eastern Europe. Desperate stuff. This is what we get served up several times a day to in order to fulfil our public duty of staying informed. Question: do we have to wallow in it? Another question: is there nothing new in the world that is good *and* newsworthy?

I jump to my feet, pace three steps to the machine and turn it off. Instantly the noise and gloom dies. Turning, I see a book on the sofa. The last time I picked it up a feather fell from its pages. I shiver. How had it got there? Surely Maggie wouldn't use it as a bookmark.

Someone put it there. Feathers don't just find themselves between the pages of books. If it was deliberate, only one person knows how that might affect me.

For chrissake, McBain. You need a dose of perspective. Leonard's not going to break into your home just to place a small, white feather between the pages of a book.

A book that Maggie gave me. I should give her a call.

Nah.

If she wanted to speak to me she would have rung.

Maybe she's waiting for you to call her, dumb-ass.

In the meantime, there is still that gigantic bar of chocolate in the cupboard. It's shouting; eat me, eat me, eat me.

I flop on to the sofa and thumb through the book. It reminds me I should meditate more. Theresa introduced me to it not long after we first met. She convinced me of its merits after proving to me that sex was spectacular afterwards. So relaxed did we become that our inhibitions melted and all that was important was now. Her skin. My hands. My tongue. Blending into each other till we all but dissolved into a puddle of sweat.

She was good.

Maggie was different. I know it's a capital sin to compare lovers. Here's the thing: try not to.

Where Theresa was all about the moment, Maggie did all she could to make *me* feel good. Where sex with Theresa centred on the flesh and organs, with Maggie the way she looked at me told me she was offering more. There's nothing more flattering than a lover who gives unselfishly.

Anyone for chocolate? I could just have a square. Two

270

squares wouldn't kill.

Tomorrow I have an appointment with the very lovely Ms Gibson. Wonder what her marital status is? Maybe I should give her office a call and cancel. Can't be arsed with all that introspection. Sensible me pipes up and says if I don't go it will give the suits the chance to put me on permanent leave.

I open the book at random. A quote in italics draws my eye. It's a line from a poem by Nicholas Boileau.

In vain he flees his troubles on a horse —
They share his saddle and see him on his course.

That's weird. I shiver. Maybe I should go after all.

For the rest of the evening I channel hop. There's nothing on all of the channels worth staying with for more than a minute. Before I go to bed I go through to the kitchen, pick the chocolate out of the cupboard and toss it in the bin. Feeling virtuous I brush my teeth, peel off my clothes and jump into bed. As I fall asleep my last thought is; I'll take the chocolate out of the bin in the morning.

My night is broken; jagged with bouts of staring into the black and periods of sleep. Eventually I dream. Colours blend into white. Then red. The red flakes off into a blizzard. This slows and congeals. A face forms in a puddle. The eyes open. Leonard stares at me and grins. His knife flashes.

I sit up, heart hammering. Fuck. That was scary. Adrenalin sparks under my skin. I allow my head to clear, gravity to register and then walk naked through to the bathroom.

Examining my face in the mirror I promise myself that I will not let Leonard win. He's history. The people who harmed his brother are all dead. There's no reason to come after me.

Besides, he's long since gone. He'll be hiding in Brazil, or somewhere. My eyes stare back at me unconvinced.

A long satisfying piss, wash of the hands and as I brush

my teeth a nagging thought tugs at my mind. I have something to do this morning and I can't quite remember what.

My mobile rings.

I run back through to the bedroom and pull it from the charger. It's Elaine Gibson.

'Did I disturb you, DI McBain?' she asks.

'Not at all.' I catch my profile in the full length mirror of the wardrobe. And immediately suck in my belly. Then I let it out again. What a tosser. As if she can see me. 'I haven't forgotten if that's why you're calling.' As I say this I'm thinking, boy is she persistent.

'There's been a change of venue. It's a wee bit unconventional, but I think it's worth it. I'll explain when I see you.'

'OK,' I say and wonder what she's up to. Then I realise that with my left hand I'm tugging at my scrotum. What's that all about? Nervous wee boy stuff? If she knew what I was doing she'd feel all *icky*. I tuck my hand under my right armpit.

'Do you know The Lighthouse in Mitchell Lane? Go up the escalator and then get in the lift. Get off at the top. You're looking for Viewing Platform Six. Oh and can you be there half an hour earlier than we arranged?' She hurries on and doesn't give me a chance to answer. 'Great. Bye.'

At the allotted time I am at the location as suggested by Ms Gibson. Before I left the house I called Bob at Medical Records. His phone went straight to answer machine. I'll try again later.

I park my car in the city centre and struggle past thousands of fierce-looking shoppers, each of them carrying bags with the names of designers blazing from them. The Lighthouse is tucked in just off Buchanan Street and is the venue for the Scottish Centre for Architecture and Design.

The lift doors open at the top and I walk out into a small space with windows on all but the wall with the lift doors.

Some of the windows are panoramic, offering spectacular views across the city while others are the size of arrow slits in some ancient tower and set into verdigris copper tiles.

'Incredible, isn't it?' asks Elaine. She's sitting on a low chair. There's another chair spaced at a comfortable distance and a small table holds an aluminium flask, a jug of milk, two white cups and a bowl of sugar.

I walk over to the main window and look over the rooftops of the city's shops and offices.

'This is amazing,' I agree. 'You'd never know this was here.' I look over at her as she tries not to look too pleased with herself. 'How, and ...why?' Then a thought occurs to me. 'This isn't a date, is it?'

'The How...I give the building a lot of business and they owe me a favour. The Why...my feeling is that I needed to get you away from the usual office surroundings,' she answers. 'Most of my colleagues would frown at this, but you are an unusual man, DI McBain. And sometimes one has to think outside the box.'

I sit. She pours. We sip.

'So where do we begin?' I ask.

'Wherever you want,' she answers.

'I take it you belong to the non-directional school of counselling?'

'I belong to the do whatever it takes to get the job done school.'

'Does that include dinner and a couple of glasses of wine?'

'Clients are out of bounds. Romantically speaking,' she answers. She couldn't be more comfortable if she was sitting in her own living room, wearing a big pair of pink fluffy slippers and sipping a warm cup of cocoa. 'Could we put that one to bed, Ray?' Then she smiles at the less than carefully chosen metaphor. Perhaps she's not as comfortable as her body language suggests.

'Tell me why you think you are here, Ray,' she says.

'In a nutshell, my bosses are pissed off at my tendency to get into trouble.'

'What's the pay-off?' She looks deep into my eyes.

'The pay-off? For my behaviour you mean?' I scratch my cheek. 'I get the job done.'

'Might it be a form of self-sabotage? By all accounts you were marked for the top of your chosen career very early on. Perhaps that's not how you see yourself.'

'Go on,' I say with a little irritation. I'm irritated because I recognise the possibility in her words and I want to buy myself some time before I have to answer the question.

'We all have an internal construct of how we see ourselves. A view of how we fit in the world. And if the image that the world has of us differs, our subconscious finds a way to re-align our internal world with the external.'

'An internal construct? Sounds a bit airy-fairy if you ask me.'

She doesn't answer with words, instead she arches an eyebrow. If she thinks the silence is going to force me to speak then she's wrong.

'How would you describe your self-worth?'

'A pot of gold.'

'Sorry?'

'At the end of the rainbow. Guarded by an army of leprechauns.'

'Interesting analogy,' she says and I curse inwardly. What started as a flippant comment has come out as a damning statement. One that she won't fail to read.

'So you ascribe it as having some value. But out of reach?'

I suddenly feel as uncomfortable as if I had a thistle stuck up my arse. My head and neck feel warm and my hands are shiny with sweat. My face is turned to the right and I study the roof of the building that houses the Gallery of Modern Art. The rows of small, glass pyramids that provide light to the rooms below have just become completely fascinating.

'Tell me three things you remember most about your parents,' she says.

274

'Between them, they excelled at absentee-ism, addictive substances and hurting each other.'

'Do you blame yourself?'

'No. Why should I?'

'Who is talking now? Ray McBain the clever policeman? If wee Ray McBain the six-year-old were to speak, how would he answer that question?'

My mind fills with images of my parents, their faces twisted with hate and anger. They turn to me and I imagine their expressions are now full of disappointment.

This time it's me who breaks the long silence. I surprise myself with my honesty. 'He'd say that the grown-ups are always right and that he must have something terribly wrong with him that makes the two people he loves most in the world hurt each other so much.'

'How about the orphanage? Tell me three words to describe your time there.'

'Scary ...lonely ...and scary again.' I attempt a laugh at my weak joke.

'How does the boy feel about being sent there?' Her expression has slipped out of neutral and has softened with empathy. I feel my throat tighten and my eyes sting.

I take a deep breath and allow the tears to fall.

'That he deserved it.'

Before I know it our time is up and in silence we enter the lift. From there we take the escalator down to the main entrance.

'I feel we made some real progress today, Ray. Thank you,' she says as she shakes my hand. Then I remember that I'm wearing the same jacket as yesterday. I pat my pocket and feel the photo. I take it out and show it to her.

'This woman is linked to a case of mine,' I say quickly. Don't want her to think that I am prone to showing women pornographic images. At first she is discomfited by the image, then her professional demeanour asserts itself.

'And you want to know what exactly?'

275

I explained how I had come into possession of the photograph, '...and this mystery woman has been trying to get it back.'

'Do you think she was being bribed by the dead nurse?'

'Makes sense. It's a piece of a puzzle and I'm trying to get some details on the personalities involved so I can understand them and work out the connections.'

'My first question is what's in it for her? At one level, it's a classic pose of male domination. We can only see one penis, but the amount of semen on her face suggests there is more than one man. She's an older woman. Is she starved for affection? Also, this is an act that is devoid of intimacy. She's lonely. Some women can only dream of getting so much male attention.' She flaps a hand at my expression of disgust. 'Yes, it's extreme, but if people continually suppress a long held longing, it will force itself out in an extreme manner.' She stares into the distance as she thinks some more. 'She's on her knees, but she's brought these men to a point where they lose control. Although the feminists might not agree, she's using her power. Perhaps she has a public life that demands moral correctness and in private she relishes another world altogether.'

Starved for affection. A public life that demands moral correctness. Sometimes all you need is to hear things said out loud. A note of alarm sounds deep in my brain. I look at the picture again. I turn it at an angle so I have a head that appears upright.

She smiles. 'However, that could all be psychological babble and the woman simply has a thing for semen.'

'Fuck me,' I say as the name to the face pops into my head. 'I know who this is.'

Chapter 44

She has been playing me for a fool all along. She pretends that I've won a victory, allows a little of her real emotion to slip through, gives me a little piece of truth and the cumulative effect is that she gets me off her back. I'm almost impressed at her performance, if only her self-serving attitude hasn't affected the life of a child.

As I drive I fumble with my mobile and headset. I really should have done this before I started to drive out of the Mitchell Street car park. Corkscrew turns are not the easiest to negotiate while steering with one hand. I consider calling Bob at Medical Records. Then decide against it for the moment. I know who I'm after. I can chase him up for verification when we come to close the case. I dial a different number.

'Hey, boss.'

'Alessandra, are you busy?'

'Up to my eyes in it, mate.'

'I need a woman.'

'Can you not pay like you normally do?'

'Very funny. This is in a professional capacity.'

'I stand by my original statement.'

'Listen. I have a strong lead on the Browning and Craig case. I need to bring a woman in for questioning. I need a female presence.'

'Right.' That's what I love about Alessandra Rossi. Immediate understanding of the implications on a case. She could have given me a row for not obeying the suits. Instead, she goes straight to thinking about how this helps us catch the perps. I hear a voice questioning what's going on. Alessandra mumbles something to someone I'm guessing is Daryl, then comes back to the phone. 'Sorry, Ray. We've got half a dozen of Glasgow's best-dressed gangsters in here for this Kay case. We're going to be here for days questioning them.'

'You'll not get anywhere with them.'

'That's what I'm worried about. This lot are tighter than a nun's...'

'Alessandra, you won't get anywhere because this is not really a gang war thing. It's a love thing.'

'Eh?'

I tell her what Dan Donovan explained over a newspaper.

'So,' Alessandra processes the information, 'if we find the gay lover, we find the killer. We stop the excuse for the gang war. The city becomes a safer place. Any ideas?'

'I only met the son once, years ago at a charity dinner. He was with a lawyer-friend and a couple of women.'

'Fag hags?' asks Alessandra.

'You own a delightful turn of phrase, Miss Rossi,' I say as I try to remember the dinner and with the benefit of hindsight I connect the dots. After the meal was served and the band struck up some tunes, the two couples were barely off the dance floor. Rarely have I seen men willing to dance quite as much. Not unusual in itself, I'm partial to a wee dance myself, once suitably relaxed. However, when the smoochy music came on, they all sat down and both genders acted as if they were on their own. I can see the men now in my mind's eye. If I had an operational gaydar I would have suspected, but my thoughts tend not to go there. I couldn't give a shit what genital equipment other people demand in a lover. Life's difficult enough without casting those sorts of judgements in my view.

I stop at a red light on West George Street. A horde of men and women in business suits cross from both directions. Almost everyone is wearing black. An occasional splash of colour from the odd tie and ladies blouse. Everyone is wearing an identical expression, focused on their internal world, worrying about the next meeting or the next deal.

'You need to find a young-ish corporate lawyer. Blond. His hair is receding, late twenties-early thirties. Slim, good-looking,' I speak my thoughts aloud.

'Keep going,' says Alessandra. 'Sounds just my type.'

'I think you're forgetting something, Alessandra. We're talking suspect in a gay lover killing.'

'There's always some kind of trade-off with the lookers,' she laughs and then sobers. 'And now I'm freaking myself out.'

'How are you going to play this one out?'

'Peters won't want to know. It's not his idea. And we're looking for the proverbial needle. Throw a stick down Glasgow city centre and you'll strike a corporate lawyer.'

'Has the father been in?'

'Yes. With a team of lawyers.'

'Make up an excuse. Get him back in. Then hit him between the eyes.'

Alessandra is silent while she processes this.

'A little bit of the truth can go a long way, Miss Rossi.' I'm thinking of a certain woman and how she played me as I say this.

'Where will you be?' Alessandra asks.

'A little bit of unofficial surveillance,' I reply and give her the address.

'Why are you going there again?' she asks. 'Is that not where Violet Hogg lives?'

Chapter 45

Jim sat outside his parents' house for what felt like hours. He couldn't bring himself to go through the actions required to go inside. Pulling at the door handle, moving his legs out of the car and walking up the path was beyond him.

He was so tired. And confused. What was going on? How did it all get to this?

Sure he had told some lies, but they were white lies; designed to help the situation. He didn't deserve to be in such an unholy mess.

If he was tired how must Angela be feeling?

Jim felt a crushing weight of guilt that his actions had contributed to the situation his wife and child now found themselves in. What he would give for a return to happier times.

He thought about the way Angela was the last time he saw her; exhausted, furious and an approximation of the woman he first met.

Then his thoughts were drawn to that first occasion as if he needed the balm of the memory of a time when the world was still recognisably round.

'Don't fancy yours much,' Billy Grant said out of the side of his mouth, while paying full attention to the blond girl dancing in the middle of the floor. Even under the strobe lighting they could see that her hair was a honey blond. It swung from side to side in a solid sheet as she moved to Luther Vandross's *Never Too Much*: a perennial favourite of the DJ.

Billy was his best mate and they were at a club in the city on a typical night out. The aim was, as usual to have a good drink and then pull a bird.

Jim was sure that this was his night. He was wearing a trendy new shirt and he was confident that this change would stand him in good stead.

Neither he nor Billy could take their eyes off the girl with the blond hair and the red blouse. With both hands she piled her hair on to the top of her head, enjoyed a breeze on her neck and then let it fall back down on to her shoulders. Her eyes were closed as she mouthed the words of the song. Locked in the rhythm and the moment, she looked as if no other place on earth could do it for her.

'Killer tits,' whistled Billy. 'You can dance with her pal.' He moved past Jim and took a step on to the floor.

'Piss off you tosser. I got the ugly bird the last time,' Jim pulled on his arm and strode past. Almost running to make sure he got there first, he kept ahead of Billy. In that well-worn Scottish male courtship movement Jim tapped blondie on the shoulder and started dancing in front of her.

'Cracking song, eh?' He shouted into her ear. She smiled, nodded, closed her eyes and continued to dance as if Jim wasn't there.

Jim looked over at Billy to see that his new dance partner had her mouth pressed against his ear. She was a good bit shorter than Billy and was straining on to her toes to do so. Up close she looked a lot better than he first thought and Jim wondered if he hadn't made a mistake. It didn't look like Billy was going to have much bother warming her up.

'Luther Vandross is the bollocks,' Jim tried to shout above the thump of the baseline. 'Love his stuff.' Inwardly he cursed, what a stupid thing to say.

Again, she opened her eyes, looked at him, nodded and then went back to her dancing. Feeling as socially inept as a man dressed only in a pair of speedos and a gold medallion, Jim danced beside her for the rest of the song, wondering if his arms were swinging too much and praying for the song to end. He'd never felt as if he'd made so poor an impression on a girl before.

'Thanks,' she said when the song ended. She picked up her bag, looked at her pal and walked off the floor.

On each of the following three Saturdays she wasn't there. She appeared, as if by magic on the fourth. Billy and Jim managed to squeeze on to a bare piece of carpet near to her and her pals. Looking through the press of clubbers, he tried to catch her eye.

Nothing.

'Just go up and talk to her, for chrissake,' said Billy.

'Shut up,' Jim sipped at his beer. 'She's not interested.'

'Aye and she never will be if you stand there staring at her like a poofy big fearty.'

'Eh? Can you even understand English?'

'Go and talk to the lassie. Buy her a drink, for fuckssake. Nobody can refuse a free drink.' And there, in a nutshell was Billy's game plan for winning over the fairer sex. The annoying thing was, his record was a good deal healthier than Jim's.

'Right, okay.' He negotiated a path through the crush of people and ignoring the swirl in his stomach he offered her a drink.

'Got one thanks,' she held up her almost full glass as proof.

'Oh c'mon, can you no make this a wee bit easier on me?' he asked.

'I'm trying to save you money.'

A grin. That was good.

'Money is something I'm not short of. Especially when it comes to a beautiful girl.' Jim heard the words coming out of his mouth as if they were in slow motion and prayed that he could reel them back in.

'You don't do this much do you?' She took a sip from her glass.

'Was it that bad?' Jim screwed up his face in anticipation of her answer.

She nodded in commiseration, like a vet telling an owner that their beloved animal was about to be put down. 'Shocking.'

'Okay. You do it.'

'What? Chat you up?'

Jim nodded and took a sip from his bottle, trying to look as cool as she did.

'What's your name?'

'Jim... Jim Hilton.'

'Okay Jim Jim Hilton, what do you do?'

'I'm a bookseller.'

'Wow, I love books. What's it like working in a bookshop, must be wonderful?'

'Oh it has its moments. Like any job I expect.'

'But to be surrounded by all those books...wow. Who's your favourite author?'

Before Jim knew it he had launched into a list of authors and books, encouraged by every nod from the girl in front of him. He stopped speaking after several minutes aware that she was now grinning at him as if he was her prize pupil and he'd just won a gold star.

'What?' he demanded.

'That's how you do it.' She waved her hand in a slow horizontal S and took a bow.

'What ...' Then it dawned on him. 'You are good.'

'The lesson for the day is over. Don't chat up a girl, chat *to* her.'

'What's your name?'

'Angela. Angela Morris.' She grinned in advance of what she knew he was going to do with her name.

'Well, Angela Angela Morris, what do you do?'

'I'm a social worker.'

'Nae luck.' He drank from his bottle and grinned.

She laughed, bending forward as she did so. 'Oh, a sense of humour as well as lots of money, how can a girl say no?'

'Say no to what?'

'A night at the pictures.'

Chapter 46

I'm sitting outside Mrs Hogg's house in Shawlands. It's two o'clock in the afternoon and there is little movement around me. This is the lull before the school run. Then the streets will be full of yummy mummies in their suburban tractors, as they go and pick up their little darlings. It must be a bummer to go and invest in a higher seating position to find out it has been nullified because everyone else has one.

There's no movement behind Hogg's windows. Nor has there been any since I arrived here two hours ago. I wonder if I should add breaking and entering to my list of police sins. Best not. I've given them enough rope to hang me. It's about time I make an effort to keep my job.

Aye, right.

I sit low in my seat. Don't want anyone to get a good look at me. Although I have been here twice already and someone's sure to have clocked me on my previous visits. Perhaps that's something I should play on.

Forty-five minutes later and a young woman leaves the house next door and walks to her Toyota Rav4 parked in her drive. She's carrying an infant that she straps into the backseat. While she's doing so I approach her.

'Excuse me,' I say while I'm still a safe distance from her. 'Do you have any idea where Mrs Hogg is?'

She stops what she is doing and faces me. There is judgement in her expression and a little wariness. And then some form of recognition when I introduce myself.

'Yes, Mrs ...I mean Violet did tell me that she was helping the police.' She formed an expression of not so polite interest. 'Something about children that were being abused by some horrible women?'

'Can you tell me where Mrs Hogg is?' I ask, ignoring the question.

'Sorry,' she replies with a smile. 'No idea. She's probably on some committee or other. Feeding the starving millions somewhere.' She says this as if Hogg's generosity is at best some form of eccentricity. 'Sorry.'

She gets in the car, starts it up and reverses down the short drive into the street. As she does so I pretend to go back to my car, with the view that as soon as she is out of sight I'll be peering in Hogg's windows looking for a way in.

She offers me a cheery wave as she passes. I wave back with one hand as I stretch my seat-belt into position with the other and watch her in my rear-view mirror. Her car turns left at the end of the street and I'm out of my car.

The back door is wood, painted white. There are three windows at street level. None of them are double glazed, in contrast to those in the front. Perhaps she ran out of money before she could replace them all.

There are three refuse bins, green, brown and blue to one side of the door and three red ceramic plant pots in a group on the other side. I check under the pots in the off chance. You see people in movies doing it all the time. Leaving a spare key in a secret place just in case. However, Mrs Hogg isn't that careless. There are no keys hidden under her plant pots.

I look behind me up the length of the garden. The boundary at the far end is marked out by a line of tall conifers. This means that I am not in view of her rear neighbours.

An unlocked window is as good as an unlocked door to a would-be burglar, they say. I check all the windows. The one that looks into the kitchen has a small panel window in the upper centre of the pane of glass, that is indeed open, and a panel to the right. Perhaps I can reach in through the upper panel, and open the side window from there. I pull the green bin over to the middle of the window and pull myself on top of it. I put my arm inside

285

and stretch down to the handle. Can't reach it. I push my body against the glass in the hope of giving me more arm room inside. Still can't reach it. I pull my arm back out of the space and lower myself to the ground. Fuck. I guess it would have been too good to be true.

I move to the side and start to push the bin back into place. Something glints in the space where it had rested. I lean forward and pick it up. Bugger me, a key. The woman is careless after all.

I replace the bin and unlock the door. The kitchen is clean and tidy. Apart from a plate and a floral mug on the worktop at the side of the sink. The plate holds a half-eaten sandwich and the tea in the mug has barely been sipped. Makes me think that our Mrs Hogg had an unplanned meeting to attend.

The rest of the house is similarly clean and tidy. In the bedroom the bed is made and no dirty linen litters the carpet. The living room is dust free and even the second downstairs bedroom that is being used as an office is an essay in tidiness.

The desk is along the far wall and is lined on either side by bookcases. The books themselves are non-fiction, stories of worthy individuals. A Dell computer sits under the desk, with a flat-screen monitor on top. I switch it on. The screen fills with light and colour and the usual music sounds from it.

The computer demands a password. I key in *Violet*. Nothing. I try *Hepburn*. Nothing. With a grin I try *Bukkake*. Nothing.

What was her husband's name? Tommy. I key it in. Nothing. I'd bet any money it was his date of birth. Where could I find that?

I hear the thunk of a car door and move to the window. It's the neighbour and her children. A small boy and a girl chatter all the way from the car to the front door, each vying for the lion's share of their mother's attention. I see her look over her shoulder towards my car as if looking to attract my attention. Good. The light must be reflecting off the windshield and spoiling her view. She must think I am still inside.

I walk into the hallway. This space is bare apart from a large wooden framed mirror and a shelf of matching wood. The shelf houses a phone, a pad of paper and a pencil. The shelf is completely free of dust. I pick the phone up and press last number redial. The phone rings out and is answered within four rings.

'Good afternoon, Royal Bank of Scotland, Shawlands branch. Molly speaking. How can I help you?'

'Jings, Molly,' I say. 'That's quite a mouthful.'

'We do have our standards, Mr ...' I can hear the smile in her voice.

'Mr Wrong Number. Sorry to waste your time, Molly.'

I replace the phone in its cradle and as I do so look more closely at the pad of paper. It's in a nice pastel shade of lilac and has the remnants of the last page still attached where it was torn off. I hold the pad up to the light. I can barely see the imprint from the missing page, but the writing forms the shape that an address might when written down on an envelope. Not many people hand write these days. If this turns out to be a clue we have to be grateful to Mrs Hogg's age.

It's a tad Enid Blyton and *The Secret Seven*, but I rub the lead from the pencil across the page in the hope that something shows. She can't be too heavy on the page when she writes as I can't make out much on the paper. I've got a capital B on the end of the first line. Strange place for a capital letter. Nothing much thereafter until the last line. Reads like Troon. Under that I can make out a pound sign. The first number is too faint, but this is then followed by what looks like three zeros.

Chapter 47

I'm back in the car after searching the house and feeling more than a little disappointed. There's nothing on view that might give me more information on how to find Hepburn. All I got for my efforts was something that might be an address in Troon and a bruise on the inside of my upper arm from the window pane.

So far I've been flying by the seat of my threadbare pants. I need to have some sort of strategy for when Mrs Hogg appears. She's sure to recognise my car when she drives into the street. That would give her time to prepare for whatever I have to say. It's best if I surprise her.

I start the car and move down a couple of houses, parking on the far side of a large blue Ford. In position I check my wing mirror. I have clear visual access to her drive. Now I just have to sit and wait some more.

A couple of boys are out on their bikes, weaving up and down the street, aimlessly passing the hours before supper and bed. They cycle a large figure of eight and then go back again. Then they stop, speak to each other, laugh and cycle some more. Thankfully neither came out of the neighbour's house, so they won't report my presence to their mother.

The neighbour is clearly the inquisitive type. Nothing to do all day but housework, daytime TV and childcare. She's no doubt spotted my change of position and wondering why the hell I've moved down here. Something she said earlier leaks into my mind: "children being abused by some horrible women". Not woman. Women. Why would Hogg detail it to her neighbour in the plural? Makes me wonder what exactly her involvement in all of this is.

As far as we know she has provided a reference for Hepburn and a safe house. Is there more?

It's now six-thirty and still no sign of Hogg. I am starving and I need a piss something fierce. Should have gone while I was in her house. There's a half-full bottle of water on the back seat. I could empty that out the window and use it as a temporary toilet. Mind you, all it would take would be for one of the boys to cycle past just as I had my dick in my hand and we'd have a full-blown paedo alert.

To take my mind off my bladder problems I give Alessandra a call. No answer. I try Daryl. No answer. Kenny? He's similarly engaged.

Just call me Ray McBain: Nae Pals.

I send each of them a text. "Call me". Doesn't sound too desperate, right?

I turn on the radio. Chirpy chappy Simon Mayo is doing his utmost to spread cheer to the nation's workers on their way home from another thankless shift. Where does he get his energy? Whatever he's on, I'll have twelve please.

A car parks in front of me. It's Alessandra. She all but bounces out of her car and into mine.

'Ray McBain, I owe you one,' she says eyes large and bright with excitement. She's wired. 'We got the bastard. Broke down and confessed there and then.' She makes a fist, punches the air and whispers. 'Yes.'

'Whoa, soldier,' I say. 'Who's the bastard and where did he breakdown?'

'The lawyer guy. Totally gave himself up. There was much wailing and gnashing of teeth. And a confession.'

'What?'

'The Kay case,' she says and looks at me as if there's dumb, dumber and then me. 'Keep up, McBain. Mind you, Rayo, it's all down to you.' She grips my knee. Looks at her hand. 'Sorry.' She pulls her hand away. 'The gay thing was the break we needed. I acted the daft lassie, paid the father a visit, asked for the girlfriend's contact details. Paid her a wee visit and she told me about where to find the lawyer guy.' Her eyes are shining. 'I'm going to be in the news.' She moves her hand in a slow arc as if it represents a banner headline. 'Promising Young Detective Solves the Crime of the Year.'

'Well done you,' I say, delighted for her. I'm equally delighted that the collar was bugger all to do with DI Peters. We get the bad guy, Alessandra gets the kudos and Peters gets the hump. A win-win situation all round.

'They'd had a lovers' tiff. Gangster's son was putting it about. Lawyer guy was totally in love. He lost it. We have one less mad shagger in Glasgow.' Her expression reads; how easy could it be?

'I've said it before and I'll say it again, Alessandra. You have a wonderful way with words.'

'Thanks.' She couldn't look happier if she'd won the Euromillions draw.

'How was Peters?' I would give my left testicle to be able to see his face.

'Well, I kinda went behind his back,' she laughs and looks at me. 'I had the best teacher. The Chief Super was delighted. Kept saying I was a credit to the Force, while Peters was standing there with a face on him. Looked like a tranny who'd gone on stage only to find out his tights had a huge ladder in them.'

'Shouldn't you be in the pub with the rest of them, having a celebratory beer?'

'That can wait,' she brings her focus to bear on me. 'We have a psycho-bitch to find.'

'Do the suits know where you are?'

'I'm thinking I have some leeway at the moment. Best to use it before you fuck up again.' She grins to show she's only joking. I let it slide. She reminds me of me when I was new and eager. There's nothing quite like cracking that first big case on your own.

'I couldn't have done it without you, Ray.' Her expression grows sombre. 'I'll let the high heid yins know that it was your tip that led to the arrest.'

'You'll do no such thing. You ran with it. You took the chance. You deserve it.'

'Okay,' she gives a delighted shrug, slips her shoes off and puts her stocking feet up on the dash. 'So, bring me up to speed.'

I reach into my pocket and pull out the photograph.

'Eeeeee,' she says and makes a face as she takes it from me. Then she turns the photo to the side. 'Ooooo.' She looks at me. 'It's the quiet ones you have to look out for every time.'

'You know who that is?' I try not to sound annoyed. 'It took me days to work it out.'

She studies the photo some more. 'That is a *lot* of man-juice.'

'Man-juice?'

'What do you want me to call it? Spunk seems too old, sperm too... bourgeois, jizzum... too crude.'

'God I feel old.' I give Alessandra a mock glare. 'Too old to be discussing the nomenclature of semen in the current situation.'

Alessandra looks at me. Opens her mouth. Closes it again and then settles for, 'Whatever'.

She looks at the photo again. Thinks. 'Let me guess. Hogg knows more about Hepburn than she's letting on. She's been giving her some sort of help ...you wanted to know why. This photo gives you the *why*. Hogg is going to lead you to Hepburn.' She says all of this without any questioning tone. I nod. She licks a finger, touches the dashboard and makes a sizzling sound.

'I am soooo hot today.'

'How would you approach the situation next?' I ask, doing my lead detective training thing. Might as well use Alessandra while she's *in the zone.*

'Does Hogg know you have this?'

I shake my head.

'Good. The way I see it we have two choices. One, we keep an eye on her and hope that eventually she leads us to Hepburn. Two, we post it through her door,' her eyes

291

gleam as if she has only just this second thought of that, 'stand back and watch the fireworks. Or three, we confront her with it and demand answers.'

'What is it with you women and numbers?' I ask.

She ignores me. 'My choice would be the latter. The less time it takes to find this Hepburn woman the better.'

Chapter 48

My belly is rumbling like the warning of an approaching storm. And my bladder is under a serious amount of stress.

'How long have you been here?' asks Alessandra.

'Long enough to grow a couple of gray hairs.'

'Want to...?'

'Think I'll go find somewhere to eat. Preferably with a toilet. Need anything?'

Alessandra shakes her head. 'I'm good.'

She gets out of my car and walks over to hers. I can't help but notice how well her trousers sit on the firm cushion of her buttocks. What can I say? I'm a guy, we notice these things.

I drive down to the main drag, walk into the first pub I see and take a leak. Next door we have a fast-food place. A kebab is the first thing I see on the menu. A large lump of meat spins in a vertical roasting position, with fat dripping on to the tray below. Why is it when you are trying to take care of what you place in your mouth, the world conspires against you? I can feel an artery harden as the meat slowly turns. I order one. And hedge my bets with a can of diet Irn Bru.

Minutes later I'm back in position with Alessandra. As I drive past the house I see Hogg's car in the driveway.

'When did she arrive?' I ask Alessandra, while wiping my cheek with the back of my hand. I can feel a line of grease from my less than healthy snack.

'The minute you drove away.'

'Figures. So she's been in there what, ten minutes?'

Alessandra nods.

'Let's go. She'll be spooked that we've arrived not long after she has,' I say.

I knock on the door. Silence. I knock again. Hard enough this time to bruise my knuckles. I can hear her coughing as she comes downstairs to answer.

'I'm very sorry, I was just looking for ...' her smile falls when she sees who has come to visit. 'DI McBain, this might be construed as harassment.' Her mouth has formed a tight line of irritation. She coughs.

'We can do this here,' I say, 'or we can take you down to the station.' I love saying that.

Without a word she stands aside to let us in. As I walk past the telephone shelf I see that the notepad is still in position. Alessandra and I pause in the hallway and allow her to lead us into the living room. Mrs Hogg walks over to the side of the fireplace. Her stance tells me that we are not welcome and this visit will not be long.

'Where is she, Mrs Hogg?'

She appears distracted. As she stands in front of me her head is moving back and forth as if she is mentally trying to track some object in the house. 'I have no idea what you are ...'

'My advice? Don't waste any more of our time. It will not look good when this comes to court.'

'My...I...' she blusters, her face red with a number of emotions; anger, fear, confusion. She knows that I know something. Her face tells me that she is hoping fervently that I don't know enough, while she fears that I do. She crosses her arms and sucks in her upper lip. I take in her appearance. Her eyes are heavy and dark. She looks like she's been on the go all day. I couldn't help noticing as I followed her into the room that her blouse had a number of creases in the horizontal, the way it might if you had been seated in the one position for a reasonable amount of time. Her trousers are similarly creased in the groin area.

'Here's the thing, Mrs Hogg,' I pause and give her The Stare. The trick is to appear confident that you have *all* the facts. The scribble on the notepad and the call to the bank gel into an enticing whole just as I speak. 'I know that you are just back from Troon. You met with Lucy Hepburn and you attempted to pay her off with a large sum of money.'

'That's ...that's nonsense. Utter nonsense.' She takes a step back and all but falls into an armchair. Then she gets louder, stronger. Desperation lends her strength. 'Who do you think you are coming to my door, time after time ...' Her speech is interrupted by a sustained bout of coughing.

'Do you need a glass of water, Mrs Hogg?' asks Alessandra. Hogg waves the offer away with her hand. I give a look at Alessandra that says now is not the time to play nice cop. Her answering look is defiant.

'This needn't involve you beyond tonight, Violet. Just tell us where she is and we'll be out of your hair,' I say.

She's gone white now. Her mouth keeps opening and closing as if she can't find the words to tell me any more lies. I watch in silence. She's played me for an idiot so far. Each time we've met she's manipulated me like a master. It ends tonight. I am not leaving this house until I know where Hepburn is.

'I didn't want to do this, Mrs Hogg, but you've left me no choice.' I stand up and walk over to her. As I do so she shrinks back in her chair. I reach into my pocket and pull out the photograph. I hold it out to her. Even from her angle she recognises it instantly. Her mouth opens. The skin on her throat flowers into red blotches. Her hand stays on her lap. I'm guessing she doesn't even want to touch it, so I drop it on to her hand. She turns her head to the side and screws her eyes shut. A tear leaks onto her lashes and I suddenly feel a class one prick. I acknowledge a hot stab of guilt as I observe the shock in Mrs Hogg's face. Who am I to be in the position of morality judge? There are things I've done that I'm not proud of, things I've done under cover of cloud and night.

I tick myself off. She played the cards, you are just using them. Time and again this woman has manipulated me so I swallow any feelings of sympathy I have and harden my expression.

'Mrs Hogg, don't you think it's about time you told us everything?'

She stares at a space on the wall above the fireplace. The only movement I notice is in her throat as she swallows against what must be a nervous dry mouth. Then she takes a deep breath. Then another. And another. Now, her chest is rising and falling at an alarming rate. The change has been rapid. It's like she can't take in enough oxygen. The sound of her breathing is like the high-pitched panic of an asthmatic. Her hands flutter on the arms of her seat. Then they batter at them as the panic eats on itself and grows. Her face is contorted with the effort of trying to breathe. She's trying to say something, but it's impossible to make it out.

Alessandra pushes me aside, puts a hand on Mrs Hogg's back and pushes her forward. 'Breath slowly, Mrs Hogg. Take your time.' The woman's head is bobbing up and down. Alessandra turns to me. 'She's hyperventilating. Go into the kitchen see if you can find a paper bag... anything that she can breathe into.'

In the kitchen I throw open all the drawers. Even from this distance I can hear the noise that Mrs Hogg is making. Sounds like wheezing.

'Hurry, Ray,' Alessandra's shout carried through to me, her voice high with fear.

'There's nothing here.' I shout back and run through to the office. A large envelope might just do the trick. I find one tucked in behind the desk and run through to the living room. Mrs Hogg is leaning over the back of a chair. Face white. Alessandra is rubbing her back and making soothing sounds.

Hogg is trying to speak. The noises coming out of her mouth are indecipherable. She cups her right hand over her mouth as if she is holding something.

'Try the bathroom or her handbag, Ray,' Alessandra says. 'See if she has an inhaler.'

I drop the envelope and run.

Her handbag is in the kitchen on top of the washing machine. I tip it upside down. There. An inhaler. Of course. It's an asthma attack. I run through to the living room and hand it to Alessandra.

Fuckfuckfuck. I wish I'd paid more attention in First Aid classes. Alessandra slides the end into Mrs Hogg's mouth and sprays. I can't help but notice that her lips have a bluish tint and the skin on her face has gone all pale and sweaty. The flesh on her face has the appearance of wax that's been kept in an overheated room.

Alessandra is hunched over her. Her hair has fallen over her face, she pulls it back. She looks at me and says nothing. There are no need for words. Then she sprays another shot into Mrs Hogg's mouth and goes back to rubbing her back.

I'm thinking hospitals.

'How far is the Vicky from here?'

I reach for the phone and dial 999. My instructions are precise. Address and strong asthma attack. I'm told the ambulance will be with me in minutes.

We're in luck. I nod at Ale.

The photograph is on the arm of the chair. I stick it in my pocket. There's no need for anyone else to see it.

Alessandra and I are sitting in Mrs Hogg's living room like the last visitors at a wake. The paramedics almost had to push Alessandra off her so they could do their thing. They arrive in a pair, a man and a woman, both lean and brisk in their professionalism. They walk and talk like every second counts 'I'm Dave. This is Lesley,' said the man.

'Cyanosis,' Dave said to his partner. She nodded and looked at us.

'We're going to have to intubate.' They nod at each other.

Alessandra and I stand side by side and watch them as they work. I'm thinking if I ever take ill I want these guys on my case.

'Are you relatives?' asks Lesley. Her tone suggests she doesn't think so, but it's safer to check.

We each shake our head. Alessandra looks as pale as Mrs Hogg. She can't take her eyes of the woman. She is still holding the inhaler. She offers it to Dave.

'We didn't know that she ...'

Dave senses her distress and takes a moment from his ministrations to reassure. 'Lucky we were so close. Next time, just get in the car and drive to the hospital. With such a severe attack, every second counts.'

'God. She nearly died,' Ale said.

'We're not out of the woods just yet,' says Dave.

'Are you guys police?' asks Lesley while Dave runs out to the ambulance for a trolley.

'How did you guess?' I ask.

'Do you know of any relatives that need to be informed?' asked Lesley.

I shook my head. 'There's no-one we're aware of.'

It seemed like seconds since the medics came in the door, but already they have Mrs Hogg on the trolley, covered in a blanket and hooked up to an oxygen mask.

As they wheel her out, Mrs Hogg catches my eye. Hers are full of loathing. I'm not sure whether the target of that emotion is me, or herself.

I make Alessandra and myself a cup of tea. It seems weird to be using Mrs Hogg's bits and pieces while she is on her way to hospital. The atmosphere in the house seems diluted by her absence. Both Alessandra and I are moving as if our own energy has been drained.

'Boy, do we live in a fucked up world,' says Alessandra before she takes a sip from her mug. 'You have men and women who kill themselves because they prefer having sex with people with the same body bits as them. Then you have Mrs Hogg who is so frightened that people might see that image that she ...I mean, really. What harm was she doing? She got her rocks off. The guys got their rocks off. No one got hurt. Everybody should be happy, right?'

I sense where she is going with this.

'Alessandra don't ...'

'Don't what, Ray?' She faces me, her expression firm with anger. 'That woman could have died.' She angrily wipes at a tear.

'Ale, look at me.' I pull her hands away from her face. It's important that she listens to me. 'We did not cause Mrs Hogg's asthma attack. We were here trying to catch a sick woman. We were doing our job. She had a condition we knew nothing about. Her dealings with Hepburn put her under a huge amount of stress.' I burp loudly. 'And that kebab is fair giving me heartburn.'

Alessandra laughs.

'Yes, Violet Hogg carried on with a sexual practice that she despised herself for. Yes, she was deeply ashamed of it. But we are not responsible. There is a whole raft of circumstances here. Her reaction to those circumstances provided the wave that tipped everything over,' I say.

'Hey, I like what you did there with the whole raft, wave and tipping thing,' Alessandra smiles, unaware of the image she presents with the mad grin, eyes bright with tears and smudged mascara.

'Got it?' I shake her hand for emphasis. She nods.

'Sure?'

'Yes, boss. I'm sure.' She takes a sip from her tea, looks around the room. 'What now? How do we find Hepburn?'

Chapter 49

My tea is cold and I've barely taken a sip from it.

'Want another one?' I ask Alessandra. She nods. I've re-filled the kettle and I'm waiting for it to boil.

Hepburn, where are you? I scan the room as if closed cupboards of china and cutlery will provide me with answers. The kitchen table still holds Mrs Hogg's empty handbag, with the contents of it strewn all over the place.

I bend down and pick a lipstick and a small mirror from the floor. At least it didn't break. Alessandra joins me. She picks up a pen and a disposable lighter. Holding the lighter, she waves it at me.

'I didn't know that Mrs Hogg smoked,' she says then throws both objects into the bag. 'Weird, innit? A couple of hours ago these items would have been crucial to Mrs Hogg's well-being. She'd never have walked out of that door without them.

'Worth a look, do you think?' Alessandra is holding a mobile phone.

'Alessandra,' I grab it from her. 'You're a genius.'

I slide the phone open.

'That would just be too lucky,' says Alessandra.

'You never know,' I answer. 'People are well used to hiding paper files, letters and memos, but the stuff we keep on our phones ...' I check Hogg's phone book, scrolling through every entry. Nothing. I check her photos and videos. Empty. The text message section is equally empty.

'How much for a clean mobile phone?' I throw it in the bag. 'So much for that idea.'

Next I pick up Mrs Hogg's chequebook. 'I thought nobody bothered with these things anymore.' It had a very lady-like blue leather cover. I fan the pages and note that there are only three empty cheques left. I fan the stubs and read, 'electricity, telephone, gas ...had this woman not heard of direct debits?'

I look at the back page. It has some hand-writing on it. Looks like a set of directions. The first word on the page is *Troon*.

'I've often said the old-fashioned ways are the best,' I say and show the page to Alessandra. 'Ya dancer!'

Chapter 50

'Mum, don't make me anything for dinner,' said Jim on his mobile phone. 'I'm working late.'

'Okay, dear,' replied his mother. 'But it's only ten in the morning. You don't need to tell me that now, silly. Just call when you're finished and I'll have something ready.'

'Look, don't bother, Mum,' he grimaced at how rude that sounded when it came out. 'I'll pick something up on the way home.' He softened his voice, feeling bad that he might have offended her. Serves her right for being so bloody nice.

Jim was lying. For one thing, he wouldn't pick up any food on the way home; he wasn't doing food right now. And for another, he wasn't at work. He was parked in his car down the street and round the corner from his own home.

He looked at the closed curtains of the front bedroom. Angela would be having a long lie. The trauma of the last few days will have no doubt knocked her out. Jim knew the feeling. He had barely slept all week and he was struggling to keep his eyes open. He reminded himself that he couldn't afford to miss a minute, he'd have to stay alert and focused.

He fished a bar of chocolate out of his jacket pocket and tore it open. Some sugar might do the trick. Through every chew of the chocolate his eyes never moved from the house.

His car was positioned in such a way that with a slight repositioning of his mirrors he could watch his house and its occupants. It was unlikely that Moira would think to look down in this direction, but if she did and spotted him, so what? He wasn't doing any harm.

He was just sitting in his car minding his own business. He even had a newspaper spread out on the passenger seat to prove it.

While he watched his house, his thoughts kept returning to Erskine. Before he left Rob's house, he'd gone up to Erskine's room to say hi. The room was in darkness and the child's small body barely made a shape under the thick quilt. He was facing the far wall and his shoulder rose and fell in a deep pattern of sleep.

'Life can be really shitty,' Jim spoke in a low voice to Rob. 'As if it's not enough for his mum to be ill in hospital ...'

Jim's stomach was in full churn, acid scoring at the lining of his stomach. His hands seemed to have a life of their own as they drummed his thighs, picked at creases on his trousers, scratched an itch with no source.

What was going on here? Sure, he didn't really like Moira at first, but he'd come round. She was so good with Angela it was hard not to. She very quickly became invaluable.

So why the switch from trusted aide to scheming betrayer? Jim was in no doubt that she had done the dirty on him. Moira had planted the condom somewhere that Angela would find it. Then she'd stood back to watch the fireworks. She was the only person who could have contacted the police.

Had she been after him all along? Realised that he would never leave his wife and sought revenge? But it all happened so quickly, from seduction to betrayal in less than a day. It didn't make sense. Nothing made sense.

Now she had him out of the way. Did she want him out of the way? Why? He had no idea why, but he began to question Erskine's fall. Was it an accident? With a dose of twisted logic it all added up. The continued lies, the manipulation, the fake backstory; no-one goes to all that trouble for room, board and sympathy. They might offer a free blow-job, and for as long as he lived he would never forgive himself for that lapse, but the rest? It was too much, too measured, too calculating.

Wasn't it?

Jim couldn't get the image of Erskine from his mind. He didn't need to see the eye-patch to see how the wee soul had been affected. The forlorn shape he made under the quilt was enough.

What to do in the meantime? Could he just stay here and watch over everyone indefinitely? It just wasn't practical. Even if Moira didn't spot him, the neighbours would. The people who knew him would be asking uncomfortable questions. The ones who didn't would be calling the police.

Another run at the police might be a good idea. If he was to lie and say that Moira had abused his son that might do it. They tend to act quickly in those situations.

Could he tell such a lie? Whatever her faults had been so far, she'd always treated Ben well, in fact thinking of this made him ashamed that he had thought her capable of harming Erskine.

Another potential problem with going to the police with such a story was that he was on record as having caused a disturbance. He'd already been threatened with a charge of wasting police time. Maybe he should try the divisional headquarters in Ayr. If he presented a calm exterior and a plausible story it might just work.

He had to get that woman out of his house. What was she up to, he asked himself for the millionth time? What did she want from them?

All she needed was for him to go away permanently and she would be in easy street. But that wasn't going to happen. He was going to be a thorn in her side, in her foot, up her arse until she pissed off and left his family in peace.

Heated by thoughts of getting his family back, Jim closed his eyes briefly. Just once for now. It wouldn't harm anyone if he closed his eyes for a moment. Would it? Soon, very soon he would be back in the house and sleeping in his own bed. He pictured the bed, the quilt, the comfort.

Soon, he thought, soon. So lost was he in thoughts of warmth and sleep and comfort that he missed the taxi draw up outside his house and a woman approach his door.

If he had seen her he would have recognised her, could have given her a name.

Kirsty.

Chapter 51

The sea rolls on to the beach with the consistency of treacle as if all the to-ing and fro-ing in the warm spring air had tired it out. Dotted here and there along the beach, couples stroll hand in hand. The high and happy voices from children in the swing park mingle with the caw of the seagulls as they circle in the air. In the jagged horizon, the Isle of Arran projects a two-dimensional outline as if from an award winning photograph.

Picture perfect.

I remember the hours spent building sandcastles here and on other beaches along this coast. In all kinds of weather. Pouring water into a moat that would empty just as fast as I could fill it. Taking that satisfying leap on to the middle of the castle at the end of the day.

The nuns urged us on to great feats of sand engineering. They clustered together on woollen, tartan blankets. In full habit. If the sun was shining their only concession was to roll up their sleeves to just below the elbow.

'Sure you're getting a grand tan,' one would say to another.

Once sufficient time had passed on the sandcastles we were urged to go for a swim. Then soaked and shivering we lined up and sandwiches were thrust into our hands.

I remember debating with another child that the grit covering each *sand*wich was where the name came from. Stands to reason even now.

Then there was the dread of the return to the convent and bedtime while the sun still shone. I kick at some sand as if trying to dislodge the negative associations from the good memories.

'Don't come crying to me when you get too much sand in your shoes, Boss,' says Alessandra from the safety of the low grey wall that runs the length of the beach.

'There's always a compensation for life's discomforts,' I reply.

'Good god, he's going all Dalai Lama on me.'

'Heard that,' I shout back.

I hear her landing on the sand, a dull grunt, then her footfall as she makes the dozen steps to my side.

'See, grasshopper, the pleasure outweighs the pain,' I say.

'As far as I'm aware, Ray, the Dalai Lama doesn't use grasshoppers to illustrate his points. That was the guy in Kung Fu.'

'Whatever. Don't you just love being by the sea?' I breathe in long and deep and study the cool flame of the sun, hanging low in the early afternoon sunshine. It's sparking off a chain reaction on the surface of the water, like a golden disco ball that has been flattened and stretched across the width of the bay.

'Don't we have a mad woman to catch?' asks Alessandra while looking at me as if I'm wearing a disguise and she's trying to find the real me underneath.

'We do.' I turn and pace back to the wall. 'Let's go. Cliché alert, Miss Rossi. Never forget to take time out and smell the roses.'

'And the sea air, and the …' she pauses looks at her right foot, '…dog shit.'

'Bring that into my car,' I'm all heart, 'and you're walking home.'

'Where will I …?' She looks back and forward. Then looks to the sea as if she might dip her shoe there.

'Patch of grass,' I point in one direction. 'Public toilet,' I point in the other.

'Wanker,' she points in mine and grins.

A clean and odourless Alessandra joins me in the car. I drive back to the bed and breakfast establishment that

307

Mrs Hogg's directions led us to. It is a grand, sandstone building, constructed in the traditional villa style standing just off the seafront to the far right of the bay. A sign in the window tells me that there is room to spare in Ettrick House.

The door is large and made of solid wood; I push it open and walk in. A short, slim woman with cropped blond hair walks towards me while wiping her hands on a white apron. Her eyes are blue and bright and hold a frank curiosity in the people before her.

'I'm Julie. Can I help you?' she asks and looks from me to Alessandra.

'DI McBain and DC Rossi. We're looking for someone.' I take out my warrant card and show it to her.

'Oh.' She goes through the changing expressions that people who rarely have contact with the police exhibit. First there's mild alarm, followed by *who me*, then relief that it can't possibly be her, followed by an all-consuming interest in who could possibly be of interest to the police. All of this in two seconds flat. Now she's mentally assessing all of her current clients.

'We are looking for a young woman, early twenties, on her own,' Alessandra says.

Julie nods. 'We have two of those actually. One is American ...'

'It'll be the other one then,' I say. 'Is she in? What does she look like?' I ask.

'She's not in at the moment. Don't know where she is. She mentioned something about having friends in the town. Says she hasn't seen them for years, since they had a baby.

'She's average height, average weight, quite pretty, short brown hair. Last I saw her she was wearing jeans and a blue cotton coat.'

'Can you check your reservation book for her name?' I ask.

'Don't need to do that, DI McBain, when someone tells me their name is Audrey Hepburn, I tend to remember.'

In the car, Alessandra and I have nothing better to do than wait.

'How should we approach this, Ale?'

'Doh!' she makes like Homer Simpson. 'Soon as we see her, we jump out and arrest her.'

'We know for sure that she's the one?'

'There's not too many people running around with the name, Audrey Hepburn, is there?' She pauses. 'I loved her movies. She was one classy woman.'

'The nuns used to make us all watch her movie about the missionaries in China. *The Inn of the Sixth* something or other.'

'*Happiness* and that was Ingrid Bergman, ya numpty,' Alessandra punches my arm for good measure.

'Like, whatever, dude.' I rub my arm as if it really hurts.

'Don't talk like that. You are, like, way too old, pops.'

'I'm not that much older that you, sweetheart. And anyway if I'm the old one how come you know the movie better than me?'

'There were lots of wet Saturday afternoons in my youth with nothing better to do than watch old black and white movies.'

'Almost makes me want to be you,' I say.

Alessandra looks out of the window and watches a seagull wheel and glide in the sky. 'We do need a positive ID for the live Hepburn. You still got my camera?'

'Did I not give you it back?'

She pulls her mobile phone from her handbag, 'Never fear, gadget girl is here.'

'If it takes clear photos, even better. Then we can send it to Mrs Browning's phone and she can give us the identification we need.'

Minutes later a woman walks in the direction of Ettrick House. She is of average height and build with short brown hair and wearing denims and a blue coat. She's walking along with the air of someone who is on holiday. There's nothing pressing, nothing important and she has all day to see to it.

As she passes the car, Alessandra aims her phone. It makes the clicking sound of a camera. She holds it up so we can both look at it.

'Crap,' she says.

'I thought you said your phone took good pictures?'

'It does. She was walking too fast …or something. Why don't we just go and arrest the bitch?'

'Alessandra, we can't afford to fuck this up.'

Ten minutes later a large Skoda draws up in front of us and beeps its horn. It has lettering on the rear window that says "Troon Taxis". The same girl runs out of the building and jumps into the front passenger seat. The car moves off into the traffic.

I start the engine and do likewise.

'Wonder where she's off to?' Alessandra thinks aloud.

'Must be local. What would be the point of coming to stay in Troon and then get a taxi somewhere else?'

The taxi drives for around ten minutes. We pass a large supermarket, a swimming pool and then a different stretch of beach.

'I didn't know Troon had two beaches,' says Alessandra. I move my eyes from the traffic to view the tall grasses, sand dunes and another stretch of sparkling sea and then go back to the traffic. Minutes later the taxi takes a left into a large housing estate full of neat modern houses with neat lawns. Suburbia by the sea.

The car takes a few turns, left and right, then pulls up in front of an identikit semi-detached house. It has a trim lawn and a couple of fir trees in front. A child's bike has been abandoned to the side of the path leading to the front door.

The car stops, the woman gets out and the car drives off. I park across the road.

The door of the house opens. The woman's head moves as if she is speaking. We can't see to whom. The door closes. The woman turns and faces the street. She looks stunned and getting angrier by the second. Whatever just happened was not in the script. She turns back to the

310

door, pauses and then puts her back to the house. She walks down the path and pauses again. She looks up at the bedroom window, thinks some more and then walks to the end of the path.

Alessandra and I look at each other. What the hell was that all about?

Whatever happened, it means that we now have a photo opportunity.

'I'll distract her,' I say to Alessandra. 'You take the picture.'

I climb out of my car. 'Excuse me,' I say while trying to think about what I should say next.

The woman is wearing a strange expression that suggests the thoughts in her head are too confusing to be tolerated. Her eyebrows are low and her chin is jutting out with the effort of trying to make sense of them. Her mouth is a tight line of pink, like a well-stitched wound.

'What?' she asks.

As she looks at me I try to take her measure. She may be confused, but she's not stupid. There's a clear and cunning intellect behind those brown eyes and while I try to assess her, she's doing the same with me. What does she see? A man in a suit. He's not a tourist then. A salesman, perhaps?

'I'm afraid I got kinda lost in this maze of houses. I'm trying to get back to the main road. Do you know how to get there?' As I say this I'm hoping that Alessandra has her phone out and she's snapping away.

A car door slams and feet thunder behind me getting closer. A man is shouting. I turn to face him. He's not looking at me. He only has eyes for Hepburn.

'Jim,' she says. 'What the fuck is going on? I tried to get in to see Angela and ...' she pauses as if catching herself about to say something, 'and that bitch wouldn't let me in.' A look passes between them, a look that shows a shared experience. It's an intimate recognition of friends, perhaps even lovers turned adversaries, with their past wound in years' worth of falsehoods.

311

Judging by her face the experience didn't end well, nor has it aged well.

He on the other hand has moved on. Or something else more important is demanding his attention. I'm not really listening to what the guy has to say, I'm wondering what his part is in all of this. He's about my age, tall and wiry. He needs a shave and he looks like he slept in his clothes. He's still talking and Hepburn is listening closely. Then she looks at me as if to say, why can't you fuck off?

Such is the force of her glare that I take a step back, despite myself. The man just called her something. It isn't Audrey, or Lucy or Hepburn.

Sounded like Kirsty.

Chapter 52

The walls are tiled in a grey cardboard-like material, the table is formica-topped and the chairs are dark blue plastic. We're in Ayr cop shop. Alessandra is beside me and Hepburn in front of me. The man we just met, Jim Hilton is sitting in the reception area like he's got a bomb hanging round his neck and it's going to explode any second.

Hepburn is sitting back in her chair, feet crossed at the ankles, hands clasped and resting on her lap. She looks like she's about to pray for all of the world's lost souls.

'Ms Hepburn, thank you for your patience,' I say. 'We need to get some clarity on the Hiltons' situation and as a close family friend you are obviously in the position to do that.'

'But I haven't seen them or spoken to them ...'

I stand up. 'Sorry. Please bear with us for a little longer? Alessandra, let's go. We need to have a word with Mr Hilton.' I assess Hepburn's reaction to this. The line of her mouth suggests she is annoyed. Good. I want to goad her into a response and there's nothing like a couple of hours of being completely ignored to fuel the fires of provocation.

Downstairs Jim Hilton grabs my hand like I'm the surgeon and he needs a new valve.

'Thank you for speaking to me. Thank you,' he says, his face bright with need.

'Coffee?' Alessandra asks.

He nods fiercely. Alessandra walks in the direction of the cafeteria and I follow to have a quick word out of Jim's hearing.

'Did you get any reply from Mrs Browning yet?' I ask. She shakes her head. 'Did we send it to Mrs Craig?' She

313

was the mother of the boy who had almost been strangled on the curtain cord.

'I'll get on to that.'

'Why don't you tell me everything you know, Jim,' I say.

He talks for over an hour. He tells me all about his wife's condition, his wee boy and this woman Moira. He actually blushes when he tells me how Moira gave him oral sex and then filled a condom with his semen so she could present this to his wife and get him out of the house. He then goes on to say how he had been dreading Kirsty coming home, because she was an old friend of his wife's and the only one who could blow his cover of them still being happily married.

Poor sod. I almost feel sorry for him. He goes through all of that and he still loses his wife and son.

'Hang on a minute. You mentioned Kirsty. Who's she?' I ask.

He fixes me with a puzzled expression. 'The woman you were talking to outside my house. Kirsty. Kirsty Maxwell.'

'She's going by another name now,' I say. 'Audrey Hepburn.'

He makes a face. 'Who goes about changing their name? Good Christ, what next? This is like living in a bad movie.'

'Aye and the cast is Moira Shearer and Audrey Hepburn,' I say. He makes a sound with his lips, like an abbreviated neighing noise.

'Yeah, crazy innit.'

'There's a connection,' I say, thinking out loud. 'Moira's surname is supposedly Shearer. Moira Shearer, old Hollywood star. Kirsty is going by the name of Audrey Hepburn. Do they know each other? Quite a coincidence with the old actresses' names, don't you think?'

'That's just a coincidence, surely,' he asks looking completely puzzled. I can see him processing the possibility. That would mean Maxwell and Shearer knew each other. He shook his head.

'In my view,' I answer, 'when it comes to crime there is no such thing as coincidence. Another name for a coincidence is a pattern. We are just too close to it at the moment to see it properly.

'You've told me about your suspicions of Moira Shearer. How certain are you of this?'

His face lightens with a thought, 'Erskine. Erskine's dad Rob. You should speak to him. Erskine lost an eye ...' My heart beats a little faster. '...Rob says it must have been an accident, but I think he's fooling himself. The alternative would be just too painful.' I nod in understanding. That your son would lose an eye is horrible enough to bear, but to consider that your actions might have set the event in motion would be too much.

'Then there's the whole condom thing and the police,' he swallows and looks at me, then tells me the rest of the story.

'There's a definite pattern here that we have been aware of for some time,' I say, then I sit back in my chair and cross my arms. 'Tell me about Hepburn or Kirsty, or whatever the fuck her name is.'

He screws his face to the side in consideration. 'It's kinda ...well ....'

'Go on,' I say thinking, how typical. Hepburn's been clever enough to leave nothing more than suspicions all the way along her trail. There's got to be something concrete, something we can touch, see or hear, something that's going to get the witch locked up for a very long time.

'This is nuts, man.' He runs a hand through his hair. Shakes his head again. 'Angela and I got together years ago. Kirsty was our friend. Angela and I broke up. Kirsty chased me. We had a ...fling,' he makes a face at the memory. 'But it wasn't much fun. We weren't happy,' he pauses, searching for the right words. 'Sex for one thing was weird. She wouldn't let me touch her, but she would ...and the only word for it is *lavish* ...she would lavish attention on my ...' he grimaced as if in apology for the

315

frankness of his words, '...my cock. Don't get me wrong, what guy wouldn't love that kind of interest. But ...it was too much, you know? Too weird. Like she had no ...' he shook his head. Then he looks at me with a look of shame and full of awareness that even the best portrayal of his past will be one that will never reassure him or anyone else involved.

'Angela and I had sex while I was seeing Kirsty.' From the way he casts his eyes to the floor I can tell there is more to that episode than he is going to detail. 'Angela became pregnant.'

He pauses. 'I'm not proud of myself, DI McBain, and I've spent the rest of my life making up for it.' He is quiet again, lost in the memory. His jaw muscle twitches. 'And I never slipped again until ...'

'Jim,' I lean forward and grip his arm. 'I'm not here to be your judge.' I release him. 'Please don't take this the wrong way, but I don't give a fuck if you screwed your Aunt Jessie from behind while she was cooking a meal for her twenty starving weans. Just tell me the facts.'

He coughs out a laugh and tells me about his mother's cat and a knife slash on his leather jacket.

'Could be just a coincidence,' he offers with a shrug.

'There's that word again,' I say.

Alessandra appears with a tray of cups and offers each of us a share of her bounty. Jim and I take a drink and we are all lost in a moment of caffeine appreciation.

Watching Jim as he drinks I can't help but notice that the man is on his last legs. His eyes are heavily lidded, his skin is grey and his lips dry and split. He looks like he's crammed ten years of hard living into one weekend.

'Jim, I want you to go home after you've drunk your coffee and rest for a few hours. We're going to need your brain again later on and you're no good to me if you're on the point of collapse.'

Jim Hilton has gone home and it's just me and Alessandra and a certain Audrey/Lucy/Kirsty. She's in for a wee sur-

316

prise. When Jim approached us in the street it was too good an offer to miss. He was desperate to speak to the police about his family; we simply took him up on it and snared Hepburn while we were at it. She thinks she's here to tell us everything she knows about the Hiltons.

As I said, she's in for a wee surprise.

Chapter 53

Alessandra received a text message from Mrs Browning an hour before we enter the interview room where Hepburn/ Maxwell is hopefully quietly simmering. The message had one word.

"Yes!"

As yet there is no answer from Mrs Craig.

The extra hour was added as an extra frustration.

Hepburn is up on her feet the second I enter the room.

'What the hell is going on here? I demand you let me go. Wait till the press hear about this. Do you treat all your witnesses like this or is it just the women?' Her nostrils are flared, a fleck of saliva is poised at the corner of her mouth.

I sit down and unwind the plastic wrapper from a cassette tape and slide it into the recorder.

'Is that what you think you are, Audrey?' I ask. 'A witness?' She remains standing, feet planted wide and arms crossed.

'Tell me about your time with the Brownings and the Craigs.'

'What?' Her posture slackens, some of her aggression bleeding from her form as she wonders where I am going with this. Then she smiles, the skin at the side of her eyes crinkles with pleasure.

'You haven't a clue, do you?'

'Pete and Dan are nice wee boys, aren't they? Must be difficult to have a mum who is suffering from MS. Must have been nice to have someone who could do stuff with them. Like throw them downstairs.'

'That,' she sits down, 'was an accident.'

I fire all sorts of questions at her. Her answer is a solid silence.

I press the pause button on the recorder. 'Anybody fancy a coffee?'

'Can I go now?' asks Hepburn.

'You can go anytime you like, Miss Hepburn. Or is it Maxwell?'

'What is it you think I've done, DI McBain?' She leans forward in her chair.

'Why don't you tell me?'

'Can I go now?'

'How well do you know Moira Shearer?' Alessandra asks while stretching beyond me to switch the recorder back on.

Hepburn studies her as if for the first time.

'Fucked him yet?' she asks Alessandra and flicks her head at me.

'How does it work, Audrey?' Alessandra asks. 'Do you pick a family for her and then she picks one for you?' Yet again, Alessandra's composure impresses me. In no way does she give Hepburn a reaction to the question.

'Bet he has a tiny cock.'

Hepburn is wearing a grin of satisfaction. She thinks by attacking us like this that we will be uncomfortable and thereby lose our edge. Sex is society's greatest sin, right? People rarely talk about it in mixed company. In single sex groups and in the dark with a lover is fine. Or even over the phone, or on the internet.

Her words have given me an insight. Her weapon has become our attack. I arrange my features into a look of sympathy.

'Who hurt you, Audrey?'

'Oh, give me a break. Pathetic.' She pushes her chair back from the table with her feet in order to cross her legs more easily. 'Nothing worse than an amateur psychologist. You think because I hurt these boys that I'm a victim of abuse.

'Do you have to use a little bit of lube, darling? Things a bit dry are they?' Again, Hepburn has a go at Alessandra.

319

'So you did hurt these boys, Audrey?' I ask.

'Aha, think you got me there? That's not what I said,' she tilts her head to the side. 'Does he give it to you up the arse, love?'

Again, from Alessandra's expression Hepburn might only have asked her about the weather. Why is she not more adamant about getting out of here? Why the attacks on Alessandra?

Hepburn will see me as the real threat, the trophy to be won, but first she has to weaken Alessandra. If she gets a reaction she wins and Alessandra is out of the game, much less effective. However, Alessandra will give no more thought to her words that she would to removing a hangnail. Still, as the higher ranking officer I have to protect my colleague.

'Miss Hepburn,' I say. 'We now have on tape several instances of personal abuse you have aimed at my colleague DC Alessandra Rossi. One more and you will be charged with Breach of the Peace. A couple of weeks with a bull dyke up at the women's prison might just soften you up for the next bout of questions. What do you think?'

She sits back in her chair, the light in her eyes lessened but still defiant.

'Everyone happy to carry on?' I ask and look at both women.

'Absolutely, DI McBain,' says Alessandra.

'For the record,' I say for the recorder's benefit. 'Miss Hepburn has nodded her head.'

I consider the behavioural patterns that we are aware of. She physically damages the boys, tries to seduce the father and in doing so undermines the mother.

Then there's her relationship with Jim Hilton and the *bukkake* with Mrs Hogg.

How can I use all of this to my advantage? We don't have any physical evidence so I need to get her to break.

I put all of the questions to the back of my mind and trust that my subconscious will throw forward an answer.

'When can I go?' she asks.

'You are free to leave anytime, Miss Hepburn, but it may be more beneficial if you answer my questions honestly.' Time for another change of direction.

'How well do you know Violet Hogg?'

She looks up sharply. 'You leave Violet out of this. She's the one person who's been kind to me.'

'And you betray that kindness by blackmailing her.'

'What are you on about?' she asks, her eyebrows are knotted together.

'When did you last speak to Mrs Hogg?' I ask. It occurs to me that she won't know Hogg nearly died.

'Saw her yesterday. How do you know about Mrs Hogg?'

'How much did she give you? One thousand, two thousand pounds?'

'Dunno what you're talking about.'

'I'm talking about this.' I bring out a piece of paper with an image on it and speak with exaggerated clarity of tone for the recorder. 'I am showing Miss Hepburn a photograph of Mrs Hogg which depicts Mrs Hogg with a face covered in semen.'

Hepburn looks from me to the image and back again, her face wreathed in thoughts and conjecture. We know a lot more than she suspected and she is beginning to worry.

She has already rushed to Mrs Hogg's defence; perhaps this is something I can capitalise on.

'Does Violet know you have this?' she asks. I nod.

Her eyes shift from mine. She works to keep her face free of expression, but I see movement in her throat as if she is trying to swallow a small piece of stale bread. Her fingers move as she picks at a small loose thread in the thigh of her denims. The moment passes and her expression goes back to stone. The face is much easier to control than the rest of your body, however. There are flashes of colour on Hepburn's neck and this gives me a better view into her state of mind.

She is worried.

Really worried.

A tone sounds out from in someone's mobile. Alessandra pulls hers from her pocket. Reads it and shows it to me. I can see that it is from Mrs Craig. Her answer reads. 'I don't know this woman. Any more suspects?'

'Tell me about your time with Mrs Hogg,' I ask, setting this information to one side.

She makes a face as if to say not again. 'She gave me a place to stay. And yes, some cash when I was broke.'

'Except you had to blackmail her to get the money, didn't you Audrey? The cash wasn't freely handed over.'

'What ...what did she say when she saw ...? How did you find the picture?' Her voice is small, she pulls the sleeves of her jumper lower as if she's trying to heat her hands. This has the effect of making her look years younger. Then she realises that I've noticed and she crosses her arms, as if hiding any evidence of weakness.

'Did you know that Violet suffered from asthma?'

She looks up quickly. 'You what?' Her face is agitated with thoughts. She's trying to work out where I am going with this. I can see concern for Hogg. There was some feeling for the woman after all. It was a form of collateral damage that she had to extort money from her.

I need to tighten the screws.

'Do you know that stress can bring on an asthma attack?'

'What happened? Is she all right?' She pauses, her eyes huge with alarm. 'You said suffered with asthma. Not suffers. You said it in the past tense. What happened?'

'She tried to get the laptop back from your old landlord. He wouldn't part with it until he got his overdue rent, but he let me have a look.'

'Oh no,' she holds a hand to her face.

'It was too much for her. She had an asthma attack. Alessandra gave her mouth to mouth.' I don't have to try and form an expression of sympathy for Hepburn. The shape my face is wearing is real. I can see her anguish

322

and guilt scored over every shadow on her face.

'She almost died.'

'Don't you dare feel sorry for me. Don't you fucking dare,' Hepburn shouts, her eyes full of the knowledge that her actions could have led to this woman's death. Her eyes are wet, her skin pale and stretched like thin grey plastic that has been shrink-wrapped over bone.

Chapter 54

'Is there anyone there?' Jim shouted up the stairs of his home. The silence felt like the moment before a storm breaks. His heart thundered in his chest. Angela? Ben? Where is everyone?

After he left the police station he had gone straight home. How he managed to negotiate the traffic safely he would never know, but he made it and ignored the questions of his mother and the open-mouthed stare of his father. He climbed the stairs to his room, like a man who'd just lost the block of concrete he'd been dragging behind him for a month. In his room he didn't pull the curtains shut or take off any clothes, he simply fell forward on to the bed.

He slept for three hours.

When he woke it was with the abruptness of a slap. One second he was in the black hole of a dreamless sleep and the next he was awake, his mind alert to his situation.

The police were involved. That's a result. Although what they wanted with Kirsty was a mystery. Soon, he hoped very soon, they would turn their attention to Moira and then he could get his family back.

In the meantime he should resume his watch just in case.

He parked in the same spot, turned the radio up loud and settled in to watch his house. Strong sunshine quickly heated the air within the car and he opened the window.

Again, the curtains for the master bedroom were closed, but that wasn't unusual. Angela needed a lot of sleep. He wondered what Ben was up to. He turned the radio off and tried to tune his hearing into the area around his home. Nothing. Ben liked to spend time in the garden. It was a nice day so why wasn't he outside playing? Might he be watching TV?

Jim stepped out of his car and looked towards the downstairs window hoping to see some movement. Ben was an active boy and even when his favourite cartoons were on he'd be flying or marching his toys across the room in conjunction with the action on the screen.

All was still.

He'd heard about the sense of foreboding that some people get when they know; just *know* that something is wrong. This was something that he had laughed at. Yeah, right, like everyone has this caveman instinct suppressed by centuries of socialisation. Give me a break.

Now, however, he wasn't laughing at it, he was listening to it. Even before he was aware of movement he was walking towards his house, head leaning forward like an antenna.

There should be some movement, some noise, something.

Nothing.

He broke into a run. The front door was unlocked. Why wasn't it locked?

'Angela? Ben? Anybody home?' He quickly searched downstairs. Living room, dining room, kitchen. Nothing. Back garden. Empty.

His breathing was laboured, his forehead slick with sweat. Where the fuck was everyone? He ran up the stairs. Ben's room was empty, his quilt with its Spiderman cover tossed to the floor.

'Angela?' He ran through to her room.

His wife struggled to sit up in bed when she was disturbed by his entry. Her expression was slack, her hair scrunched high on one side of her head as if she had slept in the same position for days.

Her speech, when she spoke was slurred. 'Jim, what you...?' She looked as if it was all she could do to remain

325

in an upright position. Jim jumped to her side and held her steady. She leaned her head into the cradle of his upper chest.

'What are you doing here?' she asked. Then her face slackened with panic. 'Is there something wrong with Ben?'

Her notebook, thought Jim.

Maybe she's written something in her notebook. Jim spotted it on the bedside cabinet. He reached for it and fanned it open to the most recent entry. Angela must have sensed his urgency. Her protest was automatic, but half-hearted.

The last entry dated the previous day read: *Why am I always feeling so tired? Remember to ask Moira if the medicine she's giving me is the right dose. Thank god she's here don't know what I would do without her — what Ben would do without her. He's so looking forward to tomorrow. He told me in that happy wee voice of his that he and Moira were going for an adventure. Something about smugglers and caves. Bless him. Must be hard for him just now. Dad's gone. And I'm a just a complete and utter waste of space.*

Chapter 55

We give Kirsty a glass of water. A moment of kindness in the rollercoaster of an interview. A change of pace is always welcome. It keeps the interviewee in an unsteady mental rhythm. Too much all out attack and they simply retreat behind a wall of self-justification and heat their defence against their dislike of you. But show some humanity and it unsettles, keeps them on the hop.

Time to speed things up a little.

'Fill in the blanks for me, Kirsty,' I say. 'Why hurt these boys? What was in it for you?'

She sits in silence, arms crossed, eyes lost in a fog of denial and half-quelled memory.

'You had a fling with Jim Hilton, didn't you?'

She ignores me.

'And he let you down like every other male in your life. Who hurt you Kirsty? Was it your father?' I watch her closely.

'Was it an uncle? A family friend?'

Her nostrils swell as she takes in more breath. The movement is so slight, if I hadn't been watching I would have missed it.

'What a bastard. To take advantage of a young girl like you.'

'You know nothing,' she states.

Her expression is closed to me. Her arms and legs crossed.

I raise an eyebrow. A simple movement that says I know everything.

'You know nothing,' she repeats, aiming for neutrality, but her eyes are twin spots of fire.

'And I'd bet you he's still out there, swanning around,

thinking he got off with it. Chances are he's done it again. People like him don't stop. There's probably a whole string of little girls that have been damaged by that monster and what do you do? Mmm? Go after innocent wee boys instead of doing what you can to stop a man who's made a career out of abusing wee girls.'

'Shut up.' Her face is twisted with denial.

'How many other women are out there? How many other Kirstys are there?'

'Shut it.' She slams a hand down on the desk.

'A classic case of abused turned abuser, that's you Kirsty,' I say. 'You feel unable to commit to a relationship. Someone you trusted, betrays you and leaves you with a twisted view of your sexuality. Jim Hilton is your first real boyfriend. You watch him with Angela and you learn from her. But the lessons already learned are too difficult to set aside. Am I right?

'A real relationship is beyond you, but you can't be failed for trying. You don't let Jim touch you. No full sex allowed, but you keep him sweet with plenty of hand jobs and oral sex. It's never enough though, is it Kirsty. Men always want more.'

'SHUT UP,' she roars, jumps up and the room fills with the scream of rubber against linoleum as she pushes her chair back.

'Because it's dirty. You're dirty. What you have between your legs is dirty.'

Kirsty collapses into the chair and slumps over the table. Her head and shoulders rise and fall as she gives way to the emotion that has been a lifetime in the making.

I open my mouth to speak again, too lost in disgust at myself, too lost in disgust at our propensity to harm each other to notice that I have Kirsty where I want her. Alessandra places her hand on my arm. Her face says it all.

Now is the time for silence.

328

Chapter 56

This is the story of Kirsty Maxwell as told to me. Her parents died when she was five. They had gone for a rare night out leaving her with her bachelor uncle. Their car was found the next morning, upside down in a ditch. There seemed to be no explanation for the accident. It was a tight bend. There had been a lot of rain. That particular road was known to be an accident black spot. There were the occasional deer spotted in the hills above. Whatever the combination of events, the young Maxwell was now in the care of her uncle.

Uncle was a quiet, studious man and he took his responsibilities to his new charge very seriously. Unfortunately, the needs of his parishioners took precedence. From a young age Kirsty came to hate that knock at the door of the Manse and the question; is the minister in?

In an effort to win Uncle's approval she watched how he dealt with his people. She studied his quiet, questioning manner and the absolutes with which he would dole out his advice. Other children found her difficult to play with. She was too serious and more than a bit strange in their view.

Arnold Baxter was a family friend. He was one of the executors of the trust fund set up on Kirsty's behalf and as such felt the need to be a regular presence in the young girl's life. Kirsty remembered the chats over coffee and cake while Arnold attempted to lecture her on the correct way through life. She remembered his tiny eyes behind thick glasses, the thatch of hair on the back of each pinkie, but most of all she remembered the smell of his breath as he bent forward to kiss her each time before he left. It reminded her of the bouquet of flowers she had stolen from her parents' funeral display. She held on to the flowers long after the colour had faded, long after mould had set inside the vase. The smell was distinctive, it was the scent of decay.

On her tenth birthday, Arnold taught her how to masturbate. Then she was made to watch while he did likewise. His reaction was so strong that the first time she thought he had died. His breathing quickened, his face coloured purple, his hand worked furiously at his penis. Then, a loud grunt and he threw his head back, and then everything was limp and silent. What was wrong with him? That must have been quite a shock to his system. She stood watching him, terrified to move.

Afterwards he took her into the bathroom and made up a solution of water and bleach. He had brought a cloth especially. They were both to scrub the sin from their genitals. It was all her fault, he told her. She was dirty. She had led him astray. This could never be allowed to happen again. No one else was to know. Then he bent forward to kiss her cheek, breathing mould on to the silk of her complexion.

Of course, the visits continued until the week of her fifteenth birthday. Here, in the telling of her tale is where Maxwell shows emotion for the first time. Her eyes are wet, a flare of red appears on the skin of her neck and then disappears.

'That was when I realised that I missed it. The attention.' She focuses on me, then moves her view back to her feet, her eyes dimmed by the memory. 'How sick am I?

'That's exactly why we did it,' she slashes the air with her right hand. 'Watch the news, read a newspaper and you'll see the violence that men dole out on women. You see it every fucking day.'

'So ...you were what, teaching these boys a lesson?'

'What was it the Jesuits used to say, give me the boy before the age of seven and we'll give you the man. Teach them young, DI McBain, and they'll treat every woman

330

they meet thereafter with respect.' Her eyes are challenging me to argue against her logic. What a wasted effort that would be. She was a radical, fundamentalist hater of men; regardless of my sympathy, nothing I could say would soften her views.

'What about the Hiltons?' I ask. The best questions to ask in an interview are the ones you know the answer to and then by the information left out you can judge the veracity of the speaker.

'Jim and I had a ...thing,' she brushed at the air as if trying to make light of their moment of romance. 'He went back to Angela. He slept with her the night her mother died. Can you believe it? We were all pals at first.' Her expression softens and I get a glimpse of the woman she might have become. 'I loved the time I spent with those two. Felt like I had a family for the first time, you know?' She is pulling at the sleeve of her jumper, stretching it down beyond her thumb. 'Then when they split up I thought I could keep that feeling going with Jim.' She crosses her arms. 'But I think he was still in love with Angela.'

'Are they still your friends?' Alessandra asks.

'You joking? After the way Jim treated me. No.' She sweeps us both with her eyes, chin tilted defiantly. 'I lost interest in them a long time ago. Ben, now that's another story. He's a great wee guy. He won't follow in his father's footsteps, not if I have anything to do with it.' She pauses, a thought pulsing behind her eyes. 'That is if Moira hasn't started without me.'

Chapter 57

I rub at my face while I consider what my next step should be. I look at who I now know to be Kirsty Maxwell, smug in her certainty. She seems almost relieved that she has unburdened herself of all this information. Whatever a suspect tells me in the interview room, I have learned over the years to listen without judgement. It makes for a much more effective interview. However the air in this room seems stained by her words, her disclosure hanging in the atmosphere above us like a soiled rag.

I feel the need to breathe some clean air.

Alessandra and I are outside the interview room.

'I need to wash my face,' I say. 'And get a breather.'

'I need to dip my ears in disinfectant. That is one disturbing woman.'

Just then a local CID officer called Dave Bishop approaches us. He's wearing a white shirt, red patterned tie and a pair of dark trousers. He has black hair, closely cropped to his skull that is flecked with grey. His wide shoulders taper down to a trim waist and his arms look thick and solid, suggesting this is a man who spends a few of his spare hours in a weight room. His skin tone also suggests he's the outdoors type. He has a line of sunburn around his hairline and the rest of his face is freckled and a mixed shade of light brown and pink.

'Hey guys,' he offers a friendly smile, which is really aimed solely at Alessandra.

Alessandra is returning the smile in kind and suddenly feels the need to check that her hair is in place, without the help of a mirror.

'Hey Dave,' says Alessandra, 'thanks for your hospitality. We really appreciate it.'

'Welcome,' he says as his smile increases in wattage. 'Anything else you need, give us a shout.' This last bit is aimed at me. It's nice to feel included. Bishop keeps walking past us down the corridor.

'If he turns and looks back at you before he gets to the double doors,' I mumble out of the side of my mouth, 'he's yours for the taking.'

'Shut it, McBain,' she hisses while not taking her eyes off him. 'I'm a married woman, remember?'

His hand stretches out for the door handle, he pulls it towards himself, takes a step through and turns and waves just before the door closes. I give Alessandra a nudge with my elbow.

'He really likes you,' I sing. 'He wants to kiss you.'

'You are out of your tree, McBain,' she pokes me in the ribs with a finger, swallows on a grin and walks away.

Walking out of the glass-panelled front door, I take a left towards the car park. The air is not so fresh around here given that a busy roundabout is right outside the station, but it beats breathing in the same stale air as our friend Maxwell.

As I pace up and down the car park I consider the story that Maxwell told me. Was she telling the truth, the whole truth and nothing but the truth?

It's just a wee bit too clichéd that she claims to have been abused, but the sad fact is that these sorts of cliché are stuffed, bound and cellophane wrapped in truth. What might be Shearer's story then? I don't really care. A child's life is in danger.

They met at the hospital Maxwell told me. They must have recognised something about the other on a purely subliminal level. I imagine they might have shared a few past horror stories; all men are bastards, that kind of thing. For most women that is enough, the act of venting sufficient to ward off their antipathy and allow them time to find something redeemable about the men in their lives.

333

Not Maxwell and Shearer. They find the energy from their past to take it on to the next level, but like all true bullies they don't address their fears, they decide to go to work on someone weaker than them. Someone that can give them the power they so badly need.

'Are you not pissed off that Shearer made it to Ben before you did?' I asked her.

'Nah,' she shook her head. I couldn't help feeling amazed at the transformation in her since she told us the truth. Whoever scripted the adage about the truth setting you free, I don't think this was quite what they had in mind. 'At first I was furious, I mean this was mine. Jim Hilton was the catalyst for my ...' she made a motion in the air with her hand as if searching for the right word, 'mission? But it made sense, kind of. After all, Moira wouldn't be who she is without me and I get the revenge without having to spend the rest of my natural being gang-banged by a lesbian cell-mate and her pals.

'Besides, she's always had a thing about Troon. Spent the best summer of her life here.' She smiled. 'Meeting the Hiltons gave her the excuse for a wee trip down memory lane.' She paused, took a deep breath and affected a face of concern. 'My only worry is how far Moira's going to take it. I mean what's the point in teaching the next generation a lesson if they are not going to be functional enough to put it into practice.'

'What do you mean?' I stiffened with alarm. I could sense her pleasure at my concern, it's like electrodes are pulsing just under the surface of her skin. I think I prefered the old nervous and more restrained Maxwell.

'I don't really know all that much about Moira. She doesn't talk much about herself. That's what drew me to her, I guess. That ...' she paused, thinking about the correct words, 'that and ...there's something *wrong* about her.'

'Wrong?' I asked.

She nodded. 'She did tell me that she adored Daddy, but Daddy was way too into Mummy to even bother with her. They went ballroom dancing, apparently. Entered competitions. But that level of neglect on its own shouldn't produce that level of disturbance in a person.'

'Disturbance,' I repeated, feeling a chill. Maxwell was hinting at something with far more destructive power than your run of the mill abuser.

'Think about it DI McBain. You're the expert, n'est ce pas? The cases that you are aware of, with the more modest violence ...and I'm hoping that this is on the record ...they were all me. The ones where the violence is becoming, shall we say, unsettling ...' her eyes took on a strange light. 'You need to find Moira Shearer.'

Chapter 58

Jim was in Moira's bedroom looking for clues of where she might be and what she might be doing with his son. First he checked the room with his eyes, skimming over every surface for paper, books, mobile phone, anything in which something could be recorded. This was always a room with a function, but without any warmth. It looked as if it had barely been used since the single divan bed had been set in place against the wall.

Then he began to investigate with his hands as if the use of another sense would augment the search. The search was systematic at first as he forced his breathing to an even pitch. It wouldn't help Ben, he reminded himself, if he was to lose it. While one side of his personality worked hard at maintaining control, another side was intoning the words *fucking bitch*, like a mantra. If she harms one hair on Ben's head ...he couldn't, wouldn't allow himself to finish the thought. What use would he be to his family from a jail cell?

He found a paperback on the floor beside the bed. It was a recent bestseller in his shop, had a Richard and Judy sticker on it. It looked as if it had never been read, the way some people might use a book as a disguise. He threw it on to the armchair by the window. Hard. He was beginning to lose his fight for control. There was nothing here. Nothing. The room was just as neat and tidy as any guest bedroom might be, with nothing to hint at the personalities of the owners of the house.

An image of Ben formed in his head. His son's trusting face looking up at him. His small hand in his. In panic, Jim pulled at the pillows ...one ...two. Nothing underneath. He ripped off the quilt. Bent over, tore the sheets off the mattress. Nothing. He placed two hands under the mattress and heaved it off the bed with all of his might. It landed with a thud on the floor and toppled to rest against the small bookcase, pushing a lamp on to the floor.

Jim collapsed to the floor, chest heaving. He was overreacting. Nothing was wrong. Moira was simply taking his wee boy out for a fun day. Somewhere.

If she harms ...

Angela was in the doorway, leaning against the wood as if it was taking all her strength to stand there. Her alarm at Jim's behaviour had tightened her face into a mask of worry.

'Jim, why are you behaving ...you don't think Moira is ...?' She was on her knees beside him, gripping his right hand in both of hers. 'Is Ben in danger?'

Jim stroked the side of her face trying to reassure her; aware of the image he was projecting. Angela knew nothing about what had been going on. To her Moira was the only friend she had in the world. And now he was in her house ripping up the furniture.

'Can you remember anything about the last couple of days, honey?' he asked. 'Anything that might give us a clue ...'

'A clue? Why do you need a clue? A clue for what?' She pushed herself away from Jim, stood up and hugged herself. 'Why are you doing this?' Her eyes flitted around the room, questioning the mess.

Jim looked at his wife standing above him. She looked as if a hard breath from him in her direction would knock her off her feet. She swayed a little and put a hand out to steady herself. Even in the few days since he had been away she looked less substantial.

'When did you last eat?' he asked her.

She shook her head as if she couldn't understand the question.

In the kitchen, Jim threw open all the cupboards. Apart from a couple of tins of soup, a mouldy loaf of bread and

337

a box of teabags, the kitchen was bare. The fridge was just as bad with a carton of unopened orange juice, a half-litre of milk and a box of eggs.

He whisked the eggs in a bowl and then scrambled them in a pan. He managed to salvage some of the bread by cutting off some mould and sticking what was left in the toaster. Maybe with some food inside her Angela would regain some of her senses. Jim made another entry in his Things-to-Hate-Moira-For list.

When he placed the food in front of Angela she began to eat as if she had forgotten what the purpose of food was. Then as the sustenance reached her stomach she all but crammed it into her mouth as if her body had suddenly informed her that she was in actual fact malnourished and should eat NOW.

While Angela washed the solids down with a cup of tea, her trusty notebook by her hand, Jim rooted around in the kitchen cupboards, looking for more clues. In the medicine drawer he found nothing but the usual headache pills, plaster and cough mixture bottles that had been there for years. It was often a joke of theirs that rarely did a cough mixture bottle get finished before the sell-by date. The last time he had reached for one, he spat the fluid into the sink with disgust. It tasted like petrol might.

What was this? There was an extra box. Antihistamine. Where did that come from? Jim looked over at Angela and the tiredness that was slowly receding from his wife's face. Of course. The box read that it held sixteen. It also read don't drive or operate machinery. He opened it. There were only two left.

He threw the box on to the kitchen table.

'That's why you are so tired.'

Angela picked the box up and studied it. Then looked at Jim with a question in her eyes.

'You've been feeling sleepy. More so than usual?' asked Jim.

'Yes, but ...'

'That's why.' Jim nodded at the box. 'Moira's been drugging you.'

Angela's hand shot to her mouth, but her face formed an expression of disbelief.

'Do you remember Erskine?' I asked.

Angela slowly shook her head. 'Erskine,' she said as if tasting the word. 'Erskine.'

'Small boy. Moira said he was her son.'

'Oh right,' said Angela as if a cloud had just cleared and an image had popped into her mind's eye. Then it clouded over again. She shook her head.

'Erskine is not her son. She was looking after him for another family. Another family where the mother was ill in hospital.'

Angela looked at Jim as if he was speaking in a different language. As if she was thinking, why was he telling her all this?

'Erskine lost an eye. The day that Moira came here to move in.'

Angela shook her head,

'She's been manipulating us, honey,' said Jim. 'She's been after Ben all along. And she knows Kirsty. Kirsty's in on it too.'

'Now you're just being crazy,' said Angela. She stood up, steadying herself against the table. 'Why are you doing this, Jim?'

Jim reached for her hand and grabbed it. 'You have got to believe me, Angela. This woman, this Moira woman, she goes round helping families, pretending to help families and then hurting their kids. She's evil, honey. She's been very clever. She's ...'

Angela was shaking her head as if making a blur of her head wouldn't allow the words in.

'No, no, no. Moira's my friend.'

'You've got to believe me, Angela. That woman is no friend of ours.'

Jim heard a knock at the door and a loud male voice. He walked through the kitchen and down the hall to answer, with Angela trailing in his wake.

He opened it to find DI McBain and DC Rossi. Jim wasn't worried to find two police detectives on his doorstep. What gave him cause for concern was the look on their faces.

'Mr Hilton,' said DI McBain. 'You need to tell us everything you know about Moira Shearer. And you need to tell us fast.'

Chapter 59

We are sitting in the living room of the Hilton home. Jim and Angela are side by side on the sofa. As close as they can be without actually touching. Alessandra and I sit on the armchairs.

Jim hands us a small photograph of their son. He has dark hair, long-lashed brown eyes and a pair of cheeks that a parent could spend all day nuzzling.

'He's a handsome wee lad,' I say.

Angela Hilton sniffs into a handkerchief.

Before I spell out what Kirsty Maxwell told me I can't help but be concerned by the boy's mother. She looks like she's been on a diet of water and air for a month. Her face is coloured a gaunt grey and her eyes look as if they are haunted by the ghost of a former self that she can never hope to equal.

I think about what Jim told me earlier about her memory loss. Even if he hadn't explained the situation I would have picked up on the fact that something was not quite right with her. She had barely spoken a word since Alessandra and I sat down, her eyes flitting around the room like the flight pattern of a wild bird in a confined space. Every now and again, she shifts her view to the window as if in an attempt to neutralise the energy around her.

'Are you okay, Mrs Hilton?' I ask.

She smiles as if her lips might burst any second, but I take it as a yes, so I tell them everything. As I speak Angela's eyes move from me to Jim and then back again.

Jim is now looking equally as fragile as his wife.

'So this is all my fault? This an act of revenge?' He leans forward. 'Bloody hell. You mean Ben might pay for

341

something I did ...' his voice trails into silence. Angela studies his face as if he has just spoken in the verbal equivalent of wingdings.

'Jim, this is not your fault. We all do things in relationships that we might not be proud of later. You are not responsible for her reactions. That lies with the people who were in a position of trust when she was just a wee girl.' I stop speaking before I say too much, but they both need to know something of what we are dealing with. Part of the *success* of both Kirsty Maxwell and Moira Shearer is down to their ability to manipulate the grownups as well as the children. 'Believe that you are not responsible and you'll get through this.

'In any case,' I raise my voice aiming to look and sound like someone who has absolute confidence. I can find their child. I can make things better. 'I need you both to go over every conversation you've had with Moira. Within your heads there is the seed of a clue, we just need to get it into the open.'

Jim starts speaking. He tells us of the entry in Angela's notebook. She nods and clasps it to her chest. Then Jim tells us of the conversation he had with another man who had dealings with Ms Shearer. This guy, Rob, told him about stories Shearer told his son that mentioned smugglers and pirates.

'Isn't that a bit of a coincidence?' he asks eagerly as if desperate to work a clue out of any scraps of knowledge he has of Moira.

I nod and think some more.

'Angela, is there anything else in your notebook about Moira? Any other conversations that you might have recorded?' Alessandra asks.

'I've read through it,' Angela answers with a shake of her head. Her voice is so weak I can barely hear her. She clears her throat. 'Sorry, I haven't been feeling so good.' Her voice is louder now, her expression deeply apologetic. 'Ben's safe isn't he?' She blinks a tear from her eye. 'If I wasn't such a ...' she stops as if unsure what she is. 'God,

342

I hate this. What have I done to deserve all of this?'

Jim reaches over and grips her hand. 'Angela, c'mon babe. We have to stick in there. For Ben's sake.'

Angela swallows, straightens her spine and pushes her shoulders back. She looks down at the notebook in her lap, then looks at her husband as if coming to a decision. Then she hands the book to him. His face heats and he accepts it, his eyes full of thanks.

'What do we know?' I say. 'We have stories of smugglers and pirates. We know Shearer spent a wonderful holiday in these parts as a child.'

'Two and two sometimes makes four, DI McBain,' says Jim. 'The Ayrshire coast was renowned for smuggling in the not so dim and distant past. Robert Burns himself was an exciseman. I know of some caves down by Culzean that were apparently used by smugglers. Could there be a connection that is specific to this part of the Ayrshire coast?'

'How would she get there?' asks Alessandra, then adds, 'wherever *there* is.'

'She doesn't have a car,' says Jim. 'She said that her so-called husband took it back along with Erskine. Whenever she went anywhere with Angela she booked a taxi.'

'What firm did she use?' I ask. Jim recites the telephone number.

Alessandra picks up the phone and dials. We hear her side of the conversation as she asks the taxi controller to check any hire from this address on the date on question. She shakes her head at us as the conversation draws to close and then hangs up.

'Nothing' she says shaking her head. 'Absolutely nothing.'

Chapter 60

'Do you need to lie down, honey?' Jim asks Angela once the detectives have gone.

'How can I possibly sleep at a time like this?' she replies. He says nothing, simply strokes the back of her hand.

'I'm sorry.' His words were quiet and unforced. 'If only I hadn't ...'

Angela held a finger to his lips. 'Don't Jim. I can't ...'

'I understand,' Jim's chin was all but touching his chest as he turned his head away.

'I'm not saying I can't forgive you, Jim. I'm saying I can't deal with this right now. It's too much. Ben is out there ...God knows where, with this crazy woman we thought ...I thought was a friend.'

'When did you start to remember stuff?' Jim asked. He needed to know how much energy he had been wasting. Energy he could have used to keep his family together. This is knowledge he can use in the small hours like a religious penitent might use a steel-tipped whip.

'Not long after Moira showed up.' She looked at him. 'You were all I had in the world. Who else could look after me? I didn't really know Moira at that point. I was terrified at the thought of you not being there. Terrified.' Her eyes were full of shadow. 'Can you understand that?

'This has all been too much.' She closed her eyes. 'It's like my life has been frozen in a mirror. Only the mirror has been shattered and each tiny fragment isn't quite big enough for me to see the whole story. And when I look too hard...and believe me I look *hard* ...the image fades. The sense of it is gone. It's all just tiny bits of broken glass that crunch under my feet. It takes me all of my time to make a cup of tea for chrissake. The thing is ...I remem-

344

ber the me I used to be. What happened to her, Jim?'

'She's still there,' said Jim and tapped her forehead and offered a small smile.

'That's why I can't talk about us at the moment. I have to know that Ben is safe first.' As she spoke she stroked the cover of her notebook. Then she opened it from the back. She lifted out what appeared to be an envelope folded in half and handed it to Jim. He folded it flat and looked at the cover. It was addressed to Angela at this address. He looked from the envelope to Angela, his eyes forming the question, what is this?

'I can't talk about us, Jim, but I want there to be no more secrets between us. No more lies. I never told you, but the first time we broke up, it was because of what was in that letter.' She stood up. 'I think I'll have a lie-down.' She left the room.

Jim pulled out the contents. He looked to see whom the letter was from. He checked for a date and then did a quick calculation. He scanned the letter quickly, heart thumping in his chest. Then again, this time more slowly, picking out the truth from the near-truth and the lies.

Dear Angela,

This letter has been years in the making and I don't quite know how to begin. Conscience is a funny old thing, isn't it? Something happens and you think you can deal with it. Only it comes back and whispers to you from dark corners.

You are my dearest, oldest friend and I know that I've been distant from you recently and it's all down to this secret — and my conscience. Don't worry, I'm not dying or anything. This isn't the confession of a woman on the edge. It's a righting of wrongs. An attempt to shut off the nagging guilt.

If you could only see me now, you'd laugh. At least I hope you would. Me, who you used to call the breezeblock 'cos I never cried at any of those sappy movies you used to love.

345

This story goes back to the time when your mother died. And I hope and pray that you don't hate me for this, but the night you found her you tried to call me and then you tried to call Jim. The reason you didn't get me was that I was with Jim.

We were in love, Angela. Please believe me when I say that nothing happened between him and me until after you and he split up. I wanted to tell you straight away, but Jim wouldn't let me. He didn't think you could handle it. But I always knew you were stronger than that.

Anyway, you eventually found Jim and he came over — and you don't need me to tell you what happened next. I could die at the thought that I was hiding in his bedroom at his parent's house while he was "consoling" you on the couch.

Then the night you met him and told him you were pregnant — and didn't he handle that with his customary aplomb — I was again with him at his parents' house.

He came back, stunned from your meeting and told me everything. He also told me that it was me he loved and that we should get married regardless. As far as you were concerned, he would do what he could to help you with the baby, hoping that you would get it adopted, but that he had no interest in you. To his credit, he didn't like the idea of abortion.

We talked and talked well into the night. Jim wanted us to stay together and I wanted you to be taken care of. After all, you had just lost your mother, you had no one.

The thing is, and I can only see this now, is that Jim is not a bad guy. He's just a man — you know. Us girls, we're made of much sterner stuff.

Anyway, I told him that he and I were over and that you and his baby should be his priority. He begged me and begged me, but I refused to listen to his arguments. By the end of the night I'd convinced him that we had no future and that he should act like a man and take care of his responsibilities.

So, he and you were married. And I moved away.

I was so pleased that you guys made a go of it, and especially pleased when Ben was born. It's great to be an aunt and I'm so looking forward to showing him how he should treat the women in his life.

My dearest hope is that you burn this letter, if I send it. I may just burn it myself. I believe that Jim regrets the actions of his youth and that eventually he came to love you in his own way.

I hope and pray that you can forgive me for my part in all of this and that we can continue to be friends.

Be safe. Be happy,
Kirsty.

Chapter 61

We reassure the Hiltons that we will do everything in our power to find their son and leave to go back to the cop shop in Ayr.

There's nothing quite like local knowledge in this situation and we know a man who can help. Alessandra is trying her best to look all calm and collected when I approach Dave Bishop. He's also doing his best to listen to me while his eyes stray to Alessandra. I feel like giving them the number for that bed and breakfast place in Troon, just so they can get past the whole first blush thing.

'We should do the tour of the local taxi firms?' Dave asks me without actually looking at me. Three guesses where his eyes are. Alessandra's hand strays to her blouse, checking that the buttons are all closed and she's not having a Janet Jackson wardrobe malfunction. Then she excuses herself to go to the toilet, probably to make sure her hair is sitting nicely.

'Dave,' I give him my elderly statesman look. 'Do me a favour, mate. Keep your eyes off the totty and your focus on the case?'

Alessandra comes back in and we divide all of the taxi firms in Ayrshire between us. The next hour passes in a blur of conversational dead-ends. If all of the people we spoke to are to be believed no one gave Shearer a lift to wherever she was going. She just vanished.

'Any car thefts in Troon recently?' I ask Dave.

'Afraid not, sir,' he answers. 'That was one of my last calls there. I called the Troon office and there's nothing.'

'Good work, Dave,' I say, impressed, and looking at Alessandra I nod my head in Dave's direction. She kicks my foot.

'What now?' Alessandra asks in an attempt to deflect attention from her efforts at bodily harm.

'We try to find out as much as we can about Troon's history,' I answer.

'History?' asks Dave. 'Why?'

'A hunch,' I say. 'Each kid that Shearer is with she mentions stuff about smugglers. And we know that she holidayed in the Troon area as a wee ...' I stop talking aware that Dave has stopped listening. Except this time his focus is on me, not Alessandra.

'Smugglers,' with a smile, 'Why didn't you say?'

Chapter 62

Dave Bishop is officially my new best pal. We'll overlook the fact that he's desperate to get into Alessandra's pants and celebrate his admission that he is a keen rambler. Not many men of his relatively tender years would admit to such a thing, blame the parents I say, but it has led to a break in the case.

It appears that hundreds of years ago the smugglers would bring their ill-gotten gains up from the beach at Troon to the town of Dundonald. The trail they trod is known as The Smugglers' Path and has recently been renovated and signposted by the local council. It's a bit tame for our Dave, but ideal for a warm-up for some of his longer walks.

As Jim Hilton said rather succinctly earlier on, sometimes two and two just makes four. So I'm happy to take the knowledge that Shearer holidayed in Troon, add in the several mentions she had made of smugglers to the various children she has cared for and extrapolate that into a search of this area.

Dave, Alessandra and I are standing at the information board for said path with the sun beating down on our heads and shoulders. Dave has arranged for some uniformed officers to check the houses and farms that are dotted along the road to where we are standing. In front of the board is enough space for one car to turn and park. It is occupied by a small Vauxhall, so we had to reverse down the hill and steal some space from one of the houses at the end of that section of path.

The board itself highlights various points of interest on the way over to Dundonald, like the reservoir, the working quarry and the castle at the far end.

Although it is still technically spring, May is when Scotland tends to get its summer weather. June, July and August are often lost under a swelter of swear words as parents of school kids and tourists wonder what happened to the fucking weather.

Today Troon is masquerading as Torremolinos. It must be in the mid-twenties.

'I'm worried about your head, Dave,' I say. 'What do you think, Alessandra? Think he's going to get burned?'

'I think if anyone's going to get burned it's you, DI McBain,' she smiles sweetly.

Beyond the board is a high, grey stone wall. It has a padlocked gate with a "No Fishing Without Permit" sign and a space for people with said permits to get through. Begs the question, why bother with the padlock?

Just as we are about to enter the space in the wall, we hear a scream and some shouting. We all look at each other and file through. A teenager in a Rangers football top is running down the grassy hill towards us, his arms wind-milling in panic.

'Somebody phone the polis. A wee boy just fell in the water.'

The three of us take off up the hill. Dave gets to the top first and I reach the crest in time to see his shoes and jacket being kicked off before he dives in. In front of me is a stone walkway, stretching left and right, from which the water leads off in a triangular shape. This part of the reservoir is man-made, the far edges of the water are edged in grass and reeds.

I take in the scene instantly.

There's a square orange stand about one hundred yards to the right of me. A young woman is running from it with a lifesaver in her arms.

In the water I can see a small head of dark hair and a tiny, white hand clutching desperately at the air.

Chapter 63

I run to the woman and pull the lifebuoy out of her arms and, turning, throw it to Dave. He pops it expertly over the head of the boy who is splashing frantically. Once the ring is secure I pull it in and help the boy out of the water. The weight of him and the ring is nothing and I soon have him gasping on the stone floor of the walkway.

I search his face hoping for recognition. It could be Ben. He's about the right age. He has the same colouring. The same long lashes.

The woman pushes me out of the way and is all over the boy in a flurry of snot, tears and remonstrations.

'Why did you go so close? I told you not to get so close.' Only when the woman has him in her arms does the boy start to cry. It's as if the strength of her reaction makes him realise for the first time that he was in real danger.

Dave clambers out and Alessandra moves to check that he is okay. Apart from a violent shiver and sodden clothes that are now sticking to him, he looks none the worse for his brief swim.

The wee boy is still crying. The woman's tone is placatory.

'There, there, wee man. Don't worry. No need to tell mum. Let's keep this our wee secret. Okay?'

Our wee secret.

'DI McBain,' I introduce myself. 'Who are you and who is this boy to you?'

Her name is Mary and she's the boy's aunt. His name is Lewis. They both live in Troon and she was looking after him while his mother was called in to work. As quickly as I showed her my warrant card, she had her purse out of

352

her handbag and was waving her bank cards under my nose. A switch card, a credit card and a blood donor card. They all have the name Mary Agnes McKee stencilled along the bottom. Then she's pulling out some letters and bank statements all with the same name.

She'd heard about the new walkway from a pal and decided, seeing as it was a nice day, to take the wee fella for a walk. Never again, she said solemnly holding a hand to her chest.

The Vauxhall beyond the wall is hers and I tell her to get the boy home and dried and to buy him the biggest bar of chocolate she can find.

'Aye, right,' she says. 'Sugar. For the shock.'

'Naw,' I say, looking at the boy. Now that he is safe, Lewis is wearing a huge smile as if he can't wait to tell someone that he nearly drowned and had to be saved by a big policeman. 'Sugar. For a bribe.'

Once they are safely on their way I turn to Dave who has just stripped off his soaking wet shirt.

'You don't happen to have a towel in your car?' asks Alessandra while scanning the lean and muscular torso in front of her. I smile. Dave's top half is coloured in what is known locally as an Ayrshire tan. Most summers the occasion for a man to take his shirt off in these parts is rare. The sun may be shining and strong enough to burn, but it can often be accompanied by a wind that feels as if it has come directly from the Arctic wastes. Therefore if you are out of doors often, you can get a tan on your face, neck and on your arms up to the halfway point of your bicep where a T-shirt sleeve would stop. It is a bizarre look and Dave is displaying a textbook example.

Alessandra is not so bothered about the piebald tan effect and is looking at Dave as if to say: fuck me, a policeman with a six-pack.

'Where do you live?' I ask him.

'Ayr.'

I throw Alessandra my car keys. 'Drive Dave home for a change of clothes and then come straight back.'

Alessandra is trying not to smile as she walks away.

'Remember, you're a married woman,' I shout after her.

Behind her back, she holds up a finger.

I walk back up the stretch of road that leads to the reservoir wall and take the path that leads off to the left. A small pine post with an inset green circle and white arrow points me in the right direction. The path is crisp underfoot with crushed stones and twigs. I loosen my collar in a vain attempt to lessen the heat. I am out of the breeze here and the wall to my left is acting like a radiator.

Nettles line the path and stretch up almost as far as my shoulders. I try to imagine a small boy walking up here. He'd be excited walking in the steps of smugglers and pirates. But he'd hate the nettles. They are part of every small boy's nightmare. Bad enough when they are up to your knees, but these would be swooping over his head.

If this is indeed where Shearer came. I'm starting to have my doubts. Ahead of me I see a tall post with arrows that show there is a distance of 1.7 miles to Dundonald and 1.3 miles back to Troon.

I follow the arrow to Dundonald and enjoy the shade from a stretch of trees on my right. The trees are tall and their slim trunks and branches shelter me like half of a corridor. To my left I can see down into the reservoir. The teenager who came charging down the hill looking for some help is sitting on the wall, his fishing rod and line stretching into the water.

This part of the path leads to the far end of the reservoir and just before the path takes a turn to the left, I turn and look back over where I've come. From this elevation I can see over the Firth of Clyde to the hills of Arran. It's such a clear day, I can see beyond that to the low and long stretch of land that is Kintyre.

The sun is the colour of red gold and it looks as if this colouring has seeped into the sea and stained the water burnt amber from one side of the wide bay to the other.

This is all very nice, but I have a child to find. I turn and follow the path with purpose.

My heart is given a charge when a blackbird bursts from a bramble thicket. The bird would think this lumbering beast on the path is a danger and she's leading me away from her nest.

The path is dry and well-maintained. Trees lean over offering shade. This must have been an ideal way for the smugglers of old. They'd have been safe from the prying eyes of the exciseman up here.

The path takes a fork, and a familiar post points to the left. Some witty vandal with a black marker has written Smuggler's Path on one side, and Fanny Path on the other.

How weak is that? Pussy path would have been much better. Alliteration is everything in the best graffiti circles.

Trees, trees and more trees. So much for the view from this part. I could be in the middle of a maze for all I know. For a stretch the shade becomes stifling rather than welcome, so little of the sun does it let through. Apart from the crunch of my feet on the ground there is no other sound. All is quiet.

I reach another stretch of sunlight and take a deep breath. It's only with that action that I realise I have been holding my breath in. Tall grass flanks the path, dragonflies zip across the air about knee height. I've never seen so many of them in the one place. The birds must love coming up here for a dragonfly feast.

Then I'm back in the shade amidst some tall trees. What are they, I wonder. Elm? Silver Birch? Larch? Over to my right a giant fungus grows out of the trunk of one. It's pale and makes the shape of a hugely inflated pair of lips, as if Mick Jagger not only talks to the trees, he copulates with them as well. Then I spot a tree with a denuded ivy stem growing up it. Criss-crosses here and there along its length give it the appearance of a wood spirit's ladder up to the sky.

Give it a rest, McBain. All this atmosphere and nature and you're coming over all fanciful. I shake my head as if freeing it from such frippery and increase my pace. A long dark stretch downhill opens up and to the right I can see the grey stone tower of what must be Dundonald Castle.

The woods come to an end at some houses. And this must be the village of Dundonald.

I pick my mobile from my pocket. Check the signal. It's weak but I should be able to get through. I call Alessandra.

'Alessandra, can you ask your man there to contact the uniforms and ask them to check the houses at the Dundonald end of the path?'

'Sure.'

'What's your E.T.A?'

'Not sure, boss, there's been a snag ...'

'You got your tongue stuck in his braces?'

'That's an inappropriate way to speak to a *married* colleague.' Then, 'Chance would be a fine thing.'

'Maybe he's shy, Alessandra. Maybe you need to do the running.'

'Anyway, boss, as I was about to say, there's been an accident on the A77. We've got the lights on and we're trying to nudge our way through, but it's a bit of a nightmare.'

'I've started without you. See you when you get here.' I hang up.

Looking back the way I came, I review the path. There was nothing to suggest any human habitation apart from the houses at either end. Where might she be? I retrace my steps. There's a couple of spots where the path detours. I follow each of them and they both lead to an open field.

Soon I'm back at the reservoir.

The boy with the Rangers top has been joined by a pal in a Celtic top. Who says never the twain shall meet? Not if these boys have anything to do with it. They're showing a maturity that is lacking in many adults in this part of the world. I'm liking them already.

In concert, the boys flick their arms and their rods out over the water with practised ease. They've done this before, I think. How often? I wonder.

A thought begins and forms as I run along the path in their direction. I clamber over a fence and climb through some fierce undergrowth before I reach the shore path and then, picking up speed, I run towards the lads.

One of them spots me and I can see his head turn to the side as he tells his pal. They both freeze. Then burst into action. They reel in their lines, pick up their bags and leg it.

'Awfurfucksake,' I shout after them. 'I'm not checking on your permits.' I run over the hill and down to the gate in the wall, where one is through and the Rangers fan is momentarily tangled in the gate. His rod stuck through some wire. He wrestles with it, trying to free it. It gives me enough time to catch him.

'What are you running for?' I ask breathing hard.

'You started it,' the boy's face is coloured with acne and embarrassment at being caught. 'If anybody runs after you up here, they're after your permit.'

'I don't give a fuck about your permit. I'm the police.'

'Even worse,' says the boy. He looks at me, forms a grimace and then a tentative grin.

'Where's your pal?' I ask.

'He'll be hiding at the end of the road. If I don't show up in five minutes he'll come back here and kick your arse.' He's giving me the meanest, scariest look he can come up with. 'He's a black belt.'

I laugh. 'Give Black Belt a shout. I need to pick your brains.'

Chapter 64

I'm sitting on a black wrought iron bench on the shore of the reservoir. The Celtic fan is called Liam and the Rangers fan is called Billy. For real. The irony is they both have roots in the same name: William.

My guess is that they are aged about twelve. Which is ideal. They'll be old enough to talk freely, but young enough not to know any better. If I were speaking to them a couple of years in the future they'd be sullen and unco-operative.

Liam is sitting on the bench beside me, arms crossed, body turned towards me. He has blond gelled hair proba-bly cut to mimic one of his footballing heroes. Billy has dark hair in a shorn, military-style cut and he's sitting cross-legged on the ground between us.

'Come up here a lot, do you?' I ask.

'Just during the holidays,' says Liam.

'There's nothing else to do, mate,' says Billy.

'Catch much?'

'Na,' says Liam.

'Don't know what we'd do with it if we did,' grins Billy.

'Eat it,' I suggest.

'You must be joking, mate.' Liam makes a gagging sound.

'My mum says if it doesn't come in wee rectangular shapes and covered in breadcrumbs then I'm no inter-ested,' says Billy.

Both boys look at each other and giggle. I smile despite myself.

'I'm looking for someone,' I say. The seriousness of my tone is enough to dampen the giggles. 'Have you seen many people out walking on the path?'

'Not really,' says Billy.

'Don't pay much attention to grown-ups,' says Liam as he makes a face.

'This is important, guys.' I lean forward and look at them both. 'A wee boy called Ben has gone missing. He's four. We think his ...' I search for a term that might mean something to these boys, 'baby-sitter is hiding him from his parents. We're worried she's going to hurt him.'

'That's rank, man,' says Liam.

'What a bitch,' says Billy. 'There was that wummin, earlier with the wee boy that fell in?'

'He's not the boy we're looking for.'

'Who would do ...' Billy sits bolt upright, his eyes large with excitement. 'Liam, 'member yesterday? 'member? I pointed at that lassie with the wee boy.'

'Nut,' says Liam as he works at his memory of the last few days. I'm anxious to press, but I don't want him to say something, anything just to please me.

''member?' says Billy. 'I laughed at her, saying it looked like she was taking her messages for a walk.'

'Oh, aye,' says Liam, but he's still wearing an expression showing his uncertainty.

'She had a back-pack on, like something I would use for school,' says Billy. 'And she was carrying like a Tesco plastic bag in each hand.' He turns to face me, his expression clouded with the effort to recall. 'Thing is, I turned away to tell Liam about them.' As he speaks he swivels in his seat as if going through the motions of yesterday. 'And when I turned back to look at them they'd gone.'

'So they'd reached the end of the path and gone on towards Dundonald?' I ask.

'They couldn't have,' he replies. 'No way were they moving that fast. It was like, just seconds. Last time I saw them they were ...' He thinks. 'See that bench on the shore, right in the middle?' I look over and follow his line of sight.

'Right.'

'See if you draw a line up to the trees from there ...that's where I saw them last.'

359

I look up to a point just over half way up that stretch of path.

'I looked away for a couple of seconds and when I looked back they were gone. Pure vanished.'

Liam makes a whooshing, disappearing noise, as if keen to have some sort of involvement.

'Did you see anything, Liam?' I ask.

'Nope,' he answers.

''Cos by the time you looked up, loser, they'd gone.' Billy reaches out and kicks Liam's foot. Liam kicks him back. Up till now the conversation has been pretty mature, but this serves as a reminder that this pair are just boys.

'Guys, I need you to do me a favour. I'm going up there for a look, but I'm expecting some colleagues to arrive soon. A man and a woman,' I say.

'Izzat the man that dived in and saved the wee boy?' asked Billy.

I nod.

'Should have seen it, man,' Billy said to Liam. 'It was well cool.'

'Watch where I go, will you? And when they arrive, can you direct them?'

They both nod and almost at the same time ask, 'Will we be on the telly?'

I shrug. 'Who knows.' Then I stand and look down at them both looking up at me, with their Celtic and Rangers shirts on.

'Want to earn a tenner?' I ask.

'Aye,' they both answer instantly.

'Swap over your tops. Billy put on the Celtic one. Liam put Billy's on.'

The each pull their shirt out from their chests and look at the other.

'No fucking way, man.'

'Not a chance.'

I walk away smiling. It seems some things are just unthinkable.

I walk back up along the path. When I get to the middle I turn and check with Billy down by the reservoir. He sees me standing and waves me on. I walk a couple more steps. Again no. I take half a dozen more steps forward and check again.

Billy rewards me with a huge smile and a double thumbs up.

I turn and face the woods. The trees are thinner here at the front, but a few yards in they thicken. The ground is covered in patches of grass, earth and weeds. Here and there a small bush survives on the meagre sunshine that reaches through the foliage. The land rises in a slope at this point, still covered with the same amount of foliage.

There's nothing here to suggest where they might have gone. Whoever *they* are. I should be doubting myself around now. I should be on the verge of going back to the car, finding a nice wee café in Troon and treating myself to an Americano.

But something tells me to keep going.

There's a breeze on the back of my neck, something's pushing me on and I can't ignore it.

Chapter 65

There. Right there among the undergrowth I can see the faint line of a path. The word path may be an exaggeration, but there is definitely an impression of some sort on the earth. It stretches in an almost straight line through the woods and up the slope at the far end.

I step out of the light of the main path and into the dark and hush of the woods. It's a few degrees colder in here, the heat and light of the day being held back by the foliage higher up. I shiver, move faster, thinking I should have brought a jacket.

The path takes a slight curve and follows the slope upwards. I walk for what must be five or ten minutes. Apart from my breathing and the noise as I crush the leaves and twigs caught underfoot, I am in a world of silence. No breeze. No birdsong. Nothing.

There's a low dry-stone wall in front of me. Why would a wall would be built here in the middle of a wood? Was it a boundary of some sort? Whatever its purpose; it is a sign of habitation. I walk faster and climb over a section of the wall that has long ago collapsed in on itself.

On the other side of the wall the path continues onwards and upwards. The ground evens out and the slope begins a downwards slide that is much more gentle than the way up.

I hear a noise. Sounds like a scream. High in the trees a large bird calls out, claps its wings and then flies off to a different perch. I still my breathing. I was just imagining things.

Then it sounds again. And again.

I start running in the direction of the noise. That was

no wounded beast of the woods. That was the noise of a child in pain.

The trees thin out into a clearing. Along one side runs the rest of the wall I climbed over earlier and just beyond that sits a low roofed, squat, white house. From here I can make out a green door and small windows on either side. The house must have two rooms at the most.

The screaming has stopped. I'm not sure if that is a good sign or not. I clear the wall and approach the house from the side so that whoever is inside can't see me.

I reach the window. The glass is filthy, streaked with bird droppings, dust and rain. On the other side my view is obstructed by a net curtain. I wipe some of the dirt off the window with my hand, trying to get a better look and what I see then sends a chill through me.

I can see the still, vertical form of a small boy in the centre of the room. His head is at the same height as mine and twisted to the side. He has no clothes on his bottom half. His feet are also bare and tied together. They are dangling in mid air.

I don't think twice. I take a step to the right and shoulder in the door. The hinges and the wood are old and rotting and give easily.

The room is dark, the only light provided by the window and the open door. The only furniture in the room is a wooden table and four crudely crafted wooden chairs. I reach the boy. He has a noose around his neck. His face is covered in what looks like burn marks. Small, circular burn marks as if they had been done with a cigarette. In the seconds it takes to reach him I can see that the same burns are on and around his small genitals.

The boy's face is pale, his eyes closed and his lips blue. But he is still warm. I drag a chair over and stand on it. I hold his small body up and take the weight off his neck. Looking up I see that the rope is attached to a light fitting. Hopefully, like the door this is in a rotten state as well.

How long has he been like this? Will I be able to get air

into his lungs before his brain is damaged by the lack of oxygen.

With one arm round Ben, I give the flex of the light fitting a hard tug. Nothing. Another tug. It remains solid. I look around the room for something sharp. I can see nothing but shadows. The spaces the light touches are as bare as the walls of a crypt.

There's another room. Might be a kitchen. Might be something sharp there.

What about Shearer? Did she vanish as soon as she heard me?

Just then I hear a noise from my right. Excellent, Alessandra and Dave must have arrived. I turn round.

'Quick, give me a hand.'

But it's no-one I know. The shape of the woman in front of me is small and slight. Her hair all but covers her eyes, but not enough for me to miss the look of hatred that is aimed at me.

'No you don't, you bastard.' She runs at me. I can see something short and sharp glint in her hand.

My options are to protect myself or continue to take the pressure off Ben's neck. In the seconds it takes for Shearer to reach me I make my choice and turn. All I can do is offer her my back as a target.

Her blade punches me in the right buttock.

'Fuck,' I let out a scream.

She's coming at me again. I lash out with my right leg. I hit something. She grunts and then comes back at me. I've got to get Ben off this rope. I pull at the electric flex again. There's a slight shift. Shearer's on me again. I can't take much more of this knife. I feel the knife enter the front of my thigh. I turn in agony. She strikes again. This time in my lower back.

'Fuck!' I scream. 'You bitch.'

My first choice was either to protect Ben or myself. If this continues I will have saved no one. I've got to stop her before she finishes us both. My trouser legs, back and front are soaked in my blood. I've no idea how much I've lost but my legs are wobbling. My arms need a rest.

The only weapons I have are my feet and my knees. Time to gamble. She has to get close enough for it to work and I have to take the risk of another knife wound. I balance on the chair to gather some strength, amazed that it hasn't toppled already.

As if she smells my weakness she stops and smiles. And then takes a step closer. Just a little closer, I pray and pretend to close my eyes and rest my head on Ben's chest, which is completely still. Ben. Poor Ben, I've got to save you. I don't bother speaking. We are beyond words. I've got to hope against hope that Ben is still in there somewhere and he knows I am here fighting to help him.

Shearer has no fear of me. She looks up at me with all the interest of a customer at a zoo. I can't hurt her, she's thinking. I can't stop her either. She has a mission and by god she'll complete it.

I look at Ben and try to judge his state. I can't feel for a pulse. I don't have time. The rope at the back of his neck isn't completely tight. There is some space. Perhaps there's hope.

Shearer edges in as casual as someone at Tesco might consider the purchase of an own brand of tomatoes. She lifts her arm up; the blade is dark with my blood and aimed at me. She brings it down. Fast.

I twist violently to the side, using the flex as my point of anchor. She misses and her momentum brings her closer to me. Then in one motion, I take my hand off Ben's chest, place both on the flex, grip as tightly as I can and pull up. As I do so I bring my right knee up with as much force as I can manage.

My knee connects with her chin. Her head shoots back. But I can't see much more as my full weight on the flex has ripped the connection from the ceiling.

I hit the floor. On the way down my back hits the chair and my wounded buttock hits the ground. Ben lands on top of me.

Just then Dave and Alessandra burst in the door,

closely followed by Liam and Billy.

'You okay, boss,' asks Alessandra, her face white.

'Don't worry about me. Ben. Needs CPR.'

Chapter 66

As it turned out, Liam and Billy did get their fifteen minutes of fame on the telly. I watched it from my hospital bed.

Still wearing their football tops, they proudly told the world how they had directed the first policeman to the wee house where the mad woman was torturing the wee boy. Then how they waited for the man and woman police detectives and showed them where I had disappeared into the woods.

Then how they watched the policewoman save the wee boy's life and the policeman put his handcuffs on the mad woman. Even though she was unconscious, she was still pure scary, they opined. A line that was repeated in every newspaper in the country.

Visitors, I've had a few, but then again, not too few to mention.

Alessandra was the first. She kissed me on the cheek as she left.

'That nurse with the moustache,' she grinned. 'She's got her eye on you.'

'Fuck off, Rossi,' was my sweet reply.

Jim Hilton also made an appearance. He stood by the bed with his arms crossed.

'Can't stay long,' he said. 'Can't take my eyes off Ben for any longer than ...'

His face was long and shadowed with guilt, relief and worry about what the future might bring. His war wasn't over yet. He still had a wife to nurse and win over. And a son to love and protect in a manner that will give him a safe yet free childhood.

How do you convince the child that the bogeyman won't

367

come and get him, when the bogeywoman already did?

'Just wanted to thank you ...' His face twisted with emotion. His eyes were wet, but he wouldn't allow the tears of gratitude to flow. Strange how with everything he had gone through that he would still care about a public display.

'I'll never forget what you've done for us, DI McBain. I'll make sure Ben knows and maybe one day he'll follow in your footsteps.'

'Oh for fuckssake, don't say that. Look at the state of me, man.' We both laughed.

We shook hands and he left.

I try to sleep. An image of Jim Hilton with his son, Ben keeps imposing itself on my mind. For all his recent trials I envy him. He has his son.

I wonder where Theresa is right now. If she has had the baby yet? If she will ever tell me the truth.

Do I deserve the truth?

I drift in and out of sleep until I feel a presence hovering over me. I am dazed with fatigue, my eyes unfocussed. It is a man's face; thin and sharp with threat. His voice is frighteningly familiar.

'It's not over yet, McBain.' I feel his breath on my ear as he speaks. 'It would be too easy to do anything now...'

'What?' I sit up, propelled with fright.

'Well, Ray,' says Chief Superintendent Harrison. He's standing over at the door. As usual he looks as if he has just walked out of a shop window. 'Been in the wars again?'

I look over his shoulder. 'Did you see anyone just leave there?' He swivels, following my line of sight.

'Nope. You were totally on your own.'

'You sure?' I ask, voice tight with panic.

'Ray, I realise that you've had some stress recently, but you need to calm down.' He walks towards me and pats my shoulder. I slump back on to the pillows fighting to keep my eyes open. I am so tired.

Harrison sits in the chair beside me and crosses one well-tailored leg over the other, displaying a leather brogue so shiny it could double as a disco ball.

'Anyway, Ray. We have other more pressing things to discuss ...' his face is severe. Fuck. What is he going to say? Acid churns in my stomach. I can't lose my job, it's all I have. It's the only thing I can do.

'Sir, I know I was out of line. I know I was supposed to stay by the desk, but a wee boy was in...'

'Ray, for chrissake shut up, man. I hate to see someone begging.'

'But, sir ...'

'No buts, DI McBain ...'

Here we go. He always gives me my full title before he goes for the jugular.

'...you're a credit to the force. A bona-fide hero.' He slaps my thigh. The good one, thankfully. 'The newspapers love you. You saved a child, man.' His face wide with glee. The men under him perform well, he looks good. The men under him save the life of a photogenic child of four, he looks like a future Chief Constable.

'So don't worry, Ray. In fact I'm sure there will be a commendation in line for you after this. We'll just forget the small fact that you were on forced desk duty and concentrate on the dogged fashion in which you hunted down a maniac.'

I am weak with relief. I seriously thought I'd done it this time. That the brass would think this was the last straw. See me, I'm a great judge of events. Not.

Harrison then looks over at the door. He raises his eyebrows in an approving manner.

'Looks like you have another visitor, Ray.' He stands up. 'We'll see you when you're fit. And the first thing you're doing when you return is a refresher on Officer Safety Training.' He wags a finger at me.

He leaves. Maggie enters.

'This is getting to be a habit,' she says.

'You look good.'

'You look like shit,' she laughs. Then, soberly. 'What am I going to do with you, Ray McBain?' Relief has lined her eyes with the beginning of tears.

'Ignore the scars and the fact that I'm crap in bed and return to being my best pal?'

Her laughter in reply is the best medicine. We look at each other. Tentative. Knowing that the worst is over. Her eyes are shiny, her smile curved with warmth. We are still friends.

I have a thought.

'Does everyone know that I got stabbed in the arse?'

She laughs, loud and unrestrained and rubs her hands together.

'Ray,' she grins. 'The whole world knows.'

Acknowledgements

A big thank you to readers, bloggers, reviewers, booksellers and all the social networkers (you know who you are) for helping to make *Blood Tears* a success. Thanks also to everyone at Five Leaves and to Derek Fyfe and John Hazlett for guidance in police matters. Any errors are all mine. Special mention must also go to my first readers on this book, Sheila Templeton and Alison Craig. Who knew those targeted Monday night sessions at The Coffee Club would end up here?